FAR-SEER

"REFRESHINGLY ORIGINAL!" —*Quill & Quire*

"SAWYER HAS RETURNED A SENSE OF WONDER TO SCIENCE FICTION." —*Tanya Huff, author of Blood Price*

"INVENTIVE AND ENGAGING!" —*New York Newsday*

"AN ADVENTURE STORY, a commentary on the conflict between truth and established faith, and a fascinating exploration of an alien society." —*Science Fiction Chronicle*

"SAWYER'S DINOSAUR-RACE MIRRORS HUMANITY." —*North York Mirror* (Canada)

"CONSTANTLY INTRIGUING!" —*The Ottawa Citizen*

"FASCINATING . . . Sawyer's understanding of both our reptilian predecessors and of astronomy is considerable . . . *Far-Seer* entertains as a fantasy about an alien culture and as an exercise in world-building."

—*Books in Canada*

"TRULY A GREAT PIECE OF FANTASY SF . . . The author, at heart a paleontologist, has never outgrown his early love for dinosaurs. It is catching!" —*Kliatt*

"ONE OF THE YEAR'S OUTSTANDING SF BOOKS!" —*Toronto Star*

Continued . . .

Then, Robert J. Sawyer returned to this fascinating world—
as Afsan's son, a geologist, discovers a mysterious artifact
that could reveal the saurians' true origins . . .

FOSSIL HUNTER

"THOUGHTFUL AND COMPELLING SF ADVENTURE!"
—Library Journal

"BRILLIANT . . . Sawyer blends hard science with effective
storytelling . . . tight and fast-paced . . . *Fossil Hunter*, like *Far-Seer*,
is not just wonderful SF, it's wonderful fiction."
—Quill & Quire

"EVERY BIT AS GOOD AS ITS EXCELLENT PREDECESSOR,
this makes me more anxious than ever to see the final volume!"
—Science Fiction Chronicle

"A WRITER TO WATCH . . . Robert Sawyer may be Canada's
answer to Isaac Asimov!"
—Andrew Weiner, author of *Station Gehenna*

"IF ROBERT J. SAWYER WERE A CORPORATION, I
WOULD BUY STOCK IN HIM." —Spider Robinson

"A FASCINATION WITH DINOSAURS and an ability to write
has been a winning combination for Robert J. Sawyer!"
—Thornhill Liberal (Canada)

Now, Robert J. Sawyer presents the third volume of this brilliantly original saga—a strange, timeless world of nature's greatest mysteries . . .

FOREIGNER

Science Fiction Novels by Robert J. Sawyer

GOLDEN FLEECE
FAR-SEER
FOSSIL HUNTER
FOREIGNER

END OF AN ERA (Coming in November)

FOREIGNER

ROBERT J. SAWYER

ACE BOOKS, NEW YORK

This book is an Ace original edition,
and has never been previously published.

FOREIGNER

An Ace Book / published by arrangement with
the author

PRINTING HISTORY
Ace edition / March 1994

All rights reserved.
Copyright © 1994 by Robert J. Sawyer.
Cover art by Bob Eggleton.
This book may not be reproduced in whole or in part,
by mimeograph or any other means, without permission.
For information address: The Berkley Publishing Group,
200 Madison Avenue, New York, NY 10016.

ISBN: 0-441-00017-7

ACE®
Ace Books are published by The Berkley Publishing Group,
200 Madison Avenue, New York, NY 10016.
ACE and the "A" design
are trademarks belonging to Charter Communications, Inc.

PRINTED IN THE UNITED STATES OF AMERICA

10 9 8 7 6 5 4 3 2 1

For Quentin and Gin Peterson,
with love and thanks

Acknowledgments

This book got off the ground with the help of my wife, Carolyn Clink; my brother-in-law, David Livingstone Clink; my brother, Alan B. Sawyer; physicist Dr. Ariel Reich; programmer Ted Bleaney; my agent, Richard Curtis; my editor, Susan Allison (and my former editor, Peter Heck, who commissioned this novel before he left Ace); and fellow SF writers Cory Doctorow, Gregory Feeley, Terence M. Green, Edo van Belkom, and Andrew Weiner.

The Equatorial Continent of LAND

Capital City

Ark Excavation Site

|— 3,837 kilometers —|

1. Jam'toolar
2. Fra'toolar
3. Arj'toolar
4. Chu'toolar
5. Mar'toolar
6. Edz'toolar
7. Kev'toolar
8. Capital

◄—— 1,000 kilometers ——►

Major Characters

Capital City

Afsan (Sal-Afsan)	advisor to Dy-Dybo
Cadool (Pal-Cadool)	aide to Afsan
Dybo (Dy-Dybo)	Emperor
Edklark (Det-Edklark)	Master of the Faith
Mokleb (Nav-Mokleb)	psychoanalyst
Mondark (Dar-Mondark)	palace healer
Osfik (Var-Osfik)	Arbiter of the Sequence
Pettit	Afsan's apprentice

Geological Survey of Land

Babnol (Wab-Babnol)	team member
Biltog (Mar-Biltog)	mate aboard the *Dasheter*
Keenir (Var-Keenir)	captain of the *Dasheter*
Toroca (Kee-Toroca)	leader, Afsan's son

Exodus Project

Delplas (Bar-Delplas)	project staff member
Garios (Den-Garios)	project staff member
Karshirl (Bos-Karshirl)	engineer
Novato (Wab-Novato)	leader, inventor of the far-seer

Others

Captain	sailor
Jawn	teacher
Morb	security chief
Taksan	eggling

Prologue

Historically, there have been three great blows to the Quintaglio ego.

First, Afsan delivered the cosmological blow by taking God out of our skies and moving us from the center of the universe to one of its countless backwaters.

Then, Toroca dealt us the biological blow, showing that we were not divinely created from the hands of God but rather had evolved through natural processes from other animals.

And, finally, Mokleb administered the psychological blow, proving that we were not rational beings acting on lofty principles but are in fact driven by the dark forces that control our subconscious minds.

—Briz-Tolharb, Curator
Museum of Quintaglio Civilization

Chapter 1

Afsan couldn't see the sun, but he felt its noontime heat beating down. With his left hand he held the harness attached to Gork, his large monitor lizard. They were moving over paving stones, Afsan's toeclaws making heavy clicks against them, Gork's footfalls echoing that sound with a softer ticking. Afsan heard metal-rimmed wheels rolling over the roadway, approaching from the right.

Afsan had been blind for twenty kilodays. Det-Yenalb, the Master of the Faith, had pierced Afsan's eyeballs with a ceremonial obsidian dagger. The priest had rotated the blade in each socket, gouging out the empty sacks. Afsan didn't like thinking about that long-ago day. He'd been convicted of heresy, and the blinding had been performed in Capital City's Central Square in front of over a hundred people, a mob packed with as little as three paces between each of its members.

The city had changed since then. The landquake of kiloday 7110 had destroyed many roads and buildings, and the replacements were often different from the originals. The growth and redevelopment of the city had left their marks, too. Still, Afsan always knew where he was in relation to the Central Square. Even now, having to walk through it made him anxious. But today's journey would take him nowhere near—

Roots!

Suddenly Afsan felt his middle toeclaw catch on something—a loose paving stone?—and he found himself pitching forward, his tail lifting off the ground.

Gork let out a loud hiss as Afsan, desperately trying to right himself, yanked hard on the lizard's harness.

From ahead, a shout: "Watch out!"

Another voice, a different passerby: "He's going to be crushed!"

A loud roar—a hornface?—dead ahead.

Afsan's chest scraped across the pavement.

The sound of cracking leather.

The hornface again.

A *snap* from his shoulder.

A jab of pain.

His muzzle smashing into the ground.

Blood in his mouth.

Two curving teeth knocked loose.

And then, an explosion within his head as something heavy kicked into it.

His head whipped sideways. His neck felt like it was going to snap.

Crunching sounds.

More pain.

Indescribable pain.

A scream from the roadside.

More teeth knocked out.

Afsan was unable to breathe through one nostril. He felt as if that whole side of his upper muzzle had been crushed.

Running feet.

Afsan let out a moan.

A stranger's voice: "Are you all right?"

Afsan tried to lift his head. Agony. His shoulder blade was a knife, slicing into his neck. His head was slick with blood.

The high-pitched voice of a youngster: "It's Sal-Afsan!"

Another voice. "By the Face of God, it is."

And a third voice: "Oh, my God. His head—Sal-Afsan, are you all right?"

More running sounds, toeclaws sparking against paving stones. *Agony.*

"You ran right over him!"

"He stumbled in front of my chariot. I tried to stop."

Chariot. The wheels he'd heard. The hornface must have been drawing it. The kick to his head—a hornface's forefoot. Afsan tried to speak, but couldn't. He felt blood coursing out of him.

"The left side of his face is smashed," said the youngster. "And look—there's something funny about his shoulder."

Another voice. "Dislocated, I'm sure."

"Is he dead?" called a new voice.

"No. Not yet, anyway. *Look at his skull!*"

Afsan tried to speak again, but all he managed was a low hiss.

"Someone get a healer!"

"No, it would take too long to fetch a doctor; we've got to take him to one."

"The palace surgery isn't far," said one of the voices. "Surely Sal-Afsan would be a patient of the imperial healer, what's his name . . ."

"Mondark," said another voice. "Dar-Mondark."

"Take him in your chariot," shouted a voice.

"Someone will have to help me," said the charioteer. "He's too heavy for me to lift on my own."

Silence, except for Afsan's labored breathing and, nearby, Gork's confused hissing.

"For God's sake, people, someone help me! I can't do this alone."

An incredulous voice. "To touch another . . ."

"He'll die if he doesn't get medical help. Come on."

A new voice, from farther away. "Make room for me to pass. I'm just back from a hunt. I suspect I can touch him without difficulty."

Shuffling feet. Afsan moaned again.

The charioteer's voice now, close to his earhole: "We're going to touch you, Sal-Afsan. Try not to react."

Even in agony, even with a broken skull and dislocated shoulder, instinct still reigned. Afsan flinched as hands touched him. Fingerclaws popped from their sheaths.

"Careful of his shoulder—"

Afsan howled in pain.

"Sorry. He's pretty heavy."

Afsan felt his head being pulled out of the thickening puddle of blood. He was lifted up and placed facedown in the back of the chariot.

"What about his lizard?" said the charioteer.

"I'll take him," said the youngster who had first identified Afsan. "I know where the palace surgery is."

The charioteer shouted, *"Latark!"* His hornface began to gallop along the road, Afsan's head bouncing up and down, the sound of metal wheels over the stones drowning out his moans.

After an eternity, the chariot arrived outside Dar-Mondark's surgery, a typical adobe building just south of the palace. Afsan could hear the charioteer disembark and the sound of his fingerclaws clicking against the signaling plate set into the doorjamb. The door swung open on squeaky hinges, and Afsan heard Mondark's voice. "Yes?"

"I'm Gar-Reestee," said the charioteer. "I've got Sal-Afsan with me. He's hurt."

Afsan heard Mondark's heavy footfalls as the healer hurried to the chariot. "God," he said. "How did this happen?"

"He tripped and fell into the roadway. My hornface kicked him in the head before I could stop my chariot."

"Those are massive wounds." Mondark leaned closer, his voice reassuring. "Afsan, you're going to be all right."

The charioteer's voice, incredulous: "Healer, your muzzle—"

"Shush," said Mondark. "Help me bring him inside. Afsan, we're going to pick you up."

Once again, Afsan was carried. He felt cold in the side of his head. After several moments, he was placed face down on a marble tabletop. Mondark had treated Afsan kilodays ago on a similar table after Afsan had plummeted to the ground from the top of a thunderbeast's neck. The surgery chamber, Afsan knew, was heated by a cast-iron stove burning coal. He also knew that the roof above the table was made largely of glass, letting in outside light, illuminating the patient.

"Thank you, Gar-Reestee, for bringing Afsan in," said Mondark. "I will do everything I can for him, but you must leave. The physical contact for treating his injuries is something you shouldn't see."

The charioteer's voice was full of sorrow. "Good Sal-Afsan, I'm terribly sorry. It was an accident."

Afsan tried to nod, but daggers of pain stabbed through his muzzle.

The charioteer left. Mondark went to work.

"Land ho!"

Captain Var-Keenir stopped pacing the deck of the sailing ship *Dasheter* and tipped his muzzle up to the lookout bucket, high atop the foremast. Old Biltog was up there, his red leather cap and the green skin of his head and shoulders stark against the purple sky. Keenir's tail swished in sadness. He'd seen it happen before on long voyages, and lookout officers, who spent inordinate amounts of time in the sun, were particularly susceptible to it. Biltog was hallucinating. Why, Land—the single known continent—was half a world away.

"Land ho!" called Biltog again, his green arm extended toward the northeast. The red sail attached to the foremast snapped in the wind. Two Quintaglios moved to the starboard side of the vessel to see what Biltog was pointing at.

Keenir looked up again. The sun, brilliant and white, was climbing in front of them. Behind, covering half the sky between zenith and rear horizon, was the Face of God, its leading edge illuminated, the rest of its vast bulk in shadow. Also visible were three moons, wan shapes in the sun's glare. But along the northeastern horizon there was nothing but waves touching sky.

Near Keenir was a ramp leading below. Kee-Toroca, a young Quintaglio male, came up it. He moved closer to Keenir than Keenir was comfortable with and said, "Did I hear a shout of 'land ho'?"

Keenir had known the young savant all his life; indeed, Toroca had taken his praenomen syllable in honor of him. "You've sharp hearing indeed, to have heard that below deck," he said in his gravelly voice. "Yes, Biltog shouted it, but, well, I think he's had too much sun. There can't be any land out here."

"Ah, but undiscovered land is exactly what we're looking for."

Keenir clicked his teeth. "Aye, the final stage of the Geological Survey. But I don't expect to find any, and doubt very much we have now."

Toroca was carrying the brass far-seer his mother, Novato, had given to his father, Afsan, the day after he had been conceived. It glinted in the fierce sun, its green patina counterpointed by purple reflections of the sky above. Toroca scanned the horizon once with his unaided eye.

Nothing.

Or was there something?

He brought the far-seer to his face and slid the tube's components apart until the horizon was in focus. There *was* a slight brown line dividing the waves and the sky.

Keenir could see it, too, now. Biltog's greater height had let him spot the land sooner than those on deck.

"Will you look at that?" said Toroca softly, passing the far-seer to the captain.

"An unknown country," said Keenir, head shaking in disbelief. Then, rotating on his heel, he shouted, "Starboard ho! Turn the ship!"

An ark.

A space ark.

Wab-Novato leaned back on her muscular tail, placed her hands firmly on her slender hips, and looked up at the vast blue structure protruding from the cliff face.

She'd spent most of the last two kilodays here in Fra'toolar province, studying this alien spaceship, trying to fathom its mysteries. But figuring out this ship was like tracking a wingfinger: you could follow the footprints in the sand, fooling yourself that you were getting closer to a tasty meal, but just when you thought you had your quarry within reach, it would take to the air, leaving you far behind. There were almost no gears or levers or springs used in this ship's construction, no pumps or wheels, nothing that Quintaglios were familiar with.

It had seemed like a Godsend, this ship of space. The Quintaglio world, innermost of fourteen moons, was doomed: within a few hundred kilodays it would be torn apart by the stress of its orbit around the giant, banded planet called the Face of God. Twenty kilodays ago, when Afsan had figured out that their moon was doomed, no Quintaglio had ever flown and the idea of traversing the void between worlds was the stuff of the wildest fantasy stories. But now the government was devoted to the exodus, the project Novato herself was in charge of.

Before this ship had been found, the Quintaglios had been making good progress on their own: after studying wingfingers and the long-extinct creatures known as birds, Novato had built the first glider, the *Tak-Saleed*. In the two kilodays since, more efficient gliders had been developed. Perhaps she'd been a fool to turn over that line of research to someone else, although back then this ark had seemed to be a shortcut to the stars. But despite the best efforts of her team, no one yet had a clue as to how the ship operated.

The cliff it was embedded in was more than a hundred paces tall, showing the best uninterrupted sequences of sedimentary rock on all of Land. Toroca had uncovered the ship while studying these layers, looking for fossils. He found lots of them above a certain point—the lowest chalk stratum, known as the Bookmark layer—but none below. It had been as if the Bookmark indicated the point of the divine creation of life. But most scholars now agreed that it was instead the *arrival* point, marking where transplanted lifeforms had first been released by other arks onto this world.

But this ark had crashed, its five-eyed crewmembers killed, its cargo of plants and animals never released. The ark had been buried in sediment that later turned to rock, but it had not been crushed: the blue material of the ship's hull was harder than diamond and impervious to corrosion. The part now projecting out of the cliff had been exposed by blasting, and, big though it seemed, it was only a tiny fraction of the total ship.

It was noon. The purple sky was shot through with silvery-white clouds. To Novato's left were choppy waves—the world-spanning body of water. In front of her, running along the edge of the cliff, was a narrow strip of beach, crabs scuttling amongst the rocks. Leading up the cliff face to the blue ark were webs of climbing ropes left over from the early excavations as well as scaffolding made of *adabaja* wood, added later to make getting up to the ark easier. Oil lamp in hand, Novato began climbing the rickety stairs of the scaffolding.

As she ascended, she could see, far overhead, the green forms of several Quintaglios working with picks at the sides of the giant ark. Others, Novato knew, were likewise hacking away at the rock on top of the ship. To date, only one entrance to the ship had been found, and passage through it was hampered because its outer door was jammed partway shut. Miners had been working steadily at uncovering more of the ship in hopes of finding another way in. So far they had failed, but as they exposed more of the ship's roof, they had found that much of it was covered with black hexagonal cells. No one knew what the black honeycomb was for, but Novato had noticed one startling thing: rather than heating up in the sunlight, as dark objects normally did, these cells remained cool, as if—Novato couldn't fathom the mechanism involved—as if the heat falling on them were somehow conducted into the ship.

At last, Novato reached the top of the stairs. She crossed the wooden platform leading to the ship's half-closed door. That door led into a tiny chamber, the far wall of which contained another door. The chamber itself was completely empty, except for some grillwork on the walls.

This double-doored room was the subject of much debate.

Some thought it was an animal trap. Bait might have been used to lure prey into the outer chamber, then the outside door would have been closed quickly and the inner door not opened until the animal within had asphyxiated or starved to death. Certainly no hunter would catch food that way, but the bodies of the ship's crew were so bizarre that one could scarcely imagine them actively pursuing food.

Others suggested the double-doored room served almost exactly the opposite function: a safety feature to prevent any of the animals aboard the ship from escaping—it was, after all, an ark—while crewmembers were disembarking.

Novato doubted both theories. She was certain there was another, more elegant explanation, but no matter how hard she contemplated it, the answer remained elusive.

Oh, well, she thought. *Just one of many things about this ship I don't understand.*

As she had countless times before, Novato squeezed through the half-closed door with her lamp, entering the vast ark, looking for a miracle to help save her people.

Afsan's recovery was remarkable. His shoulder had been easy enough to reposition, but getting the broken pieces of his skull to line up properly had been difficult and painful. Mondark had used gut ties to sew shut the gashes on Afsan's muzzle and head, Afsan having remained stoically silent as the surgeon's needle repeatedly pierced his skin.

Afsan had spent the night of the accident, and the one that followed, lying on Mondark's surgical table, slowly regaining strength. Finally, when he was well enough to move, Afsan's assistant, the lanky Pal-Cadool, had come to take him home.

That had been twenty days ago. Mondark had insisted that Afsan return every ten days so that his injuries could be checked.

"How do you feel today?" asked the healer.

"All right, I suppose," said Afsan, "although the new skin itches, and the side of my head is still tender to the touch."

"That's to be expected. Frankly, you're doing much better than I'd have thought. I didn't think you were going to make it."

Afsan clicked his jaws together. The gaps in his sawtooth dentition where teeth had been knocked out had begun to fill in with pointed buds. "No one is more pleased than me that your diagnosis was in error. How do I look?"

Mondark's turn to click his teeth. "Well, nothing I could do would make you pretty, Afsan. If you want miracles, you'll have to see a priest. But on the whole, you look remarkably well. Your scars are bright yellow, but the scabbing has diminished. Your back is still bruised around your shoulder blade, but that will clear up in time. Does it still give you pain?"

"Yes. But it's getting better."

"Good. And you've been following my advice about no heavy lifting?"

"Right," said Afsan. "I've been skipping my usual shift on the docks."

"Good. Now, let me remove your stitches. I'm going to touch your face."

Mondark used a tiny pair of scissors to gently lift and cut each of the gut strings. Then, using his claws as pincers, he pulled the little threads out. Despite his efforts at stoicism, Afsan winced slightly as each one came free.

After removing the stitches on Afsan's muzzle, the healer repeated the process for the ones on the side of his head. Eventually he stopped, but for some reason he didn't move away from Afsan's face. After a few moments, Mondark said, "How are your eyes?"

Afsan's voice was cold. "Your repartee is slipping, Doctor. That's not very funny."

"I mean, there's something different about your eyelids. It's almost as if . . . Afsan, forgive me, but can you open your eyelids?"

"I never do that. It hurts to have the sockets exposed."

"I know, but . . . forgive me, I'd like to open them myself. I'm going to touch your face."

Afsan flinched at the sensation of Mondark's fingers on the side of his head. He felt a strange coldness as his left eyelid was peeled open.

The healer sucked in his breath. "By the eggshells of the hunters . . ."

"What? What is it?"

"Afsan, can you see me?"

"What?"

"Can you see me?"

"Doctor, what *are* you talking about?"

Without any warning, Mondark's fingers were on Afsan's other eyelid, prying it open. "God," he said.

With Afsan's green lids peeled back, Mondark could see into his eye sockets. From the bottom of each pink fleshy well, a wet all-black sphere, about half the size of a normal Quintaglio eye, stared out at him.

Mondark had Afsan force his eyelids open while he brought a candle close to Afsan's face. Quintaglio pupils were hard to discern against the all-black sclera, and light played across the wet surface making it all the more difficult to see, but there could be no doubt: Afsan's pupils were contracting in response to the candlelight.

"Eyes don't regenerate," Afsan said, incredulous. "They're like internal organs. Damage to them is permanent."

Mondark moved across the room; too much closeness was bad for both of them. "Usually, that's true. But very, very rarely, an organ, even an eye, will grow back. It usually only happens to young children, but it's not unheard-of in adults."

"But it was twenty kilodays ago that I was blinded. Why would my eyes be coming back now?"

"No doubt your recent head wound has something to do with it. You had to regenerate a lot of bone, a lot of flesh, a lot of muscle. Somehow your body went on to regenerate your eyes, too. Of course, they're not fully back yet; they're only about half normal size."

Afsan shook his head. "That's incredible." And then, after a moment, he spoke again, his voice tremulous, as if he feared the answer. "So when the eyes have finished regenerating, will I be able to see again?"

Mondark was quiet for a time. "I don't know. Your eyes have already regenerated in all functional aspects. Oh, they're still too small; presumably they'll continue to grow to fill the sockets. But the lenses are clear, the pupils are responsive, and both eyes track left and right in unison. Whether the eyes will actually work for vision, I don't know." Another pause. "You say you can't see anything now?"

"That's right."

"Nothing at all?"

"Nothing."

"Not even when I brought that candle flame close a moment ago?"

"No, not a thing. It's pitch black, just like it's been since . . . since Yenalb did this to me."

"Well, come back in ten days. And come immediately if you

get any hint of vision—a flash of light, a blurry image, anything."

"I will, Mondark." Afsan faced him from across the room, his eyelids open, the half-size black spheres appearing to look at him from the bottoms of their sockets.

Chapter 2

The *Dasheter* continued to sail in. It was clear that they were approaching a small group of islands. Discounting the icy polar caps, until moments ago Land and its attendant archipelagos had been the only known dry ground in the world.

But now there was someplace else: a new land with possibly untold riches. Not gold or diamonds; those weren't the types of riches Toroca was looking for. No, his Geological Survey sought valuables of another kind: things that could be used to aid in the effort to get the Quintaglio people off their doomed world.

The chain of islands—Toroca could see six discrete bodies now—seemed to be volcanic. Each was conical, a ragged mountain rising out of the water. Lush vegetation covered the flat lands around the bases of the volcanoes and much of the volcanic cones, as well.

"Drop anchor!" shouted Captain Keenir. Four members of his crew struggled with the big wheel that paid out the chain. They put their backs into it, channeling the territorial anger such close proximity would normally engender. They were still two thousand paces from the nearest island, but Keenir wouldn't risk bringing the *Dasheter* closer until he was sure the waters were free of obstructions.

Two crewmembers were working on the foresail booms, untying the huge red sheets. The snapping of the sails had been a constant background; its end made for a curious reverse-deafness. Toroca cocked his head and listened to the quieter sounds of the anchor chain uncoiling, of waves slapping against the wooden hull, and—was there something else on the wind? Briefly there, but now gone? A rhythmic pounding, like hunting drums? No, of course not. Doubtless it had just been Toroca's own heartbeat thundering in his earholes as his senses adjusted to the change in sound quality.

"That's as far as it'll go!" shouted a voice. Toroca turned to see a mate, her red leather cap bright in the white sunlight, indicating the wooden wheel that held the anchor chain. Toroca thought briefly that the bright red caps worn by Keenir's crew suggested inflated dewlaps, like those of males in full mating display. He shook his head; he'd been on board the ship much too long.

Keenir made a hand signal indicating he understood that the anchor had failed to find bottom. It mattered little: with the sails down, the *Dasheter* wasn't going anywhere. "Shore boats!" shouted the captain in his gravelly voice. Sailors began pulling back the leather sheets that covered the *Dasheter*'s four auxiliary craft.

Keenir turned to Toroca. "I hope there's game on those islands," he said, claws dancing in and out of their sheaths. "I'm sick of fish and salted thunderbeast."

Keenir knew of Toroca's . . . *condition* was perhaps the best word for it. Toroca lacked the native sense of territoriality and the urge to hunt. Oh, he ate meat, and enjoyed the taste of it, but he preferred, whenever possible, not to have to take part in the killing. Still, to stand on solid ground; to drag toeclaws through dirt; to feel something other than splintery wood beneath his tail—it would be wonderful to get off the *Dasheter,* even for a short time.

Only four individuals would go ashore on the first excursion; it wasn't wise to pack Quintaglios tightly together. Keenir and Toroca clambered into one shore boat, and two other surveyors, the females Babnol and Spalton, got into a second. Sailors on the *Dasheter* worked the winches that lowered the boats into the water.

The nearest island was perhaps six hundred kilopaces in diameter. It had two adjacent beaches, separated by a finger of jungle that came to the water's edge. Keenir and Toroca would land on the northern beach; Babnol and Spalton would take the southern one.

Quintaglios grew throughout their lives, so Toroca naturally wasn't as big or strong as Keenir. Their boat was taking a decidedly curving course toward the island. Keenir clicked his teeth

and switched to paddling on the same side as Toroca, causing
the boat to arc in the opposite direction.

Finally, the two of them made it to shore. At first glance,
Toroca was disappointed. The vegetation that rose up like a wall
behind the sandy beach seemed familiar. Why, that was a stand of
keetaja trees over there, and the ubiquitous orange flowers were
common starweed. Toroca had formulated his theory of evolution
while visiting the south pole, having seen all the startling forms
inhabiting the ice pack that had developed from the wingfinger
body plan, and he'd hoped to find similarly bizarre life here. But
this could have been one of the resort beaches along the north
shore of Chu'toolar province back in Land.

They began walking toward the jungle, looking for a break that
might indicate a path trampled by animals. Toroca glanced back,
saw his and the captain's footprints and the marks made by their
tails, saw, too, far out in the water, the twin diamond-shaped hulls
of the *Dasheter*. Then he turned, and—

Something was very wrong. Keenir's claws were extended. His
body had tipped forward from the waist; his torso was bobbing
up and down, up and down . . .

Toroca looked in the direction Keenir's muzzle was pointing
and felt, just for an instant, his own claws leap out in surprise.

Up ahead, someone—some*thing*—had stepped out of the jungle and was staring at them.

No matter how much time she spent inside the ark, it never
ceased to make Novato uneasy. The thing was huge, bigger than
any structure Quintaglios had ever built. And it was ancient:
assuming it was the same age as the Bookmark layer, the ark
was *millions* of kilodays old.

But most chilling of all was the *alienness* of the ark. In a thousand ways it screamed that its makers had not been Quintaglios:
the straight corridors; the rooms with multiple beds that made
no concession to territoriality; the tools designed for six-fingered
hands; the remnants of fabric on the floors; the bowl-shaped
chairs with no notch for a tail.

And strangest of all were the ark crewmembers themselves,
with five knoblike eyes; long, flexible trunks; three pairs of
legs—the front pair for locomotion, the middle and hind pairs
successively smaller and used for God only knew what.

Today, Novato was cataloging the contents of storage locker
412. The ark-makers had been fanatical about numbering things:

doorways, beds, lockers—everything had a number on it. Their system of counting was the only part of their written language that had been deciphered. They used six numerals, plus a horizontal line to represent zero.

Novato set her lamp on the slightly canted floor. She tried to concentrate on her task, but, as usual, found her mind wandering and her heart pounding. Except for the pool of light made by the lamp, the vastness around her was blacker than Quintaglio eyes. Her claws hung half out of their sheaths, ready in case an alien trunk should reach out of the darkness, seizing her by the neck.

Novato was particularly edgy today. She'd been hunting earlier and things had not gone well. Although she'd managed to fell a small shovelmouth, her kill had been stolen by a pack of terrorclaws. Novato had escaped by climbing a tree but she was still rattled by the whole affair. Here, in the darkness, deep within the alien ship, her imagination was running rampant.

Light from the lamp flame seemed to lap at the walls. Quavering specters danced behind her. Novato tried to shut it all out, to concentrate on her work. She'd been here a thousand times, she reminded herself. A thousand times. There were no ghosts here. Nothing to fear.

Those terrorclaws *had* rattled her . . .

Be calm. There was no reason to be afraid.

What was that?

A sound?

Ridiculous.

But there it was again.

Someone calling her name, perhaps?

Novato's tail swished as she turned around—

Her heart skipped a beat—

God, no!

But it was too late.

She knocked over her lamp, the glass housing shattering. Thunderbeast oil spilled everywhere. Flames shot up as the puddle ignited. Novato backed away from the inferno.

A voice.

Just at the limit of perception, a voice.

Afsan craned his neck, trying to hear. Around him all was darkness, but from somewhere in that abyss came the voice.

The tone was doleful, plaintive, and the words were elusive. Afsan thought he could catch the occasional pronoun—"I," "you," "we"—but that was all. The rest was a lilting blur, rising and falling like heavy sighs.

Afsan ran toward the voice, ran the way he had ages ago when he could see. The sound of his feet slapping the ground echoed behind him, drowning out the very words he was desperate to hear. He stopped, but his heart was pounding deafeningly now. Cupping a hand behind each earhole, he tried to isolate the mournful voice. Earlier it had been to the left. Now, maddeningly, it seemed to be behind him. He ran again, back the way he'd come.

More snatches of speech: "I." "You." "We." The rest was a smudge of sound, unintelligible, lost on the wind.

Afsan stopped running again, cocked his head, strained to listen. It seemed now that the dim voice was up ahead. He hurried in that direction but already it was clear that the source was moving yet again. "Wait!" cried Afsan as the source of the sound shifted again. "Wait for me!"

He ran until he could run no more. The voice was still too far away for him to catch anything more than the odd isolated word.

"I—"

From behind him now. Afsan pivoted and ran to the rear.

"You—"

The left! He hurried in that direction.

"We—"

The right.

Again and again, forever.

The creature staring out at Toroca and Captain Keenir looked something like a Quintaglio. All the same parts were there: two arms ending in five-fingered hands; two legs ending in feet with three toeclaws and a heel spur; a tail, triangular in cross section, hanging off the back; a thick, dexterous neck with, in males, as this one apparently was, the folds of an uninflated dewlap suspended from the front; a head looking round in full view but front-heavy with a drawn-out muzzle in profile; two nostrils at the tip of the muzzle; small earholes; forward-facing eyes.

And yet, at the same time, the—the *other* didn't look like a Quintaglio at all. The leathery hides of Quintaglios are predominantly green, shaded with yellow and brown, and, in the very old, mottled with black. But this being was almost completely yellow, with gray highlights. And its eyes, rather than being the black of Quintaglio orbs, were pale yellow with gold irises and clearly visible pupils. The earholes, instead of being the kidney-shaped openings most Quintaglios had, were vertical slits. And the shape of the muzzle, well . . . it was pinched, caved in on either side, coming to a narrower and sharper point than normal for a Quintaglio. The head also seemed big for the body, and the body was thin and puny by Quintaglio standards. The net effect of all these differences in color and shape and proportion was to make the other look *wrong,* malformed.

Quintaglios usually sported a decorative sash, and possibly a hat or tool belt. This creature was completely naked save for a copper necklace, two bracelets on one arm and three on the other, and a small band around his right ankle.

The Other just stood there, head tilted slightly, hands hanging free, claws retracted. But Keenir, Captain Var-Keenir of the good ship *Dasheter,* continued to bob in territorial display.

Toroca thought the sailor's reaction a bizarre one and wondered fleetingly if the captain was only feigning the display as a form of greeting, but, no, the extended claws and the jaws hanging loosely open showing curving, serrated teeth made clear that this was a true instinctive display.

The Other was thirty paces away, too distant to constitute an encroachment on Keenir's territory, and he was giving no sign of replying to Keenir's bobbing. Surely the combination of a lack of response and the distance between them would snap Keenir out of it—

Not a chance. Keenir burst into action, his body tipped over so that his torso was held horizontally, parallel to the sands of the beach, his tail flying out behind him.

The Other took a few beats to react . . . a few fatal beats. By the time he had turned around, ready to retreat into the vegetation, Keenir was almost upon him. The captain crouched low, then leapt, hurtling through the air. He landed on the Other's narrow yellow back, slamming him into the sands.

The captain was more than twice the Other's size. Keenir arched his own neck, preparing for a killing bite, but the Other managed to roll the two of them onto their sides then jab his elbow into the underside of Keenir's muzzle. Quintaglio lower jawbones aren't fused at the front; they can split to facilitate the bolting of meat. By bringing his elbow in underneath Keenir's jaw, the Other forced the two halves to separate—excruciating when not done under voluntary control. Keenir yelped and scrambled for his feet. The Other clawed sand, also trying to regain his footing.

Toroca had stood frozen, startled by the sight of the Other, and confounded by Keenir's bizarre reaction, but now he, too, sprang into action, running toward the combatants. The Other seemed not to be in the territorial frenzy of *dagamant* which now gripped Keenir; his elbow-to-the-chin trick had been a calculated, intelligent move. Toroca hoped that if the Other could get away, he'd do just that instead of turning to attack. Toroca ran toward them, divots of moist sand flying out behind his footfalls. He'd broken up a territorial fight once before but this would be a lot harder. Keenir was huge and powerful. A shearing bite from his massive jaws could decapitate Toroca; a blow from his arms could crush Toroca's throat.

Toroca was about to leap onto Keenir's back when another strategy occurred to him. Bending low, he scooped up a handful of sand. Here, back from the breaking waves, it was mostly dry. He tossed it in Keenir's face. Instinctively, Keenir brought his hands up to try to get the grit out of his eyes, and, in that moment, the Other made it to his feet and began to run toward the wall of vegetation. But Keenir was only momentarily distracted. Although he kept one black eye closed, grit presumably still stinging him, he rose up, a mountain of green flesh, and gave chase.

There was no contest at all. Keenir's stride was half again as long as the Other's. He was upon the hapless yellow being in a few moments, the captain's jaw swinging wide, the lower jawbones splitting apart (this time under Keenir's direction), his curving white fangs, slick with spit, glinting in the harsh sunlight. And then, with a dart of the neck, Keenir scooped a vast track of flesh from the Other's shoulder and back. Death was instantaneous; the Other crumpled, blood surging onto the sands. Keenir tipped his head up and let out a long, primal roar.

Toroca surveyed the scene. The beach was covered with footprints, dents left by bodies slamming into the sand, and splatters of blood. And here, at the end of the trail, Captain Keenir crouched on top of a strange yellow corpse, his muzzle shiny and red, stringy meat caught between his teeth.

The first encounter between Quintaglios and Others had not gone well.

Chapter 3

Emperor Dy-Dybo was constantly busy. His principal concern
was the exodus project, but he knew it would be many kilodays
before the world came to an end—indeed, the world would doubtless outlive him. That meant he could not ignore more prosaic
matters. During a typical day, Dybo dealt with many issues related to the economy, including, for example, improving bilateral
trade with Edz'toolar province, whose storm-swept coast made it
difficult for ships to land.

He was also trying to resolve the dispute between the peoples of Chu'toolar and Mar'toolar. The citizens of the latter
claimed that the *Hahat Golarda*—the ancient scroll that apportioned territories—had been misinterpreted, and that their border
should run along the northern, rather than southern, edge of the
Hoont'mar mountain chain. Dybo's scholars had determined that
the Mar'toolarians were correct, but it remained for him to get
Len-Honlab, the ancient and stubborn governor of Chu'toolar, to
concede the point.

Judicial matters also made demands on Dybo's time. In addition
to being the highest level of appeal, the Emperor had to approve
or reject all laws proposed by the legislature. For instance, he'd
been wrestling with a new rule that would require anyone killing
an animal for food purposes inside a city to drag the uneaten part
of the carcass outside the municipal boundary.

Despite these pressures, Dybo always cleared ample time to
eat. Unlike most Quintaglios, who ate a major meal only every

five days, Dybo liked to dig his muzzle into a steaming haunch every other afternoon. Many people requested mealtime audiences with the Emperor, common belief being that he reacted more favorably to requests when his stomach was not growling. Still, there were certain friends and advisors with whom Dybo dined regularly, and, by long custom, on every fortieth day he shared his meal with Afsan.

In his youth, Dybo had been fond of scatological insults. His age and his office had changed that, but, as Afsan entered the private room at the back of the imperial dining hall, it sounded briefly as though the old Dybo was back. "Why, Afsan," declared the Emperor, his rich voice filling the large chamber, "you look like a pile of hornface droppings."

Afsan responded in kind. "Ah, my friend, but one of the few joys in being blind is *not* having to be constantly reminded of what it is that you look like."

But it turned out that Dybo wasn't really looking to engage in a humorous exchange. "I'm serious," he said, pushing up off his dayslab, which was angled over the food table. "Your tail is dragging like a dead weight and your skin is grayish. Are you sure you didn't pick up an infection because of your accident?"

"No, it's not an infection," said Afsan. "I'm afraid I haven't been sleeping well."

"What's wrong?"

"Dreams," Afsan said. "Bad dreams."

"What about?"

Afsan leaned back on his tail. His whole body seemed weary. "There's a dayslab two paces to your left," said Dybo.

Afsan found the angled marble sheet and lowered himself onto it. "Thank you," he said. He seemed too tired even to settle in comfortably.

"What are your bad dreams about?" Dybo asked again.

The words came out as protracted hisses. "I'm not sure. Just disjointed images, really. Trying to listen to people I can't quite hear, for instance, who maddeningly stay just out of reach."

"That does sound frustrating."

"That it is. And every night it's a different dream. I lie on my floor trying to sleep, but the dreams keep waking me. There's always some point at which they become unbearable and I wake with a start, my heart pounding and my breath ragged. It happens over and over throughout the night."

"Maybe you need to eat more before you go to bed," said Dybo. "I never have trouble sleeping."

"I've tried that. I've gorged myself before retiring in hopes of forcing torpor, but the dreams come nonetheless."

Dybo slapped his belly. Although it was substantially reduced from its once-legendary girth, he'd put back a good hunk of what he'd lost before the challenge battle with the blackdeath. "I imagine your idea of gorging is something less than mine. Still, I take your point. Are you still sleeping only on odd-nights?" Just about everyone, except the very young and the very old, slept only every other night, but Afsan had long had the habit of sleeping on the night that most people were awake.

Afsan shook his head. "I've tried altering my sleep schedule: I've slept even-nights, I've tried sleeping every night, and only every third night. Nothing has helped."

Dybo grunted. "Have you consulted Dar-Mondark?"

"Yes. I've been seeing him every ten days so he can check on the healing of my injuries. He's better with broken bones than with something as mundane as sleep. He simply said I'd eventually be so tired, my body would force itself to sleep."

"I suppose that's true," said Dybo. "But if I can apply a lesson you taught me, that would be dealing with the effect rather than the cause, no?"

Afsan found the strength to click his teeth lightly. "Exactly. The real problem is the dreams."

Dybo was silent for a moment. "Have you tried the talking cure?"

"The what?"

"Afsan, you've got to have that apprentice of yours—what's her name?"

"Pettit."

"Her. You've got to have her read to you on a wider range of subjects. The talking cure is all the rage, so they tell me. A savant named—oh, I never can remember names. Moklub, Mokleb, something like that. Anyway, she's worked out this system in which people simply talk about their problems and, *poof!*, they go away."

Afsan sounded dubious. "Uh-huh."

"Really. She calls herself a, a—what was the word? A psych-something. Means a healer of the mind, apparently. There was a fellow from Jam'toolar who came clear across Land to see her. He was constantly depressed. Said he felt as if the weight of his tail were hanging off the front of his head instead of his rump. Turned out that as a child, he'd stolen some jewels from his Hall of Worship. He'd completely forgotten doing that, but not only did talking with Mok-whatever help him recall it, he was even able to remember where he'd buried the stones. He dug them up, returned them to the Hall, walked the sinner's march, and apparently feels better than he has in kilodays."

"I haven't stolen any stones."

"Of course not. But this Mok-person says there are always hidden reasons for why we feel the way we do. She could help you uncover whatever it is that's causing your bad dreams."

"I don't know . . ."

"Ah, but that's the whole point! You don't know! Give it a try, Afsan. You certainly can't go around looking like something a shovelmouth spit out."

"I thought I looked like hornface droppings."

"Depends on the light. Anyway, I need the old Afsan back. Can't run this crazy government on my own, you know."

"Well—"

Dybo raised a hand. "No more objections. I'll have a page round Mok-thingy up and send her to you this afternoon. You'll be at Rockscape?"

"No, I've got to see the healer again this afternoon. Send her tomorrow."

"Very good."

"One thing, though," said Afsan. "If I'm sleeping when she arrives, tell her not to wake me. I can use the rest."

Dybo clicked his teeth. "Fine. Now, where's that butcher?" The Emperor's voice sang out. "Butcher! Meat! Meat, I say! My friend and I are hungry!"

Inside the ark, flames licked the ceiling. For once, the interior of the alien ship was brightly lit. For once, Novato saw—really saw—what it looked like.

Its blue walls appeared green in the fierce light of the flames. Their perfect smoothness was unmarred, even after all these millennia. Here and there columns of geometric markings were incised somehow into the obdurate material.

Novato was terrified, her breathing ragged, her claws glinting in the roaring flames.

Calm, she thought. *Be calm.*

She couldn't douse the flames—the water in her canteen would do little against an oil fire. But the fire couldn't really spread, either. She'd done tests on the blue material; no matter how much she heated it, it never burned. No, the blaze would exhaust itself once the oil had been consumed.

The heat was tremendous.

Novato put a hand to the tip of her muzzle, covering her nostrils. Thunderbeast oil normally burned cleanly, but with so much going up at once there was an acrid smell.

She couldn't stay here. Quintaglios had learned much about air recently; Novato knew that open flames consumed some part of it that she needed to breathe. To remain here was to risk fainting, and although the material of the ship would not burn, Quintaglio flesh most certainly could. She backed away from the dancing flames, away from the light, into the darkness, the all-consuming darkness of the vast and empty ship.

She couldn't hear anything except the thundering of her heart, the crackling of flames, and the clicking of her toeclaws against the floor. Turning, she confronted her own giant shadow, a shuddering silhouette on the far wall. Next to it was an open archway. Novato stepped through, the heat now on her back and tail, the normal coolness of the ship's interior a welcome sensation on her muzzle. Her shadow moved with her, dancing along the wall like a living tapestry.

Left or right?

Why, right, of course.

No—left.

Left, yes, that was correct. Left.

She turned and took two steps forward. Her shadow disappeared as everything faded to uniform blackness.

Novato placed her left hand on the wall. Her claws were still extended. She tried to retract them but they would not return to their sheaths. So be it. She let the fluted cones lightly scrape along the wall as she began down the corridor. The sound of the spluttering flames gradually disappeared.

And then, a bend in the corridor.

Should there be a bend here?

Yes. Surely yes, she thought. A bend to the right here, one to the left not much farther after that. Be calm!

Total, absolute darkness now. No trace of light from the fire. She removed her hand from the wall and held it in front of her face. Completely invisible. She closed her inner and outer eyelids. No difference. Utter, complete, soul-devouring blackness.

Novato walked slowly, afraid of losing her footing on the too-smooth, slightly angled floor.

The ship groaned.

She stopped dead, held her breath.

Again: a moaning sound, coming from all around her.

She touched her hunter's tattoo and then her left shoulder, an ancient gesture of obeisance to God.

Once more: a low, sustained, mournful sound.

The ship . . . alive? Alive, after all this time?

Impossible. It had been buried millions of kilodays ago. Novato hadn't realized her hands were shaking until she tried to bring them together.

Groaning, rumbling—like, like *digestion*. As though she'd been swallowed alive . . .

But then she slapped her tail loudly against the floor.

Be rational, she thought. *Rational.*

She'd heard this sound before, but never so clearly. Most of the ship was buried in a cliff. As the day wore on, the rocks of the cliff's face heated and expanded. Their shifting against the unyielding hull caused sounds like these. She'd never been so close to the outer hull when the shifting had occurred, but that must be it. It *must* be.

She touched her teeth together and shook her head. *If Afsan could only see me now—*

Afsan, so rational, so logical. Why, he'd click his teeth until all the loose ones had been knocked out if he saw Novato being so foolish . . .

But then it hit her. *If Afsan could see me now?* Afsan sees nothing, nothing at all.

Novato began walking again, her claws still unsheathed, although she was certain—*certain!*—that should she now command them to, they would slip back into her fingers, out of view.

Out of view.

She thought again of Afsan. Was this what it was like to be blind? Did Afsan feel the kind of fear she felt now, unsure of every step, unaware of what might be lurking only a pace away? How could one get used to this? *Was* he used to it? Even now, even after all this time?

He had never seen their children, never seen the vast spaceship Novato was now within, never seen the statue erected in his honor in Capital City.

And never, except that one wonderful time when he had come to Pack Gelbo all those kilodays ago, had he seen Novato.

Of course he must be used to the darkness. Of course.

She continued through the void, the image of Afsan giving her strength. She felt, in a strange way, as though he, with all his experience in navigating in darkness, walked beside her.

Her footfalls echoed. The ship moaned again as its rocky tomb heated further.

Suddenly her left hand was touching nothing but air. The corridor had opened into another corridor, running perpendicular to it. Novato exhaled noisily. Her teams had marked every intersection with a circle of paint on the wall, color-coding the various paths through the ship's interior. Of course, she couldn't see the colors—or anything else—but surely she could find the circle. She felt at shoulder-height. Nothing but smooth, uninterrupted wall, until—yes, here it was. A roughening of the wall surface, a round area of a different texture. Dried paint.

Novato scraped the paint with her claws, catching tiny flakes of pigment on their tips. She brought her fingers to her nostrils and inhaled deeply.

A scent, faint but unmistakable: sulfur. Yellow pigment. Yellow marked the corridor designated major-axis 2. She stopped, picturing the layout of the ship. Yes, major-axis 2 . . . that made sense. She *had* been going the wrong way, but she knew how to get out from here, although it would require more time. She would take the right-hand path here, and in what—a hundred kilopaces?—she'd come to another intersection. Another right and then a left and eventually she'd be back at the strange doubledoored room that led outside.

She paused for a moment, relaxing. Her claws slipped back into their sheaths. The panic of moments before was forgotten. She stepped—

What was that?

A flash of light?

Light?

Here, inside the ship?

Madness . . . unless a firefly or glowgrub had made its way into the interior.

She looked in the direction from which she'd seen the flickering.

Nothing. Of course not. Why, hadn't Afsan once said he still occasionally saw little flashes of light? The mind hated to be deprived . . .

There it was again . . .

Novato brought the side of her head right up to the wall and stared into the darkness.

The ship was old, inconceivably ancient.

But there it was once more, a flash of greenish-white, gone almost before she'd even noticed it. A line of geometric shapes, flashing in the dark. Incredible.

Novato wanted to mark this spot so she could find it again. She undid the neck chain that helped hold her sash on, then lifted the wide loop of leather over her head and set it on the floor in front of the flashing symbols on the wall. The sash settled with little clinks as its brass and copper ornaments touched the deck.

Alive. After all this time, at least some small part of the ship was alive.

Novato went down the corridor as fast as she dared in the darkness, anxious to get a fresh lamp and return to examine whatever she had found. Finally, she caught sight of a pale rectangle of light along the corridor: the double-doored room. The inner door was wide open; the outer one jammed half-closed, just as it had been ever since her son Toroca had first entered the ship three kilodays ago. Novato shouldered her way through, cool night air pouring in from outside. The fit was getting tighter all the time; eventually the growth that would go on until her death would prevent her from squeezing into the ship.

She stumbled out onto the wooden scaffolding. It was early evening, the sun having just set. Still, after so long in absolute darkness, the five moons visible overhead blazed like wild flames.

Captain Keenir of the *Dasheter* slowly regained his senses. He pushed himself off the carcass of the bizarre yellow being and staggered back a few paces along the beach, a look of horror on his face.

"What have I done?" he said, leaning on his tail for support, his gravelly voice a half-whimper. "What have I done?" The captain looked down. His arms were covered with drying blood up to the elbows, and his entire muzzle was crusted over with red. He brought his hands to his face and tried to wipe the blood from there. "What have I done?" he said once more.

Toroca looked at the dead body. It had been badly mauled. Before coming out of the territorial madness, Keenir had bolted down three large strips of flesh, cleaning the neck, shoulders, and most of the back of meat.

Toroca had backed away and was now about twenty paces from Keenir. "Why did you kill it?" he said.

The captain's voice was low. "I—I don't know. It—it must have invaded my territory . . ."

Toroca's tail swished in negation. "No. It was nowhere near you. You saw it, and went, well, berserk."

"It was evil. It had to die. It was a threat."

"How, Keenir? How did it threaten you?"

Keenir's voice was faint. "It had to die," he said again. He staggered toward the lapping water at the edge of the beach, crouched down, and tried to wash his hands. The water turned pink, but his hands weren't really coming clean. He scooped up some wet sand and rubbed it over them, scouring the blood away. He kept rubbing his hands, so much so that Toroca thought they'd end up covered in the captain's own blood, but at last he stopped. He splashed water on his face in an attempt to clean his muzzle.

There was a point where the lush vegetation stuck right out to the water's edge. Suddenly there was movement in that brush, and for one horrible moment Toroca thought it was another of the strange yellow creatures, come to avenge its comrade's death. But it was only Babnol and Spalton, the other two surveyors, who had made their own landing south of here.

But then he saw their faces.

Muzzles slick with blood.

"Toroca," said Babnol, her voice tremulous. "I think Spalton and I just did a terrible thing . . ."

Chapter 4

By now, Afsan's eyes had grown back to full size, black orbs filling the once-empty sockets. His lids had sagged for so long that they'd developed permanent fold marks that showed as yellow lines now that they were filled out from underneath.

And yet, despite his new eyes, Afsan still could not see.

After his lunch with Dybo, Afsan walked the short distance to the imperial surgery and once again opened his lids so that Dar-Mondark could look at his new eyes.

"And you still can't see anything?" said Mondark.

"That's right."

"Not even vague shapes? No hint of light? Nothing?"

"Nothing."

"Your eyes look fine, Afsan. They look like they should work."

Afsan's tail swished gently. "When I was young, I once traded some time tutoring mathematics for a toy boat that I was enamored with. The boat was beautifully carved from soft stone and looked correct in every way. Only one problem: when I put it in a pond, it sank. It was good at everything except the one thing that defined its purpose." He tipped his head. "Eyes that do everything well except see aren't of much value, are they?"

Mondark nodded. "That's true. But, Afsan, your eyes *are* seeing: they are responding to light. Now, yes, perhaps there is some problem with the way your new eyes are connected to the rest of your body. But as far as I can tell, your eyes are fully restored."

"Then God is having Her revenge on me," said Afsan, his tone only half-jesting. "A cruel joke, no? To give back eyes, only to have them not function."

"Perhaps."

"Perhaps nothing, Doctor. I'm not a medical expert, but clearly there's something wrong with the nerves that connect my eyes to my brain."

"In ordinary cases of blindness, I'd concur. But this isn't ordinary. Your eyes *are* responding to light, and they're tracking as though they can see. They would do neither of those things if there were extensive nerve damage."

"But I tell you, I'm not seeing anything."

"Exactly. Which brings us to another possibility." Mondark paused, as if reluctant to go on.

"Yes?" said Afsan impatiently.

"Do you know the word 'hysteria'?"

"No."

"That's not surprising; it's a fairly new medical term. Hysteria refers to a neurosis characterized by physical symptoms, such as paralysis, that don't seem to have any organic cause."

Afsan sounded suspicious. "For instance?"

"Oh, there have been several cases over the kilodays. A person may lose the use of a limb even though the limb appears to be uninjured. And yet the person simply stops being able to move, for instance, his or her right arm."

"I've never heard of such a thing."

"Well, it does happen. It used to be if your arm stopped working, they'd hack it off in hopes that the regenerated arm would function. Sometimes that worked—if there had been damage to the nerves in the arm. But sometimes the arm would grow back just as dead as it had been before."

"But surely the paralysis would have been caused by a stroke or something similar."

"Ah, there's the rub," said Mondark. "When paralysis is caused by a stroke, it affects *general* parts of the body. Oh, the right arm might be completely paralyzed, but there will also be numbness in the right leg, and perhaps the right side of the face. But in hysterical paralysis, only the arm seems dead. The loss of sensation is quite abrupt, beginning, say, precisely at the shoulder, and affecting no other part of the body."

"Go on," said Afsan.

"Well, there are also cases of hysterical blindness: eyes that are in working order that simply no longer function."

"And you think that's the case here? That my blindness is caused by . . . by hysteria?"

"It's possible. Your eyes physically *can* see, but your mind *refuses* to see."

"Nonsense, Mondark. I *want* to see. I've wanted to see since the very day I was blinded."

"Consciously, yes. But your subconscious—? Well, this isn't my area of expertise, but there is a doctor who has had some success curing these matters, Afsan. She's helped several people regain the use of arms or legs."

"This is ridiculous," said Afsan. "If my eyes are malfunctioning, the problem is physical. It's that simple."

"Perhaps," said Mondark. "But what have you got to lose by visiting her?"

"Time," said Afsan. "I'm getting old, Mondark, and there is much that I wish to accomplish still."

Mondark grunted. "Humor me, Afsan. Meet with this person."

"I *have* been humoring you. I've been coming here every ten days to let you look at these useless eyes."

"And I thank you for that. But consider how lucky you are: almost no one who loses eyes gets them back. To give up now would be a horrible mistake. If there's a chance—any chance at all—that you might be able to see again, you owe it to yourself to pursue it."

"I owe it to myself to be a realist," said Afsan. "That's the principle that has guided my entire life. I'm too old to change now."

"Do a favor for an old friend, Afsan. Indeed, do yourself a favor. At least arrange a consultation with Nav-Mokleb."

"Mokleb?" said Afsan, startled.

"You've heard of her?"

"Well, yes. Dybo has been after me to talk with her as well. Says she might be able to do something about the bad dreams I've been having."

"Those continue to plague you?"

"Yes."

Mondark's tail swished across the floor. "That settles it. Go to Rockscape. I'll contact Mokleb and send her out to see you."

"Dybo already has her coming out tomorrow morning."

"Good," said Mondark. "Who knows? Maybe she'll be able to cure both your bad dreams and your blindness."

• • •

There was no need for Novato to wait until morning; working inside the alien ark could be done as easily at night as day. It was even-night, anyway, the night upon which Novato usually did not sleep. She went to find Den-Garios, an old friend from Capital province who had long worked with her on the exodus project. They fetched two fresh lanterns and re-entered the ship, moving quickly down the corridors.

Soon they were at the intersection marked by the circle of yellow pigment on the wall. Beneath the yellow circle was the ark-maker's own numerical designation for this intersection. And there, down the perpendicular corridor, just as she'd left it, her sash. Heart pounding, she jogged over to it.

"Right here," said Novato, pointing at the wall. "This is where I saw the flashing."

Garios was about Novato's age. He had an unusually long muzzle that gave him a melancholy look, and eyes that were small and close together. He peered at the wall. "I can't see anything."

"No," said Novato. "The lamp flame must be drowning it out. Here." She stepped close enough to proffer her lamp to Garios. "Take this and walk down that corridor and go around the bend."

Garios set down the roll of leather he'd been carrying, dipped his long muzzle in acknowledgment, and did as Novato had asked. In the darkness, Novato pressed the side of her face against the wall. Nothing. Either the flashing had stopped, or perhaps her eyes hadn't had enough time to adjust to darkness.

She waited for a hundred beats, then tried again. Still nothing.

It had been daytime when she'd been here before. Daytime and the flashing was happening.

Now it was night, and there was no flashing.

That made no sense. One lit lights at night, doused them during the day. This was exactly the opposite.

Suddenly she thought of the matrix of black hexagons on the ship's roof. They conducted heat from the sun somewhere, but only during the day, obviously. Could this have been where that energy was channeled?

She called Garios back. He came, holding the pair of lamps in front of him, two long shadows following behind.

"I can't see the flashing anymore," Novato said. "Hold the lamps steady, please. I want to examine this wall."

Novato turned her back so that Garios couldn't see what she was about to do, then she forced her claws from their sheaths. Keeping them out of Garios's view, she felt along the wall, looking for anything out of the ordinary.

There.

A seam.

A juncture where two plates were joined.

No one had ever found a seam before. The whole ship appeared to have been made inside and out from one continuous piece of blue material.

Novato used her middle fingerclaw to trace the seam's height. It came to a right-angle intersection and then continued along about a handspan below the top of the wall. By the time she was finished, Novato had outlined a rectangle going almost from floor to ceiling. Its width was about equal to Novato's arm-span.

"No wonder we missed that," said Garios, his little eyes peering intently. "It's difficult to see, even with two lamps."

Novato nodded. "Maybe this panel was originally painted differently from the rest of the wall," she said. They'd found colored dust in the ship that seemed to be dried pigment that had peeled off the walls; the blue material wasn't porous, so paint probably didn't stick to it well even under the best of circumstances.

"And where exactly did you see the flashing?" said Garios.

Novato's sash was directly below the middle of the rectangle. She pointed to the panel's center.

"May I?" said Garios.

Novato scuttled out of the way. Garios came in, a lamp in each hand, and peered at the wall. "Maybe," he said at first, and "Maybe" a little later. Then: "Yup, there it is. God, it's hard to see! But there are little bits of glass inlaid into the wall here, absolutely flush with the wall material. A string of those geometric shapes the ark-makers used for writing. Seven, no, eight shapes. A word." Garios sighed. "I guess we'll never know what it said."

" 'Emergency,' " said Novato. "Something like that."

Garios sounded surprised. "What makes you think that?"

"Have you ever been on a hunt that's gone badly? Lots of injuries? When healers arrive, they prioritize whom to treat. Those who have the most critical need for attention are tended to first. Of all the things on this ship, the only one that we've seen any sign of still working at all is this panel, whatever it is. It's obviously the priority now that a little power is somehow trickling into the ship. I'm no sailor, but I suspect Keenir would say that if he had to prioritize things aboard a ship, lifeboats, fire-fighting buckets, and other emergency equipment would be the most important."

Garios grunted, not convinced. He had brought plans of the ark with him. He set his lamps on the floor and proceeded to unfurl a chart, kneeling down to read it. "According to this, there's just another one of those multi-bed rooms on the other side of this wall. Now, yes, the wall is thicker than normal here—it's about a third of a pace thick. That's not unusual, though. There are lots of places where the walls are even thicker. But surely there can't be any lifeboats stored behind here. Whatever is back there can't be very big."

Novato nodded. "Let's see if we can get the panel off. It must open somehow."

"Maybe it's a sliding door, like the others we've seen."

Novato's tail swished in negation. "Those doors are recessed and apparently normally were moved by an arrangement of gears that must have required some power to operate. No, if I'm right— if this is a hold for emergency equipment—it'll be designed to open without any power." She paused. "If you were one of those five-eyed creatures, how would you open something?"

Garios looked at the floor. "Well, I'd only have one useful limb—that long trunk—so the method would be something that you or I could do with one hand. And, let's see, those creatures only came up to about here on me." He held a hand at the middle of his chest. "They've got a lot of reach with those trunks, but I imagine if they wanted any real leverage, they'd have to fold the trunk over."

Novato nodded. "So, if we're looking for a handle, it would be in the middle of the panel, right about here." She pointed.

"But there isn't anything there," said Garios.

Novato, ever the empiricist, pressed her palm against the center of the panel. Nothing. She tried again, leaning all her weight against it. As soon as she stopped, the panel popped forward as though it had been on springs. Garios surged in and grabbed one side of the heavy sheet. Novato took the other side, and they lowered it to the floor. From the back they could clearly see the little array of glass inlays that had caused the flashing.

A shallow closet had been revealed. Inside were three metal boxes. Each had embossed on its side the same word Garios had traced out on the wall panel. The boxes had handles sticking out of their sides. Novato pulled on one of the handles, and the box came out of its holder. A tail of flexible clear strands stuck out of its back connecting it to the rear of its holding compartment, but as Novato pulled a little harder, the strands came loose. At the end, they were bundled together in a little plug, as if they'd been designed to come out this way.

The box itself had clamps on its side, holding the lid securely on. Novato had seen clamps like this several times aboard the ark. They required an uncomfortable backward bending of the fingers to undo, but she'd gotten the hang of it over time. She opened the box.

Inside was orange dust.

Garios loomed in for a peek. "Rust," he said. "Whatever was in there decayed long ago." He backed away.

Novato put her hand in the box and wiggled her fingers, looking for any fragment that hadn't completely decayed. The orange dust felt strange. Warm. A lot warmer than it had any right to be. And it wasn't sharp like iron filings. Rather, it was soft, like talcum, and slightly heavier than it looked, as if the material was very dense. Novato didn't bring it too close to her face; she was afraid of inhaling the powder.

Just dust, that's all it was. Ancient dust.

She knelt down and upended the box onto Garios's floor plan, hoping there would be something inside all the dust. But the orange grains just sifted out; it seemed to be a uniformly fine grade. The dust made a good-sized mountain in the center of the plan. Individual grains spilled toward the sheet's edge.

Disappointed, Novato turned her attention to the two boxes still embedded in the wall. The second one had apparently been damaged in the ark's crash and its contents had long since escaped through a crack in the container's bottom. The third box was rusted or fused to its holder. They tried again and again for an extended period, but no amount of tugging by either her or Garios could dislodge it.

Novato sighed and turned around.

What the—?

The mound of orange dust was no longer centered on the floor plan. In fact, the center of the plan was completely clear and the mound was now half on and half off the sheet of leather.

It must be flowing downhill, thought Novato.

And then she realized that wasn't right at all.

The dust, the ancient orange dust, was flowing, all right, but it was flowing *uphill,* heading toward the corridor that led to the double-doored room.

"They weren't just dumb animals, were they?" said Captain Keenir of the *Dasheter,* his tail swishing back and forth across the beach. "They were people."

Toroca pointed at the body of the Other, lying in a pool of blood. "That one was wearing copper jewelry," he said.

"And the one we, ah, encountered was also sporting jewelry," said Babnol, who had removed her sash and was using it to wipe her face clean of blood.

"The braincases were bigger than those of any animal," Toroca said. "So, yes, they were people, of a kind. Thinking beings."

"And we've killed two of them," said Babnol, shaking her head. "I—I don't know why I reacted the way I did. It was as though the sight of the—the *thing* was enough to trigger *dagamant.* I felt as if my territory had been invaded. My claws popped out, and then everything became a blur. Next thing I knew, Spalton and I were standing over the dead body." She paused. "What was left of the body, that is."

"You didn't feel the same thing?" Keenir said to Toroca, almost imploringly, as if seeking absolution.

Toroca's tail swished. "No. The appearance of the Other was startling, but it didn't trigger any rage in me."

"You're unusual, of course," said Babnol matter-of-factly. "You're free of the territorial instinct."

"True."

"Something about these Others sets off that instinct," said Babnol. "The sight of them, or maybe their pheromones. Something."

"It wasn't pheromones," said Keenir. "The one Toroca and I saw was downwind of us." He looked out over the waters. "The sun is setting. We should get back to the *Dasheter.*"

"What about the bodies?" said Toroca.

"What do you mean?" asked Babnol.

"I mean, what do we do with them? Do we just leave them on the beach?"

"What else?" said Keenir, aghast. "You're not suggesting we take them back to the ship as food?"

Toroca wrinkled his muzzle in disgust. "No, of course not. But we should do something with them." He leaned back on his tail. "If we're going to have any further contact with the natives here, we've got two choices. Either we try to explain to them what happened—offer our apologies and let them do with the bodies whatever they normally do. Or we hide the bodies and hope that suspicion for the disappearance of these two individuals never falls on us."

Babnol looked at Toroca. She was an unusual Quintaglio herself, having retained her birthing horn into adulthood. The fluted cone cast a shadow across her muzzle. "I suggest we simply hightail it back to the *Dasheter* and get as far away from these islands as possible. They're evil, Toroca."

Toroca looked surprised. "Evil? That's the same word the captain used before you joined us. In any event, we've got to explore these islands; that's the whole point of the Geological Survey. But as to whether we, ah, admit involvement with these deaths . . ."

"Don't do it," said Keenir. "How could we explain what we did? We can't even fathom it ourselves. No, we'll take the bodies back out in the shore boats, tie rocks to their ankles, and dump them overboard when we're far from shore."

Babnol's voice was distressed, and her tail moved in agitated ways. "I don't feel right about doing that."

"Nor do I," agreed the captain. "But since we don't know anything about these people, it's best we not make our initial presentation of ourselves to them as . . . as . . ."

"Murderers," said Toroca.

Keenir sighed. "Yes."

Toroca's turn to sound uncomfortable. "If we are going to take the corpses, please don't dump them overboard. I'd like to, ah, study them."

"Very well," said Keenir. A pause, and then, his voice heavy: "Let's fetch them."

And they set out to do just that. The one that Keenir had killed was still nearby. Wingfingers were picking at the gaping wounds, but they took flight as soon as the Quintaglios approached. Spalton and the captain carried the corpse to the shore boat and began paddling back to the *Dasheter*. Toroca and Babnol covered the bloodstained ground with clean sand, then headed down the beach. They came to where the vegetation jutted into the water and made their way through the growth until they arrived at where Babnol and Spalton had encountered their Other.

"Uh-oh," said Babnol, her head swiveling left and right.

The second body was gone.

Chapter 5

Nav-Mokleb's Casebook

Word of the talking cure is spreading, apparently. I've received an imperial summons asking me to take on a new patient. I'd hoped that the subject was going to be Emperor Dy-Dybo himself. I thought he might be having emotional difficulties, stemming from the challenge to his leadership two kilodays ago. True, he'd acquitted himself well in the battle with the blackdeath, but I wouldn't be surprised if there were residual problems. After all, he did see six apprentice governors die in front of his eyes, and, as if that weren't bad enough, he'd had to chew his own arms off.

But, no, my new patient isn't *quite* that highly placed in the government. Still, Sal-Afsan should be an interesting case nonetheless. I've been reviewing what is generally known about him. Afsan is middle-aged, having hatched some thirty-four kilodays ago in Pack Carno, part of Arj'toolar province. Extremely gifted intellectually, he was summoned to Capital City at the age of thirteen to be the latest and, as it turned out, the last in a series of apprentices to Tak-Saleed, the master court astrologer.

Afsan has certainly lived an interesting life. He was aboard the sailing ship *Dasheter* when it made the first-ever circumnavigation of our world. He is credited with figuring out the true nature of the Face of God, and with discovering that our world is doomed to break up into a ring of rubble. Originally his idea was denounced as heresy, and the late Det-Yenalb, Master of the Faith back then, used a ceremonial dagger to poke out Afsan's eyes in punishment. But an underground of Lubalite hunters declared that Afsan was "The One," the great male hunter that Lubal had prophesied as she lay dying. Afsan's hunts—before he was blinded, of course—were indeed spectacular: he killed the largest thunderbeast ever seen, defeated a great water serpent, and even brought down a fangjaw.

Because of this, all eight of Afsan's children by Wab-Novato were allowed to live. The bloodpriests, an order closely allied with the Lubalites, refused to devour any of The One's egglings.

And now, apparently, this remarkable fellow is having nightmares.

I've long suspected that genius and madness were closely allied. Well, I'll soon learn whether the individual pushing us to the stars is merely troubled, or, as some of his detractors have always claimed, completely insane . . .

Rockscape had lost some of its appeal. Oh, visitors to the Capital still trekked out to see the ninety-four granite boulders arranged in patterns, spread across a field of tall grasses by the edge of a cliff overlooking water. No one knew exactly when the boulders had been laid out in these designs, but it had been in a time before written history.

Still, Rockscape seemed insignificant compared to the ancient spaceship unearthed by Toroca in Fra'toolar. That giant ark was millions of kilodays old. Rockscape, even if it was the oldest known Quintaglio settlement, couldn't compete with that.

Nonetheless, Afsan continued to visit Rockscape most days, using it as an open-air classroom for his students, and, when alone, as a restful, isolated spot for quiet contemplation.

Except, of course, he was rarely alone. His lizard, Gork, was usually with him, lying on its favorite Rockscape boulder, warming in the sun. Afsan also had a boulder he was partial to. He was straddling it now, tail hanging off the back, his sightless eyes turned toward the cliff's distant edge. He could hear the *pipping* calls of wingfingers as they rose and fell on the air currents and the sounds of crickets and other insects in the grass. Although he was a good piece north of Capital City's harbor, Afsan could also make out the identifying drums and bells of ships and occasionally the shouts of merchants arguing over what constituted a fair trade for newly arrived goods. There were many smells, too, including a salt tinge to the wind and a rich variety of pollens and flowers.

"Permission to enter your territory?" called a voice Afsan didn't recognize.

He turned to face where the words had come from. *"Hahat dan,"* he said. "Who's there?"

The voice grew closer but the wind was blowing the wrong way for Afsan to catch any whiff of pheromones, so he couldn't tell whether his visitor was male or female.

"My name is Nav-Mokleb," said the voice, now, judging by its volume, no more than fifteen paces away. "Late of Pack Loodo in Mar'toolar province."

There was no need for Afsan to reciprocate with introductions. There were few blind people in Capital City, and his sash, half black and half green, the colors of the exodus, removed any possible confusion about which blind person he might be, even if one didn't know that he frequented Rockscape. Still, with typical modesty, Afsan identified himself, then bowed concession and said, "I cast a shadow in your presence, Nav-Mokleb. Dybo said he would send you out to see me." Dybo had referred to Mokleb as female, yet she was still downwind of Afsan, so he'd had no evidence of that himself.

"It's my pleasure to serve," Mokleb said. Then, after a moment, "I hear, ah, you are having difficulty sleeping."

Afsan nodded.

"And I received word today from Dar-Mondark that your eyes have regenerated, but you still cannot see."

"That, too, is true." Afsan was quiet for a time. "Is there anything you can do for me?"

"No," said Mokleb at once, "nothing at all." She raised a hand to forestall Afsan's objection, then clicked her teeth, realizing that Afsan couldn't see the gesture. "Don't misunderstand me, though. The talking cure can indeed help you, but *I* do nothing. The problem is within you, and so is the cure. I just facilitate the process."

Afsan scrunched his muzzle. "I don't understand."

"What do you know about psychology?"

"It's the study of the mind," said Afsan. "The ancient philosopher Dolgar is often thought of as its founder."

"That's right," said Mokleb. "But Dolgar was way off base. She thought of the head and tail as being discrete repositories for opposing forces in our personalities—the artistic and sensual residing in the head, and the strong and insensate in the tail."

"Yes, I remember that," said Afsan.

"That's an outdated view, of course. Oh, there are two opposing forces—the high mind and the low—but they reside in our brains, not various parts of our bodies. The high mind contains the conscious, the understood, the learned—that of which we are aware. The low mind consists of instincts and base impulses, of drives; it's the province of the subconscious. The struggle between high and low mind produces the personality."

"But surely the high mind is who we really are," said Afsan.

"No. The high mind may represent who we want to be, or who the church says we should be, but we are just as much our low minds as we are our high; the low mind shapes our behavior, too."

"But if the low mind is unknowable, then it's as if it didn't exist," replied Afsan. "Dolgar's contemporary, Keladax, said nothing is anything unless it is something. In other words, a concept without material reality is meaningless."

"Ah, indeed," said Mokleb. "Perhaps I've spoken imprecisely. The low mind is *normally* unknowable, but together we can explore it. Just as the far-seer allowed you to learn things about the heavenly bodies that previously had been secret, so my technique allows us to see that which is normally hidden. There, Sal-Afsan, if you are willing to undertake the journey, in the part of yourself that you don't really know, the part that is suppressed and hidden, that's where we'll find the cause of your problems."

It looked like the ark was *melting*.

The alien ship still jutted from the cliff face, but the rocks immediately beneath it were now the same blue as the ship itself, as if melting residue were flowing down the steep slope. Except the ship wasn't melting at all—it still had sharp edges. And yet the blue stain on the cliff continued to grow.

Novato scrambled down the precipice like a green spider, using the web of climbing ropes attached to the cliff by metal spikes. She was overtop of plain downrock layers, but about fifteen paces below, the web crossed the lowest lobe of the amorphous blue. She continued down, tail hanging off her back, until she was over the blueness.

The coarse ropes of the web normally shifted slightly in the breeze, but here they seemed to actually be stuck in the blue material coating the cliff. Novato negotiated her way to where the blue stopped and the cliff face was exposed again. She ran her fingertips over the join between the rock and the blue material. She'd expected the blue stuff to have stood slightly proud of the cliff, the way rivulets of sap do on a tree, but it seemed, if anything, to be recessed. Still, that could make sense: the blue material must surely have been liquid before it hardened. It would naturally have flowed into the declivities in the wall of sandstone.

But if the material had been fluid before it had congealed—the melting-wax analogy still seemed appropriate—it was completely dry now. There was no tackiness to it at all, no sense that it had ever been anything but solid.

The stuff had to be leaking out of the ship, so the blue material surely only formed a thin veneer over the rock. Except for the orange dust that had marched outside, nothing had left the ship, and even if the material comprising the blue coating was only eggshell-thin, there still was much more of it than the total volume of all the dust grains.

Novato lowered herself farther down the climbing ropes, moving with difficulty over the part where the ropes had become mired in the blue material. She was at eye level with one of the spikes that anchored the ropes to the cliff face. But this spike was now completely surrounded by blue stuff. Proof, she thought, that the blueness had originally been liquid: it had flowed right around the spike, which was buried in the rock except for its flared head.

Here, at the spike hole, it should be easy to see how thick the blue coating was. Novato was wearing a tool belt, held up by her tail. She used the splayed end of a hammer to grab the spike's crown. She bent her legs up and planted her feet flat against the vertical cliff face, then used the strength of flexing her knees to lever the hammer.

It took several yanks, then suddenly the spike popped free, Novato flying away from the cliff like a rappeller. She dropped her hammer and the spike, and they skittered down to the beach far below. The climbing web, no longer anchored by the spike, billowed away from the cliff. Novato held on tightly, twisting and turning with the ropes. At last she regained control and maneuvered over to the spike hole. It was hard to get a good view inside; whenever she brought her face close, the shadow of her head put the hole in darkness. But at last she managed it.

It was blue all the way down.

It was just barely possible that the spike had been loose enough in its hole to allow the liquid blueness to trickle in and harden there, but in a flash of insight Novato realized that that was not what had happened at all. She would confirm it later by digging into the sandstone right at the edge of the blueness, but even now she knew what was going on.

The blueness wasn't a stain, wasn't a congealed liquid that had dripped off the spaceship.

No, the blueness was the cliff itself. Somehow the entire cliff face was slowly turning into the same incredibly strong material from which the ancient spaceship was made.

By the time Toroca and Babnol returned to the *Dasheter,* the body of the one Other that Keenir and Spalton had brought back had already been laid out on Toroca's dissection table. During the various voyages of the Geological Survey, Toroca had collected many biological specimens, and in this room—a cabin converted to a laboratory—he often dissected animals. It was here that he'd examined the body of a diver, the Antarctic swimming creature built on the wingfinger body plan that had first suggested to him the idea of evolution.

In the center of the room was a worktable, its top made of two wide wooden boards that gently sloped toward each other. The boards didn't join in the middle, though. Rather, there was a small gap to allow body fluids to drain into a ceramic trough underneath.

Toroca had intended to let each person have a look at the body, this likely being their one chance to see an Other up close. He was surprised at the vehemence of the response, though. Individuals were emerging from his lab with claws extended, and one—old Biltog, the *Dasheter*'s longest-serving mate—came out with a distinct bobbing motion to his steps. Over the protests of those who hadn't yet seen the corpse, Toroca barred further access to the room. Anything that aroused even a hint of territoriality could not be permitted. Toroca had always been haunted by the story of the *Galadoreter,* the ill-fated vessel that had blown back to shore near Parnood, its decks littered with the rotting corpses of its crew, many of them still locked in the death struggles that had killed them all.

It was well into the evening, but this was even-night, the night that Toroca and half the crew were supposed to be awake while the others slept—another precaution against triggering the territorial reflex—so he decided to begin his dissection by lamplight.

The Other's shoulder bones and several of its vertebrae had already been exposed by Keenir's jaws. Toroca picked up a scalpel, but hesitated before making an incision. He'd dissected hundreds of animals before but although he'd studied Quintaglio anatomy, he'd never carved into the body of a person. And even though its skin was yellow instead of green, this clearly had been a person; the copper jewelry it wore reflected the flickering lamplight.

When a Quintaglio died, a series of rites were performed, including a service at the Hall of Worship, five days of mourning, and the laying of the body at a prescribed funereal site so that it could be reclaimed by nature.

But this Other was being denied whatever customs his people had concerning death. Indeed, assuming they'd made good their escape, the Others wouldn't even be sure for some time that this one was dead, and only eventually would conclude that his disappearance must be proof of his demise.

Toroca didn't feel right about treating this body as a mere specimen. He put his scalpel down and made a brief trip to his cabin to fetch his book of Lubalite prayer. Finding an appropriate passage, he spoke softly over the body:

"I mourn the death even of one unknown, for the chance to make that stranger a friend has come and passed. In heaven perhaps our paths will cross, and although we were not acquainted in life, perhaps there we will hunt side by side. Your journey will be a safe one, stranger, for we are both formed from the hands of God."

Toroca was silent for a moment afterward, then picked up his scalpel and went to work.

The Other's skeleton was similar to a Quintaglio's. Its arm articulated with its shoulder the same way a Quintaglio's did, and the vertebrae had similar processes on the superior surface for anchoring the back muscles. Toroca rolled the body on its side and carved into the upper chest. Most carnivorous reptiles had two types of ribs: large ones projecting off the vertebrae and a secondary set along the belly, attached to the back ribs by ligaments. The Other had such chest riblets; indeed, by pressing his fingers into the skin, Toroca was able to count the same number of vertebrae, back ribs, and chest ribs as one would find in a Quintaglio.

Before examining the lower body, Toroca spent some time on the head. Here, there were some subtle differences in structure. The neck muscles weren't as strong as in a Quintaglio. That made sense, since the jaws were much less pronounced, meaning the neck had a smaller weight to support. And the eyes had a scleral ring of bone, something that blackdeaths and other carnivorous reptiles had, but Quintaglios lacked. Also, the Other's snout had several hornlets and bony knobs, making it look more like a blackdeath's head than the smooth head of a Quintaglio.

Toroca repositioned the corpse so that he could work on the lower abdomen. The riblets would have made a simple ventral incision difficult, but, as in Quintaglios, there was a gap between the front and rear rib sets, covered only with skin, muscle, and ligaments. Toroca made a long vertical slice there, and then intersected it with a deep horizontal cut. He peeled back the four resulting flaps of skin, exposing the belly cavity.

There was something hard and blue-green inside.

A gizzard stone? Surely not in a carnivore! And surely not so big!

And then he realized what it was. In shape and size it was just like those of a Quintaglio, but the odd color had prevented Toroca from immediately recognizing it.

An egg.

An unlaid, unhatched egg.

But this Other had appeared to be male; it had a dewlap sack. Had it been eating eggs?

Toroca tilted the creature onto its side and examined the flaps covering the genitals. No doubt—this was a *female*. Perhaps both sexes had dewlaps. Amazing.

He gently repositioned the corpse and reached into the opening he'd made in its belly. His hands were slick with bodily fluids so he was careful not to lose his grip as he pulled out the egg. Along its major axis, the orb was just a bit longer than Toroca's handspan.

There was another egg behind it.

Toroca carefully set the first egg on the floor, lest the rocking of the ship knock it from his dissecting table. He got the second one out as well.

There was a third egg behind the second. He removed that one, too. Behind it were shards of a fourth egg, and an interior pocket smeared with yellow egg-fluid: that egg had been smashed inside the body, probably when Keenir had propelled the Other to the ground.

There were no signs of additional eggs.

Quintaglios normally laid clutches of eight. Assuming this Other wasn't anomalous, these people only had four eggs to a clutch.

The three intact eggs were fully formed, with tough, soft shells, as if they'd been ready to be laid. Indeed, Toroca wondered whether the Other they'd encountered had been walking the beach looking for a suitable spot to deposit her eggs. If that was the case, then the eggs were probably still alive. He'd heard stories of eggs being rescued from the body of a dying female.

Toroca hurried off to find leather blankets to wrap the eggs in.

Chapter 6

"The talking cure is not always pleasant," said Nav-Mokleb, leaning back on her tail. She was standing about fifteen paces downwind of Afsan's rock. "You will have to bare your innermost thoughts to me. Further, the cure takes a great deal of time. We must meet for a daytenth every other day for a protracted period—perhaps as long as a kiloday."

"Five hundred sessions!" said Afsan. "Five hundred daytenths." And then, as was his wont, he extended the mathematics: "That would mean the aggregate of our sessions would total fifty days."

"Yes."

"Mokleb, I don't have fifty days to spare. I'm old."

"To invoke math, as you are so famous for doing, you are not old. If you survive an average span, your life is a little less than half over." Mokleb let out a long, hissing sigh. "Look, this is an unusual case for me. Normally, patients seek me out on their own. They believe in my techniques and are eager to be cured. You, however, are here because the Emperor and your physician recommended it. I see that you are skeptical, and reluctant to undertake the process."

"Skepticism is the mark of a good scientist," replied Afsan. "As for reluctance, as I said, I don't have fifty days to spare."

"The Emperor asked me to take you on as a patient," said Mokleb, "and I am a loyal subject of Dy-Dybo. But if you are reluctant now, it will only get worse as our explorations take longer. You must be committed to this process, or it cannot work."

"Then it will not work," said Afsan.

Mokleb shrugged. "The loss is yours. I sleep well at night, Afsan, and I can see. I don't expect you to envy me for that, but I had been led to believe that you desired those same things yourself. I see that I was mistaken. My apologies for taking up some of your precious time."

Mokleb began walking away. Insects buzzed. She passed three Rockscape boulders before Afsan spoke. "Wait," he said. And then, a moment later, "Come back."

Mokleb walked back toward Afsan's rock.

"I'm sorry," Afsan said. "I understand you are trying to help me. Please—I *do* want to be cured."

"Good," said Mokleb. "That brings us to the question of compensation for my labors."

"I have an unlimited imperial endowment," said Afsan. "Please talk with Dee-Laree at the palace; he'll make sure you are well looked after."

"I will speak to Dee-Laree," said Mokleb. "But simply having a third party provide me with recompense is insufficient. We are about to embark on a long and difficult road, Afsan. There must be a contract directly between us. Normally, I wouldn't say this to a patient, but I'm sure you would figure this out for yourself—and I know that the moment I leave, you will send an assistant to the library and have him or her bring back my writings and read them to you anyway." She paused. "I have found that, as therapy progresses, patients begin to skip appointments. They wish to avoid facing difficult questions. Therefore, I will charge you a personal fee for every session, to be paid whether you attend or not, said fee to be dear enough to make you reluctant to waste it."

"A fee! On top of what the palace will give you?"

"Yes. You've already made clear how valuable your time is to you, Afsan. Mine is equally valuable to me, and I won't be trifled with."

"But a fee! Doctors don't trade directly with patients, Mokleb. Surely you already receive a stipend."

"That's irrelevant. You must be committed to the therapy, and a fee helps ensure that. Plus, there's another reason to charge you a fee. Again, I wouldn't normally mention it, but you will be savvy enough to see it, anyway. During the course of the therapy, you will have many different reactions to me. At times, those reactions will be ones of aggression and hate. Paying me a fee will help assuage your guilt over having those feelings. You must have no humiliating debt of gratitude to me for tolerating such outbursts; rather, you must feel that you have bought the right to make them."

Afsan was silent for a time. Then: "Although Dybo looks after my needs, Mokleb, I personally own little. My endowment is mostly to finance research. I have no precious stones, no percentage interest in any ship or caravan, and only a few trading markers. How would I pay you?"

"What do you own that you value most?"

"I have few possessions. My greatest prize, I suppose, was the far-seer that Novato gave me. But that is in the custody of my son, Toroca."

"What else do you treasure?"

Afsan's tail, hanging off the back of the rock he was straddling, waggled back and forth. "Well, to my astonishment, my old teaching master, Tak-Saleed, left me a complete set of his *Treatise on the Planets,* the most famous of his works."

"What good are books to a blind person?" asked Mokleb.

"Oh, occasionally I have a student read passages from them to me. But simply owning them, running my fingers over the *kurpa* leather binding, smelling the musty pages—that gives me pleasure."

"How many volumes are there?"

"Eighteen. Three per planet, other than the Face of God."

"Excellent," said Mokleb. "And how many times does eighteen go into five hundred?"

Afsan tipped his head. "A little less than twenty-eight: 27.778, to be precise."

"Very good. You will pay me in advance. Today, you will surrender the first volume of the treatise. After every twenty-eight sessions, you will surrender another volume. If you are still being treated after five hundred sessions, we will renegotiate the contract. Agreed?"

"I cherish those books," Afsan said softly.

"Agreed?" said Mokleb harshly.

Afsan tipped his head down, blind eyes looking at the ground. "Agreed," he said at last.

Novato mentally whipped herself with her tail for not having come up with the idea. After all, it was a logical extension of her own invention, the far-seer. The far-seer used lenses to make distant objects appear close, and this device, the small-seer, used lenses to make tiny objects visible. The small-seer's inventor, Bor-Vanbelk of Pack Brampto in Arj'toolar, had discovered amazing things. Tiny lifeforms in a drop of water! Little disks within blood! Minuscule chambers in the leaf of a plant!

Novato, balancing again on the side of the cliff, clinging with one hand to the rope web, was using a small-seer to examine the spreading blueness.

Here, right at its very edge, she could see shifting patterns of dust. Even through the lenses, the grains were all but invisible. But unlike the random jostling in a drop of water, these motes moved in regular patterns, back and forth, up and down. It was as though Novato were watching a dance from the back of an impossibly high amphitheater, the individual dancers virtually impossible to discern but the mathematical precision of their movements still a thing of beauty.

Dancers, thought Novato. Dancers smaller than the eye could see.

But they weren't just dancing. They were working, like ants building an anthill, moving with determined insectile exactness.

Part of her said the little things must be alive, and part said that that was ridiculous, that nothing so ancient could be living. But if they were not lifeforms, then what could they be?

Whatever they were, they were making phenomenal progress. Already, almost the entire cliff face was blue.

If further contact was to be made with the Others, Toroca would have to go ashore—and he would have to do so alone. The *Dasheter* had sailed south and was now approaching the archipelago from a different direction so that the ship's arrival would not immediately be associated with the death on the westernmost island. The ship stayed below the horizon, the islands out of sight.

This part of the world never knew real darkness. By day, the sun blazed overhead. True, for a good part of the day, the sun was eclipsed by the Face of God (although they were far enough north of the equator that the sun's path behind the Face was a chord much shorter than the Face's diameter). But even when the sun was eclipsed, and the Face was completely unilluminated, the purple sky grew no darker than it did at twilight. And at midnight, when the sun shone down on the other side of the world, the Face was full, covering a quarter of the sky, lighting up the waves in shades of yellow and orange.

Because of this, there was no time at which the *Dasheter* could sneak in to let Toroca off. Toroca, therefore, was going to swim to shore. He'd removed his sash; it would have interfered with swimming. But he was not completely naked: around his waist he wore a swimmer's belt, with waterproof pouches made from lizard bladders in which he carried supplies.

Standing near him on the deck of the *Dasheter* were Babnol and Captain Keenir. There was no way for them to keep in touch with Toroca once he left the ship. They'd simply agreed that the *Dasheter* would sail farther out, then return to this spot in twenty days to pick up Toroca; if he did not rendezvous with them, Keenir would then set sail for home, rather than risk further disastrous contact.

Babnol's tone was full of concern. "Be careful, Toroca."

Toroca looked at her wistfully. He'd always wanted their relationship to be so much closer. "I will."

"We'll be back for you, lad," said Keenir.

"Thank you."

Toroca moved to the side of the ship and began to climb down the rope ladder that led to the shore boats tethered below. He could have paddled one of those to the island instead of swimming in, but the boats were pretty big for one person to manage; swimming would be easier and faster. When he got to the bottom, he managed a little tip of his torso and saw, up on deck, Keenir and Babnol likewise executing ceremonial bows.

The waves were high enough that Toroca had been splashed up the calf by the time his foot reached the bottom rung. Without further ado, he let go and slipped beneath the waves.

They were far enough north that the water was cooler than what Toroca was used to, but it wasn't cold enough to pose a hazard. He put his arms flat at his sides, stretched his legs out behind, and undulated his tail. His body sliced through the water. He passed a school of silvery fish at one point and later saw a couple of limpid floaters bobbing on the surface. The Face of God waned visibly during the course of the long swim in, and the sun moved closer and closer to its edge.

In the distance, Toroca could see a few of the Others' own sailing ships, but they tended to stay close to shore. That wasn't surprising; the Others presumably long ago determined that there was nothing except empty water for thousands of kilopaces around.

Even from far away, Toroca was surprised by how different the Others' ships looked. Quintaglio vessels had diamond-shaped hulls, square sails, and an even number of masts (the *Dasheter* had four). The ship passing Toroca far to the left had a rounded hull, three masts, and overlapping triangular sails.

Toroca was now a hundred paces from shore. He was approaching what seemed to be a small coastal city made of wooden buildings. Right off, that seemed alien. Quintaglios normally built from adobe or stone; surely wooden buildings were at risk of fire from lamp flames. And these buildings were such odd shapes! The Others seemed to avoid right angles; it was hard to tell from this vantage point, but most of the buildings appeared to have eight sides.

Toroca stopped swimming for a moment. There were fifty or sixty people walking along a broad wooden pier built along the contours of the water's edge. So many! Why, it was as if they had no territoriality at all. And then Toroca saw something that amazed him: two individuals walking side by side down the pier. He could see them clearly, and there could be no doubt about what they were doing.

Holding hands.

Incredible, thought Toroca. Absolutely incredible.

He began to swim again, his tail propelling him over the remaining distance.

Finally, somebody noticed him. He saw a hand pointing in his direction, and a shout went up. Others turned to look out at the waters. More arms pointed at him. One person turned and ran toward the octagonal buildings. Two large Others grabbed a juvenile and, against the juvenile's apparent wishes, dragged the child away from the edge of the pier. One Other was shouting gibberish. Two Others shouted back; more gibberish. Toroca was about ten paces from the pier now.

Someone pointed a blackened metal tube at Toroca. A flash erupted from its open end and a sound came from it like the bellow of a shovelmouth. The water exploded next to Toroca as something crashed into the waves. Someone ran to the Other holding the tube and motioned angrily for him to put it down.

There was a rope ladder dangling from the side of the pier into the water. Toroca grabbed it. The rope itself was of a material Toroca had never seen—perhaps some kind of waterweed fiber—and the knots along its length were tied in a complex style he'd likewise never encountered. Still, it was clearly meant for accessing the pier from the water, or vice versa, and so he pulled himself up, rung after rung, his body feeling cool as the air ran over his wet form. At last he was up on the pier; it, too, was bizarre, made of long planks that went lengthwise instead of crosswise, the way a Quintaglio would have built it.

Toroca stood there, dripping, hands on hips, looking at the Others, and they stood looking at him. Some were pointing at his swimmer's belt, and Toroca was reminded of how he had made much of the fact that the first Other they'd encountered had been wearing jewelry. They must know he was intelligent. These Others all sported copper jewelry, but some were also wearing vests made of a material that looked too pliable to be leather.

The Other with the metal tube was near the front of the crowd. He held the tube in such a way that he could raise it again in a fraction of a beat.

One of the Others stepped forward and spoke, a string of nonsense syllables emanating from its mouth.

At the back of the crowd, Toroca could see someone trying to get through. Incredibly, he was actually tapping people on the shoulder to get them to move, or gently pushing them aside. On Land, this fellow's throat would have been ripped out by now, but people were gladly making way for whoever this was. Once he'd gotten to the front, Toroca saw that this Other also was brandishing a metal tube, but it was smaller and more compact. He was wearing black bands around both his arms; no one else had such bands.

"Hello," said Toroca, and then he bowed. The moment seemed to call for some sort of speech, but if the Others' language sounded like gibberish to Toroca, his words would likely sound the same to them. "Hello," he said again, simply.

The Other with the armbands said "Hello" back at him. For a moment, Toroca thought that the Other understood him, but it was soon clear that he'd simply repeated the sound Toroca had made.

If this Other had been a Quintaglio, he'd have been a good piece younger than Toroca, but none of the Others seemed as large as an old Quintaglio. Either this wasn't a location frequented by the elderly, or Others simply didn't grow as fast or as big as Quintaglios.

Toroca made a gesture toward the city, indicating, he hoped, that he wished to go there. The Other with the black armbands looked warily at Toroca, then stepped aside. Toroca began to walk down the pier, and this Other walked silently beside him. There was a hubbub among the spectators. Some had claws out; others had them sheathed. If these were Quintaglios, that would mean some were frightened and others were just curious—exactly the mix of emotions Toroca himself was feeling as he continued down the pier.

Chapter 7

"Normally, I sit where the patient can't see me," said Mokleb. "Otherwise, they spend too much time watching for my reactions. Therapy is not a performance, and I am not an audience. Also, there may be times when the most effective response to something you say may not in fact be the truth. By sitting out of view, the patient cannot see my muzzle. In any event, since you are blind, it doesn't matter where I sit. However, you should be as comfortable as possible. That rock you are straddling is your favorite, yes?"

"Yes," said Afsan.

"You should relax as much as possible. Rather than sitting up, you may find it more comfortable to lie on your belly. Why don't you try that?"

Afsan obliged, settling himself down on the top of the boulder, his arms and legs dangling a bit over the sides and his tail, semi-stiff, sticking up into the air.

"Good. Now, I'm going to sit on another boulder. I take copious notes; using a system of simplified glyphs, I can record both sides of our conversation verbatim. You'll occasionally hear the sound of my fingerclaw dipping into a pot of ink or solvent, or the sound of me getting a new sheet of paper. Pay no attention, and don't worry about whether I'm writing something down or not. I assure you, I will dutifully record everything—there's no telling what is important. And I further assure you that my notes will be kept confidential. Do you understand all that?"

Afsan nodded.

Mokleb dipped her left middle fingerclaw into ink and started writing. "In our early sessions, I may do a lot of talking, but as the therapy progresses I may go for great lengths without saying anything. Fear not: I am listening intently, and if I have something to say, I will. You must adopt the same principle: if you have something to say, don't worry about manners. Interrupt me freely. Let no thought, however fleeting, escape. Understood?"

Again, Afsan nodded.

"Good. Now, to your dreams. As you may know, dreams serve one fundamental purpose: they prolong sleep."

"Mine certainly aren't doing that," said Afsan. "It's the dreams that are waking me up."

"It only seems that way. If it weren't for dreams, we'd constantly be waking, perhaps thrashing over in our minds something that had been worrying us the previous day, or else we'd awaken because we feel vulnerable and want to look around and make sure we're still safe. Dreams prevent this from happening, and, since sleep is necessary to life, in a very real sense dreams allow us to go on living."

"But my dreams, Mokleb, are *preventing* me from getting a good night's sleep."

"Ah, yes. So it appears. I'll come back to that. First, though, let me ask if you've ever had a dream that went something like this: you are trying to get somewhere or do something, but are frustrated in your attempts. Nonetheless, you keep trying, and keep being frustrated."

"Oh, sure. I suppose everyone has dreams like that. One I recall is trying to find my way out of a corridor. The corridor was the standard kind, zigzagging to keep other users out of sight. I kept trying to open doors along that corridor, but they wouldn't work. One would have rusted hinges, another had a broken opening bar, a third was obviously barricaded from the other side, and so on."

"And yet, eventually, you woke up."

"Obviously."

"And what did you do immediately after awakening?"

"I don't remember."

"I'll tell you exactly what you did; next time you have such a dream, observe for yourself and you'll see that you'll do the same thing then, too. You pushed up off the floor, left your sleeping chamber, found your household bucket, and urinated into it."

"So? Nothing unusual about that."

"No, of course not. But don't you see the function the dream was performing? Your bladder was uncomfortably full. Part of you wanted to get up so you could relieve yourself. But your low mind constructed a dream that said, in its most basic form, 'I'm aware there's a problem, and I'm trying to deal with it.' That keeps you from waking up, thereby prolonging sleep."

"But at some point I *did* wake up."

"Exactly. For a while, the attempts in the dream to solve the problem placate the real physical need, but eventually the urge to urinate overpowers the dream, and you find yourself no longer sleeping."

"But what about the bad dreams I'm having? How can such horrible images be attempts to prolong sleep?"

"You know that stage actors wear face masks?"

"Of course. They have to; otherwise the audience would be distracted by the performers' muzzles turning blue whenever they spoke an untrue line."

"Precisely. Dreams are like those masks: they disguise the truth of things. Your dream of the corridor is an example. Your mind was fooling itself that you were dealing with the desire to urinate. It was masking the fact that you were just lying there, resting, with a story of you trying to find a working doorway. The bad dreams you are having likewise are masks. The dreams obliquely represent, in ways your mind finds easier to deal with, the underlying things that really distress you. The dreams may seem horrible, but I stand by what I said earlier—they are attempts to prolong your sleeping state. However unpleasant the dreams appear, the real thing that torments you, beneath the mask of those images, is something your mind finds even more unpleasant, and therefore refuses to face directly. We must remove the mask, Afsan, and see the true face of your dreams."

The sky above Fra'toolar was a mix of sun and cloud. Novato was straddling a broken tree trunk on the beach, a piece of drawing leather on top of a board resting on her knees. She was sketching the cliff face and its metamorphosis from rock into the blue material.

Garios approached to within about twenty paces. Ten would have been a normal territorial buffer, especially considering how long, and how well, they had known each other. Added distance often indicated hesitation about broaching a subject.

Novato saw him approaching; whenever possible, one always approached so as to be visible well before arrival.

"Hello, Novato," he said. "I cast a shadow in your presence."

"Greetings, Garios. But *hahat dan,* for goodness' sake. Come a little closer."

Garios took a few steps nearer, then said awkwardly, "I have a question to ask you."

Novato put her charcoal drawing stick in a pouch on her sash. "Oh?"

"Yes," said Garios, his long muzzle tipped down at her. "You are now thirty-six kilodays old."

Novato clicked her teeth. "Aye, and these old bones are feeling every bit of it."

"We've known each other for a long time," said Garios. He paused. "Indeed, we've known each other *well* for eighteen kilodays." He paused again. "A year."

"Yes," said Novato.

"And now you are *two* years old."

"Yes," she said again.

"Soon," said Garios, "you will call for a mate."

"I imagine so," she said, "although I feel no stirrings yet."

"Eighteen kilodays ago, when you were completing your first year of life, you called for a mate, as well." He paused. "And I responded."

Novato's voice seemed a little wary. "You did, yes."

"Normally," said Garios, "that would have been your first mating."

"Normally," repeated Novato.

"But you had mated once before, a couple of kilodays prior to your normal time."

"It's not all that unusual," said Novato, a defensive note in her voice.

"Of course not. Of course not. But you mated with Afsan."

"Yes."

"It is not, ah, out of the ordinary for a female to mate twice with the same individual."

"It is the female's choice," said Novato. "Some do it one way, some another."

"Indeed. But now that you are coming into receptivity again, I, ah, I've been wondering if you will mate with one of your previous partners."

"The thought has crossed my mind," said Novato.

"Normally, at this stage in your life, I would have been your only previous partner."

"That's true."

"But you have had, ah, *two* previous partners: Afsan and myself."

"Yes."

"You laid clutches of eggs by both of us."

"Yes."

"You know who your children by Afsan were; they were spared the culling of the bloodpriest."

Novato nodded.

"And after your second clutch was culled, one of the egglings went on to be a member of Capital Pack; that person would be a young adult now. Of course, we don't know which one of the Pack members he or she is."

Novato looked as though she were about to say something, but checked herself. A moment later, her tone devoid of emotion, she simply repeated the old saw "Children are the children of the Pack."

"Oh, I know," said Garios. "Forgive me, I'm just rambling. Anyway, when you mate again, good Novato, you, ah, have three choices, no? You could call for Afsan, call for me, or call for someone new. I know it is premature, and it's wrong for me to ask regardless, but the thought plagues me. Whom will you call for?" He wrinkled his long muzzle. "I, ah, I hope it will be me."

"Garios, we have worked together for a long time. We are friends. My thoughts toward you are always warm."

"But?"

"But nothing. I don't yet feel the stirrings, although I imagine they will start soon. Who knows how I'll feel then? I honestly don't know whom I'll call for."

"But I'm in the running?"

"You are intelligent and strong and good of heart. Of course you are in the running."

"Thank you," said Garios. "Thank you very much."

The Other with the black armbands took Toroca to one of the octagonal buildings. As soon as he got inside, Toroca understood how they could safely use wood as a building material; the roof was made of glass, letting in light from outside. Since there was never total darkness here beneath the Face of God, there was no need for open-flame lamps.

Toroca had to wait a long time. An Other brought flagons of water and a pink transparent liquid with bubbles in it. He'd had his fill of water on the swim over and was reluctant to try the pink liquid, afraid it might be some kind of plant juice. The Other also brought a platter covered with small pieces of meat. At first glance, Toroca thought the meat was dried—he was used to such fare—but then he realized it had been ruined by exposure to heat. And yet the Other waiting with him had no compunctions about eating the stuff. Toroca decided to be sociable and tried a small piece. It was still warm, but not with the warmth of a freshly killed body. Toroca changed his mind about the water, downing a massive gulp.

Finally, whoever they'd been waiting for arrived. Toroca tried to imagine who would have greeted a stranger who swam up to the docks on Land. Emperor Dybo? Surely not at first. The imperial guards? Maybe. He'd now gathered that all those wearing black armbands—this particular octagon was full of them—were the equivalent of that. Toroca remembered when a huge tentacled mollusk had washed up after a big storm many kilodays ago, its shell a good four paces across. It was a savant who was summoned, old Osfik, the Arbiter of the Sequence. Perhaps this new arrival was likewise a respected thinker, come to puzzle out the nature of the green apparition that had appeared in their midst.

The newcomer was about Toroca's size; meaning, given the overall smallness of the Others, that he or she was probably quite old. There were pheromones coming off the Other, but Toroca couldn't interpret them; he wished he knew how to differentiate the sexes. The newcomer looked at him with an intensity Toroca found uncomfortable. The golden eyes made clear *exactly* where it was looking; such staring would be considered a challenge display amongst Quintaglios. The newcomer spoke briefly with the fellow with black armbands, then turned to Toroca and uttered a few words.

Toroca shrugged his shoulders and said, "I don't understand."

The Other savant looked fascinated. It spoke again, and the arm-banded fellow looked up sharply. Toroca guessed that the oldster had said something incendiary as a test to see if Toroca was faking not knowing their language. Toroca shrugged again and said, amusing himself, "May a thousand wingfingers fly up your anus."

Satisfied, apparently, that there really was a language barrier, the savant pointed at his own chest and said, "Jawn."

Ah, thought Toroca. Now we're getting somewhere.

The savant gestured at Toroca, his hand extended in a loose fist.

Toroca opened his mouth to reply, then realized that he didn't know what the reply should be. Was Jawn the savant's own name, or the name of his people? Toroca pointed at the fellow wearing the black armbands.

The savant seemed disappointed to not have his question answered, but after a moment, he pointed at the security fellow as well and said, "Morb." He then indicated a copper tag he was wearing on a chain around his neck. Large geometric characters were embossed into it. "Jawn," he said.

Jawn's cartouche, thought Toroca. Or at least, some representation of his name. He pointed at his own chest, and said, "Toroca," and then, more slowly, "Toe-*roe*-ka."

Jawn pointed at himself and said "Jawn" again, then he pointed at Toroca and said "Toroca."

Toroca clicked his teeth and pointed at Morb. "Morb," he said.

It was a start.

Chapter 8

"The imagery in most dreams," said Mokleb, "comes from the hunt. We revel in the desire to overtake and vanquish, to release pent-up violence, to gorge on fresh meat."

Afsan clicked his teeth. "Either you are wrong or I'm abnormal," he said. "I rarely dream of the hunt."

"Perhaps not directly," said Mokleb. "But tell me: are you often running in your dreams?"

"Running . . . why, yes, I suppose so."

"That's pursuit. Do you often leap?"

"Through the air, no." Afsan clicked his teeth again. "Leaping to conclusions, sometimes."

"It's still leaping, whether it's literal or metaphorical, and it represents the attack."

"But I almost never gorge myself in my dreams, Mokleb. Indeed, all my life people have teased me over my lack of interest in food."

"Again, the gorging doesn't have to be literal. Any excess—whether in eating, in sexual congress, in claiming and defending a giant territory—anything like that represents the gorging, the final culmination of the hunt. Almost everyone reports at one time or another having the dream of defending a huge piece of land, bobbing up and down to deter interlopers who are kilopaces away. Territoriality is just another kind of hunt. When stalking prey, we are satisfying current needs; when defending a territory, we are ensuring that future needs will be met. Broadly, you could say dreaming is about fulfilling needs, and all needs, at their most basic level, are related to hunting and killing and establishing territory."

"I just don't see that."

"No, of course not. It takes training to interpret dreams. The low mind uses symbols and metaphor. Some are obvious. Any long, curved object represents a hunter's tooth: a bent tree trunk, a broken wheel rim, a rib, a crescent moon, wave caps seen in profile, even, I daresay, the convex lenses of a far-seer. And any prone object, or object out of its normal orientation—a table lying on its side, say, rather than standing on its legs—or any object leaking liquid—a bucket with a hole in it, perhaps—represents felled prey."

"It all strikes me as rather unlikely," said Afsan.

Mokleb was unperturbed. "Tell me a dream you had prior to the onset of your current bad dreams. Anything."

Afsan was quiet for a moment, thinking. "Well, there's one I've had a few times. There's a big, fat armorback waddling by, and— okay, this one *is* about the hunt, I see that now—and I leap on its back, but there's no place to dig in tooth or claw; the whole animal is encased in a bony carapace. I struggle for a time, but end up exhausted and finally just lie down on the thing's back, close my eyes, and go to sleep, as it ambles along, carrying me with it."

Mokleb looked up. "I'm sorry—I didn't get all that. Could you repeat it?"

Afsan sounded annoyed. "I said, there's a large armorback. I jump on its back and try to dig into its carapace, but can't find anything to tear into. I struggle and finally fall asleep on its back."

"Thank you," said Mokleb. "You'll note that your description of the dream changed the second time you told it. This is very significant in dream interpretation. The first time, you referred to the animal as 'a big, fat armorback.' The armorback is often a symbol of the unassailable in dreams. Although they eat plants, such creatures are almost impossible to kill. And a big, fat armorback—those were your words—could refer to only one person: Emperor Dybo, whose girth is legendary, or at least was so the last time you actually saw him. The power of Dybo's office makes him impervious to almost all attacks, just like an armorback. And again, you changed your words when you described the dream a second time: in the first description, you specifically said you closed your eyes at the end; the second time you left that detail out." Mokleb paused. "The interpretation is simple: your dream is an expression of your anger with Dybo for allowing your blinding."

Afsan's tail moved in the air.

"Telling a dream twice is very instructive," said Mokleb. "In the dream world, we explore thoughts that we'd rather not openly face. The mind censors these thoughts completely when we're awake, but while we sleep the censorship mechanism relaxes along with the rest of the body. Oh, in a healthy mind, even in dreams it won't allow direct expression of an unpleasant thought, so it couches such things in symbols and metaphors. When you first put the story of your dream into words, part of your mind suddenly realized what you were really talking about. That's why by the time you came to relate the dream a second time, the most important clues to what you were actually dreaming about were removed—the reference to the armorback being fat, and the reference to your eyes. The censorship mechanism was hard at work, keeping you from facing unpleasant thoughts.

"I see you're not attempting to interrupt. Of course not; you see the correctness of what I'm saying. Now, for our therapy to work, you must understand this well: *everything* is significant, every thought, every image, has at least one determining cause, and sometimes several. You must pledge to hold nothing back, to share every thought and picture that comes into your mind, no matter how embarrassing, unpleasant, or just plain irrelevant it may seem. The mind is just as complex, but also just as comprehensible, as the movements of the heavenly bodies you study. Together we will explore a new universe, the one that exists inside your head, and by so doing, we'll rid you of the horrors that have been plaguing you."

"And restore my sight?" asked Afsan.

"Perhaps. Perhaps. How successful the therapy will be is entirely up to you."

"I want to succeed at this," said Afsan.

"Good. Our time is up for today. I will see you in two days." She paused. "Eventually, I hope, you'll be able to say the same thing to me."

Novato wanted to know how deeply into the rocks of the cliff the blueness went. The cliff was more than a hundred vertical paces tall. At its base was a narrow expanse of sandy beach. At the top of the cliff, several gnarled trees precariously clung to the edge. Leading to the cliff's edge were wide plains covered with tall grasses. And sitting in the middle of the plain were buildings made of stone blocks. In successive turns, the buildings were occupied by Packs Derrilo, Horbo, and Quebelmo, all of whose ranges overlapped this area. Currently, Pack Derrilo was making use of them.

Novato enlisted some of the Pack members to help with an experiment. She had them dig down through the loose topsoil near the edge of the cliff. She wanted to see which they'd come up against, solid rock or the blue material. Down a fair bit, they came to the blue stuff.

Fascinated, Novato had them back off to five paces from the edge of the cliff. They dug again, and again their shovels struck blue.

They tried again ten paces back. Blue.

Twenty paces. Blue again.

Novato asked them to try again from another ten paces farther back, but at this point, Gatabor, one of the Pack members doing the work, held up a hand. "Humor me," he said, and walked another hundred paces away from the edge of the cliff. Here he had to dig down a considerable distance before he reached the bottom of the soil, but finally his shovel rang in his hands. He crouched down and cleaned away the dirt.

Blue. Solid, unrelenting blue.

A total of a hundred and twenty paces back from the edge of the cliff. And the cliff face itself was now blue through almost its entire height of over a hundred paces.

Gatabor stood by the hole, hands on hips, shaking his head.

Novato walked to the other side of the hole, facing him, and, incidentally, facing the expanse behind him leading to the edge of the cliff. And so, she saw it happen . . .

Saw the blue mass poke out of the ground thirty paces closer to the cliff's edge, grass and dirt erupting out of its way as if pushed aside by a shovelmouth's prow.

Novato's jaw dropped, and Gatabor's claws slid out in response to the breach of protocol. But then she pointed and Gatabor swung around and he, too, saw it, whatever it was, rising out of the ground.

Jawn deposited a handful of copper disks on the table. Some of them had an engraving of an Other in profile; others had an engraved crest. He moved one of the disks to the center of the table. Pointing to it with palm closed, he said, *"Bal."* He then raised his hand with one finger extended. *"Bal."* Toroca repeated the word.

Next, Jawn picked up a second disk and placed it beside the first. Originally, the disk had been showing a crest; now, flipped over, it showed a profile. Toroca realized that all the disks were identical. *"Lod,"* said Jawn, indicating both of the disks. He held up two fingers. *"Lod."*

Toroca found this easy, and soon Jawn had taught him the names of the numerals from one to ten. It was time for the next step. *"Bal eb bal tar lod,"* said Jawn. One and one is two. Jawn demonstrated this by moving disks around.

Toroca nodded and repeated the sentence: *"Bal eb bal tar lod."*

Jawn then demonstrated two more constructions. *"Bal eb bal eb bal tar ker."* One and one and one is three. *"Bal eb lod tar ker."* One and two is three.

There was a little more practice with basic math, but then it seemed they were back at square one. *"Bal eb bal tar lod,"* said Jawn: one and one is two. But then he added a new word: *"Sek-tab."*

Jawn next said two and two equals four, and again appended *"Sek-tab."* Toroca dutifully repeated each phrase.

Then Jawn said, *"Bal eb bal tar ker."* Toroca looked up. Had he misunderstood everything so far? *"Bal eb bal tar ker,"* said Jawn again. One and one is three? Then, stressing the word, Jawn added, *"Sek-na-tab."* He then made the hand motion that meant he wanted Toroca to repeat what he'd said.

Toroca shook his head, trying to convey that something was wrong here. *"Bal eb bal tar* lod," he said. And then he repeated the answer: *"Lod."*

Jawn opened his mouth, exposing teeth. Toroca had come to understand that this was the Others' way of showing amusement. Jawn's expression indicated he wanted Toroca to bear with him. He said again, *"Bal eb bal tar lod, sek-tab."* Toroca repeated that. Then Jawn said, *"Bal eb bal tar ker, sek-na-tab."*

Toroca slowly repeated the phrase: *"Bal eb bal tar . . . ker."* Jawn's eyelids blinked, an expression of astonishment shared by both Others and Quintaglios. *"Sas lesh,"* he said, using words Toroca had learned in an earlier lesson. Your face.

Toroca was frustrated. "Well, of course my face is turning blue," he blurted in the Quintaglio language. "You're making me say something that's not true."

In that instant, Toroca realized what was going on. *Sek-tab* meant "correct" or "true" and *sek-na-tab* meant "incorrect" or "false"; the addition of the syllable *"na"* to the middle of the word implied negation, the first Other grammatical rule Toroca had been able to divine.

But in the same instant, Jawn clearly realized something, as well. He pointed at his own chest and said, "Jawn." Then he pointed at himself a second time and said, "Toroca."

It was Toroca's turn to be astonished, his own eyelids beating up and down. Jawn's face had remained its usual yellow. He indicated for Toroca to repeat the same thing. Toroca pointed at his own chest and said, "Toroca," then pointed at his chest again and said, "Jawn." When he uttered the second name, he felt tingling as his muzzle blushed blue.

And so, Toroca realized, a significant fact had been communicated by this simple math lesson. The Others now knew that Quintaglios could not lie without their faces betraying them. And Toroca now knew that the Others *could* lie.

Jawn and Toroca stared at each other, both of them clearly astonished.

Garios and Novato were sharing a meal of water turtle; the beast had been killed when it had waddled up onto the beach. Casually holding the flipper he was gnawing on, Garios said, "I see you've dispatched a letter to Afsan."

Novato spit aside a hunk of bone, then: "Along with the usual missives to the Emperor, yes. It went out with a rider last night."

Garios seemed engrossed in the anatomy of the flipper. His tone was offhanded. "May I inquire about the letter's contents?"

"Oh, just bringing him up-to-date on what's been happening. You know: the cliff turning blue, and the blue pyramid erupting out of the ground."

"Did you, ah, perhaps ask him to come here?"

"Here to Fra'toolar? Goodness, no. That's a long trip, and he's got plenty of other things to do."

"Of course," said Garios, tearing some more flesh from the flipper. After a moment, he added, "Will you be going to the Capital soon?"

"I don't know. I should report in person to Dybo at some point. We'll need new equipment to investigate this pyramid. Of course, Delplas could go back to take care of that; she's got a fine head for details. So, no, I have no immediate plans to return to the Capital. Why do you ask?"

"Just curious," said Garios, again examining the flipper as if he somehow expected there to be some meat on it that had evaded his earlier investigations. "Just curious."

"I call this the listing game," said Mokleb. "It works like this: I suggest a category of thing, and you list all the items that fit into that category."

"A memory test?" said Afsan. "There's nothing wrong with my memory."

"No, I suspect there isn't. But please indulge me. Could you, for instance, give the names of the original five hunters?"

"Sure. Lubal, Belbar, Katoon, Hoog, and, ah, Mekt."

"You hesitated before Mekt. Why?"

"I couldn't remember if I'd said her yet."

"Of course. Of course. And can you name the five original mates?"

"Dargo, Varkev, Jostark, Takood, Detoon."

"There, you had no trouble with that list. What about the names of the seven principal branches of government?"

"Oh, easy. The judiciary. The church. Civil works. The exodus. Interprovincial trade. Portents and omens. Tithing."

"Very good. And the names of the eight provinces?"

"Not only will I give you the names, Mokleb, but I'll give them to you in order from west to east: Jam'toolar, Fra'toolar, Arj'toolar, Chu'toolar, Mar'toolar, Edz'toolar, and Capital."

"You missed one," said Mokleb.

"Did I? Which one?"

"You tell me."

"Let's see: Jam'toolar and Fra'toolar on the west coast. Then Arj'toolar. Chu'toolar to the north, with little Mar'toolar beneath it. Edz'toolar. And Capital."

"You missed it again."

Afsan sounded irritated. He held up his fingers as he named them off. "One: Jam'toolar. Two: Fra'toolar. Three: Capital. Four: Chu'toolar. Five: Mar'toolar. Six—did I say Arj'toolar yet? Arj'toolar. Seven: Edz'toolar. And eight, ah—number eight is—"

"Yes?"

"Isn't that funny?" said Afsan. "For the life of me, I can't remember number eight."

"Would you like a hint?"

"Um."

"Its provincial color is light blue."

Afsan shook his head. "Sorry. It's right on the fork of my tongue, but—"

"Kev'toolar," said Mokleb.

"Kev'toolar!" cried Afsan. "Of course. How could I forget that?"

"Now, quickly, Afsan, tell me the words that pop into your mind when you think of Kev'toolar."

"Len-Lee. She's the governor."

"No, don't explain unless I ask you to. Just say whatever words pop into your head."

"Coastline." A pause. "Kevpel."

"Kevpel?"

"Yes, you know. The planet. Fourth planet from the sun."

"Kev'toolar and Kevpel: they both start the same way."

"That's right. It's a coincidence, of course. The province is named after Kevo, one of the fifty original Packs. The 'kev' in the planet's name is just an old word for 'bright.' "

"And what does Kevpel make you think of?"

"Well, Novato, I guess. When we first met, she showed me her sketches of Kevpel. And phases, of course: you can see Kevpel's phases clearly, even with a small far-seer. Oh, and rings: Kevpel has rings around it."

"There's another ringed planet, isn't there?"

Afsan nodded. "Bripel. But it's not as easy to see through a far-seer. And it's farther away from the sun than we are, so it doesn't go through phases."

"Novato. Tell me about her."

"Well, she's head of the exodus project now."

"But more than that, if I recall the stories I've heard correctly, she and you mated."

"Yes."

"Now phases. Tell me about phases."

"Well, they're cycles."

"Cycles?"

"You know: periodic occurrences."

"And rings. What things are ring-shaped?"

"A *guvdoc* stone."

"Yes. Anything else?"

"Certain trading markers, no?"

"I suppose. Anything else?"

"No, well—eggs are laid in a circle with empty space at the center. A clutch of eggs looks like a ring."

Mokleb nodded. "You couldn't remember the province of Kev'toolar, because your mind was blocking out the similarly named planet Kevpel, and Kevpel makes you think of Novato, cycles, and rings."

"Oh, be serious, Mokleb. Those are just random connections, surely."

"Cycles and rings. Rings of eggs. And Novato, whom you once mated with. Let me ask you a question, Afsan. Tell me: is Novato about to be an integral number of years old? That is, is she about to cycle into her receptive phase, and take a mate?"

Afsan's jaw dropped. "Mokleb—!"

"Forgive me if I'm wrong."

"No, no, you're absolutely right. She'll be in heat anytime now."

"And again forgive me, but have you perhaps been wondering if you and she will couple again? If the two of you will produce another clutch of eggs?"

Afsan's claws slipped out for a moment, but then slid back into their sheaths. "Yes, Mokleb, as much as I have no right to wonder about such things, the questions you ask have indeed been disturbing me. I mean, normally I'd have a good chance at it, having been the first person she coupled with. But, ah, I'm blind and far away from her, and, well, there is the matter of Garios."

"Garios?"

"Den-Garios. A fine fellow, really. Novato and I coupled prior to what would have been her normal first estrus; she mated with Garios about two kilodays later. So, yes, Mokleb, I have been wondering whether she and I will mate again. It's not a proper thing to think about, I know, but . . ." He lifted his hands helplessly.

"As you can see," said Mokleb, "the most insignificant-seeming slip can be of major importance. We're beginning to gain access to your mind, Afsan; soon we'll have our prey in sight."

Chapter 9

Toroca's lessons in the Other language progressed rapidly. He soon had a vocabulary of perhaps two hundred words, mostly nouns. The pace had picked up once he realized that when Jawn pointed at an object with his palm open, the word he spoke was the general term (furniture, say), and when he pointed with his palm closed, the word was specific (table, for instance). Jawn was a good teacher, with inexhaustible patience; Toroca guessed that teaching the Other language to youngsters had once been his job. Nonetheless, Toroca found the language confusing. In the Quintaglio tongue, related nouns usually ended in the same suffix: *-aja* for kinds of wood, *-staynt* for types of buildings, and so on. But the Other language didn't seem to have any such simplicity; a sailing ship was a *ga-san* whereas a rowboat was a *sil-don-kes-la*.

Eventually, some questions could be asked. There were six standard interrogatives in the Quintaglio language: who, what, how, why, where, and when. It became apparent, however, that there were *eight* in the Others' speech, six corresponding to the Quintaglio ones, plus two more that Toroca gathered meant "with what degree of certainty?" and "how righteous is this?" He'd picked up the latter by Jawn repeatedly asking questions and pointing through the glass roof at the gibbous Face of God; the Other religion centered on the Face, just as the Quintaglios' own discredited Larskian faith had.

The first question Jawn asked was the one Toroca had expected. Jawn leaned back on his tail—Toroca had decided to refer to Jawn as "he"; it was too difficult maintaining a mental image of a "she" with a dewlap—and said in his own language, "Where you from, Toroca?"

Toroca had to answer with a question of his own. "Picture land," he said, and made the beckoning hand sign that meant "give me."

Jawn looked momentarily confused, then apparently realized that "picture land" must refer to a "map," a word the Other equivalent of which Toroca didn't know. Jawn spoke to Morb, the fellow with the black armbands, and a map was brought in. It was made of neither leather nor paper, but rather a pinkish material that had a waxy feel to it; perhaps a plant derivative. Once the map was unfurled, Toroca was surprised to see that although the page it was printed on was square, the image was perfectly circular. Rather than having the Others' archipelago in the center, it was displaced toward the upper left. In the correct relative positions the northern and southern polar caps were indicated.

Suddenly it hit Toroca: the circular view showed all of the back side of their moon, everywhere from which the Face of God was visible. Had the Others never sailed farther than that? Perhaps with a religion built around the Face, they refused to sail beyond its purview. Indeed, the glass roofs of their buildings might be for more than simply letting in light; perhaps they ensured that the Others were never out of sight of their god.

Toroca used his hands to make the map bulge up from the tabletop into a dome, in hopes of indicating that it represented one hemisphere. Then, with an exaggerated gesture of his muzzle, he tried to show that he came from around past the borders of the map.

Jawn looked shocked. He glanced over at the guard, but Morb was paying little attention. Jawn said just two words, the two interrogatives unique to the Other language: With what degree of certainty? How righteous is this?

"Loud," said Toroca in Jawn's language, and then, realizing he was using the wrong word, "Much."

Jawn shook his head. "How you here?"

Toroca hadn't learned many verbs yet, but that sentence was easy enough to decipher even without them. *"Ga-san,"* he said. Sailing ship.

"No see," said Jawn.

Toroca gestured in the direction of the water, then curved his arm down, hoping to convey that the ship was below the horizon. "No far," said Toroca, wanting to make clear that it hadn't gone all the way back to Land.

Jawn touched his own chest. "Jawn," he said. He pointed at Toroca. "Toroca." Then, wrinkling his muzzle in a way that Toroca had come to associate with asking questions, *"Ga-san?"*

"Dasheter," said Toroca. *"Ga-san Dasheter."*

Jawn pointed at himself, then Toroca, then Morb, the guard. "Three," he said in his language. "Three here. *Ga-san?"*

Toroca only knew the numerals to ten. "Ten and two," he said.

"Farg-sol," said Jawn.

Toroca briefly wondered what "eleven" was; he hated gaps in his knowledge. But Jawn pressed on. "Few," he said.

And that was the key point. Yes, there were only a few people aboard the *Dasheter,* even though it was a big ship. Toroca had never thought the ship particularly empty, but by the standards of these people, it would be. How to explain territoriality? For God's sake, he was the least expert of all his people on that topic.

With one hand he lifted the corner of the map and flicked the edge. With the other, he made the beckoning gesture. Jawn understood immediately and fetched blank drawing sheets and graphite sticks. Toroca drew a circle and then put a dot in it. He pointed at the dot, then pointed at himself, palm opened, conveying, he hoped, that the dot represented one Quintaglio rather than him in particular. He said, *"Bal,"* the Other word for one, followed by *"hoos-ta,"* the Other word for good. Then he put in a second dot, but far away from the first, and said *"hoos-ta"* again. Then he added a third dot, close to the first. *"Hoos-na-ta."* Bad. And a fourth dot, even closer. *"Hoos-na-ta, hoos-na-ta"*—repetition being the way the Others showed successive degrees.

Jawn looked dismayed. He gestured with his hand, showing how much room was still left in Toroca's circle.

"Bad, bad," said Toroca again.

Jawn wrinkled his muzzle and said that word, *"Glees,"* meaning, how righteous is this?

Not very, thought Toroca, but he didn't know how to say it.

"All right," said Novato to the group assembled on the hillside. "It seems that whatever was being built is finished. Let's review what's happened." Garios and the other five members of Novato's staff were lying on the grass. Early morning sunlight sporadically punched through the clouds.

"Some orange dust escaped from the ark and came into contact with the cliff," said Novato. "It—the dust—seems to have undertaken a two-stage project. In the first stage, it converted a cube of cliff material into the same super-strong stuff the ark is made of. That cube, which was originally almost entirely buried in rock, measures roughly a hundred and thirty paces on a side, and one face of it roughly corresponds with what was originally the face of the cliff. In and of itself, that single cube constituted the largest artificial structure in our entire world.

"But after completing the first stage—construction of the central cube—a second stage began. That involved expanding the cube on top and on its four sides by adding new material to turn the overall structure into a pyramid, with a base approximately three hundred paces on a side. Making the central cube was relatively straightforward, if such words can be applied to miracles: it only involved converting existing rock into the blue material. This second stage has required bringing in new material, and we've all seen that going on: rocks seeming to liquefy, but without giving off the heat we expect of molten material, then flowing into new shapes, and, as they resolidify, turning blue.

"Gatabor and I watched as part of the pyramid's crown pushed up from under the ground, and you've all seen the one sloping side of the pyramid projecting out of the cliff face.

"The pyramid doesn't come to a point at its apex. Rather, there's a central shaft dropping straight down into the structure. The opening is square, about fourteen paces on a side. Gatabor and I only had time for a brief look down into the depths of the pyramid's interior before the apex was lifted too high off the ground for us to be able to see within it. Things are moving around down at the bottom of the pyramid: things with wheels, things with metal jaws, things with long prows that coil to a point. Incredible as it may seem, we can only conclude that these things were somehow built or grown by the same orange dust that escaped from the ark."

Novato shuddered, recalling the wonder of it all.

"As I said, the apex of the pyramid is now too far off the ground to reach, but it's easy to measure the angles of its sides. One can draw an imaginary line right through the remaining rocks of the cliff and it would join up perfectly with the part of the pyramid's base now projecting out of the cliff face, across the strip of beach, and into the water. As you've all no doubt observed by now, a large part of the material of the cliff has been consumed, so the total pyramid is only partially buried in rock now.

"And what about the ark? It seems intact, although most of it is now buried within the pyramid. The door is still exposed, although there's no cliff face left near it to get hold of, and the blue material provides no footholds of any kind. However, we could lean a very tall ladder against the side of the pyramid to gain access to the ark. I was hoping to put the crafters of Pack Derrilo to work constructing such a ladder, but the pyramid burst through the plain on which their old stone buildings existed. First the buildings fell apart, and then the stone material—which had been quarried out of the cliff face, after all—was absorbed into the structure. The Pack has moved on; the pyramid has scared off all the shovelmouth herds.

"You will have noticed that the sides of the pyramid aren't completely solid. Rather, there seems to be a tunnel entrance in the middle of each face. I forbade anyone from entering these until construction stopped. However, it seems now that the pyramid is complete. It's not getting any taller, although it may still be growing down and wider beneath ground level; there's no way to tell. If it remains quiescent for another day, I'll authorize the first teams to go inside. Any questions?"

"I have one," said Garios, lifting his long muzzle to look at her. "What do you make of that stuff projecting out of the top of the pyramid?"

"What stuff?" said Novato.

"Oh, you must have seen it. The stuff rising toward the sky. It's been going up since this morning."

Without a word, Novato ran to where she could get a decent look at the vast, blue pyramid.

The third stage had begun.

A hunt! Simple, primal, soothing . . .

Afsan stalked his prey through tall grass. He couldn't see exactly what it was he was pursuing—the grass hid it from view—but he could smell it and he could hear it. Afsan moved quickly through the grass, the sound of his passing hardly more than an undercurrent beneath the steady east-west wind.

At last his quarry moved into a clearing. It was a small shovelmouth—a juvenile, no doubt, not much larger than Afsan himself—moving along on all fours, its pendulous gut waggling back and forth as it walked. The beast's head was drawn out into a flat prow and atop its skull was an ornate three-pointed crest. Its pebbly skin was a mixture of light green and yellow.

Afsan crouched down in the grass, then leapt, his legs unfolding, his jaws swinging wide for the killing bite.

But the leap seemed to stretch out, and time itself appeared to slow down. Everything happened ponderously, as if the whole scene were taking place underwater. The juvenile shoveler swung its head around to look at Afsan and its prow opened wide to let out a thunderous yell.

And then the impossible happened. As the call spewed forth, both the upper and the lower halves of the shoveler's prow split apart and grew longer and longer, great fleshy globs pulling away from them. The globs, light green and yellow, like the rest of the beast's skin, soon resolved themselves into four tiny Quintaglio heads, black eyes round with terror. Meanwhile, the triple points of the head crest flared out into tiny greenish spheres that sprouted saw-toothed muzzles and obsidian eyes.

The shoveler's thunderous cry split into a choir of seven Quintaglio screams as Afsan continued to sail through the air, now on the downward part of his parabolic leap. As the distance between himself and the shoveler closed, Afsan thought for an instant that he recognized the tiny faces, but then he hit, the impact knocking the wind from his lungs. With a single darting movement of his neck, Afsan scooped out a tract of flesh from the shoveler's shoulders and throat. The beast fell to the ground, dead. Afsan scrambled to his feet and rolled the creature's head over so that he could clearly see it.

The tiny Quintaglio faces were gone. The prow was back to normal, and the crest had re-formed into its original triple-pointed configuration.

Afsan stood stupefied for a moment. A shadow passed over him. Above, a giant wingfinger was circling, its purple wings vast and amorphous, billowing up around its body, waiting for its chance at the carcass.

Afsan rolled the shoveler onto its side so that he could get at the belly. With a great bite, he opened the abdomen wide, blood spilling out like water from a sluice. He pushed his arms into the warm flesh, spreading open the chest to expose the tasty organs within.

Suddenly a second pair of arms appeared. He couldn't see whom they belonged to; indeed, they seemed to be coming from his own chest, although for some reason his muzzle refused to tip down so that he could see the precise source. These intruding hands pulled at the shoveler's flesh, too, their claws raking into the outer layer of yellow fat and the red meat beneath.

Afsan tried to pull the mysterious hands out of the body cavity, but soon another pair appeared, and then another and another, all trying to grasp a piece of the kill, greedily tearing out chunks of flesh. Afsan tried to slap them away, but they began to tear at his own arms, the claws scratching his skin, long blood trails running along his forearms all the way from wrist to elbow.

More arms appeared. They seized Afsan's own upper arms, their sharp clawpoints digging into his skin. Afsan fought to free himself, but stringy tendons and bones—his own radius and ulna—were now glistening gray-white beneath his torn flesh.

Afsan brought his muzzle down and chomped through one of the foreign arms, then shook his head, flinging the thing aside. He heard a scream coming from somewhere, and the shadow of the purple wingfinger moved again and again across the scene. Afsan's neck darted once more and another arm snapped off. Meanwhile, he fought with all his strength to twist free of the arms holding his own. Finally, after chomping through five, ten, twelve, fourteen phantom limbs, Afsan, his own arms reduced to articulated skeletons, dug into his meal, getting every last bit of meat for himself.

Chapter 10

"Your name is Sal-Afsan, correct?" asked Mokleb.

"Of course," said Afsan, irritated.

"Tell me about that," Mokleb said.

"Tell you about what?"

"Your name. Tell me about your name."

Afsan shrugged. "It means 'meaty thighbone.' "

"Unusual name for a skinny person."

He sighed. "You're not the first to have observed that. But what choice did I have? The name was given to me by the creche masters in Pack Carno. I had no say in the matter."

"Of course not. But what about your praenomen syllable?"

"Sal? Ah, now, that I did get to choose, of course. It's in honor of my mentor, Tak-Saleed."

"Tell me about your relationship with Saleed."

"Well, I didn't meet him until I was—what?—twelve kilodays old. I was summoned to Capital City to be his apprentice."

"How did that make you feel, to be summoned clear across the continent?"

"It was, and still is, an honor to serve at the imperial court."

Mokleb waved her hand. "Doubtless so. But you were torn from your friends, your creche-mates. Creche-mates are as one."

Afsan nodded. "I rarely think of my creche-mates. There was Dandor and Keebark. And Jostor, who became a famous musician."

"Yet you were torn away from them—ordered to leave your

home and undertake the long and arduous journey to the Capital."

"I've made much more arduous journeys since."

"Granted," said Mokleb. "But this was your first time traveling."

"Pack Carno traveled all the time. We moved along the shore of the Kreeb river, following the herds of shovelmouths."

"But on those journeys you moved with your Pack and your creche-mates. I'm asking what it was like to have to leave all that and set out on your own. You're avoiding the question."

Afsan's tone carried a slight edge. "I never shy away from questions."

Mokleb clicked her teeth. "Oh, no, not from questions about the stars or the planets or the other moons. But you do shy away from *personal* questions. Why?"

Afsan was quiet for a time. Then: "I value my privacy."

"As do we all. But for this process to work, you must be forthcoming."

He nodded. "Very well. I was frightened and disoriented by the move. But when a rider brings an imperial summons, one has no choice."

"And what about leaving your creche-mates? Your friends?"

A scrunching of the muzzle. "Creche-mates I had, yes, but friends? No, I had few of those."

"Why?"

"Why?" Afsan sighed again. A single question that brought back all the pain of his youth. "Why?" he repeated. "Because . . ." He turned his head, facing vaguely in Mokleb's direction. "Because I wasn't very good at athletics. Because I *was* very good at mathematics. Whatever problem the teaching master gave us, I had no trouble solving it."

"And this irritated your classmates?"

"I guess so. That certainly wasn't my intention."

Mokleb dipped her muzzle. "The sad truth, Afsan, is that often what we intend has little to do with what we achieve."

Afsan was silent.

"So it would be fair to characterize your childhood as unhappy?"

"If one had to characterize it, yes, I suppose that word would be as good as any."

"What word would you use?" asked Mokleb.

"Alone."

"That's an unusual word. One rarely hears it applied to people."
Mokleb was silent. "I mean, as a race, we like being separate.
We like the distance that keeps us apart, the territorial buffers we
maintain."

"Indeed," said Afsan. "But we also do like some interaction.
Not for long periods, of course, but we do like spending time
with others, and we take comfort in knowing that those others
enjoy the time they spend with us."

"And?" said Mokleb.

"And, of those my age back in Carno, none of them wanted
to spend time with me. It . . ."

"Yes?"

"It didn't seem fair, that's all. It seemed that somewhere there
should have been people more like me, people who shared my
interests, people to whom my mathematical skill was nothing
special."

"But there was no one like that in Carno."

"No. Except perhaps . . ."

"Yes?"

"Nothing."

"No, you must share your thoughts."

"It's . . . it's gone now. I've forgotten what I was going to
say."

"You were suggesting that there perhaps was someone in Carno
who would have been more like you," said Mokleb patiently.

"No, there was no one like that. I—I just wish there had been,
that's all." Afsan turned his head so that Mokleb could clearly
see his muzzle. "That's all."

Rising up from each corner of the square hole at the apex of
the blue pyramid were thin poles, each about as thick around as
Novato's leg. These poles, too, seemed to be made of the super-
strong blue material. They were being pushed up as new material
was added from underneath, the strange machines Novato had
briefly glimpsed presumably manufacturing them. Their growth
was shockingly quick: on the first day that they appeared, they'd
already pierced the bottoms of the clouds.

Every forty paces or so, the poles were joined by cross struts,
making the whole thing look like four absolutely vertical ladders
arranged in a square. And every fifth crosspiece had a large cone
attached to it, made of copper-colored metal instead of the blue
stuff. Each cone was affixed to the strut's outermost edge by its

apex, so that the open funnel faced away from the tower.

Novato guessed that the vertical tubes were hollow, meaning they'd not require much material to build. Still, given the tower's height, a huge amount of sand or rock must have already been converted into the blue building material. Indeed, the cliff had now been devoured for a large distance on either side of the giant base of the pyramid and was still receding. The pyramid itself was now standing free at the edge of the beach. And from the square hole in its center, the four ladders continued to grow toward the stars.

"You know, Mokleb," said Afsan as she made herself comfortable at the beginning of their session, "you've chosen an unusual boulder to sit on. Most of those who come to talk with me sit there." He indicated a boulder about ten paces upwind from the one he was straddling. "It's nothing major, but I've been meaning to mention it since we began these meetings."

"I—prefer it here," said Mokleb. "The view . . ."

Afsan shrugged slightly as he lowered his belly onto his own rock. "Of course."

"Today, I want you to talk a bit about your . . . family," said Mokleb, "although I admit it's strange to use the word in relation to any except the imperial clan."

"Tell me about it," Afsan said dryly.

"You have four surviving children, is that right?"

"Yes."

"And you know them all personally?"

"Yes."

"Remarkable," said Mokleb. "Tell me about them."

"Well, there are my two sons, Af-Kelboon and Kee-Toroca. Kelboon is a mathematician; Toroca is leader of the Geological Survey of Land. Then—"

"Did you say Af-Kelboon?"

"Yes."

"Is his praenomen syllable in honor of you?"

Afsan sighed. "Yes."

"How does that make you feel?"

Afsan's tail moved. "It embarrasses me a bit. It had never crossed my mind that anyone would take that praenomen."

"Interesting," said Mokleb. "And what about your daughters?"

"Well, there's Nov-Dynax, a healer—"

"Nov, in honor of her mother, Novato?"

"Yes."

"Fascinating. Forgive me for interrupting."

Afsan tipped his head in mild concession. "And, lastly, Lub-Galpook, the imperial hunt leader."

"Galpook is your daughter?"

"Yes. There were many in my youth who said I should become a full-time hunter. Well, Galpook has done just that. And let me tell you, she's a much better hunter than I ever was."

"How did it happen that she entered that profession?"

"The usual way."

"The usual way for average citizens—through vocational exams? Or the usual way for hunt leaders?"

Afsan turned his head slightly away. "The latter."

"So she is perpetually in heat? She doesn't have a set mating time?"

"That is correct."

"I should like to meet her."

Afsan clicked his teeth lightly. "A few males have said that over the kilodays. I'm surprised to hear it from a female."

Mokleb let that pass. "Do you see her often?"

Afsan's voice was a bit wistful. "That would not be . . . prudent."

"Why not?"

"I should think that would be obvious."

"Oh?"

"It would not be appropriate. I'm her *father,* for God's sake."

"Yes?"

"Look: there are no other fathers in this world—fathers who know who their children are, that is. Emperor Dybo knew his father, of course, but Ter-Reegree had been killed long before I came to the Capital. And Dybo himself has yet to have offspring. I understand that, I think: after his right to rule was challenged by Dy-Rodlox, Dybo had agreed to let his own clutch, the imperial hatchlings, undergo the culling of the bloodpriest. But I suspect that he's chosen an even simpler path: not to be responsible for any eggs at all." Afsan paused. "So, without any models to follow, I've had to make up this fatherhood business as I go along. And mating with one whom I know to be my daughter does not seem appropriate."

"Oh?"

"Oh, indeed. And since she's perpetually giving off signs of receptivity, I, I prefer not to spend much time with her."

"But those who are constantly in heat do make exceptional hunt leaders," said Mokleb. "They have an energizing effect on the members of the pack."

"I am blind, Mokleb. I cannot hunt anymore."

"But you could mate."

"Of course."

"Have you recently?"

"No. No, not in a long time. A male normally has to be in the presence of a female in heat to become aroused, after all." He clicked his teeth. "I don't get around as much as I used to."

The wind continued to blow across Afsan from behind.

"It's an interesting occupation, I should imagine," said Mokleb. "Being a hunt leader."

"I'm sure it is," said Afsan.

Mokleb was quiet for a time. "I once toyed with the idea of that profession, but I developed knee problems in my early adolescence. I cannot run fast. They tried hacking off my leg when I was young, to see if it would grow back without the impediment, but it did not."

"Ah," said Afsan. "I'm sorry."

"Nothing to be sorry about," said Mokleb, with finality. "If the problem had been solved, I wouldn't have been allowed to pursue my studies. They would have made me become a hunt leader."

"Nonsense," said Afsan. "Why, they wouldn't have done that unless . . ."

She got off the boulder she'd been sitting on and walked around to the other side of Afsan's rock, letting the wind blow over her and onto him. Afsan's nostrils flared slightly. "Oh, my," he said.

"Beautiful day," said Garios.

Novato, who had been making more sketches of the pyramid and the strange tower growing up out of its apex, looked up at the sky. Clouds covered most of it. "Looks like rain," she said.

"Oh, perhaps, perhaps. Still, beautiful day."

"Since when is rain beautiful? Especially here, where we get more of it than we need."

"Oh, maybe the weather isn't great. I guess I'm just in a good mood."

"Ah," said Novato, noncommittal.

At this point, Delplas ambled by about thirty paces away—far enough that normally no territorial gesture was required. But

Garios waved at Delplas anyway with a wide sweep of his arm. "Beautiful day!" he called.

Delplas shook her head. "You're crazy," she said good-naturedly, but then she splayed her fingers in a conspiratorial gesture aimed at Novato.

Novato sighed. She'd felt the first tinglings herself this morning, but hadn't expected anyone else to be able to detect her new pheromones yet. It'd still be a few hundred days before she was fully receptive; given that receptivity came only once every eighteen thousand days, it took its time coming into full bloom.

"Beautiful day," said Garios again, to no one in particular.

Males, thought Novato.

Chapter 11

The twenty days on the island of the Others passed quickly, and now it was time for Toroca to check in with the *Dasheter*. Jawn offered a boat and rowers to take Toroca out, but Toroca repeated what he'd tried to make clear over and over, although his speech was more fluent now: "Do not come near the *Dasheter*," he said in the Other language. "To do so would be bad."

"I still do not understand," said Jawn. "I am curious about your sailing ship."

"Accept my words," said Toroca. "I will return soon. I am sorry you cannot see my sailing ship."

Jawn didn't seem satisfied, but he let it go. "Swim safely."

"I will," said Toroca, and, with that, he climbed down the rope ladder and entered the water. It was a long swim out to the *Dasheter*, but the weather was good. His tail propelled him along.

Toroca's mind was full of thoughts as he swam. The Others were so unlike Quintaglios. Cooked food; "cooked" being a word Jawn had taught him. No territoriality; even to Toroca, the open displays of physical contact the Others exhibited were distasteful. And they used tools to kill animals; Toroca had seen many of those metal fire sticks. Toroca shuddered as he swam along: he hadn't realized just what had happened that first day. Someone had shot at him as he'd approached the shore. Jawn had apologized later; the person on the pier had mistaken Toroca for an alligator.

An alligator! Oh, the ignominy!

Toroca continued to slice through the waves, occasionally using his feet to steer in the direction he wanted to go. With the giant Face of God hanging stationary overhead, navigation was easy. The Face was waning gibbous now, its unilluminated limb looking dark purple against the lighter violet of early morning sky. The water was still cooler than Toroca would have liked. Part of him was sad to be leaving the Others, even though he fully intended to return, but it would be good to see faces that were green instead of yellow. He'd missed Keenir's gravelly voice, and Babnol's gentle clicking of teeth, and even old Biltog's endless stories about days gone by. Why, soon he'd—

What was that?

Something big was coming toward him, wave tops churning in its wake. Toroca went below the surface and saw it front-on: a body circular in cross section, thicker than Toroca's own torso, with three equally spaced tapered projections, one on top and two at the lower sides. He kicked sideways to get another angle on the animal.

Oh-oh.

From the side, he could see that the upper projection was a stiff dorsal fin, and the two side projections were flippers. The body was streamlined, starting with an elongated snout and ending in a large vertical tail fin. At the pelvis, two more small flippers projected from the creature's sides.

A fish-lizard. The *Dasheter*'s fishing nets often caught small ones; they provided a welcome dose of reptilian flesh in the diet. But this one was half again as long as Toroca. The body was slate gray in color and the visible part of the eyes looked like tiny mercury drops in the middle of raised scleral bone rings. Its nostrils were just in front of its eyes. And projecting forward from its face was that long, tapered snout, lined with sharp teeth.

The beast quickly turned so that Toroca saw it head-on again. There was no doubt: it was coming after him. Toroca swam well for a land creature, but this animal was in its native element. There was no chance that he could outdistance it.

Suddenly the fish-lizard was upon him, its long, narrow jaws opening wide. Toroca felt a hundred little daggers tear into him as the jaws closed on his thigh. Clouds of red appeared in the water. Toroca pounded his fists on the creature's snout. That surprised it; it was not used to battling prey that had hands. The fish-lizard rotated around, its giant tail slapping Toroca. Toroca struggled for the surface, gulping air as soon as he broke through the waves. The animal twisted its body and tried to bring its needle-like prow to bear again.

Toroca had eaten enough small fish-lizards over the kilodays to know their anatomy: the dorsal fin had no bones in it at all, and the giant tail fin was only supported along its lower edge by an extension of the backbone. The upper prong of the fin was pure meat. Toroca's jaws were still open wide from taking in air. He chomped down on the upper part of the tail fin, his curving teeth easily slicing into it. The fish-lizard, which had been about to bite into Toroca's leg, opened its own jaws wide, letting out a silent underwater scream.

Toroca filled his lungs once more. The fish-lizard was an air-breather, too, but it was cold-blooded and could go much longer between breaths, especially since its body, unlike Toroca's, was built for subsurface maneuvering. The creature moved almost effortlessly, a little flick of a paddle here, a gentle movement of the tail there. Toroca looked up at the Face of God overhead. He wished for a moment that it really was the countenance of the deity; he most certainly did not want to die out here.

The fish-lizard was swinging around to attack again. Toroca felt the sharp teeth cut into his tail. Blood was clouding the water, some his own, some the lizard's. Toroca hadn't had a chance to examine his own wounds yet; he didn't know if they were superficial or if he was hemorrhaging to death. And, he thought, God help me if there's a shark in the area; about the only thing that made Quintaglio *dagamant* look tame was a shark driven to frenzy by blood.

Toroca tried beating on the thing's gray torso with his fists in hopes of driving it away, but it seemed determined to make a meal of him. Perhaps he could gouge its eyes out; but no, the scleral rings of bone afforded a lot of protection.

Toroca lashed with his tail to get out of the way. The lizard changed trajectory, barreling toward him. Its jaws were closed, perhaps to better streamline its form when moving quickly.

Suddenly Toroca had an idea. Instead of trying to swim away, he surged forward, his tail undulating, his legs kicking. He almost thought he was going to be impaled on the thing's long snout. But as the fish-lizard came close, he grabbed the snout, one hand gripping it near its tip, where his handspan was easily enough to wrap around the snout's circumference, the other hand grasping it at its base, where it joined the reptile's head. He then brought his right knee up directly under the middle of the snout and, with all the strength in his arms, bent the snout downward. It took everything he had, but at last he felt the long jaw bones snap. New blood mixed with the cool water. Now that there was only ligament and flesh holding the snout together, Toroca finished the job with a massive bite from his own jaws, severing the fish-lizard's long prow cleanly from its body. The lizard's tail was smashing wildly left and right, but Toroca kicked out of the way, letting go of the snout, which slowly began to drift downward. The lizard, completely disarmed, tried to butt Toroca with its bloody front end but soon tired of that and swam away.

Toroca doubtless had mortally wounded the animal, but he wondered if the reverse was also true. Treading water, he examined the bites on his thigh and tail. Both were still slowly oozing blood, but neither seemed particularly deep. Now that the fish-lizard was gone, the water was relatively calm—calmer, in fact, than it had been when he'd swum in the opposite direction twenty days before. He rested his head on the surface, and, with slow movements of his tail, glided gently onward.

"We spoke before about the names of your children," said Mokleb, "but didn't really get into your relationship with them. This is a unique area; I'd like to explore it."

The sun was sliding down the western sky toward the Ch'mar volcanoes. Two pale moons—one crescent, one almost full—were visible despite the glare. A few silvery-white clouds twisted their way across the purple bowl of the sky.

Afsan's face showed a mixture of emotions. "My children," he said softly, adjusting his position on his rock. "And Novato's, too, of course." He shook his head slightly. "There were eight of them to begin with."

"Yes."

"One died in childhood. Helbark was his name. He succumbed to fever." Afsan's voice was full of sadness. "I was devastated when he died. It seemed so unfair. Like all of my children, Helbark had been spared the culling of the bloodpriest. It was as though God had given him the gift of life, but then snatched it away. Helbark died before ever saying his first word." Afsan's tail moved left and right. "You know, Mokleb, I've never seen any of my children; I was blinded before they came to Capital City. I felt I knew the other seven because I knew the tones they used, knew what caused their voices to sing with joy and what caused their words to tremble with anger or outrage. But Helbark . . . if there is an afterlife, Mokleb, I sometimes wonder if I would recognize him there. Or whether he would recognize me."

Mokleb made a small sound, noncommittal. Afsan went on. "After Helbark died, Pal-Cadool and I had gone to the site of that kill everyone keeps talking about—the place where I helped bring down that giant thunderbeast. We found a stone there and took it back to the mountain of stones upon which the Hunter's Shrine is built. You know the old legend? That each of the original five hunters had brought one stone there for every kill they'd made during their lives? Well, I wanted to bring a stone from one of my kills. Poor Helbark was far too young to have acquired a hunt or pilgrimage tattoo. I thought that maybe if a kill was consecrated in his name, it might help his passage into heaven. Pal-Cadool helped me climb the cairn so that my stone could be placed right at the summit, inside the Shrine—the structure made out of past hunt leaders' bones. Most people don't know about it, but on the far side of the stone cairn, there's a hidden stairway leading to the summit. I couldn't have made it otherwise."

"A priest advised you to do this?"

Afsan shifted uncomfortably. "I rarely speak to priests," he said.

"Of course, of course," said Mokleb. A topic for another time. "But Helbark isn't the only one of your children to have passed on, is he?"

Quietly: "No."

"There was Haldan and Yabool." A pause. "And Drawtood." Still quiet: "Yes."

"How do you feel about what happened to them?"

Afsan's tone was bitter. "How would you expect me to feel?"

"I have no expectations at all, Afsan. That's why I ask."

Afsan nodded, and then, "They say I'm gifted when it comes to solving puzzles, Mokleb." He fell silent, perhaps reluctant to continue.

Mokleb waited patiently for several beats, then, as a gentle prod, she agreed: "Yes, that's what they say."

"Well, most puzzles don't count for anything. Whether you solve them or not doesn't really matter. But that one . . ." He fell silent again. Mokleb waited. "That one mattered. That one was for real. Once Haldan had been murdered"—the word, so rarely spoken, sounded funny, archaic—"once she had been murdered, the puzzle was to figure out who was responsible."

"And you did," said Mokleb.

"But not in time!" Afsan's voice was full of anguish now. "Not in time. Don't you see? It wasn't until Drawtood killed again, taking the life of my son Yabool, that I figured it out."

"Murder is such an uncommon crime," said Mokleb. "You can't blame yourself for needing more data."

"More data," repeated Afsan. He made a snorting sound. "More data. Another body, you mean. Another dead child of mine."

Mokleb was silent.

"Forgive me," Afsan said after a time. "I find these memories difficult to deal with."

Mokleb nodded.

"It's just that, well . . ."

"Well what?"

"Nothing." Afsan's blind face turned toward the crumbling edge of the cliff.

"No, you had a thought. Please express it."

Afsan nodded and apparently rallied some inner strength. "It's just that I always wonder *why* Drawtood committed those murders."

"You were with him when he passed away."

"Yes."

"It's commonly believed that he confessed to you before swallowing the poison that killed him."

"I've never discussed the specifics of that night," said Afsan.

Mokleb waited.

"Yes," said Afsan at last, "Drawtood did speak of his reasons. He . . . he did not trust his siblings. He was afraid of them."

"Having siblings is unheard-of, Afsan. Who knows how one is supposed to react?"

"Exactly. But if having siblings is unknown, so is, is—let me coin a word: so is parenting."

"Parenting?"

Afsan clicked his teeth. "Saleed would have scowled fiercely at me for turning a noun into a verb. He hated neologisms. But, yes, *parenting*: the job of being a parent. And I mean 'being a parent' far beyond just having been involved in fertilizing or laying eggs. I knew who my children were, had daily contact with them, was in part responsible for their teaching and upbringing."

"Parenting," said Mokleb again. The word was strange indeed.

"That's the worst of it," said Afsan. "I was Drawtood's parent, his father. All children have something in common with their parents; studies in plant and animal heredity make that clear. But my role in Drawtood's composition was greater than that. I knew him! And yet he ended up a killer."

"I don't see your point," said Mokleb.

"Don't you? Maybe some responsibility goes along with being a parent. Maybe I failed in some way at what I should have done."

Mokleb shrugged. "There's so little data in this area."

"Data again," said Afsan. "Perhaps if I'd seen my children more *as* children and less as data, things would have been different."

"But most children have no parents, not in the sense that you're using the word."

"That's true," said Afsan, although he didn't sound mollified. "Still, it's something to think about: the relationship between parent and child."

Mokleb stared out over the precipice at the choppy waters beyond. "It is indeed," she said at last.

The four ladders finally stopped growing; no new rungs emerged from the apex of the pyramid. The ladders stood silent, stark against the harsh gray sky of stormy Fra'toolar, rising up and up until they faded into invisibility. The whole pyramid seemed dead: nothing was happening at all. Still, Novato waited a full day before she, Garios, and Delplas finally entered. The openings in the centers of each of the pyramid's sides were fourteen paces wide: wide enough that three of them could walk abreast with a minimally acceptable seven paces between each other. The sounds of their toeclaws echoed loudly as they made their way down the long blue tunnel, a tunnel that was miraculously lit with dim red light from panels in the ceiling. The floor, although made of the obdurate blue stuff, was roughened to provide traction, as if inviting people to walk down this terrifying path into the very heart of the structure.

Novato's pulse raced. She glanced left and right, saw that Garios and Delplas had their claws exposed, saw the nervousness in their expressions. The whole pyramid was about three hundred paces wide, and Novato was silently counting off paces as they continued into its heart. The tunnel continued right into the center: a hundred and forty paces into the vast structure. Novato tried not to contemplate the huge weight of alien material over her head.

At last they came to the central vertical shaft. The inside base of the tower was square, fourteen paces on a side. The sides of the interior shaft were the bases of the four great ladders. They rose up and up, as high as Novato could see, converging to a point some fantastic distance above her head. Novato was sure the apparent convergence occurred long before the actual top of the tower was reached.

She looked at the stretched ladders, large open rectangles running up their impossible lengths. A brave wingfinger, apparently not perturbed by the alien structure, had built a nest on the crosspiece at the bottom of one of the ladders, and the flying reptile's white droppings streaked the gleaming blue material.

Novato tried to picture the kind of giant being that might climb such a ladder, but she knew, of course, that it had not been physical giants who were responsible for this structure. Indeed, the absolute opposite was true: incredibly tiny engineers had built this. And yet the image of giants would not leave her mind. The builders of this tower to the sky were giants in comparison to the Quintaglios. She leaned back on her tail, looking up, humbled.

And then her heart began pounding erratically; she had to force herself not to run out of the structure. Something was approaching from up above.

The thing moved silently. Only moments ago it had emerged from the vanishing point far overhead, but already it was looming larger and larger, coming down one of the corners of the shaft. It was big and metallic, and it was moving quickly although it wasn't actually falling.

Soon it began to slow—and a good thing, too, for otherwise it would have smashed into the floor. Novato could hear a faint descending whistle as the object came closer. It was as big as a shed or large carriage, and its bottom fit perfectly into the right angle made by two adjacent inner tower walls. The rest of it was rounded, like a beetle's body.

Novato, Garios, and Delplas quickly moved across the tower's base so they, quite literally, would be on the safe side. The giant beetle came to a stop at ground level. There it sat for a few moments, then its whole surface seemed to turn brighter, more shiny, as if it were liquefying, and suddenly a large rectangular opening appeared in its side, revealing that its interior was almost completely hollow. Once the door had appeared, the structure's surface became duller, more solid-looking.

And there it sat.

Novato moved over to it and cautiously peered through the doorway. There didn't seem to be much inside, but—

Incredible.

She could see right through the walls. From the outside, the thing was opaque, built from thick metal, but in looking through the walls from the inside, she could see right through to the blue material of the tower itself. She was terrified to step inside the beetle lest its walls grow liquid again and the door disappear, trapping her within. But she did stick her head into the doorway briefly to confirm that she could indeed see out in all directions. Looking up, she could see the four ladder-like sides of the tower stretching impossibly high overhead and, craning her neck around, she could even see her own palm pressed flat against the beetle's outer hull.

A few opaque objects were visible within the beetle's walls, but basically from the inside it seemed to be made of glass while from the outside its appearance was that of burnished metal. Novato had spent a lot of time working with various materials in her studies of optics, but she'd never encountered anything with properties like this. She pulled her head out of the doorway and extended a fingerclaw. The beetle wasn't made of harder-than-diamond stuff, anyway: she had little trouble scratching its metal outer hull.

Garios was leaning back on his tail, his long muzzle looking up. "You were right," he said softly.

Novato looked at him. "What?"

"You were right. Emergency equipment, that's what it was—emergency equipment for the ark-makers." He pointed at the silver beetle. "There it is—a lifeboat to take them back to space." He paused. "Only one of the three emergency kits was still . . . still *viable* after millions of kilodays. Perhaps the second would have built a flying machine to take the ark-makers back home, and the third . . . well, God only knows what the third would have built. But this one, the one that survived, has made some sort of lifeboat."

Novato realized in an instant that Garios was correct. And she also realized a more wondrous, a more terrifying, thought: that soon she herself would have to take a ride aboard this lifeboat.

Chapter 12

Back aboard the *Dasheter,* old Biltog tended to Toroca's injuries. There was nothing major. Toroca was irritated by the glee his shipmates took in his story of the attack by the fish-lizard, but, after enduring his disdain for the hunt for so long, they were entitled to some fun at his expense now that he'd single-handedly killed a formidable predator.

And, of course, everyone was interested in the Others.

"Tell us, Toroca," demanded Keenir, "what were they like?"

Toroca, still exhausted, supported himself by leaning against the foremast. "They are good people," he said. "I hope that, despite our differences, there is some way that we can become friends."

Keenir looked out over the water, perhaps thinking of the slaughter he'd been part of back on the Others' island. He made no reply.

"Tell me more about the murders of your two children," said Mokleb.

Afsan shifted uncomfortably on his rock. "Both of them were killed the same way," he said. "Their throats were slit."

"Slit? With a knife?"

"No, with a broken piece of mirror."

"Broken mirror," said Mokleb. "And they were killed by their brother, Drawtood, correct?"

Afsan clicked his teeth, but it was a forced gesture, with little humor behind it. "Yes. Even I saw the symbolism in that, Mokleb. Broken mirrors, distorted reflections of oneself."

"Where did the killings take place?"

"In their apartments. The killings occurred several days apart. Haldan was murdered first. Drawtood snuck up on each of them, or otherwise was able to approach them closely, and then he did the deed."

"Snuck up on them?"

"So I presume, yes."

"Fascinating," said Mokleb, and then: "You discovered one of the bodies."

"Yes." A long pause. "I found Haldan. If anything should have given me nightmares, that should have been it. In fact, I can't think of a more terrifying scenario for a blind person than slowly coming to realize that the room he's in isn't empty but rather contains a horribly murdered body."

"And you say Drawtood snuck up on his victims?"

"Well, he was doubtless let into the apartments by them. They did know him, after all. But to manage the close approach, yes, I presume he did that by stealth."

"Fascinating," said Mokleb once more. She wrote furiously on her notepad.

It was the end of the day. Novato was ambling back toward the camp, located a few hundred paces from the base of the blue pyramid supporting the tower. Garios had caught up with her and was now walking about ten paces to her left.

There was some small talk, then Garios asked, in a tone of forced casualness, "What will happen to your eight egglings if you mate with Afsan? Will they be spared the culling of the bloodpriest again?"

Novato turned her muzzle sideways, making clear that her gaze was on Garios. She held it just long enough to convey that she felt he was stepping into her territory. "I doubt it," she said at last. "I mean, there are a lot fewer people who think Afsan is The One today than there were twenty kilodays ago."

"Ah," said Garios, again in a tone that would have been offhand where it not for the slight quaver underlying the words, "so you've been contemplating the question."

"Not really, no."

"But you didn't hesitate before answering," he said.

"I'm a bright person." Novato clicked her teeth. "I can answer questions without meditating on them for daytenths on end."

"Oh, then you *haven't* been contemplating this issue."

"Not directly."

"Afsan already has four children."

"He *had* eight," said Novato, a little sadly. "Four survive."

"Still, I've had but one."

"Well, if this is a contest, I win," said Novato gently. "I've had nine, five of whom still live. I'm the mother to more adult Quintaglios than anyone else alive."

"Granted," said Garios. The sky overhead was rapidly growing darker; a few stars already pierced the firmament. "But I'm talking about just Afsan and me. He's had four. I've only had one." He held up a hand. "Yes, there are those who would argue that Afsan is a great person, that our species is enriched by having more of his offspring. Still," he said, and then, a little later, "still . . ."

"I'm not the only female around," said Novato. "Delplas will be in heat in another two kilodays."

"Oh, I know, but . . ."

"In fact, there are many tens of females who might choose you at some point during the remainder of your life. You're a male; you can breed whenever called upon to do so. Me, I've got one or maybe two more opportunities to lay eggs."

"True," said Garios.

"I'm hardly your only chance."

"Oh, I know. Still . . ." he said again.

"I *am* flattered by your interest," said Novato. "But as to whom I'll call for, even I don't know. Believe me, though, it'll be either you or Afsan; I have no doubt about that."

"You do have four children already by him," Garios said again.

"I know."

"And, after all, those children weren't necessarily that great. Oh, yes, one became a hunt leader and another directs the Geological Survey, but, well, one was a murderer, too."

"Eat plants, Garios."

"I only meant—no, forgive me! I'm sorry! I just—I didn't intend to say that. Oh, Novato, forgive me! *Roots,* your pheromones are everywhere. I, ah, I'm just going to go away now, go for a little walk. I'm sorry. I'm very, very sorry."

"You know, Mokleb," said Afsan, his voice sharp, "you remind me of my old teaching master."

Mokleb lifted her muzzle. "Oh?"

"Yes. Tak-Saleed. Not as I came to know him at the very end, but as I first knew him."

"Indeed."

" 'Indeed.' He'd talk just like that, too. You'd never know what he was thinking. Only one thing was clear. He was judging you. He was evaluating you. Every day, every moment, he was watching your every move. I wasn't his first apprentice, you know. He'd had many others before me."

"But you were the one that survived," said Mokleb.

"He sent all the others back, dispatching them home."

"Dispatching."

"You know—sending."

"The word has no other connotations for you."

"What word? 'Dispatching'? No."

"It's the euphemism used by bloodpriests for what they do: in order to keep the size of the population in check, seven infants are killed. But the process is referred to as 'dispatching,' not killing."

"I suppose I knew that," said Afsan, "but that's not my point. Saleed judged each of us, each of his young apprentices. And all of them, save me, were sent back to the Packs from which they'd come."

"And that disturbed you?"

"It was frightening—not knowing if I'd be sent back next; whether I was the one he'd been looking for, or whether he'd get rid of me, too."

"But you never met any of the other apprentices?"

"No." A pause. "Saleed used to talk about them from time to time, though. Always in disparaging terms. The fellow before, his name was Pog-Teevio. I had to wear his leftover sashes. But he'd been older than I was, so the sashes had been altered to fit me. You could tell where material had been removed—since the sashes were tapered, the pieces didn't line up properly and had to be trimmed." A pause. "God, how I hated those sashes."

"How many apprentices did Saleed have before you?"

"Well, let's see. There was Pog-Teevio. Before him was Adkab. Before him was, um, Rikgot. Before her, Haltang. You know, as an aside, I wish I hadn't known their names. It made it a lot harder, contemplating what happened to them, knowing their names."

"Was Haltang the first?"

"No, there were two before him. Females both: Lizhok and— oh, what was it now?—Tasnik."

"That's a total of six before you."

"Yes."

"And you were number seven."

Irritated. "That follows, doesn't it? Yes. The seventh."

"It bothered you that your future at the palace was unsure."

"Wouldn't it bother you? When I'd been summoned to Capital City, I'd had no idea that Saleed had had all those previous apprentices, all of whom had proved unsuitable."

"But as your time at the palace grew longer and longer, surely the fear that you'd be sent back must have diminished?"

"Diminished?" Afsan clicked teeth derisively. "That shows how little you know, Mokleb. It grew worse. I kept waiting for the eighth apprentice to arrive."

"How did you know there would be an eighth?"

"Well, of course, it turned out there wasn't, but I felt sure, sure in my bones, that there would be one more."

"Six before you, you as the seventh, and one more, for a total of eight," said Mokleb.

"And they call *me* a mathematical genius."

"Eight, of whom seven would be sent back."

"Yes."

"Of whom seven would be *dispatched*."

"As you say."

"And Saleed sat in constant judgment of you."

"Yes. Just like you do."

"I don't judge you at all, Afsan. It's not my place. But you felt judged by Saleed. Six had already been sent back. If you failed, you'd be sent back, too."

"It wasn't so much a question of 'if.' I eventually became sure I'd be sent back; I knew there had to be one further apprentice."

Mokleb was quiet for a time, waiting to see if Afsan would offer anything further. At last she said, "Do you see the pattern you're describing?"

A sneer. "What pattern?"

"Eight youngsters, judged by a vastly older authority figure. Seven of them dispatched—your word, that—and only the eighth surviving."

"Yes. So?"

"It sounds precisely like the culling of the bloodpriest. Seven out of eight hatchlings in every clutch are devoured."

Afsan clicked his teeth derisively. "You're way off base,

Mokleb. By God's own tail, I knew this whole process was a waste of time. Roots, you see patterns in everything! For your information, *Doctor,* I knew nothing at all about bloodpriests until *after* I'd left Saleed to go on my journey around the world. It wasn't until I was on my return trip to Capital City, when I stopped off in Carno for a visit, that I first learned about the bloodpriests. For God's sake, Mokleb, the nonsense you spout!"

Bos-Karshirl, a young female engineer Novato had requested some time ago from Capital City, arrived by boat on a foggy even-day. The two of them stood on the pebbly beach and looked up at the massive blue pyramid and the tower rising out of its apex. The tower disappeared after a short distance into the gray gloom.

"Incredible," said Karshirl. She turned and bowed to Novato. "I agree: this is a fascinating thing for an engineer to study. Thank you for requesting me—although I'll admit I'm surprised you asked for me. I'm young, after all; there are much older and more experienced engineers who would enjoy a chance to examine this."

"You're not that young, Karshirl," said Novato. "You're eighteen or so; I was just eleven, an apprentice glassworker, when I invented the far-seer."

"Still . . ." said Karshirl, then, evidently deciding not to press her good fortune, "Thank you very much. I do appreciate the opportunity." The younger female leaned back on her tail and looked up at the tower, lost in the fog. "How tall is the tower?" she asked

"I have no idea," said Novato.

Karshirl clicked her teeth. "Good Novato, have you forgotten your trigonometry? All you have to do is move a known distance from the tower's base—a hundred paces, say—then note the angle between the ground and the top of the tower. Any good set of math tables will give you the height."

"Of course," said Novato. "But that's predicated on the assumption that one can *see* the top of the tower. But we can't, even on the clearest of days. The tower simply goes up and up, straight to the zenith. I've seen it pierce right through clouds, with the cloud looking like a gobbet of meat skewered on a fingerclaw. The tower is sufficiently narrow that it fades from view before its summit is reached. The best time to view it is on clear mornings just before dawn, when the tower itself is already illuminated by the sun, but the sky is still dark. Still, I can't make out its apex. I've looked at its upper reaches with a far-seer, and, again, it fades from view rather than coming to a discrete end."

"That's incredible," said Karshirl.

"Indeed."

"But wait—there's another way to measure it. You've said there is a vehicle of some kind moving up its interior?"

"Several, as it turns out. We call them lifeboats."

"Well, all you have to do is mark one of the lifeboats, so you can be sure to recognize the same one later. Measure the distance between two of the tower's rungs—you can do that, at least, with trig, even if you can't actually reach the rungs. Choose a couple of rungs that are a good distance apart and also are a good ways up the shaft so that the lifeboat will be up to speed by the time it passes them. Then simply see how long it takes for a lifeboat to traverse that distance. That will give you its traveling speed. After that, all you have to do is wait for the lifeboat to make a round trip up and down the shaft. Assuming the lifeboats do indeed go all the way to the top, and assuming they travel at a constant speed, you'll be able to calculate the tower's height by dividing half the total elapsed time by the lifeboat's known speed."

If Karshirl had been looking at Novato, instead of tipping her muzzle up at the tower, she'd have stopped before getting to the end of her explanation, since Novato's face made it clear that she'd already thought of all this. "We tried that, of course," said Novato. "The lifeboats accelerate quickly at first, but almost immediately seem to reach their maximum velocity. It seems the lifeboats are moving at something like one hundred and thirty kilopaces per day-tenth."

"Good God!" said Karshirl, her eyelids strobing up and down. "That's faster than even a runningbeast can manage."

"Twice as fast, to be precise," said Novato. "And it takes the lifeboats—wait for this—*twenty* days to make the round trip. Now, granted, there's a lot of room for error—these are just back-of-a-sash calculations—but if you do the math, that would imply that the tower is on the order of thirteen thousand kilopaces tall."

"But, good Novato, our entire world has a diameter of only twelve thousand kilopaces," said Karshirl. "You can't be seriously suggesting that the tower is taller than our world is wide. Something must be going on that we can't see. The lifeboats must stop at the top for days on end, or else slow down once they get out of sight."

Novato felt slightly surprised. She'd selected Karshirl for her own reasons, but was beginning to regret the choice. "Surely you wouldn't discard data just because it doesn't fit your expectations."

"Oh, indeed," said Karshirl, somewhat piqued. "I'm a good little scientist, too. However, I am also a structural engineer, which is something you are not. And I tell you, Novato, based on well-established engineering principles, that the tower cannot be as tall as you say. Look: stability is a real concern when building towers. You know the old story of the Tower of Howlee, told in the—the fiftieth, I think—sacred scroll? That was a tower that would reach up to the sky so that one could touch the other moons."

Novato nodded.

"But Howlee's Tower is utterly impossible," said Karshirl. "A sufficiently long, narrow object will buckle if it is held straight up." She raised a hand. "Now, I know you've said that this tower is made out of stuff that's harder than diamond. That's irrelevant. No matter how great its compressive strength, such a tower will buckle if the ratio of its length to width goes above a certain value. In the old scroll, which was written long before we knew just how far away the other moons were, Howlee's Tower was said to be twenty-five kilopaces tall, and had a base fifty paces on a side. You couldn't build a tower like that out of any material. In fact, one can't even build a scale replica of Howlee's Tower, *at any scale*. It will buckle and collapse."

"Because of the buffeting of the wind?" asked Novato.

"No, it's not that. You can't even build a scale model of Howlee's Tower inside a sealed glass vessel, in which there are no air currents at all."

"Why not?" said Novato.

Karshirl looked around vaguely, as if wishing she had something to draw a picture on. Failing to find anything, she simply turned back and faced Novato. "Let's say you build a tower that's a hundred paces tall and has a base of, oh, one square centipace."

Novato's tail swished in acceptance. "All right."

"Well, visualize the top of this structure: it's a flat roof, one square centipace in area."

"Yes."

"Consider the corners of that roof. There's no way they will be perfectly even. One of them is bound to be a small fraction lower than the others. Even if they are all even originally, as the ground shifts even infinitesimally under the tower's weight, one corner will end up lower than the others."

"Ah, I see: the tower, of course, will lean toward the lowest corner, even if only very slightly."

"Right. And when the tower does lean, that makes the lowest corner even lower, and the tower will lean some more, and on and on until the whole thing is leaning over like a tree in a storm— no matter how strong the building material is."

"So the tower can't be thirteen thousand kilopaces high," said Novato.

"That's right. Indeed, it can't be anywhere near that high."

Novato leaned back on her tail. "Obviously the pyramidal base gives the tower some stability, but the actual tower itself is only fourteen paces wide. How high could a tower that wide be?"

"Oh, I'm no Afsan," said Karshirl. "I'd need to sit down with ink and writing leather to figure that out."

"Roughly, though. How high? Remember, this tower extends well above the clouds."

"And how high up are the clouds?" asked Karshirl.

"Oh, it varies. Say ten kilopaces. Could a tower fourteen paces wide be even that tall without collapsing in the manner you've described?"

Karshirl was silent for a time. "Ah, well, um, probably not," she said at last.

Novato nodded. "So some other factor is at work here." She gestured at the vast blue pyramid and the narrow four-sided tower thrusting up from its apex toward the vault of heaven. "Somehow, impossible as it seems, this tower *does* stand."

Chapter 13

No one normally sat in the *Dasheter*'s lookout bucket when the ship was at rest. Still, even when just walking the decks, old Mar-Biltog couldn't keep himself from occasionally scanning the horizon, so it was no surprise that he was the first to catch sight of them. He thumped the deck with his tail. The fools! Toroca said he'd warned them! Cupping his muzzle with his hands, Biltog shouted, "Boats approaching!"

Toroca, who happened to be passing fairly near, ran as fast as he could with his healing leg to the railing around the *Dasheter*'s edge. Biltog had already made his way across the little bridge that joined the *Dasheter*'s forehull to its aft, and Toroca could hear his now-distant voice shouting again, "Boats approaching!"

And so they were: two long, orange boats. Typical Other designs. The lead boat contained five Others, each operating a pair of oars. They were packed in more tightly than Quintaglios could ever manage. The rear boat was too far away for Toroca to count its occupants, but it was likely a similar number.

In response to Biltog's calls, Quintaglios were coming up the ramps onto the top deck. That was the worst thing that could happen. "No!" shouted Toroca. "Go below! Stay below!"

Babnol was emerging about ten paces away. Toroca pointed at her. "Get everyone below!"

"What's happening?" she said.

"Get everyone below now! *Others are coming!*"

Babnol reacted immediately, turning tail and heading back

down the ramp. Toroca heard her entreating sailors to go to their cabins.

Toroca hurried toward the ropes that led up to the lookout's bucket. He began to climb. When he got four body-lengths up, where he was sure the Others could see him, he waved his arm widely. "Go back!" he shouted in the Other tongue. "Stay away!"

The *Dasheter*'s sails were furled, so he didn't have to compete with their snapping, but the wind was in his face, stealing his words. "Go back!" he shouted again, and then, more plaintively, "Please! Please go back!"

The orange boats sliced through the water, approaching fast. Toroca thought about ordering the *Dasheter*'s sails unfurled, for rowboats were no match for a sailing ship, but by the time the ropes could be untied and the red leather sheets had billowed out, the Others' boats would have already arrived.

Toroca stopped waving. Even if they couldn't hear him, they could surely see him. He made go-away gestures with his left hand. He hoped the sign of pushing away was universal, but in his lessons with Jawn such things had never come up. "Go back!" he shouted again in the Other language.

It was no use. He looked down toward the deck and saw three red leather caps. "Get below," he shouted. "For God's sake, get below."

The crewmembers were tarrying. They were curious about the Others, and perhaps doubted the stories of the effect the Others' appearance would have on them. Still, respect for Toroca ran deep, and two of the three heeded his words, heading below. The third, farther away, perhaps couldn't hear the order.

The nearer of the orange boats had now pulled up beside the *Dasheter*. From Toroca's vantage point, he couldn't see it at all, since the raised sides of his ship blocked it from view. He scurried down the ropes, getting a nasty burn on his right hand in doing so, and hurried toward the gunwale.

Below was Morb, the Others' security chief, his black armbands stark against his yellow limbs. He was waving up at Toroca, and had his mouth open in that way that the Others considered to be friendly. "Go back!" shouted Toroca in the Other language. "Go back!"

Morb made a dismissive motion with his hand. "Nonsense!" he shouted up from the waves. "You have been out to visit us. It is time we did the same!"

Morb's boat was bobbing on the waves alongside one of the *Dasheter*'s own shore boats; they'd been used for fishing while the *Dasheter* waited for Toroca. Morb had his hands on the rope ladder used to access these boats, a ladder that led up to the *Dasheter*'s foredeck.

"It is not safe!" shouted Toroca.

Morb's tone was a bit sharper. "It is wrong for you to know all about us with us knowing almost nothing about you. I am coming aboard!" The Other began climbing. Toroca was near panic. In desperation, he brought his jaws down on the rope ends that tied the ladder to the gunwale. The rope was tougher than he'd expected. Some of his looser teeth popped out. He smashed his jaws together again, and this time did sever one of the two heavy lines. But Morb was already most of the way to the top.

Suddenly a green arm shot out from the *Dasheter*'s side, gripping Morb's ankle. Toroca leaned over the gunwale and saw an open porthole on the deck immediately below. Someone had been watching through a window, had seen this Other as he passed by.

Morb twisted as the ladder, anchored now by only a single rope, swung madly to the left. He smashed his other foot down on the arm grabbing his ankle. Whoever was holding on screamed and let go. Morb took hold of the *Dasheter*'s gunwale just as Toroca brought his jaws together on the remaining rope anchoring the ladder. As before, two massive bites would be needed to sever the braided cord, but before Toroca could get his second bite in, Morb had hauled himself over the railing and was standing on the deck of the *Dasheter*.

Suddenly old Biltog appeared at the top of the ramp, his right arm bloodied and hanging limply at his side, but the rest of his body moving up and down, up and down, bobbing in full *dagamant*.

Toroca shouted, "Into the water, Morb! For your own safety, jump into the water."

Morb stared at Biltog for a moment, the murderous fury in the old sailor's expression obvious to Toroca but apparently less clear to the Other. "What is wrong?" asked Morb.

Toroca caught a movement out of the corner of his eye. Something had sailed over the rear hull of the *Dasheter*. Ropes, metal hooks. The Others in the second boat had brought their own climbing equipment. Their ropes were pulled tight, and the hooks caught in the railing around the ship's edge.

What to do? Push Morb over the side? Try to draw Biltog's attention away from the Other? Or run to the rear of the *Dasheter* and try to dislodge the Others' rope ladder before more boarded the ship?

And then, all at once—

Biltog charged—

Morb ran across the deck—

An Other appeared at the top of the ladder on the *Dasheter's* rear hull—

And one more Other appeared at the top of the rope ladder adjacent to Toroca, anchored at only one side, half-severed but still holding.

Captain Keenir emerged at the mouth of another access ramp—too proud, too stubborn, too foolish to not try to intervene in what was happening . . .

Biltog intercepted Morb, leaping through the air, jaws split wide, landing on the Other's back, the two of them smashing into the deck hard enough to rock the ship, Biltog's jaws tearing into the Other's spinal cord . . .

Keenir caught sight of the Other at the top of the ladder near Toroca. The Other's face was wide with terror and he quickly reversed himself, scrambling over the gunwale and grabbing at the damaged rope ladder. Keenir's footfalls echoed like thunder. "Captain, no!" shouted Toroca, but Keenir was too deep in the bloodlust to heed any words.

The Other on the rope ladder was having a hard time getting down. The rope twisted and—

It snapped!

The Other and the rope ladder went crashing toward the waves.

Keenir, not to be deterred, leapt over the railing, diving down toward the water.

The Other below was flailing about, trying to make it to the orange boat.

Keenir sliced into the water. Toroca, gripping the railing, hoped that the impact would be enough to break the old mariner out of *dagamant,* but soon he was on the surface again, his muscular tail propelling him through the waves. Within moments he was upon the swimming Other, jaws digging into the Other's neck, tearing it open. The water turned red.

Toroca pivoted and saw Biltog, his muzzle covered in blood, still bobbing up and down. The sailor began running toward Toroca, toeclaws splintering the wooden deck.

Biltog was substantially older than Toroca, much too strong for Toroca to fight. Toroca looked left and right, but he was trapped against the railing; Biltog could alter his course to intercept him no matter which way he decided to run. But suddenly Biltog was airborne, a giant leap pushing him up off the deck. It turned out that he wasn't after Toroca, but rather had decided to join his captain. Biltog sailed over the edge of the ship, his red cap flying off, the tip of his tail slapping into Toroca's head as it passed him. Toroca swung around. Biltog was in the water now, swimming toward the orange boat, which was trying to escape, the three remaining Others aboard it rowing with all their might.

Biltog chomped through an oar and then, grabbing the little boat's side and pulling hard, he capsized the ship, tossing its occupants into the water.

Suddenly a large red stain began spreading across the waves. Keenir was out of sight; he must have come up on one of the Others from underneath, jaws tearing into its body. Biltog had another's tail in his mouth. His jaws worked, muscles bulging, and the tail sheared off.

Pounding on the deck behind him.

Toroca swung around—

A ball of limbs and tails, some green, some yellow, locked in mortal combat. More Quintaglios had come up from below.

Toroca watched, helpless to intervene. Sounds of splitting bone and smashing teeth filled the air, punctuated by screams from both Others and Quintaglios.

He thought again of the story of the *Galadoreter*, blown aimlessly by the wind, its decks covered with the dead . . .

"Toroca!"

Deep, gravelly—Keenir's voice, from over the side. Toroca looked over the edge. "Are you all right, Captain?"

Keenir was moving up and down, but with the bobbing of the waves, not in territorial display. "They're all dead down here," he called, his tone aghast.

Biltog was floating next to him in the red water. And next to the two of them, five yellow carcasses bobbed up and down, in death returning the challenge.

"Stay down there!" Toroca shouted. "It'll be safer!"

Behind him, the battle raged on, the planks of the deck slick with blood.

Looking over the gunwale, Toroca saw the second orange boat, off in the distance. Only two of its crew were still aboard, but they were already a good part of the way back to their island, where doubtless they'd report that their eight comrades had been torn limb from limb by the strange green visitors.

Toroca wondered if the Others had a word for war.

Chapter 14

An endless beach of sand, spreading to every horizon. No waves were visible, but their pounding against the shore formed a constant background, a steady, rhythmic pulse like the beating of many hearts.

Lying on the sand were several large broken eggshells. Each egg had opened and was cracked roughly in half. The halves were all sitting in the sand, rounded ends down, like beige bowls. Afsan walked over to the nearest shell half and looked inside. The edge was clearly visible, with a fringe of shell fragments still adhering to a tough white membrane. He couldn't quite make out what was inside, though. He tipped forward from the waist, his tail lifting from the ground, and picked up the egg, cradling it in both hands. It was surprisingly heavy.

He tipped back, letting his weight rest on his tail, and looked down into the egg.

It was full of thick, dark liquid, bowing upward slightly into a meniscus. He rocked the egg gently back and forth, watching the liquid move inside the shell.

And then it hit him.

Blood.

The liquid was blood.

Afsan's claws leapt out in alarm, piercing the eggshell in ten places.

Blood flowed onto Afsan's hands.

He should have thrown the shell aside, but somehow he couldn't, not until the dark red liquid had completely drained through the holes. He felt it begin to crust along the edges of his fingers, along the backs of his hands.

At last the egg was empty. He put the fragment back down on the sand.

He knew he shouldn't look, but he had to. He moved a few paces over, found the next egg half, prodded it with his middle toeclaw. The egg tipped over, blood pouring out onto the ground.

Afsan's heart was racing. He hurried over to another bowl-shaped egg half. It, too, was filled with crimson blood. He ran across the sands to a fourth egg-bowl. This one was so full that the vibrations caused by Afsan's movement made blood slosh over the ragged edges.

Afsan spun around, terrified, and in so doing, his tail swept through a large arc, knocking over a trio of blood-filled eggshells, the dark fluid soaking the sands.

Everywhere he looked there were eggshells filled with blood sticking out of the sand, balanced precariously on their rounded ends. Afsan spun around again, his tail knocking over more of the shells, more blood pouring out.

The beach beneath him was saturated now. As he moved, his toeclaws sucked out of the wet sand, sounding like a dying gasp or like meat sliding down a gullet. Another step, another gasp.

Blood was pouring in from everywhere now. The upended eggshells had become bottomless cups, an endless torrent of red liquid flowing out of them onto the sands, sands that were rapidly turning into a bloody quicksand. Afsan tried to run, tried to get away, but with each step his body sank deeper and deeper into the sodden ground. Soon only his head and neck were above the surface, and then just his head, his long green jaw resting briefly on the sand.

Overhead, a giant wingfinger circled, its vast purple wings swirling about its body.

As he slipped below the surface, his last sight, brought to eye level as he continued to descend, was the broken eggshells, now empty, lying on their sides, scattered across the surface of the bloodied sands.

Afsan was growing progressively more annoyed with Mokleb. "Why don't you say something?" he snapped.

"What would you like me to say?" said Mokleb, her voice calm, reasonable.

"Anything. That you're happy with my progress. That you're *unhappy* with my progress. Anything at all."

"I don't pass judgments," said Mokleb gently.

"Oh, yes you do," Afsan said with a sneer. "You sit there day in and day out, and you judge me. You hear the intimate details of my life, and you judge them. I used to like you, Mokleb, but I'm getting sick of you. Sick to death."

Silence.

"No response, Mokleb? Surely that merits a reply."

"Why is it important that I reply to you?"

Afsan's tone was quarrelsome. "It's just good manners, that's all."

"I see."

" 'I see,' " said Afsan, mocking. " 'I see.' God, I'm getting tired of these sessions."

"I've never heard you so angry before, Afsan."

"Yeah? Well, things are changing, Mokleb. I've been going easy on you, but from now on, you're going to hear *exactly* what I think."

Mokleb reached for a fresh pot of ink.

Fra'toolar's sky was leaden. It had been threatening to storm all day, but so far the clouds hadn't given up their burden. When the sky was overcast like this, the material of the tower looked more gray than blue, the ladders like a column of vertebrae, the backbone of some giant creature that had come and gone before the Quintaglio race was born.

"I'm going to go up the tower," said Novato. "I'm going to get in one of those lifeboats and ride up."

Garios's tail swished. "That could be dangerous," he said. "It's—you know the old children's story from Mar'toolar? *Rewdan and the Vine*. It's just like that. The little boy, Rewdan, gets some magic seeds and plants them in the ground. A vine grows from them, and it keeps growing and growing and growing, up and up into the sky."

"A child's story," said Novato. She waved her hand dismissively.

Garios pressed on. "And do you remember what happens? Rewdan climbs the vine, up into the clouds. And there he's confronted by the most gigantic blackdeath anyone has ever seen, all fangs and rotten-smelling breath."

Novato clicked her teeth. "He also finds the wingfinger that lays eggs of gold, no? Maybe there is a giant beast up at the top, but if we're to save our people we need the golden eggs—the knowledge that perhaps is waiting for us up there."

"I—I worry about you," said Garios.

"Thank you. But, as you know, we've tried putting cages containing lizards in the lifeboats, and they came back safe. Now we need to send somebody up who can come back down and describe what's at the top."

"Very well," said Garios, his close-together eyes seeking out Novato's. "I will concede territory on the necessity of the trip. But should you be the one to go? You're very important to the exodus."

"I am, in fact, *in charge of* the exodus, Garios. And that gives me no choice. I can't order someone to do something I would not do myself."

Garios considered. Then: "I want to go with you."

Novato shook her head. "You can't. No one can. We'd kill each other in there."

"But maybe with the see-though hull, maybe the territorial instinct wouldn't kick in. If we kept our backs to each other . . ."

"I'd still know you were there, Garios. I'd be able to smell your pheromones, just as you could smell mine."

"But we've seen how air is somehow recirculated through the lifeboat—the gentle breeze that comes through the vents in its walls. Maybe our pheromones would be washed away."

"I doubt it, and even if they were, it's just too small a space. The round trip takes twenty days, Garios. Oh, the things you mention might let us survive together for a few days, but not for twenty. Long before then just the sound of your breathing would be enough to put me in *dagamant*—and vice versa, of course."

Garios looked like he was going to make another objection, but apparently thought better of it. "Very well," he said at last. "But—"

"Yes?" said Novato.

Garios dipped his long muzzle, looking at the ground. "Come back, Novato," he said. "Be safe, and come back to us." A pause, then he lifted his muzzle. "To me."

Novato turned away. "Help me start gathering supplies," she said.

Chapter 15

Nav-Mokleb's Casebook

Afsan is proving to be quite a challenge. His mind is remarkable, but instead of his bad dreams abating as he undertakes the talking cure, he tells me they are getting worse. The dreams he describes are horrifying, full of blood and death, and yet they seem unrelated to each other, with no common theme. The only element that has repeated itself is an image of a wingfinger with purple wings flying above the scene. Offhand, I don't know of any species of wingfinger that has purple wings, but I'll research the matter as soon as I get some time.

I got another letter today from Anakod, who is apparently vacationing on Boodskar. He's pooh-poohing my theories again. Dreams have no meaning, he says, dismissing them as just random activity by a tired mind. Anakod is a fool; he'd seemed so promising as a student, but his rejection of my research shows him to be even blinder than Afsan. I'm sure I'll be able to interpret Afsan's dreams, if only I can decipher his symbolism.

On another point, I've noticed an interesting effect lately. I've seen hints of it before in my dealings with other patients, but here it's clear-cut: Afsan has been responding to me not as Mokleb, but as he used to respond to, or used to *want* to respond to, his old teaching master, Saleed. It's as if he's transferred his feelings for Saleed onto me.

I'm going to try something different, something I've always avoided, in our next session. If his repressed feelings toward Saleed are so strong, I have a hunch that there's someone else for whom his feelings may be even stronger.

Mokleb found a different rock for herself this time. Instead of straddling a boulder downwind of Afsan, she chose one upwind of him.

"You've changed positions," said Afsan abruptly.

"Think nothing of it," said Mokleb. "It's of no importance."

"I thought everything was important," said Afsan. More and more lately, he'd been starting their sessions in a snit, no doubt aggravated by his ongoing sleeping difficulties. "Time and again you've stressed that every action is significant."

Mokleb ignored that. "I want to talk today about one of the relationships in your life that we haven't explored so far."

Afsan sighed. "Well, there is a fellow up in Chu'toolar who once helped me across a street. We haven't beaten to death all the ins and outs of that relationship yet."

"I was thinking of someone closer to home," said Mokleb patiently. "I was thinking of Novato."

"What about her?" said Afsan, suspicious.

"Well, she has filled many different roles in your life. It was with her that you worked out the fact that the world was doomed."

"Yes."

"And she is the mother of your children."

"Biologically, the mother. Biologically, my children. Of course, all children are the children of the Pack."

"Of course," said Mokleb. "Of course. Tell me about your relationship with Novato."

"We see each other frequently, perhaps every fifty days or so, when she's not off working at the ark in Fra'toolar. I cherish the time we spend together." Afsan lifted his muzzle. "Are there no clouds today? It's awfully warm."

"There are some clouds," said Mokleb. "There are almost always clouds."

"I suppose."

"Are there clouds in your relationship with Novato?"

"By the Eggs of Creation, Mokleb, you *do* have a thing for metaphors." But Afsan clicked his teeth, as if his ill humor from before was draining away. "But to answer your question, no. There are no clouds in our relationship." Afsan lowered his voice. "In fact, if you want to know something, I'll tell you what her last words were to me, before I left her the morning after we had first met. I'd greeted her with the old 'I cast a shadow in your presence.' She replied—I cherish these words still, Mokleb—'We cast shadows in each other's presence, Afsan. And when we're together, there is light everywhere and no shadows fall at all.'"

"That's beautiful," said Mokleb.

"Yes," said Afsan peacefully. "Yes, it is. And she's beautiful, too, Mokleb. A delightful person. There's not much that gives me joy in life, but my relationship with her does. In fact, I'll tell you a secret: when I'm falling asleep, to clear my mind of the troubles of the day, I conjure up a memory of her face, her beautiful face, the way I remember it from the one time I saw it, all those kilodays ago. No image is more calming for me than the face of Novato."

Mokleb dipped her claw into the inkpot. "She is older than you," she said.

"By a few kilodays. Irrelevant now, of course; as a percentage of our current ages, the difference is trivial. But back then, when we met in Pack Gelbo, yes, there was something fascinating about a female who was older, who had long since gone through the rites of passage." A small pause. "And yet, I guess, there's one rite of passage we went through together."

"You're talking about sex," said Mokleb.

Afsan wasn't offended. "Yes. It was my first time, and hers, I suspect, too. I mean, she *was* older than me, but she was still shy of eighteen kilodays—one year—the age at which a female normally first gives signs of receptivity." Afsan sighed contentedly. "Those pheromones, Mokleb. Those wonderful pheromones. It's almost as if I can smell them now."

"No doubt," said Mokleb, deadpan.

"I really like Novato," said Afsan. "She's so intelligent, so pleasant to be with. She makes it seem like, like, oh, I don't know, like there's no territoriality. I don't mean that she comes physically close to me or to others. Nothing like that. But when I'm with her, there's a relaxing feeling of not being crowded, of not being wary. The territoriality is still there, I'm sure, but it's in the background. I'm not—say, here's an observation you'll like— I'm not *consciously* aware of it." Afsan clicked his teeth. "It's a comfortable relationship."

Mokleb had an array of noncommittal sounds she made, including grunts, the touching of teeth, the tapping of fingerclaws on stone—anything to show, especially to her blind patient, that she was still listening. This time, she lifted her tail a bit and let it gently bounce against the boulder.

"The relationship between you and me, Mokleb, can be comfortable, too," Afsan said. "I know it isn't always, but when things are going well, when we're talking about our innermost thoughts and there's no sense of judgment or derision, just gentle acceptance, that reminds me of when I'm with Novato. You came from a good egg, Mokleb."

"Thank you."

"You know, I don't know that much about you, really," said Afsan. "How old are you?"

"What difference does that make?"

"Oh, I don't know. Say—maybe this is inappropriate, I don't know—but perhaps someday we should go for a walk or something, just the two of us. Nothing to do with our formal sessions, you understand. Just a chance to get to know each other better."

"Perhaps," said Mokleb. For a time, she simply let the wind waft over herself and blow onto Afsan. "Was there ever an occasion when you weren't comfortable with your relationship with Novato?"

"No, although I was sad after I left her in Pack Gelbo. I thought I'd never see her again."

"But you did."

For one moment, the bitter Afsan was back. "No, not really. I've been in her presence since then many times, but I've never seen her again."

"Of course," said Mokleb. "Forgive me. Tell me a bit about your reunion."

"It was on the *Dasheter*. There had been riots in the Central Square, the land was shaking, the Ch'mar volcanoes were erupting, and I was badly injured. Pal-Cadool saved my life, spiriting me to safety aboard the *Dasheter*."

"Where you were reunited with Novato."

"Yes, and discovered that I had eight children by her. There was a bad moment there, actually. I was lying on the deck, exhausted, and the children were crawling on me. It was wonderful, absolutely wonderful, and then, with a start, I realized that seven of them would have to die. It was the most crushing moment of my life, to have met them only to realize that seven of them would be killed by the bloodpriests."

"But then Novato explained to you that the bloodpriests weren't going to touch your children, that they'd made a special dispensation because they thought you were The One."

"Yes. That's the only time I was ever glad of that silly title. Because I was *The* One, more than one of them would get to live."

"And if it had turned out that Novato's and your children were not to be spared, that seven of them were to have been killed, how would you have felt?"

"I don't want to think about that," said Afsan.

"Hypothetically," said Mokleb. "How would you have felt?"

A long pause. "At the time, I was reassured by her so quickly that I don't think I gave it much thought. Today, though . . . today, I don't know. I was appallingly naïve as a youngster, Mokleb. Old Cat-Julor, one of the creche mothers back in Carno, made fun of me for that when I paid a return visit there after seeing Novato that first time. I didn't know what happened to extra babies. I accept the necessity of the bloodpriests, but if Novato had introduced me to my children so that we had made . . . made *impressions* on each other, and then she'd told me that seven of them were to be killed, I'd have resented it. I'd have resented her."

"I'm sorry to have upset you," said Mokleb. "Let me take a moment to review my notes. Just relax, Afsan." Mokleb was quiet for a time, shuffling papers. The steady wind continued.

After a while, Afsan said, "You know, I do find you fascinating, Mokleb. You've got a keen mind."

"Thank you."

"I wish we could spend more time together." A pause. "Novato and me, I mean."

"Of course," said Mokleb.

"It *is* warm today," said Afsan. And then: "We spend so little time interacting, one with another. There's so much about other people that we don't know. I wish . . ." Afsan trailed off.

"Yes, Afsan?"

"I, um, I've got to go. Excuse me, please."

"Our session isn't over yet."

"I know, but I—I really should be going."

"Do you have another appointment?"

"No, it's not that. It's just—" Afsan pushed up off the boulder. He nonchalantly brought a hand to his neck, feeling the slight puffing of his dewlap. "You shouldn't have sat upwind of me, Mokleb."

"Too many pheromones?" she asked in an innocent tone.

"I've—I've got to go," said Afsan. Gork, who had been sunning himself nearby, took note of the fact that Afsan had risen and padded over to him, rubbing against his legs. Afsan groped for the beast's harness. "I've got to go," he said again, and with that, he began to walk away.

An average Quintaglio life span was four years, each of which was eighteen thousand days long. Novato was about to become officially middle-aged, her life half over. And for almost one full year now, she had been wrestling with her emotions.

She had laid a total of sixteen eggs so far in her life: eight by Afsan, eight by Garios.

She remembered laying them. For the first clutch, she had gone into the creche in Pack Gelbo, had squatted over the birthing sands, and, one by one, the soft-shelled eggs had come out. Without any instruction, she'd known exactly how to move, taking a sideways step after each egg had been deposited so that they ended up in a circle, their long axes pointing toward an empty space in the center. Passing the eggs had been painful, but there had been a deep satisfaction in knowing that she was contributing to the ongoing development of the Quintaglio race.

Other clutches of eggs had already been laid there. As she stood at the exit to the chamber, Novato had looked back one final time into the room. If it weren't for her fresh footprints across the sand leading to her own clutch, she wouldn't have been able to identify her eggs.

She'd never expected to see those eggs again. But word soon came, from one no less famous than Var-Keenir himself, that Afsan might be The One foretold by Lubal. The eggs were rescued from the creche (the creche masters, it turned out, kept meticulous records), and Novato and her clutch were taken aboard the *Dasheter* to Capital City for a rendezvous with Afsan.

And so it came that all eight members of that clutch got to live, and that Novato knew exactly who they were. It was a bizarre feeling at first, going against everything she'd been taught. According to the eighteenth sacred scroll, children are the children of the Pack, not of any one individual. But these children *were* her children; there was no question of who their parents were.

She had known them all: Kelboon and Toroca, Dynax and Drawtood, Yabool and Galpook, Haldan and poor little Helbark.

Her children.

Not just the Pack's.

Hers.

Novato had been moved to mate with Afsan when she was just sixteen (and he was thirteen). For two kilodays, she'd wondered what would happen when she became the normal age for reproduction. Would she be moved to mate again?

The answer, it turned out, was yes.

By that time, Novato had taken up residence in Capital City, where she was director of the exodus project. And when Novato found herself calling for a mate again, Afsan, now blind, was far away, touring Land with Emperor Dybo, trying to rally support for the exodus.

And so she had coupled with Den-Garios. He was a fine fellow, a good fellow, a fellow who in all ways was desirable, a fellow who—and still it hurt to contemplate this—was not Afsan.

By Garios, she'd laid another eight eggs, this time in Capital City's much larger creche.

But there had been nothing special about those eggs. Seven of the eight hatchlings were swallowed whole. The only special treatment they got, because Novato was a minister now in Dybo's government, was that the culling had supposedly been performed personally by Mek-Maliden, the imperial bloodpriest.

So one hatchling remained.

But seventeen clutches of eggs had been hatched at approximately the same time.

That meant there were seventeen possible candidates for being Novato's son or daughter.

Seventeen.

Statistics were easy to obtain. There were nine females and eight males. But specifics about parentage were unavailable. Novato had thought she might be able to find out by using her newfound authority, assuming records had been kept. Dybo had said that she could issue any orders she deemed necessary. But people would want to know why she required the information and, well, she wasn't exactly sure how to answer that.

As the kilodays went by, Novato wondered less and less frequently who her ninth child was, although she did find herself keeping track of the seventeen hatchlings. Two of them died in childhood, one of the same kind of fever that had earlier claimed little Helbark. One more was killed on his first hunt, and two eventually left Capital City for other parts of Land. Still, she followed the lives of the thirteen who remained in the Capital with interest.

But as Novato approached the end of her second year of life, she found the question of who was her unknown child occupying her thoughts more frequently. Was it Retlas? Unlikely; her light coloring was nothing like Novato's own. Jidha? No, his wide, moon-like face was unlike either Novato's or Garios's. Colboom? Perhaps. He was a gifted artist, as was Novato herself, and his long, drawn-out muzzle was much like Garios's own. But eventually she'd come to realize that it must be Karshirl, a female structural engineer. It wasn't just that Karshirl's body shape and general facial features bore a striking resemblance to Novato's own. More: Karshirl had the same distinctive and very rare mottling of blue freckles on her back and tail as Novato herself had.

Novato could request the services of just about anyone for the exodus effort. And so, on a whim, she had sent word to Capital City that Karshirl was needed here, in Fra'toolar.

It was a crazy thing to do. Sure, they could always use another engineer to help fathom the blue pyramid or to try to puzzle out the functions of the various devices removed from the ark. But to have called Karshirl here was madness. Novato could have no special relationship with her.

Of course not, Novato kept telling herself. Of course not.

Not unless Karshirl wanted the same thing.

Madness. The very idea was insane.

Or was it?

Novato had to know.

A private meeting, a quiet chat.

Today would be the day. She'd waited long enough.

Today.

Novato went looking for her daughter.

The Others were apparently determined to destroy the *Dasheter*. A veritable wall of wooden sailing ships had appeared on the horizon. The ships were small by Quintaglio standards—the Others didn't need to build massive vessels, since they didn't mind being crowded together.

The *Dasheter* began to sail away. Captain Keenir called for Toroca.

"Tell me what they know about us," demanded the captain.

Toroca scratched his jaw. "Not much, I suppose. I talked mostly about mathematics and science."

"What about Land itself?"

"I don't understand," said Toroca.

"Land, boy! What did you tell them about Land?"

"Nothing, really . . ."

"Did you tell them how big it is?"

"What?"

"These Others live on a tiny group of islands. Land is *thousands* of times bigger than that. Did you give any indication of that?"

Toroca was puzzled by the questions. "Not that I can recall. I mean, that was so obvious to me, I don't think it ever occurred to me to mention it."

Keenir thumped his tail in delight. "Excellent!" He cupped hands around his muzzle and shouted down the deck. "Ahoy, Biltog! Set course for Capital City—the most straight, most direct course you can manage!"

Biltog bobbed concession. "Aye! Full speed ahead!"

"No!" shouted Keenir. "I want sails two and four furled. Don't let us get out of sight of the Others!"

Toroca's tail swished in bewilderment. "What are you doing?"

"Don't you see? Obviously, I'm not going to let that flotilla of ships engage us. No, they're going to have to chase us all the way home. But Land has thousands of kilopaces of shoreline, most of it unsettled and unguarded. If we let the Others simply stumble on Land, they could storm any part of it. But they've no reason to think Land is very big, so they won't deviate from whatever course we set. They'll follow us straight back."

"And?"

"We'll send word ahead. Dybo will be ready for them. We will destroy every one of their ships."

"Destroy them? Why?"

"It's them or us, lad! Think about it—by our mere existence we pose a threat to them. They'll want to sink the *Dasheter* before we can get back home; if no other Quintaglios know about them, they're safe. Well, by God, there's no way I'll let them sink my ship! So their only other option is to try to wipe out all the Quintaglios; they've no idea how big Land is—they probably think that armada of ships will be enough to do it."

"They've got those tubes that shoot metal I told you about," said Toroca. "And I've counted forty or so ships out there. They might indeed be able to wipe us out. Luring them back to Land might spell the end of our race. Perhaps we should surrender."

"Surrender, lad? With those sticks that fire metal, they'd kill us all."

"Perhaps," said Toroca softly, "that would be for the best."

Keenir looked at his young friend. "What in God's name are you saying?"

" 'In God's name,' " repeated Toroca. "That's exactly right." He was quiet for a moment, then: "Consider our history, Keenir. Life is not native to this world. Rather, it was transplanted here. Why was that? Well, certainly one possible interpretation is that we were in danger of being killed off wherever it was that we came from."

Keenir couldn't see where Toroca was going. "I suppose," he said.

"And then what happens when we arrive here? At least one of the arks crashed into this world; that's the blue ship we found buried in Fra'toolar."

"Yes."

"And since that time, what has happened? Why, our world is in the process of destroying itself, tearing itself apart."

"So?"

"You don't see it, do you? What happens when overcrowding occurs amongst our own kind."

"*Dagamant*," said Keenir. "The territorial frenzy."

"Exactly. We lose all reason, all restraint, and simply kill and kill and kill until either everyone is dead or the survivors are too exhausted to continue fighting."

"You paint it in an unfavorable light," said Keenir meekly.

"And what has happened now that we've met other intelligent beings? Why, even when there is no overcrowding, our basest feelings come to the fore and we kill again—kill thinking beings with no more regard than we have for killing dumb animals for food."

"Make your point."

"Don't you see, Keenir? We're poison. As a race, we're vicious. We kill our own kind, we kill others. And what's happening? Why, God keeps trying to snuff us out! On our original home, wherever that was, we were apparently threatened with extinction. The arks that carried us here, rather than being blessed by God, were buffeted in their voyage, with at least one of them falling out of the sky before its cargo of lifeforms could be let loose. God had almost destroyed us once, on our original home world, but a few of our ancestors escaped. God almost destroyed them en route, but enough of them survived to give rise to us. And now God shakes the entire world and is about to crumble it into dust, all to prevent the further spread of the poison that we represent."

"Toroca, I never thought I'd have to say this to you, of all people: don't be silly. Even if what you say is true, our own people must be our first priority."

"Even if, as in this case, we were the original aggressors? Remember, Var-Keenir, it was you who made the first kill."

Keenir spread his arms. "I couldn't help myself, Toroca. I was moved to madness."

Toroca's tail swished slowly back and forth. "Exactly."

"Quickly, now," said Mokleb. "Name the five original hunters."

Afsan looked startled, then: "Lubal, Hoog, Katoon, Belbar, and, uh, Mekt."

"Thank you. Now, on with our session . . ."

It was a typically overcast day in Fra'toolar, the sky gray rather than purple, the sun a vague smudge behind the clouds. Karshirl was sitting on a log on the beach, looking out at the waves lapping against the base of the blue pyramid.

Novato regarded her daughter from a distance. She was almost exactly one-half Novato's age and soon would be coming into receptivity for the first time. Karshirl was a lot smaller than Novato, and she was proportioned differently, too. The difference in proportions wasn't a sign that they were unrelated, but rather had to do with the ways in which a Quintaglio body changes in order to support its ever-increasing bulk. Novato had much thicker legs than Karshirl, and whereas the younger female's tail was a narrow isosceles triangle in cross section, Novato's was stocky and equilateral. Novato remembered wistfully when her own appearance had been like that.

She closed the distance between them. "Hello, Karshirl."

Karshirl rose to her feet. "Hello, Novato. *Hahat dan.*"

Novato was quiet for several beats, then asked, "How much do you know about me?"

Karshirl looked surprised by the question. "What everyone knows, I suppose. You invented the far-seer."

"Yes, I did. But that's not the only, ah, creation I'm responsible for."

Karshirl kept her muzzle faced toward Novato, attentive.

"I'm Toroca's mother, did you know that?"

"Yes," said Karshirl. "I'm not much for gossip, but I suppose everybody's heard the story of your eight children by Afsan."

"Indeed. But, actually, I have nine children."

"Oh? Was that clutch of unusual size?"

"No. The clutch with Afsan was normal. But I had a second clutch by someone else later on. I, ah, had two clutches in my youth."

"Oh." Karshirl clearly didn't know what to say.

"And one individual lives from that second clutch."

"So one would presume," said Karshirl.

"How old are you, Karshirl?"

"Eighteen kilodays."

"Do you know how old I am?"

"No."

"Go ahead, guess. I'm not particularly vain."

"Thirty-four?"

"Actually I'm thirty-six."

"You don't look it."

"Thank you. You don't see what I'm getting at, do you?"

"No, ma'am, I don't."

Novato drew a deep breath, then let it hiss out slowly. "You, Karshirl, are my ninth child."

Karshirl's inner eyelids blinked. "I am?"

"Yes."

"Fancy that," she said.

Novato waited for something more. Finally, when she couldn't take it any longer, she said, "Is that all you've got to say?"

Karshirl was clearly trying to be polite. "Um, well, I guess if I take after you, I'll age well."

There was frustration in Novato's tone: "I'm your *mother*," she said.

"Yes, I guess that's the term, isn't it?" Karshirl was quiet for a time, then added again, "Fancy that."

"Don't you want to ask me questions?" said Novato.

"Well, as an engineer, I've long wondered where you got the inspiration for the far-seer."

"Not that kind of question. Questions about myself. About you. About us."

"Questions, ma'am? Nothing comes to mind."

"I'm your mother," Novato said again as if that said it all.

Karshirl's tail swished expansively. "I guess it's interesting to know. I'm sure some people idly wonder about who their parents were, but I never have myself."

"Never?"

"Not really, no."

Novato sighed, air whistling out between her pointed teeth. "I suppose I should have expected this. Before I left Pack Gelbo, I never knew who my mother was, either. Now that I've been gone for twenty kilodays, I wonder about it a lot. I try to recall the females who were eighteen, thirty-six, or fifty-four kilodays older than me, to see if any of them resemble me. But the memories are dim; I keep hoping for an excuse for a trip back to Gelbo. I'd like to see her, whoever she is." She paused. "As I thought you might like to see me."

"I see you often already, Novato. Forgive me—I'm not normally this dense, but I don't seem to be getting the point of all this."

"We're a family," said Novato.

" 'Family,' " repeated Karshirl. "And 'mother.' I'm sure you're using these words correctly, although I've never heard them applied thus. Oh, I've heard of 'The Family,' of course—Dy-Dybo and his ancestors. And the term 'creche mother' is sometimes used. But the way you're using them . . ."

Novato leaned on her tail. "Don't you see? I know my other children."

"Yes?"

"Know them in special ways."

"That's very strange."

"I want to know you."

"You *do* know me."

"I mean, I want to know you as my daughter."

"Now, that's a word I don't know at all."

"Daughter: female child."

Karshirl spread her hands. "We can't know each other any better than we already do. You have your territory and I have mine."

"But there's so much I could tell you. About what it's like at ages you haven't yet reached."

"I've always thought that discovering those things for oneself was part of the joy of growing up."

"Yes, but you'll be calling for a mate soon."

Karshirl nodded. "Probably, although I haven't felt the stirrings yet."

"I can tell you about that."

Karshirl's eyelids blinked. "I don't want to be told about it."

"I'm your mother," said Novato again.

Karshirl spread her hands. "I accept that."

Novato sighed once more. "But that's all, isn't it?"

"What else could there be?"

"Nothing," said Novato, growing angry. "Nothing at all."

Karshirl said, "I'm sorry if I've upset you somehow."

"Just go," said Novato. "Go away. Leave me alone."

Karshirl turned around and walked down the beach, her tail swishing in open bewilderment.

Chapter 16

Wingfinger fanciers had long been thrilled by the ability of certain of the flying reptiles to find their way home no matter how far away one took them. Over time, using such wingfingers to carry messages had become common.

The *Dasheter* originally had two large homing wingfingers living in its cargo holds, swooping over the wooden crates. One of them had been used earlier to send a list of needed provisions. The supply ship had been carrying a replacement wingfinger for the *Dasheter,* but it had died en route.

Still, there was one wingfinger left. It had been raised at the maritime rookery north of Capital City and would return there if set free. A fish-eater, it would have no trouble feeding itself on the long journey home.

Toroca wrote the following on a small strip of leather, which Keenir affixed to the animal's left leg:

> *From Kee-Toroca to Dy-Dybo, urgent. Found chain of islands at 25 percent north latitude, 75 percent back-side longitude. Inhabited by beings similar to Quintaglios but smaller in stature. Mere sight of them triggers* dagamant *in all of us except me; by contrast, they seem to have no overt sense of territoriality at all. We killed many of them and now 40 of their ships are pursuing* Dasheter *back to Land. We are traveling under only two sails, luring them toward Capital City. Will arrive around 7131/03/81. The Others use tools to kill and can lie. Prepare defense.*

Keenir strapped a padded rest onto his arm. The wingfinger perched on it, its claws tearing tufts out of the padding. Toroca and Keenir headed up on deck. The wingfinger's inner and outer eyelids snapped up and down; it wasn't used to the daylight. The captain lifted his arm and the flyer took to the air. It rose above the *Dasheter*'s masts, circled the ship as if getting its bearings, then headed west at precisely the right angle.

"Let's hope it gets there," said Keenir.

Toroca watched the animal fly away with leisurely flaps of its wing membranes. He made no reply.

Although worship of the original five hunters no longer had to be practiced secretly, it still wasn't something one paraded in public. After all, anyone associating with it now had likely been a secret practitioner earlier, and to have been involved with cabals and deceit would not do one credit. Still, some were open in their current or past worship of the original five. Among them was Afsan's aide, Pal-Cadool. Perhaps he could answer Mokleb's questions.

Cadool was easy to spot. Tall, thin, ungainly, he stood head and shoulders above Quintaglios tens of kilodays older than himself. Mokleb found him making his way down the Avenue of Traders, one of Capital City's main streets. She had met Cadool a few times but had only previously seen him walking with Afsan, taking small steps beside the blind sage. But here, out on his own, Cadool's spider-like legs and brisk pace carried him down the paving stones at an amazing rate. Mokleb risked jogging up behind him. She came within five paces, knowing that by the time he reacted, he'd have put another few between them. "Pal-Cadool!"

Cadool came to a halt, his long body swaying like a ship's mast as if eager to get back into motion. He turned. "Yes?"

"It's me, Nav-Mokleb. I need to talk to you."

Cadool nodded, but there was no warmth in his voice. *"Hahat dan."*

"Your tone is harsh," said Mokleb. "Have I done something to offend you?"

Cadool's muzzle was angled away from Mokleb, making clear that his black eyes were not looking at her. "You've been spending much time with Afsan."

"Yes."

"His work is backing up. His students are not getting enough time with him."

"I'm trying to cure him of his bad dreams."

"He's been seeing you for hundreds of days now and his dreams are no better. Indeed, they might even be worse. He looks haggard. His lack of sleep is obvious."

"A cure takes time."

Cadool did swing his muzzle to face her now. "And to cure someone as famous as Afsan would be a boon to your career."

"Doubtless so," said Mokleb. "But I'm not deliberately protracting the therapy."

"I've looked into your work," said Cadool. "I can't read myself, but Pettit—Afsan's apprentice—was kind enough to read a book about your techniques to me. You believe we do not always consciously know what we are doing."

"Just so."

"So you *could* be stretching out your dealings with Afsan; that you consciously claim not to be is irrelevant. After all, the more difficult you make it appear to cure Afsan, the greater the glory you get."

Mokleb's nictitating membranes beat up and down. She clicked her teeth. "Why, Cadool, that observation is positively worthy of me! But I'm afraid it does take a long time to find the underlying causes of problems. Nothing would make me happier than to have Afsan cured. I remain detached during our sessions—it's important that he reveal himself directly, rather than simply react to a tone I set—but I *do* care about him, and it pains me to see him continuing to hurt."

Cadool seemed unmollified. "You ask him a lot of questions."

"Yes."

"And he tells you many things."

"Ah," said Mokleb. "That's it, isn't it? Prior to my arrival, you were Afsan's confidant. It bothers you that he now shares the intimate details of his life with me."

Cadool lifted a hand so that Mokleb could see the pointed tips of his claws peeking out of their sheaths. "Not everyone," he said slowly, "wishes to be analyzed by you."

Mokleb took a step back, conceding territory. "Of course. I didn't mean to upset you."

"If that's all you wish to say, then please excuse me. I have business to attend to."

"No, wait. I did seek you out for a purpose. I need your help."

"My help?"

"Yes. I need some information."

Cadool's voice was firm. "I will not betray Afsan's confidences. Not to you or anyone."

"I'm not looking for that kind of information. I want to know about the five original hunters. You are a Lubalite."

"Yes."

"I need to know about Mekt."

Cadool sounded intrigued despite himself. "Why?"

"To help me with my work with Afsan."

"Afsan has mentioned Mekt to you?"

"Not exactly."

"Then what?"

Mokleb decided there'd be little harm in telling Cadool. "Whenever Afsan discusses the Original Five, he mentions Mekt last."

"Afsan has an orderly mind," said Cadool. "It doesn't surprise me that he recites lists in the same sequence each time."

"Ah, but that's just it. He recites the other four names in no particular order at all, but Mekt is always last. Indeed, sometimes he hesitates before mentioning her name."

"And this is significant?"

"Yes, indeed. It's through such things that we can catch glimpses of the forces that move us."

Cadool looked unconvinced. "Whatever you say, Mokleb." He paused for a moment, then: "Like the other original hunters, Mekt was formed from one of the five fingers of God's severed left arm. Some scholars—ones like you, who emphasize the order in which things are said—suggest that she was the second hunter formed, after Lubal, since her name is mentioned second in the first sacred scroll. Mekt was a great hunter and is probably best remembered for killing an armorback, as told in the fourth scroll. When the original five hunters and original five mates began laying claims to specific territories, legend has it that Mekt took much of what is now Capital province's northern coast and part of eastern Chu'toolar."

"Anything else?"

"Not really, except the famous part, but surely you already know that."

"Know what?"

"Why, that Mekt was the first bloodpriest."

"She was?"

"Goodness, Mokleb, surely you know at least the first sacred scroll? 'The ten who had been the fingers of God came together and produced five clutches of eight eggs. But God said soon all of Land would be overrun with Quintaglios if all those egglings were allowed to live. Therefore, She charged Mekt with devouring seven out of every eight hatchlings, and Mekt was thus the first bloodpriest.' "

"I thought bloodpriests were all male."

"They are now. The seventeenth scroll is all about that." Cadool shook his head. "I'm surprised, Mokleb: I can't read, and even I know these things."

"What does the seventeenth scroll say?"

"That Mekt refused to continue being the bloodpriest. She said it was inappropriate for one who lays eggs to be involved in the devouring of hatchlings. By that time, there were many more Quintaglios than just the original ten, and Detoon the Righteous—you *do* know who he was, I hope—established a secondary priestly order, exclusively male, to look after culling the infants."

"Fascinating," said Mokleb.

Cadool shook his head again. "You know, Mokleb, given that you *can* read, you really should do it more often."

Mokleb, her mind racing, bowed concession. "That I should."

Novato and Garios finished loading the lifeboat with supplies: dried meat and fish, amphoras full of water, books in case the journey up the tower proved boring, paper for making notes and sketches in case it did not, leather blankets in case it got cold, and, of course, one of Novato's best far-seers.

Although from the outside the lifeboat's hull was rounded, the interior was all a simple rectangular hollow. As she loaded her last carton of meat, Novato shuddered. The lifeboat had seemed roomy when empty, and now, filled with provisions, it perhaps could be described as cozy, but twenty days within might make her mad with claustrophobia. Still, that was the round-trip value: after ten days, the lifeboat should reach the summit of the tower. Perhaps she'd be able to get out then and walk around.

Finally, it was time to go. Garios and Karshirl stood just outside the lifeboat's open doorway, ready to say goodbye. Novato bowed at them, then said simply, "See you later."

But Garios was not one to let such a moment pass without something more. He handed a small object to Novato. It was a traveler's crystal, six-sided and ruby red. "Good luck," he said, then, bowing deeply, he quoted the Song of Belbar: " 'If beasts confront you, slay them. If the elements conspire against you, overcome. And if God should call you to heaven before you return, then heaven will be the richer for it, and those you leave behind will honor you and mourn your passing.' " He paused. "Travel well, my friend."

Novato bowed once more, then leaned back on her tail and touched the part of the wall that controlled the door. From the inside, the lifeboat's walls grew momentarily foggy, and she knew that from the outside they would have appeared to liquefy. When the walls cleared again a moment later, not even a faint etching on the transparent hull material marked where the door had been.

The lifeboat began to move up the tower. Looking down through the floor, Novato could see Garios and Karshirl rapidly diminishing from view—father and daughter, although they probably didn't know that. It was only because of the difference in their sizes, Garios being twice Karshirl's age, that Novato could tell them apart.

After just a few moments, the lifeboat had passed through the apex of the blue pyramid and was now rising up in the open air. The pyramid was sitting in a hollow scooped out of the cliff. The strip of beach on either side of the pyramid's base looked like a beige line.

The coastline of Fra'toolar was enjoying a rare day of reasonably clear skies. Novato's view continued undiminished, except for the parts blocked by the four ladder-like sides of the tower. She could soon see huge tracts of Fra'toolar province and, stretching off to the south and east, the vast world-spanning body of water, each wave cap an actinic point reflecting back the fierce white sun.

The lifeboat had accelerated briefly, but now seemed to be moving at a steady rate: equal intervals elapsed between the passing of each rung of the ladders. Novato had seen ground from the air before, when flying aboard her glider, the *Tak-Saleed,* and its successor, the *Lub-Kaden.* But she'd never been this high up. Looking straight out, she could see that she was passing the levels of distant clouds. Looking up, the four sides of the tower converged infinitely far above her head.

Novato had worked with charcoal and graphite to capture images of planets and moons observed through her far-seers. But those illustrations had been made over daytenths, with objects crawling across her field of view. She wanted to sketch what she was seeing now, but with each moment the ground receded further and previously invisible parts of the landscape appeared at the edges.

Rivers and streams cut across Fra'toolar like arteries and veins. Tracts of forest and open fields were visible. And what was that? A series of rounded brown hills—hills that were moving! A thunderbeast stampede!

Novato felt dizzy as the heights grew greater. She could now see well into the interior of Fra'toolar, although clouds obscured much of it to the north, their tops fiercely bright with reflected sun.

A flock of wingfingers was moving by the tower: imperial jacks, judging by the colors. She hadn't realized they flew this high up. But already they were disappearing below, although she could easily make out the flock's distinctive tri-pronged flying pattern as it passed by, heading east.

Novato was high enough now that the blue tower itself vanished into nothingness before it reached the ground. Although she assumed the tower was of equal width all the way to the top, it was as though she were in the middle of an incredibly elongated blue diamond, a diamond that tapered to infinitely fine points above and below.

The sun had moved visibly toward the western horizon now. Looking down, Novato could see a thick black shadow at the eastern end of the forest tracts. The whole interior of the lifeboat darkened and brightened in turns as it passed the blue rungs of the giant ladders. Occasionally, she saw a puff of white gas erupt from one of the cones projecting from some of the ladders' rungs.

Novato let her eyes wander out to the horizon line—which, she realized with a start, was no longer a line at all. Instead, it was bowing up. Her heart pounded. She was seeing—actually seeing—the curvature of the world she lived on. She'd long known that the Quintaglio moon was a sphere, but she'd known it indirectly—from seeing ship's masts poke above the horizon before the ships themselves became visible, from seeing the circular shadow her world cast on the Face of God, from experiments done measuring the angles of shadows cast at different latitudes. But to actually see the curvature, to see the world's roundness—that was spectacular.

And then, a short time later, she became aware of something even more spectacular. It was late afternoon, the sun still well above the horizon. Nonetheless, the sky was growing darker. It had started as lavender and, without Novato really noticing it, had deepened to violet. Now it was well on its way to black. What could make the sky black while the sun was still out? A flaw in the optical properties of the lifeboat's metal hull, perhaps? Unlikely.

Novato mulled it over while the lifeboat continued its steady climb, Fra'toolar's coastline now visible all the way to Shoveler's Inlet. She knew that water droplets could refract sunlight, splitting it into a rainbow of colors, and she'd long suspected that the sky was purple because myriad droplets in the air scattered light. But if no such scattering was going on, then there was no humidity in the air this high up. Well, water was heavy, of course, so moisture would tend to settle toward the ground. She was well above the clouds now—perhaps they marked the highest level at which water vapor was a constituent of air.

Later that day, Novato watched the most spectacular sunset of her life: the brilliant point of light touched the curving limb of the world, the world-spanning body of water stained purple for hundreds of kilopaces along its edge. The sun's setting was protracted by the lifeboat's continual upward movement, and Novato savored every moment of it.

With the sun gone, moons blazed forth in full nocturnal glory. Myriad stars became visible, too. Soon, in fact, there were more stars than Novato had ever seen before. The great sky river was thick and bright, instead of the pale ghost she was used to, and the stars were so numerous that to count them all would be the work of a lifetime. She thought of Afsan, dear Afsan, who had enjoyed no sight more than the night sky. How he would have been moved to see stars in such profusion!

But once again Novato was puzzled. Why should so many more stars be visible? And suddenly she realized something else: the stars, all those glorious stars, were rock-steady, untwinkling. From the ground, stars flickered like distant lamp flames, but these stars burned steadily. With so many visible, it was hard to get her bearings; the normal patterns of constellations were all but lost amongst the countless points of light. But at last she found bright Kevpel, the next closest planet to the sun after the Face of God. She got out her far-seer and, steadying herself by leaning back on her tail, brought it to bear on that distant world.

Spectacular. Kevpel's rings were visible with a clarity Novato had never before experienced. The planet's disk was clearly striped, its latitudinal cloud bands more distinct than she'd ever seen, even with bigger far-seers. And Kevpel's own coterie of moons—why, she could count six of them, two more than she'd ever glimpsed with an instrument this size.

Had this first day of her trip up the tower taken her that much closer to Kevpel? Nonsense. Indeed, the angle between the tower's shaft and Kevpel's position along the ecliptic was obtuse: she was in fact slightly farther away from that planet than if she'd observed it from the ground.

But, why, then, did the heavens blaze forth with such clarity?

And then it hit her: the black daytime sky, the incredible sharpness of the stars, the lack of distortion when viewing the planets.

No air.

This high above the world there was no air.

No air!

She felt her chest constricting, her breathing becoming ragged. But that was madness: she could hear the gentle hiss of the air within the lifeboat being recirculated and replenished. She was sure that at least some of the opaque equipment she could see within the transparent hull was somehow maintaining breathable air. She tried to calm down, but it was terrifying to think that only the clear walls around her separated her from, from . . . *emptiness*.

But Novato did manage to steady herself, and as she did so her heart grew heavy. The *Tak-Saleed*. The *Lub-Kaden*. Wasted effort. Gliders couldn't help get her people off their doomed moon. An airship was of no more use for traversing the volume between worlds than was a sailing ship. A whole new approach would be needed.

A whole new approach.

The lifeboat continued its ascent.

Chapter 17

"Angle the sails!" shouted Keenir. "Slow the ship!"

Crewmembers ran to do the captain's bidding. Toroca was up in the *Dasheter*'s lookout's bucket, the far-seer Afsan had given him in his hands. He scanned the waters to the stern. There still seemed to be some forty ships in pursuit. By letting them approach more closely, Toroca and Keenir hoped to be able to get a count of how many Others might be aboard each of them. It took a while for the ships to draw visibly nearer. There, on that ship—decks crawling with Others. And on that one, a line of perhaps fifty Others leaning against the ship's wooden gunwale. And on the lead ship, Others furiously scrambling to one side and struggling now with a piece of heavy equipment.

As he scanned ship after ship, Toroca's heart leapt as he saw one Other who looked a bit like Jawn.

Suddenly, thunder split the air. The view in Toroca's eyepiece shook wildly. The mast tipped way over. Toroca was slammed against the sides of the lookout's bucket. He lowered the far-seer.

Another thunderclap. Smoke and flame erupted from a large black cylinder on the foredeck of the lead Other ship. For an instant, Toroca saw something large flying—*flying!*—through the air, then the water just astern of the *Dasheter* went up in a great splash. Something round and heavy had fallen short of hitting the ship by a matter of paces.

Keenir's gravelly shout, from below: "Full speed! Increase the gap!"

Footsteps pounding on the decks.

The snap of the two unfurled leather sails.

Another explosion from the tube on the lead ship, but this time the object—something round—smashed into the waves perhaps twenty paces astern. Toroca carefully placed the far-seer in its padded shoulder bag and made his way down the web of ropes to the deck below. Keenir was waiting.

"What was that?" shouted the captain.

Toroca, still rattled, held on to the mast for support. "They're like those handheld fire tubes I told you about, but much bigger."

"Did you see the smoke?"

Toroca nodded. "Thick and dark, like from the blackpowder we use for rock blasting. But they . . . they *channel* the force of the explosion, and use it to hurtle metal balls."

"Aye. If they'd connected, the *Dasheter* would have been halfway to the bottom by now. We'll have to be careful not to let them get that close again."

"Eventually," said Toroca, "they'll be close to Land itself. Are you sure we're not setting up our own people for slaughter?"

"There will be a slaughter," said Keenir, "but not of Quintaglios."

"I wish," said Toroca, his voice barely audible above the snapping of the sails, "that there didn't have to be any slaughter at all." He took his leave of Keenir and went back to his lab to put the far-seer safely away.

As he opened the door, he saw cracked eggshells.

Had the ship been rocked that badly? Were the eggs broken? And then he saw the little yellow head of a baby Other who had tumbled out onto the leather blankets the eggs were resting on. A second egg had a hole in it, and Toroca could see a little birthing horn occasionally poking through. The third egg hadn't cracked yet, but it was rocking back and forth.

Toroca crouched down beside the blankets and watched, his eyes wide in wonder.

It was pouring in Capital City. All trace of purple was gone from the leaden sky. Fat drops pounded the ground, and the sun, normally a brilliant point in the heavens, was completely invisible behind the clouds. Mokleb and Afsan held their session today in Afsan's office, the sound of driving rain punctuated by cracks of thunder and jagged bolts of lightning visible through the windows.

"When we first started our sessions, you told me you'd been having bad dreams for some time," said Mokleb, who was lying on the visitor's dayslab, located as far across the room as possible from Afsan's own. It was by the window; a cold breeze kept Mokleb's pheromones from washing over him. He doubtless could smell the ozone in the air, but would catch only an occasional whiff of her. "Can you be more precise about when the bad dreams began?"

Afsan was prone on his own dayslab, which was angled over the worktable. His tail, sticking up in the air, moved slowly back and forth. "I'm not sure," he said. "They've gotten more frequent as time has passed. I suppose the first bad dream was two kilodays ago. But it was so long before the second that I'd assumed the first was an isolated event."

Mokleb examined Afsan's office. It was the kind of place one might expect a blind person to have: the walls were free of art, there weren't enough oil lamps to properly illuminate the room, and there were no lamps at all over the worktable, which was devoid of writing material and had no ink or solvent pots in the little wells designed for them. Two brass figuring rods with raised numerals sat on the marble desktop.

"And what significant things," said Mokleb, "were happening in your life two kilodays ago?"

Afsan clicked his teeth. "It'd be a shorter list to tell you what wasn't happening then." He rubbed the underside of his throat. "Let's see. There were the murders, of course."

"The murders committed by your son Drawtood."

"Yes. Certainly they were dominant in my thoughts."

"What else?"

"Well, of course, everyone was on edge: the bloodpriests had been in disrepute for some time by then."

"They were shunned because they'd not dispatched seven of the eight imperial egglings."

"That's right. People felt it unfair that The Family didn't have to undergo the culling of the bloodpriests, when all other clutches of eggs were subjected to it. But banishing the bloodpriests caused the population to swell enormously."

"And how did that affect you?"

"Well," said Afsan slowly, "I went into *dagamant* for the second time in my life."

"The second time? You'd felt the territorial madness once before?"

"Yes. Aboard the *Dasheter* during my pilgrimage voyage."

"We shall explore that later. What else was happening two kilodays ago?"

"The challenge, of course."

"Challenge?"

"You know: by Governor Rodlox of Edz'toolar. The challenge to Dybo's leadership."

"Ah, yes. You had a role in that?"

"Yes. In fact, I suggested the way to resolve the challenge."

"Indeed?"

"Yes. Secretly, all eight hatchlings from Empress Len-Lends's clutch of eggs had been allowed to live. Seven of the hatchlings became apprentice provincial governors, and the eighth was Dybo, who became Emperor upon the death of his mother."

"I remember that," said Mokleb. "Rodlox claimed that Dybo, who he thought was the weakest child, had been put on the throne as part of a plot to have a malleable emperor, and that he, Rodlox, was the strongest, and therefore the rightful ruler."

"Exactly. I simply suggested the logical test: that Dybo, Rodlox, and their siblings replay the culling of the bloodpriest, with an appropriately scaled-up carnivore acting in the role of the priest."

"Ah, I remember that, too. I wasn't living in Capital City then, but the newsriders were full of the story. A blackdeath was used, no?"

"Yes."

"And seven members of The Family died in that replaying."

Afsan raised a hand. "Only six. Spenress from Chu'toolar was still alive when Dybo finally forced the blackdeath to retreat; she lives here in the Capital now."

"Still, six deaths . . ."

Afsan's tone was defensive. "There are many who said that only one of them should have been alive in the first place."

"Of course," said Mokleb. "Of course." Then, a moment later, "Nonetheless . . . six deaths." She tilted her head to one side and looked at Afsan. His forehead was high, his muzzle strong and firm. Perhaps this was it . . . "Do you," she said casually, "feel guilt over the death of those six people?"

A lightning bolt illuminated the room, throwing everything into stark relief. Mokleb felt her heart skip, but Afsan, of course, did not react at all. "It's an interesting question. Certainly, I dislike seeing anyone die—even someone as nasty as Rodlox." And then the thunderclap came, loud and long, shaking the adobe walls of the building. Afsan waited for the reverberations to fade before he spoke again. "But it was necessary for the good of our people that both Dybo's authority and the credibility of the bloodpriests be restored."

Mokleb shook her head. She felt she was getting closer, but still, maddeningly, the answer was out of reach.

At first Novato thought she'd been imagining it, thought it had been a by-product of her excitement.

But it wasn't. It was really happening.

She stood firmly on the lifeboat's transparent floor and dropped a small metal tool she was holding in her left hand.

It fell.

But it fell *slowly*.

A day and a half had elapsed since her journey up the tower began. If she was right about the lifeboat's speed, she was now some two thousand paces above the ground, a distance equal to one-third of the east-west length of Land.

There could be no doubt. The apparent gravity was less. Much less. The tool had seemed to fall with only half its normal speed. She stooped over and picked it up. It felt light in her hand.

Lower gravity, thought Novato. Incredible.

The tower continued up.

Novato decided she liked this lightness. It made her feel kilodays younger.

Chapter 18

The eggling Others presented a problem.

Traditionally, shortly after a clutch of Quintaglio babies had opened their eyes, a bloodpriest would be summoned to visit the creche. The priest would meditate for daytenths, drink a sacred potion, don the purple *halpataars* robe, and enter the creche chamber. And then, by the flickering light of the heating fires, he'd let loose a loud roar and break into a run, sending the hatchlings scurrying to get away. One by one, he'd pounce on the egglings, slurping them down his gullet, devouring them until only one, the fastest, was left.

But in kiloday 7126, the bloodpriests had been banished from most Packs for collusion in allowing The Family's hatchlings to forgo the culling. The bloodpriests had eventually been reinstated, but Dybo had decreed that a new selection criterion—something other than physical strength—would be used in future. Toroca, originator of the theory of evolution, was charged with finding an appropriate criterion.

Toroca hadn't done that yet, arguing that such a monumental change required considerable thought, and so, at least temporarily, the bloodpriests were culling hatchlings in the traditional way again.

And now Toroca had three baby Others in his care.

In a Quintaglio clutch, only one would be allowed to live.

Should the same hold true for these Others?

Toroca had seen what had happened when the bloodpriests had

been banished from their Packs, when, for a time, every hatchling had been allowed to live. The population had swollen, youngsters were underfoot everywhere, and mass *dagamant* had gripped all of Land.

The people had been willing to accept the bloodpriests so long as they thought every clutch was subjected to their culling. But once an exception had been found, the people rose up in anger, banishing or even killing the *halpataars*.

And now into their midst had come a special clutch. Granted, there were only three hatchlings in it instead of the Quintaglio norm of eight. Still . . .

Toroca leaned on his tail, deep in thought. To risk once again to be seen playing favorites, to be killing seven out of every eight babies from Quintaglio clutches, but to let all of these offspring live . . . The public would be incensed, especially so soon after the scandal involving Dybo and his brothers and sisters.

And to make matters worse, Toroca was, in effect, leader of the bloodpriests until such time as he had developed a new culling criterion. For what amounted to the head bloodpriest to be seen again to be flouting the customs of the people . . .

And yet, these were *not* Quintaglio hatchlings. Their mother had been killed by a Quintaglio, the eggs had been taken, albeit accidentally, from their native land. Surely a dispensation could be made in this case, surely all three could be allowed to live . . .

Surely . . .

No.

The risk was too great. Quintaglio population controls *had* to be kept in place, and that meant nothing could be allowed to discredit the bloodpriests.

Toroca hated himself for what he did next, but he had no choice. At least, since the babies were only a few daytenths old, their eyes weren't yet open; Quintaglio egglings opened their eyes about a day after leaving their shells.

Toroca swallowed one of the hatchlings, the squirming form moving down his gullet. It took a while for him to regain his nerve, but when he did he swallowed a second hatchling, leaving only one alive.

Afsan and Mokleb's next session was held at Rockscape. The ground had not completely dried from the downpour of two days ago. Mokleb's feet were covered with mud and her legs were soaked after making her way through tall grasses to the rock that she used, downwind of Afsan's rock.

"You mentioned in our last session," she said, "that the first time you'd experienced *dagamant* was kilodays ago, aboard the *Dasheter*."

"That's right," said Afsan, stretching out on his boulder. "We were sailing on beyond the Face of God, something no ship had ever done before. Emperor Dybo—he was Prince Dybo back then—and I were sunning ourselves on deck when a sailor named Nor-Gampar came charging between us, in full bloodlust. Bobbing up and down from the waist, glazed eyes, claws exposed—the whole thing."

"You were with Dybo, you say?"

"Yes."

"But it was you who killed this Gampar?"

"Yes."

"So you saved Dybo's life."

"I never thought about it that way, but, yes, I suppose I did."

"Dybo did not repay you well."

A few moments of quiet. "No, he did not."

"But you killed Gampar so that the prince could live."

"Yes."

"Surely this went beyond simple territoriality," said Mokleb. "You weren't just responding to the fact that Gampar was threatening you and Dybo. There was a larger issue at stake: the need to know. You'd convinced Captain Keenir to sail around the world, something no one had ever done. Gampar objected to that."

"Yes."

"He stood in the way of that knowledge."

"Yes."

"He stood in the way of a better life for Quintaglios."

"Yes."

"And, well, if a few people die now and then for the good of society as a whole, that's all right, isn't it?"

"No."

"Strides are never made without sacrifices. People will always die so others can live better lives."

"No."

"Don't you believe that?"

"No. No, there should be alternatives. Death shouldn't be necessary."

"Sometimes it is," said Mokleb.

"Not like that," said Afsan. "Not because of bloody instinct.

Living our lives should not require killing others of our own kind."

"But it *does*," said Mokleb.

"But it *shouldn't*," said Afsan. "By the very Egg of God, Mokleb, it shouldn't!"

On the fifth day after Novato had left, the land in Fra'toolar began to shake. Wingfingers took flight, and the calls of animals split the air. Tails flying behind them, Garios and Karshirl ran along the heaving sands. They were a good distance south of the blue pyramid, but the base of a cliff was the last place one wanted to be during a landquake. Farther along, though, the cliff face gave way to more gentle slopes. On their right, layers of rock were shattering, sending a rain of fragments down onto them. On their left—Garios looked out at the waters and his muzzle dropped open in a silent scream. A wall of water was lifting from the waves. Garios tried to run faster, the ground shifting beneath his feet.

The giant wave was barreling in. Garios risked climbing the rocky slope. He panted out the words of a prayer. In places, debris showered down heavily, but he found a pathway up that was shielded by an overhanging rock layer. Garios had lost track of Karshirl. He hoped she was finding a comparatively safe hiding place, too.

A slab of rock tumbled toward Garios, bouncing sideways under the overhanging ledge. He didn't get his right leg out of the way in time. The impact was excruciating.

Garios looked out again and screamed in terror. The incoming wall of water was higher—much higher—than the height he'd climbed to. It would—

He was slammed against the cliff by the wave's impact. Agony sliced through his battered leg. He felt as though his abdomen was tearing open, forced against sharp rocks.

The water was bitterly cold, as if it had welled up from far below the surface. Submerged, Garios kept his eyes tightly shut. His lungs were bursting, desperate for air. Somehow he managed to hold on to the rocks. A boulder bounced against his back and tail, but its movements were slowed enough by the churning water to keep it from doing much damage.

Garios's lungs ached unbearably. Darkness was gripping him. His consciousness began slipping away—

But then the wave subsided. His maw gaped wide, taking in gulps of air as if they were bolts torn from a carcass. The ground had stopped shaking, at least for now. The beach below was covered with waterweeds deposited by the wave. Wet sand had been lifted up onto the rocky slope, partially covering it. A litter of boulders overlay the ground below.

Garios scanned the beach. There was no sign of Karshirl.

His heart sank. Her body must have been washed out with the receding wave.

Garios's right leg was battered, and he had a shallow gash diagonally across his belly. Maneuvering carefully, so as not to lose his precarious footing, he turned around and looked back up the beach, toward the cliff face and the sky tower—

—which was—

My God!

Vibrating.

Oscillating.

Like a plucked string. Back and forth.

What if it fell down? What if the tower collapsed?

God protect us!

God protect Novato!

Chapter 19

Toroca was the discoverer of evolution. As the current conflict with the Others bloodily demonstrated, the Quintaglios, through the traditional culling process, had not been selecting for the most desirable traits. In trying to devise a new selection criterion, Toroca had spent considerable time in creches, learning about the process of hatching and the early days of childhood.

He hadn't expected that information to have any practical applications for him personally. But now the little Other eggling was making loud peeping sounds. It was hungry.

Creche workers could regurgitate at will, feeding hatchlings directly from their mouths. Toroca had no idea how to voluntarily bring food back up; it was said a fist inserted in the back of the throat could trigger such a reaction, but the accompanying convulsion might cause the jaws to snap shut, severing one's arm just below the elbow. Instead, Toroca took little cubes of dried hornface meat in his mouth and, glad that no one was around to see the disgusting sight, *chewed* the meat by popping it from side to side with his tongue as he slid his jaws forward and back. When the meat was well worked over, he opened his mouth wide and, using his fingers to help dislodge it, collected the meat in a bowl. He poured some water onto it and mixed it together until he had a soft mass. He then put the bowl on the floor near the peeping eggling. The baby was stumbling about.

Nothing happened. Toroca had expected the eggling to smell the concoction and make his way over to it. Perhaps it was the gastric odor in regurgitated food that attracted infant Quintaglios; this meat had no such pungent odor. Toroca crouched on the floor and used his left hand to scoop up some of the meal he'd made and presented it directly to the eggling. He used his other hand to gently prod the baby toward the food. Once its little yellow muzzle was up against the stuff in Toroca's hand, the baby apparently realized what it was and began to use its tongue to maneuver bits of it into its mouth. Toroca crouched contentedly as the hatchling ate, gently stroking the baby's back with his free hand.

Afsan looked haggard. His tail seemed stiff and dead, one of the claws on his left hand was sticking out as if he'd lost conscious control of it, his head was tipped slightly forward, and his muzzle hung half-open as though the effort of keeping his teeth covered, something protocol required, was too much for him. The little membranes at the corners of his mouth were that ashen color one gets when feverish. It was clear that he was exhausted.

Mokleb dipped a fingerclaw into the pot of ink she'd brought with her and began the transcript of the day's session. Writing her words down as they were spoken, she said: "We've come close to the territory of this issue before, but never actually crossed the boundaries. Some call you Sal-Afsan, some just Afsan, and some call you by a third name: The One."

Afsan sighed. "You really have a thing about names, don't you?"

"Do I?" Mokleb's inner eyelids blinked. "Well, I guess I do, at that. They are an important part of our identity, Afsan. And, as I said, some call you by a special name: The One."

"And some call me fat-head, among other things."

Mokleb refrained from clicking her teeth. "I'm curious about the effect it has on you to be called The One. It's a reference to the prophecy made by the ancient hunter Lubal, isn't it? When she was dying after being gored by a hornface, she said"——Mokleb stopped transcribing her own words long enough to find the quote she had written down—" 'A hunter will come greater than myself, and this hunter will be a male—yes, a male—and he shall lead you on the greatest hunt of all.' "

"Yes, that was the prophecy," said Afsan. A pause. "I don't believe in prophecy."

"Many take your proposed journey to the stars to be the great hunt Lubal spoke of."

Afsan waved a hand dismissively. "Metaphor again. You can make anything mean anything else."

Mokleb read from her notes once more. "And yet Lubal also said, 'One will come among you to herald the end; heed him, for those who do not are doomed.' Isn't that your story in miniature? You did herald the end of the world, and had we not listened to you and begun work toward the exodus, we would indeed have been doomed."

Afsan, prone on his boulder, made a noncommittal grunt.

"And," continued Mokleb, "Lubal said, 'The One will defeat demons of the land and of the water; blood from his kills will soak the soil and stain the River.' You did kill the giant thunderbeast and you also slew the water serpent, ah,"—checking notes once more—"Kal-ta-goot."

"I'd forgotten that Lubal had said that," said Afsan. "It's been an awfully long time since I've been able to read the Book of Lubal, after all, and . . ."

"And?"

"And, well, it's not the sort of thing my apprentice would expect me to ask her to read to me."

Mokleb inventoried her possible responses, chose a click of the teeth. "No, I suppose that's true."

"In any event, the thunderbeast wasn't a demon. And Kal-ta-goot . . . well, chasing it was what allowed the *Dasheter* to complete the first circumnavigation of the globe. If anything, Kal-ta-goot was a savior."

"Var-Keenir would not agree."

"As much as I like and admire the old sailor, Keenir and I often disagree."

Mokleb was silent.

"Anyway, Mokleb, this is just another case of you forcing the words to mean something they don't really say. I killed no demons."

" 'Demons,' " repeated Mokleb thoughtfully. "Strictly speaking, demons are defined as those who can lie in the light of day."

"Exactly. And I've never killed anyone who could do that. I've never even known anyone who could . . ."

"Yes?"

"Nothing."

"Once again, you are hiding your thoughts, Afsan. I must know what you are thinking if I'm to help you."

"Well, it's just that Det-Yenalb, the priest who put out my eyes—I'd never thought about it this way before, but he once hinted to me that he could lie in the light of day. He implied that it went with being a successful priest. I never knew whether he was serious about it, or was just trying to frighten me, but . . ."

"Yes?"

"He was killed in 7110, during the skirmish between the palace loyal and the Lubalites. I didn't kill him myself, but, well, if he could lie without his muzzle turning blue, then I suppose he was a demon and, in a way, he was killed in my name."

"And in any event," said Mokleb, looking down at her notes, "the word Lubal used was 'defeat,' not 'kill.' You personally did indeed defeat Det-Yenalb, for society now pursues your goal of spaceflight instead of following Yenalb's teachings." She paused. "Besides, what about all your great hunts?"

"All of them? There were only three of any significance before I lost my sight."

"But such hunts!" said Mokleb. "The giant thunderbeast. Kal-ta-goot. And a fangjaw!"

Afsan made a contemptuous motion with his hand. "You don't understand. You're just like the rest of them. No one seems to understand." He turned his head so that his blind eyes faced her. "I have *never* hunted. Not really. Not like a true hunter. Mokleb, the one time I really needed to hunt in order to save myself, I failed miserably. As a child, I was lost in a forest. I couldn't catch a single thing to eat. I was reduced to trying to eat plants. Plants!" He snorted. "Me, a hunter? I'm nothing of the kind."

"But your kills . . . ?"

"Those weren't examples of hunting prowess. I honestly believe I have little of that. Don't you see? They were instances in which I solved problems. That's all I've ever done. That's the only thing I'm good at." He paused. "Consider the thunderbeast hunt—my first ritual hunt. The other members of the pack were taking bites out of the thing's legs and sides." He shook his head, remembering. "That's how you kill a small animal, not a living mountain. No, it was obvious to me that the thunderbeast's vulnerable spot was the same as yours or mine—the underside of the throat. So I shimmied up the thing's neck and bit it there. *Anyone* could have done that; I just happened to be the first to think of it."

"And Kal-ta-goot?"

"A great hunt? Please. Even Det-Bleen, the *Dasheter*'s blow-hard priest, had reservations about that one. He wouldn't consecrate the meal at first. Mokleb, I used tools for that kill. I wasn't interested in ritual hunting at all. I realized that the animal had to breathe, just as we do, so I wrapped the anchor chain around its neck, constricting its flow of air. Again, that had nothing to do with athletic skill or hunting prowess or stealthful tracking. It was the application of the tools at hand to a specific problem."

"Ah, but what about the fangjaw? That animal is rarely killed by any hunter, yet you felled one on your first attempt."

Afsan spread his arms. "That's the most obvious example of all. Pahs-Drawo and I stalked the fangjaw on the backs of runningbeasts. It was the runners that gave us the edge, not any skill of our own. And when it came time to actually attack, Drawo and I leapt off the runningbeasts, aiming for the fangjaw's back. Drawo missed, landing in the dirt. I succeeded. Don't you see? That kill wasn't a result of hunting skill. Rather it was because I was able to calculate the trajectory properly to leap from one moving body onto another. Mathematics, that's all that was. Mathematics and problem-solving. The same as my other hunts."

"But other Quintaglios would have failed in your place. Isn't it the results that matter?"

"Oh, possibly. But the real point is simply that I kept my head during those hunts, that I was *thinking*, always thinking, while the others were letting their instincts guide them. Rationality is the key. No matter what's going on around you, you have to keep your logic at the fore."

"That's something our people aren't very good at, I guess," said Mokleb.

"No," said Afsan, his voice heavy. "No, they're not."

"Still," said Mokleb after a moment, "prophecy *is* a metaphorical game. It does sound to me as though you've fulfilled most of the requirements of being The One."

"Nonsense," said Afsan, annoyed. "Words mean what they mean. 'The One will defeat demons of the land *and of the water*,' Lubal said. Maybe, just maybe, the death of Det-Yenalb could be construed as having defeated a demon of the land. But demons of the water? No such things exist, and, even if they did, I'm hardly likely to ever come into contact with them, let alone be the one who defeats them."

• • •

Novato's lifeboat continued its long ascent up the tower.

She'd been traveling for almost five days now. That meant she was some six thousand kilopaces above the surface. By coincidence, six thousand kilopaces was the radius of her world; she was as far away from the surface of Land now as she would have been if she'd burrowed all the way to the center of her moon.

The gravity continued to diminish. Things fell in leisurely slowness, as though settling gently through thick liquid. If Novato tucked her legs under her body, it was several beats before her knees gently touched the transparent floor. She guessed that the apparent gravity was only one-sixth of what it had been on the ground.

Novato thought about the reduction in gravity. There were three forces involved: two pulling her down and one trying to push her up. The moon's gravity and the gravity from the Face behind it were both drawing her down. But the tower itself was rigid, swinging through a vast arc once per day. It was as if she were a weight at the end of a six-thousand-kilopace rope being swung in a circle. The centrifugal force would be flinging her upward. Although the gravity from the Face and the moon would have lessened somewhat because of her travel away from them, she would have weighed substantially more if it hadn't been for the centrifugal force.

The lightness was wonderful, but Novato was anxious nonetheless.

Five days.

Five days locked in here.

She needed to get outside, to run, to hunt! She couldn't stand the thought of another meal of dried meat and salted fish. Yet she was still less than halfway to the tower's summit.

Clear walls pressed down on her, invisible yet claustrophobic.

Five days.

Novato sighed.

Still, in that time she'd seen a lot of wonderful sights. While looking down, she'd seen a streak through the night sky, over the vast body of water. She realized it must have been a large meteor, seen from above. And, with the aid of the far-seer, she was able to make out the crimson points of erupting volcanoes in Edz'toolar—something Toroca had said was long overdue. She even saw an eclipse from in the middle, as another moon, the Big

One, passed directly overhead at noon, its circular black shadow moving rapidly across Land.

She looked down again.

Her blood ran cold.

The tower, this marvelous tower to the stars, now appeared to be bowing out as if it were about to fold over and break in half. She'd thought at first that it was an optical illusion: the curving horizon line made it difficult to tell by sight if the tower was truly straight, but as the bowing became more pronounced, there could be no mistake.

She'd known what her daughter Karshirl had said: the tower was unstable. There was no way for something so tall and so narrow to stand without buckling, and yet she'd been fool enough to think that whatever magic had held it against its own weight so far would continue to keep it erect for the duration of her voyage.

Her first thought was that she was going to die, plummeting back to the ground at a dizzying speed. Her second thought was that hundreds of people would die when giant pieces of the tower fell out of the sky.

She felt herself slowly being pushed up toward the ceiling. She saw now that the tower was bowing the other way farther down, as if it were a great blue snake, undulating its way to the stars. After a time, she began drifting toward the floor again.

And then Novato realized what was happening.

Erupting volcanoes in Edz'toolar, the province next to Fra'toolar, where the tower was anchored.

Landquake.

What she was seeing was the rippling of the landquake being transferred up the structure of the tower. The first wave had yet to reach her. She could see another huge wave rolling up behind it, the tower bowing first to the east then to the west like a string plucked by a giant's hand. In addition, the tower was moving up and down in longitudinal compression waves.

But something else was happening. White gas was shooting out of the copper cones that projected from every fifth strut up the tower's length. She'd seen little puffs shoot out from time to time during her ascent, but these were massive exhalations, geysers against the night.

Novato saw a dent appear in the crest of the wave that was hurtling toward her, saw the tower material bow inward, moving in the opposite direction of the gas plume, saw the one giant wave become two smaller ones, with lesser crests and shorter lengths. And then it happened again, slowly, majestically, the waves splitting once more into new waves half as long and half as tall. When the disturbance did reach her, the lifeboat simply rose and fell gently, like a sailing ship rolling on a swell.

The waves continued to dampen out. Soon, the jets of white fog coming from the copper cones became smaller and less frequent.

And it hit her, all at once: how the tower had remained standing, and what those occasional puffs of gas she'd seen venting from the cones had meant.

When the tower began leaning to the left, compressed gas nudged it to the right. When it began to topple to the right, a jet of air pushed it to the left. Along its whole length, the tower was constantly adjusting its orientation. Karshirl had been correct: no normal structure as long and thin as this one could stand. Like the mythical Tower of Howlee, it would buckle, regardless of the strength of the building material. But that had assumed that the tower was passive—and this tower was not. It was—the thought was incredible—it was *alive,* in a very real sense, constantly detecting shifts in its attitude and compensating for them with jets of air. Even the giant shifts caused by a landquake rippling up its length were dampened by this process.

Whoever had built the ancient blue ark had been incredibly advanced. They had plied the distance between stars, something Novato was only beginning to comprehend the difficulty of doing. They had created the strange and wonderful dust that had built this massive tower, an object longer than the world was wide. Nor was it any ordinary object; it was *smart,* reacting to changes in conditions.

And yet, whoever the ark-makers were, they, too, had failed. One of their arks had crashed, the crew killed, its cargo of lifeforms never released. If something could defeat the ark-makers, what chance did Quintaglios have against the fate that awaited them?

Novato hugged her arms to her body and tucked her tail between her legs. She settled slowly to the floor, afraid.

Chapter 20

The *Dasheter* continued to race back toward Land, the armada of Other ships in hot pursuit. The Face of God was already half submerged below the waves. Right now, the sun was touching one horizon, and the Face, completely full, was sitting on the other. Toroca, standing on deck, cast a long shadow away from the sun, but the shadow itself was partially filled in by the soft ocher light reflecting from the Face.

Captain Keenir approached Toroca from up ahead. Even though he knew Toroca was free of territorial feeling, Keenir couldn't overcome the ingrained protocols: whenever possible, approach from the front rather than behind.

"Beautiful sunset," said Keenir, stopping ten paces shy of the younger Quintaglio.

Toroca nodded. "That it is."

Keenir leaned against the gunwale. "You know," said the captain, his gravelly voice carrying an unusual tone of reflection, "I've been lucky. I'm eighty-three, a lot older than I have any right to be. I've probably seen more sunsets from aboard a ship than any other Quintaglio alive." He gestured at the thin line of cloud, stained dark purple against the purplish-red sky, and at the swollen egg of the sun. "Even so, I never get tired of looking at them."

They watched the sun slip below the waves. Almost at once, the sky began to darken. Toroca turned to face Keenir. "Did you want to see me about something?"

"Yes," said Keenir, the standard gruffness returning to his voice. "The Other infant."

"Taksan," said Toroca.

"You've named it?" said Keenir, surprised.

"Of course. And he's a him, not an it. There is no creche master around; who else would name him?"

"I suppose," said Keenir. Then: "What are you going to do with him?"

"What do you mean?"

Keenir exhaled noisily, as if he felt Toroca was being dense. "I mean, good Toroca, we are at war with his people. Surely the child should be disposed of."

"What?" said Toroca, shocked.

"You made a good start when you got rid of the other two," said Keenir. "After all, taking prisoners isn't normal procedure."

"There are no 'normal procedures,'" said Toroca. "There has never been a war like this."

"No, no. But in the ancient territorial conflicts, before the time of Dasan, prisoners were never taken. I mean, you can't put a bunch of Quintaglios into a cell together; they'd kill each other."

"Taksan is not a Quintaglio; his race is not territorial."

"I know that," said Keenir, a hint of exasperation in his tone. "Still, we have no facilities on this ship for holding a prisoner—"

"Stop calling him that," said Toroca. "He is not a prisoner."

"Well, use whatever term you want. But he is one of the enemy, and has no place aboard this ship."

"What would you have me do, Keenir?"

"I don't know," said the captain, scratching the underside of his jaw. "Toss him overboard, I suppose."

"*What?* Keenir, you can't be serious."

"Of course I'm serious. Look, you've had to keep him in your lab as is. No one else has even seen him. But you can't keep him there indefinitely. And soon enough one of my crew *is* going to lay eyes on him. Whether the sight of an infant Other will be enough to trigger *dagamant* I don't know, but we can't risk it. Not in the close confines of a sailing ship. I won't have the *Dasheter* become another *Galadoreter*."

"But Taksan—Taksan is my . . ."

"Your what?" said Keenir.

"Nothing. You can't make me get rid of him."

"You may direct the Geological Survey, Toroca, but *I* am captain of the *Dasheter*. I can allow nothing to put my ship or crew at risk." Keenir turned his back and looked out over the waves.

Toroca's tone was matter-of-fact. "I will not harm Taksan. If you try to do so, or allow anyone else to, I will kill you."

Keenir clicked his teeth. "Oh, come on, Toroca. Be serious."

Toroca raised his hands to show that his claws were unsheathed. "I *am* being serious, Keenir. I shall kill anyone who harms Taksan."

Var-Osfik was the Arbiter of the Sequence, the person responsible for keeping Quintaglio knowledge in order. Osfik was a fussy old thing, but lately she'd had to make a lot of changes. Astrology, for instance, had originally come right after prophecy in the Sequence, since both dealt with the revelation of hidden truths. But after Afsan's discovery about the Face of God, Osfik moved astrology to in between physics, which dealt with the way things work, and geology, the study of the world, thus making astrology the study of the way the worlds work. That had been a major move, and librarians across Land probably cursed her for it. Mokleb thought about this as she scratched the signaling plate—gold, befitting Osfik's station—next to the arbiter's door.

"Who is it?" came a gruff voice, muffled by the wood.

"Nav-Mokleb, undertaking business requested by the Emperor."

"Hahat dan."

Fortunately, Osfik was female; Mokleb's pheromones would have less effect on her. Mokleb was amazed by how crowded the room was. Objects of all types covered the floor, tabletops, and shelves. On one wall were cases containing insects on pins, arranged from right to left in ascending order of beauty. On Osfik's desk, an assortment of smith's tools. Mokleb couldn't discern any order to their sequence, unless—perhaps in ascending order of strength needed to wield them. On the floor, planks of wood from various trees, with a few set aside, apparently not yet fitted into the progression. The Sequence for wood was old and well established. That Osfik was mulling it over was a sign of the times: all knowledge was subject to reinterpretation these days.

"I'm a busy person," said Osfik without preamble. "I'm sure you can appreciate that. Do me the courtesy, therefore, of dispensing with protocols. I accept that we have bowed at each other, that we've acknowledged how we cast shadows in each other's presence, that you wouldn't have bothered me if it wasn't important, and so on. Now, quickly and precisely, Nav-Mokleb, what do you want?"

Mokleb felt off balance, as though someone had lifted her tail and she was tipping forward. Niceties were *always* observed; every encounter was an intricate social dance. She was not quite prepared for this, and, on the whole, she thought she didn't like it. Nevertheless: "I've but one question, Osfik: is there such a thing as a purple wingfinger?"

Osfik looked up, nictitating membranes fluttering. "This is the Emperor's business, you said?"

"Indirectly. His Luminance has asked me to treat a member of his staff. I'm a healer of sorts."

"Oh, I know who you are, Mokleb. You've taken more than a few daytenths of my time, what with these books and tracts you've published. The study of the mind always fit neatly under philosophy before, but I could not see putting your works on the same shelf as those of Dolgar or Spooltar—no offense; quality is not the issue. Content is. You treat the study of the mind more like a medical matter."

Mokleb was surprised that her work had attracted Osfik's attention. "I don't wish to add to the burden I've already created for you. I simply need to know whether there is any species of wingfinger with purple wings."

"You're in luck," said Osfik. "I've got most of the books on wingfingers right here. Since Toroca discovered those unknown wingfinger forms on the southern ice cap, I've been trying to fit them into the Sequence." She snorted briefly. "He's another who has made my life difficult. His evolutionary model has required a complete reordering of the sequence of life."

Osfik rummaged around until she found a large, square book bound in leather. "Here it is. *The Wingfingers of Land,* a collection of paintings by Pal-Noltark." She handed the heavy volume to Mokleb. "Have a look. It's not a great book; Noltark ordered it by geographic region when properly wingfingers are arranged by increasing maximal adult wingspan. Still, he boasts to have painted every species. If a purple one exists, it'll be in there."

Mokleb began turning the stiff paper pages. There were more varieties of wingfinger than she'd ever imagined: some had pointy crests off the backs of their skulls, others did not, but all had wings supported on incredibly elongated fourth fingers, and all had fine hair covering most of their bodies. There were scarlet wingfingers, green wingfingers, copper wingfingers, white ones, black ones, ones with striped bodies and ones freckled with colored dots, but nowhere was there one that was purple. She closed the cover.

"Find what you were looking for?" asked Osfik.

"No—I mean, yes. I found that there is no such thing as a purple wingfinger."

Osfik nodded. "I never saw a purple wingfinger," she said, "and I never hope to see one, but I can tell you anyhow I'd rather see than be one." Then the old arbiter clicked her teeth. "Say, that's good. I should write that down."

Mokleb thanked Osfik and left. The purple wingfinger was symbolic, obviously, of something that was troubling Afsan. But what? The sky was purple, of course, and some kinds of flowers were purple, too. Some shovelmouths and thunderbeasts had purple markings on their hides. The blue-black pigment used in hunting tattoos could look purple in certain light.

And what about wingfingers? Flying reptiles, they came in all sizes. They laid eggs. Some ate insects, some ate lizards, many kinds ate fish, and many more fed on carrion.

Purple.

Wingfinger.

Mokleb shook her head.

Novato had dreamed of flying before. Indeed, after a ride in one of her gliders, she often found herself feeling as though she were still soaring. But that sensation of flight had always been accompanied by a feeling of forward motion, of slicing through the air. Now, well, it was simply as if she were hovering, floating, a cloud.

And then she awoke, with a start, as her head banged against the lifeboat's ceiling.

Banged against the ceiling . . .

Novato's heart skipped a beat, and she scrunched her eyes tightly closed. She felt her whole body go rigid as she prepared to crash back to the floor. But that did not happen. Instead, her back touched the ceiling again, gently this time, like a piece of wood bobbing in a calm lake. She opened her eyes. At first, she'd thought perhaps she'd been slammed against the roof by rapid deceleration, but in the light of the countless stars and eight visible moons she had no trouble making out the rungs of the tower's ladder-like sides as they passed. They were going by at a steady rate.

She was neither accelerating nor decelerating.

And yet she floated.

Floated!

She wasn't completely weightless. She was drifting slowly downward, and her equipment still sat stolidly on the floor. Still, she now weighed so little that her tossing as she slept had been enough to lift her off the floor and send her drifting toward the ceiling.

It was a giddy sensation. Her arms were spread like loosely folded wings, her legs were bent gently at the knees, and she could feel her tail swaying behind her.

She'd been aboard the lifeboat for almost nine days now. The world below looked like a giant ball, filling most of her field of vision. About two-thirds of it was illuminated; the other third was in the darkness of night. Breathtaking as that sight was, even more spectacular was what was slowly becoming visible *behind* the world. Orange and yellow light spilled past the edges of the illuminated disk, and already she could see a hint of the vast colored bands of cloud.

The Face of God. The planet around which the Quintaglio moon orbited.

The lifeboat continued upward. As the sight of the world with its single equatorial landmass diminished, more of the Face of God beyond became visible. Her world looked now like a vast blue-green pupil in the center of a yellow eye. As time went by, she could see the two superimposed spheres—the Face and the Quintaglio moon—waxing and waning through phases in unison. When they were both full, as they were at high noon, the glare from the ring-shaped Face behind was so intense that Novato had trouble looking at it without her inner eyelids involuntarily sliding shut.

It was spectacular. When seen from the deck of a pilgrimage ship, the sight of the Face, with its roiling bands of cloud, its infinitely complex array of swirls and vortices and colored whirlpools, its vast majestic grandeur, was enough to induce an almost hypnotic state in a Quintaglio. But to see her own world, with its cottony clouds, its shimmering blue waters, and the endlessly convoluted shoreline of Land, and at the same time to also see beyond it the glory of the Face of God—that was almost too much beauty, too much wonder, for the mind to grasp. Novato found herself transfixed, mesmerized. If she hadn't already been floating on air, she would be now.

Emperor Dy-Dybo was lying on his dayslab in his ruling room, hearing the appeal of a young Quintaglio who had been accused of theft. He couldn't deny the crime, of course: his muzzle would betray his lies. Still, he sought clemency on the basis that what he had taken—spikefrill horn cores from the palace butchery, items often used in Lubalite ceremonies—would simply have been thrown out anyway. Penalty for theft was to have one's hands amputated. This fellow's lawyer contended that such an act would be cruel punishment, for the youth apparently had a flaw that would prevent the hands from regenerating. As proof, he offered his client's left foot, which had only two toes; the third had been lost kilodays ago and had never regrown.

The ruling room's doors burst open and in ran an elderly female Dybo didn't recognize. The imperial guards quickly stepped forward, interposing themselves between the emperor and the intruder; there was always the chance that someone mad with *dagamant* would get into the palace. The stranger was panting hard, but her torso was steady. She held up a hand, showing that her claws were sheathed, and caught her breath. Then: "Your Luminance, forgive me. I'm Pos-Doblan, keeper of the maritime rookery north of the city."

"Yes?" said Dybo.

"A homing wingfinger has just arrived. I wouldn't have interrupted you, but the message is urgent." She held up a coil of leather. Dybo was recumbent on the slab, tail sticking up like a rubbery mast. He flicked it, and a guard moved forward, retrieved the leather strip, took it to Dybo, then backed off to a respectful distance. Dybo unwound the strip and read it quickly. "God protect us," he said softly.

One of Dybo's advisors rose from a *katadu* bench. "Dybo?" she said, the lapse into informality within the throne chamber betraying her concern.

Dybo's tone was decisive. "You, page"—he never could remember names—"summon Afsan right away. And send word to Fra'toolar that Novato should return as soon as possible. I'm going to need my best thinkers." He pushed off the dayslab and began to leave the chamber.

"Emperor," called the lawyer for the youth. "What about my client?"

"No punishment," snapped Dybo. "We're going to need all the hands we can get."

"I have a feeling we have not gone back far enough," Mokleb said to Afsan. "What's the earliest memory you have?"

Afsan scratched the loose folds of the dewlap hanging from his neck. "I don't know. I remember, well, let's see . . . I remember my vocational exams."

"Those would have been when you were ten or eleven. Surely you remember older things."

"Oh, sure. There's that time I got lost in the forest; I've mentioned that before. And, let's see, I remember getting in trouble for biting off the finger of one of my creche mates when I was young."

"Did you do it in anger?"

"No, we were just playing around. It was an accident, and the finger grew back, of course."

"What else do you remember?"

"Learning to cut leather. Catching butterflies. Let's see . . . I remember the first time during my life that Pack Carno picked up and moved itself along the shores of the Kreeb River. I remember—what else?—I remember all the commotion when some dignitary came to visit the Pack. I didn't know who it was at the time, but I later learned that it was Dybo's—ah, what would the term be? Dybo's grandmother, the Empress Sar-Sardon."

"You remember an imperial visit to Carno?"

"Vaguely, yes. They took us youngsters down to the Kreeb and washed us off so we'd look clean for her. I remember it because it was the first time they'd actually let us near the river; they were always afraid the current would sweep us away."

"What else?"

"Learning to play *lastoontal*. God, what a boring process that was: walking up to the game board to make my move, then backing off so the other player could come up and make his or her move."

"Anything else?"

"Oh, many things, I suppose, but they all seem trivial. A great thunderstorm. The first time I experienced a landquake. Finding a dead wingfinger."

"A wingfinger? Was it purple?"

"No, it was white with pale orange stripes. A banded swift, I think."

"What else?"

"Learning to read; memorizing endless series of glyphs and the words associated with them."

"And do you remember which of these things came first?"

"It's hard to say. They're jumbled together in my mind."

"What about anything that disturbed you, or frightened you, when you were a child?"

"Well, I mentioned the landquake: that scared me. Of course, one gets used to them. And I was quite frightened when I was lost in the forest. But no, nothing really shocking, if that's what you're looking for."

"Yes," said Mokleb. "That's *exactly* what I'm looking for."

Chapter 21

Finally, it was about to happen: the moment Novato had been both waiting for and dreading. The four blue sides of the ladder were no longer simply fading into nothingness. Instead, she could see where they ended. Far, far above, she could see the actual summit of the tower. Novato's claws hung half out of their sheaths, and her tail, floating in the air behind her, twitched left and right.

She thought of *Rewdan and the Vine*.

A giant blackdeath.

A wingfinger that laid eggs of gold.

Which would it be?

The four sides of the tower flared into a vast blue bulb at the top. Long panels were extended from the sides of the bulb, panels so dark as to be visible only because they blocked the stars behind them. The whole thing looked like some deathly daisy with black petals and a blue, impossibly long stem.

The lifeboat began to slow, preparing to stop at the summit. Novato drifted toward the roof.

Any moment now.

The lifeboat slid up, farther and farther, past the bottom of the bulb, into the cavernous interior. It jerked slightly as it came to rest.

Novato was breathing rapidly. It took a while to absorb what she was seeing through the transparent walls: a vast chamber with a myriad of levels, all constructed of the blue material.

She steeled her courage as the lifeboat's interior walls fogged over. Then the door appeared. The successful return of the test lizards notwithstanding, she'd been terrified that there'd be no air inside the chamber up here. But everything seemed fine. She gave a gentle kick off the lifeboat's rear wall and floated out the door.

Ten days had elapsed since she'd first entered the lifeboat. If she was right about its speed—one hundred and thirty kilopaces per daytenth—then she was now some thirteen thousand kilopaces above the surface of her world. Here at last she felt no tendency to drift downward at all; she was completely weightless, the centrifugal and gravitational forces in perfect balance.

She floated along, kicking gently off walls to keep herself moving. At last she entered a massive cubic chamber.

Her heart pounded.

Eggs of gold.

There were nine windows on one wall arranged in three rows of three. Thick black lines connected the eight outlying windows to the one in the center.

Novato tried to take it all in, but couldn't. For a time, she simply floated there, numb, the bright colors in the windows hypnotic but devoid of content. Slowly, though, her mind began to make at least a small amount of sense out of what she was seeing.

Somehow, each window was looking out on a *different* scene. As if that weren't strange enough, the scene each window was showing changed every forty beats or so. Some of the scenes at least were partially comprehensible—why, that one showed a grassy plain and cloudy sky, and this one showed water lapping against a shore, and surely those things in that window over there were buildings of some sort. But the views through other windows were so strange, Novato could make nothing of them.

Each window was numbered in its upper left corner using the six numerals of the ark-makers. But they weren't numbered one through nine. Rather, the one in the center had the simple horizontal line the ark-makers used for zero, and the other windows had numbers that changed each time the view through them changed.

She scanned the nine windows, looking for something—anything—she recognized.

And suddenly she found just that: something familiar in the maelstrom of confusion.

Emperor Dybo.

Yes, the right-hand window in the bottom row was looking in on Dybo's ruling room. The number in the window's upper left was 27.

Except—

There was no window in the ruling room at that point; indeed, there were no windows in the ruling room at all.

And yet here was a view of that room from above, as if standing on a ladder, looking down on Dybo, who was lying on the marble throne slab. To his left and right were the *katadu* benches for imperial advisors. Three elderly Quintaglios were sitting on these. Dybo had a long strip of leather in his hands that appeared to have writing on it. The Emperor looked worried.

Still—Dybo! How good to see him again! But how was this window here, on the top of the space tower, able to look into Dybo's ruling room? What magic made this possible?

She stared through the window, trying to make out details. And suddenly she realized that these glass-covered squares were not windows. If they had been windows, the view would shift as she moved her head left and right, but that did not happen. Also, Dybo was in sharp focus, but the background was not. The tapestries on the rear wall were simply a blur. If she'd been looking through a real window, she could have focused on whatever she wanted. An optical process was at work, then, as though—as though she were looking through the eyepiece of a far-seer, perhaps. A far-seer that could see through walls.

And then her heart soared as someone else walked into the picture.

Afsan.

God, it was wonderful to see him again. Novato found herself calling out his name, but he didn't turn, didn't react. Dybo was speaking with great agitation, but Novato couldn't hear the words. And then—

The view in the window changed. Novato scanned all nine squares, hoping to find Afsan again, but each of them was showing something unfamiliar.

Her mind was reeling. The cascade of images was incredible, hypnotic. It was all so much to absorb. She decided to concentrate on just one window. She choose the bottom right, the same one that had shown Dybo's ruling room.

But what she was seeing now through that window was nothing at all like Capital City. Nothing at all, in fact, like any part of her world.

There were no familiar objects in the picture—nothing to give any sense of scale. Still, Novato eventually realized she was seeing a portion of a city. But what a bizarre city! Everything seemed to be made of one continuous piece of material, as if the whole thing had been . . . been *grown* all at once. The material was pinkish-tan and pockmarked, reminding Novato of the coral reefs she'd seen off Boodskar. But this was no random atoll; if it was coral, it had somehow been made to grow in a specific pattern. At regular intervals, dome-like buildings rose out of the gently undulating surface—they were clearly buildings, for they had windows arranged in neat rows and wide openings for doors. Elsewhere, ornate spires stretched toward the sky, and in some places deep circular pits were sunk into the material, their interior walls also lined with windows. There were no seams anywhere, no dividing lines between where one part ended and another began.

Suddenly Novato's claws popped out. A quivering red glob was emerging from one of the doorways. It seemed as if the skin had been flayed from its body: the flesh was completely naked and a reticulum of yellow circulatory channels was visible on or just below the surface. Locomotion was provided by smaller lumps underneath the main body. These lumps had many fine tendrils projecting from them, tendrils that constantly rippled like blades of long grass in the wind. Novato had the feeling that these underbodies weren't securely attached, and this was confirmed when one of them scampered off on its own into a nearby building. She couldn't see any sensory organs on the central red glob, but there were *things* moving over it: hideous leech-like worms with sharp yellow teeth. Other things, like skinless snakes, writhed at the glob's sides. These, too, were clearly not attached to it, but rather were separate entities, roaming freely over the amorphous red surface.

Another of the red globs moved into view from the right, the tendrils on its underbodies rippling back and forth. Novato watched, amazed, as one of the naked snakes left the first creature and slithered over to take up residence on the second.

Suddenly, the view changed again. This time it seemed to be a night scene. Large creatures were moving around in the blackness, but Novato couldn't make out what they were. She turned her attention to the central window—the one labeled as window zero.

At least the creatures visible through it had some slight resemblance to Quintaglios. Like Quintaglios, they had a pair of arms ending in five-fingered hands, a pair of legs, and a head with a mouth and two eyes. But that's where the resemblance ended. They weren't reptiles, whatever they were. These creatures stood impossibly erect, like the columns used to support buildings. They lacked tails. And their skin seemed to be yellowish-beige. Their heads were round, with only a tiny nose and no muzzle at all. The eyes were slanted. Some of them were wearing headgear, but others apparently were not, although Novato couldn't be sure. There was a black something crowning each head, a mass of . . . of fibers, perhaps . . . that blew around in the wind. There were hints of these same black fibers above the eyes and some of the creatures had traces of the black stuff around their mouths.

The sky was a bright blue and there was something yellow and huge blazing in it. A sun. But, by the very Egg of God, it was not *the* sun. If she hadn't been floating, Novato would have staggered back on her tail.

The view in the central window changed, but the number in the upper left remained zero. A group of strange quadrupeds were in the middle of the picture. Startling beasts: they were covered with vertical black and white stripes. The view moved, as if whatever eye was capturing these images was scanning, looking for something else. At last it settled on a trio of bipeds. These were like the yellowish ones Novato had already seen, but had skin so dark brown as to be almost black. They also had black fiber on the tops of their heads, but these fibers seemed more coiled than straight. The three of them were wearing pieces of leather cloth around their waists. Obviously they killed animals, then—but how? These brown ones still lacked any sort of muzzle, and—my God!—one had its mouth open now, and Novato could clearly see the yellow-white teeth.

Flat, square teeth.

The teeth of a herbivore.

Novato's mind reeled. Nothing made any sense. And yet, these creatures were obviously intelligent: in addition to the waist cloths, one of the three was wearing some kind of jewelry. The jeweled one was interesting. Its chest was completely different in construction from that of the other two; a pair of large growths hung from it. What could they possibly be for?

Novato shook her head, then glanced at the window to the left. Ah, at least the creature it was showing was reasonable. A reptilian biped, a bit like a runningbeast, with green and brown skin, two arms, two legs, and a long, drawn-out face. It was much less stocky than a Quintaglio, and its hands had only three fingers. The eyes were huge and silver, and its body was held horizontally, with a thin, stiff tail projecting directly to the rear, like the balancing-bar tail used by terrorclaws. Again, this was an intelligent creature, for in its hand was some sort of complex device. The creature seemed to stare directly at Novato for a moment, blinked its eyes, then turned and walked away, its neck weaving back and forth as it moved.

The view changed. Novato's mind reeled again, but eventually images coalesced for her. She was seeing an underwater landscape, but seeing it clearly, without the blurring normally associated with opening one's eyes while submerged. A herd of creatures was moving by on the bottom. Each had seven pairs of stilt-like legs and seven waving tentacles in a row down its back. The tentacles each ended in little pincers. Novato thought she must be hallucinating, the creatures looked so strange.

Her head spun, unable to sort out all the images. She fought waves of disorientation and confusion.

What was she seeing? What did it all mean?

Chapter 22

Toroca stood on the *Dasheter*'s rear diamond-shaped hull, leaning over the gunwale. It was late afternoon. Far astern he could see the strange triangular sails of the Other ships spread out in a line. Behind them was the top of the Face of God, just a sliver of it sticking above the horizon now, a tiny dome of yellow and orange and brown, all but submerged beneath the waves. In front of it, though, the water was stained red, as if slick with blood, reflecting the light of the setting Face.

Toroca's tail swished in sadness. How could it have gone so wrong? He'd sought knowledge, only knowledge, and instead had found death.

There hadn't been a war amongst Quintaglios since the time of Dasan. Toroca had thought his race had outgrown such foolishness, had evolved in spirit and morality as well as in physical form.

But no. The Quintaglios were as bloodthirsty as they'd always been. Instinctive killers, killers to their very cores.

The Face of God continued to set, its apparent movement caused solely by the *Dasheter*'s own motion through the water.

Toroca watched the Other ships, illuminated from the front by the setting sun behind him and from the back by the light reflected from the sliver of Face. It was some time before he realized what was happening, but soon there could be no mistake. Several of the ships on the left and right of the wall of pursuing vessels were turning. He could see them sideways now instead of bow-on. And soon, he saw their sterns. They were going back! They were heading for home!

Of course, thought Toroca. They worshipped the Face of God and did not want to travel beyond its purview. Perhaps no Other ship had ever sailed onto the back-side hemisphere before.

Two more ships were turning now.

Toroca glanced up at the lookout's bucket atop the foremast. Somebody was up there, but his back was to Toroca, scanning the waters ahead of the *Dasheter*. Babnol was crossing the deck behind Toroca, though. He called out to her. She looked up, her strange nose horn casting shadows fore and aft in the light of the setting sun and the setting Face. "Please get Captain Keenir for me," he shouted.

Babnol bowed concession and hurried across the joining piece to the *Dasheter*'s other hull. Moments later, old Keenir came thundering toward Toroca, his giant stride carrying him quickly across the deck.

"What is it?" called the captain, his gravelly voice full of concern.

"The Others!" said Toroca. "They're turning back!"

Keenir put a hand up to shield his eyes. "So they are," he said, sounding disappointed.

"They must be afraid to sail out of sight of the Face," said Toroca. He looked at the captain, hoping the oldster would catch the irony. When Afsan had taken his pilgrimage voyage aboard the *Dasheter,* Keenir had supposedly had a similar fear, for no Quintaglio ship had yet sailed beyond the Face in the other direction.

"Perhaps we should turn and give chase," said Keenir.

"What?" said Toroca. "Good captain, they have weapons; they could sink us. Let them go."

Keenir was quiet for a moment, then nodded. "Aye, I suppose you're right." The Face of God slipped below the horizon, although the sky was lit up with Godglow. But then the captain pointed. "Look!"

Toroca turned. A few of the Other ships had given up and gone back, but most of the attack force continued in hot pursuit.

"I guess their fear of sailing beyond the Face wasn't that great," said Keenir.

"Maybe," said Toroca. "Or maybe, since they're in the right, most of them believe their god won't forsake them even if they sail beyond its view."

The captain grunted. Night came swiftly.

• • •

The images in the nine windows continued to change every forty beats or so: red blobs, tailless bipeds, strange reptilians, stilt-legged creatures, other things Novato couldn't begin to categorize.

And occasionally an oasis in all the madness: something familiar. Dybo's ruling room.

Still, it was too much to absorb, too much to take in. Floating in midair in front of the bank of windows, Novato's eyes glazed over, the windows becoming just nine squares of colored light flashing in front of her eyes, hypnotic, spellbinding, flashing, flashing . . .

She shook her head violently, trying to gain control of her faculties again. She decided to *not* look at the windows, to avert her eyes for a while, to concentrate on something—anything—else.

To the left of each window were three vertical strips of glowing red characters that changed each time the view in the window changed. The first and second strips were gibberish in the arkmaker's script, but the third was a simple diagram. In almost all cases it consisted of a single large circle at the top with a series of smaller circles trailing off below it. In every set, one of the smaller circles was white instead of red. The design seemed vaguely familiar to Novato, and she finally realized what it meant when the lower right window displayed the inside of Dybo's palace again. Beneath the big circle was a series of three small dots, then three big dots, and finally two more small dots. Rather than one of these being white, though, a tiny white point was glowing next to the second of the three big dots.

It was a chart of the solar system, Novato realized, grateful at last to have something else she recognized, something her mind could grasp. The big circle was the sun. The three small dots close to it represented the inner rocky worlds of Carpel, Patpel, and Davpel. The string of big dots were the three gas-giant worlds, Kevpel, the Face of God, and Bripel. And the final sequence of two small dots was the outer rocky world of . . . well, Gefpel, of course, and . . . and . . . a hitherto unknown eighth planet. The single white point next to the Face of God represented the location this window was looking in on—the Quintaglio moon.

She looked at the other windows, and her mind made the glorious leap. *All* of them were solar system maps—but of *other* solar systems, alien solar systems, solar systems never even dreamed of before this moment.

There were the strange bipedal reptiles again: the string of dots indicated that they lived on the fourth planet of a system of eleven worlds. And the beings with the seven pairs of stilt legs: the second planet of five. Novato was shocked to see that almost all of these creatures lived on small planets, rather than on the moons of giant worlds. The upper right monitor switched back to the world of the bizarre red globs that seemed to work in cooperation with other lifeforms. Incredible: that world had two large circles at the top of its display—*two* suns.

Although the view in the central zero window changed periodically, sometimes showing the black bipeds, sometimes the yellow, and sometimes a third variety that was beige, the little system map always remained the same: a sun circle, four small worlds—the third of which was illuminated—four large worlds, and a final small one.

Novato's mind was still reeling, still trying to deal with the onslaught of images and information. She realized that the central window never changed to show a different world, but, judging by the system map, simply showed different views of the same third planet. Yet that particular window was connected to all the others by thick black lines. No other connections were drawn between any of the other windows.

She stared at the windows and the interconnecting lines, her brain aching.

And then it hit her.

What she was seeing.

What it meant.

Home.

The world in the center.

It was the home world. The *original* home world.

The ark-makers had brought life from there to here. That's what the black line connecting the central window to the one that sometimes showed Dybo's ruling room indicated.

But the ark-makers had also brought life from the home world to that fourth planet in the system of eleven, to that second planet in the system of five, to the single planet that somehow orbited a double sun, to . . .

Novato's whole body was shaking. Floating in the air, she hugged herself tightly.

The home world.

Life scattered from there to stars across the firmament.

It was incredible.

Eyes wide, she watched the windows change, cycling from world to world.

Sometimes, the windows came up black.

Not just night, but solid black.

Novato's heart fluttered.

Black.

Windows onto nothingness.

Maybe the magic had failed after all this time. These windows were new, of course, but surely at the other end there were eyes of some sort that sent back these pictures. It had been a long time since the ark had crashed here. Maybe some of the eyes had failed in that time.

Or maybe whole worlds had died in the interim.

Novato's head pounded. She turned her attention again to the glowing white numbers overlapping the upper left corner of each window. The number that showed when the window looked in on the Quintaglio moon was 27. When showing the other bipedal reptiles, the number 26 was displayed. Ah, there were the stilt-legged aquatic creatures again; number 9. The red globs with their city of coral was number 1. She saw four numbers higher than 27, and all of them showed bipedal lifeforms covered with brown shag. And the central window always showed the horizontal mark of zero.

Slowly, it began to make sense. Her overloaded mind cleared, the fog lifting.

She'd seen the Quintaglios removed from prominence twice in her own lifetime. First, Afsan had taken them from the center of the universe. Then Toroca had shown they weren't divinely created from the hands of God. And now—this.

A total of thirty-one different worlds had been seeded with life from the home planet. And, if the numbering was in the order in which the life was transplanted, then the Quintaglios had been moved not first, nor last, but twenty-seventh—twenty-seventh out of thirty-one. No pride of place, just one of many.

Floating there in the vast chamber, she watched, fascinated, as the strange lifeforms were paraded by her. Red globs. Stilt-legged creatures. Intelligent reptiles. Tailless bipeds. Flying things. Crawling things. Things that had twenty arms. Things that had none. Windows cycling from world to world, the light of alien suns playing across her face.

She tried to absorb as much of it as she could.

But eventually she was left numb by it all, unable to take in anything further. The windows became a blur again, just nine colored squares.

She needed to take a break, needed to let her mind sort it all out. She decided to explore, to look at other parts of the vast structure at the top of the tower.

And that presented a problem.

She was too far away from any wall or from the floor or ceiling to reach out and touch it, and so she just floated there in the middle of the cube-shaped room. She tried flapping her arms, like a wingfinger, but that didn't seem to do any good. She soon realized she was in quite a predicament: she could starve to death floating here in midair, unable to make it back to the lifeboat, which held her food supplies.

But, after a moment, she calmed down, undid the chain that helped hold her sash in place and bit through the leather of the sash so that she had one long piece of green and black material. Cracking it like a whip against the wall containing the bank of windows, she was able to start herself tumbling slowly across the room. She made her way out into a corridor and continued along, kicking gently off walls. Most of what she saw was baffling, but at last she came to something she recognized: one of the ark-maker's doors, just like the one on the outside of the ark itself. It was a panel twice as tall as it was wide, with an incised orange rectangle with bold black markings on it set into the door's center.

Novato floated toward it—

—and the door opened. Of its own volition, the door slid aside. Incredible. She'd long suspected this was how such doors were supposed to work, having seen the gears and other equipment inside the ones down below. But they were all dead; the Quintaglios had had to remove orange faceplates from the center of the ark's door panels, exposing metal handles that could be cranked around by hand. Novato was sure now that those manual handles were for emergencies, when no power was available. That's why they were kept out of the way behind the orange panels.

Novato's inertia had carried her right through the door, but to her surprise she found herself hitting a wall almost at once. No . . . it wasn't a wall. It was a second door. This was another one of those confounded double-doored rooms.

But surely this door should have opened on its own, too? Oh, well: she'd operated enough of these things manually down below. She extended her claws and flicked back the little clips that held the orange panel in place. It popped forward, revealing the handle.

Novato reached for the handle and began to crank it around—

Suddenly, the door behind her began to slide shut, but her tail was sticking out through it. The door pushed against her tail, but before the pressure got too great it reversed itself and slid open again.

Novato heard—or perhaps felt was a better word—a sound. It was very high pitched, making her teeth rattle in their sockets and her claws itch. The door behind her had reversed again, touching her tail once more.

The sound was cycling back and forth, like a repetitive call.

Novato pulled again on the handle.

And then—

A sliver of blackness down the right side of the door.

A torrent of wind—

Incredible pain in her ears.

Her hands went to the sides of her head, completely covering her earholes.

Blood spurted from her nostrils.

Stars were visible down the black gap.

Stars.

Her skin tingled.

She slammed her eyes shut, inner and outer lids crunched tightly against the pressure mounting within her orbs.

Like a vast storm, air rushed through the opening.

Blood was leaking from her anus and her genital folds.

The evacuating air was pulling her toward the partially open door, but the opening was too small for her to be carried outside.

There was great pain, searing pain, claw-sharp pain . . .

And then the pain began to subside.

Everything began to subside.

Novato's consciousness ebbed away . . .

Chapter 23

Afsan came at once to the ruling room. The Emperor read the leather strip containing Toroca's message to him. Afsan had Dybo repeat the text twice. Finally, he shook his head. "We don't stand a chance."

"Why not?" said Dybo. "My imperial guards are well trained; our hunters have great prowess. Granted, victory will be difficult, but I don't see why it should be impossible. Besides, if these . . . these Others are coming here, we have the advantage of fighting on terrain familiar to us."

"That's irrelevant." Afsan's tail swished. "Consider this: our people are constrained by territoriality. Toroca says the Others are not. We might be able to bring ten or fifteen hunters together, but they can bring a hundred or even a thousand."

"They're only bringing forty boats," said Dybo. "Even a big ship like the *Dasheter* carries less than twenty people."

"That's territoriality again," said Afsan. "The *Dasheter* could carry a hundred people if they could be crowded together in multi-bunk rooms like those aboard the alien ark. Those forty ships could contain more people than in all of Capital City. If what Toroca says is correct, they could swarm over us, like insects over dead meat. We will be hopelessly outnumbered."

"Ah, but we are still true hunters, Afsan. Toroca says these Others need tools to kill animals. We kill with claws and teeth. We don't need tools."

Afsan nodded as if Dybo had just made his point for him. "The

First Edict of Lubal: 'A Quintaglio kills with tooth and claw; only such killing makes us strong and pure.' "

"That's right," said Dybo.

"Don't you see, though? The use of tools gives the Others advantages. We have to physically connect with our prey, putting ourselves at risk. They may have God knows what to aid them. Pointed sticks launched through the air, perhaps—when I was battling Kal-ta-goot aboard the *Dasheter,* I wished for such a thing. Or perhaps they use knives not just to strip and cut hides but actually to perform the kill."

"I've never heard of such things," said Dybo.

"No. Our religion forbids them. But they may use them. And these tools and weapons could amplify their individual abilities, Dybo."

"We must learn to do the same, then."

"Easier said than done. Recall the twenty-third scroll: 'Take not a weapon with you on the hunt, for that is the coward's way.' Your brave imperial guards will find it difficult to adopt what they've always been taught is a craven approach."

"So they will outnumber us and be better—what is the word?— equipped?" Dybo looked at Afsan. "Is there nothing in our advantage?"

Afsan leaned back on his tail, thinking. "Well, in his polemic on battles, Keladax once said that the most important thing you can have on your side is moral rectitude: being right in the eyes of God. But even that, I'm afraid, falls to the Others. If I understand Toroca's note properly, we attacked them first, and—"

"Nothing supersedes my people's right to survive," snapped Dybo. "I'd be a poor leader if I didn't hold that as a sacred truth." The Emperor's tail moved left and right. "We are killers to our very core, Afsan. That's our biggest advantage. That's why we will be victorious. We kill gladly. We kill easily. We kill for fun. The Others, judging by Toroca's missive, do not have that trait." Dybo had a faraway expression, as if visualizing the coming battle. "It's not often that I can say this, but you are wrong, good Afsan—totally and completely wrong. I know the Quintaglio people." His voice was determined. "The Others won't know what hit them."

Peace. Incredible peace. Calmness, like a still lake. Novato felt no pain, no angst, no guilt, no fear. Just tranquillity, a sense of halcyon simplicity.

And then an image. Like the space tower, with the sun at the top, but not quite. Something similar, yet different. A—a tunnel, with a pure white light at its end, purer and whiter and brighter than the sun itself, but visible without squinting, without pain.

Drifting, as she had within the lifeboat, without weight. Effortless movement. Drifting toward the light, the beautiful, perfect light.

She wasn't alone; Novato knew that. There were others here, others whom she knew. Familiar presences. Lub-Kaden, the hunt leader from her home Pack of Gelbo. And Irb-Falpom, first director of the Geological Survey of Land. And, and, why, yes, it was! Haldan. Dear sweet Haldan, one of her children by Afsan. And there, a youngster . . . why, could it be?

And then it came to her, softly, gently, a thought surprising, but not really, a thought that should have been disturbing, but wasn't disturbing at all.

Lub-Kaden had died on the hunt.

Irb-Falpom, huge and ancient, had passed peacefully in her sleep.

And Haldan—Haldan's passage had been hastened by her insane brother.

And the child . . . surely this was little Helbark.

Helbark, who had died of fever.

Dead.

All of them.

Dead.

Just like me.

But then another form appeared, a familiar form. Why, it was Karshirl, her daughter by Garios. She was all but lost in the glare of the strange white light. Ah, then this *was* a dream, surely, for Karshirl was still alive, was waiting for her down at the base of the tower. Strange, though, the way the younger female stood there, as if now, at last, she wanted to talk, to spend time with Novato, to know her mother.

Such beautiful light.

The dream didn't frighten Novato. Nothing, she thought, could frighten her so long as she was in the presence of that hypnotic, wondrous light.

The light's edges were diffuse and yet she thought that maybe, just maybe, she could discern a shape in that light, a form in the illumination.

A Quintaglio. A giant Quintaglio, bigger than the biggest

thunderbeast. Maybe, just maybe . . .

It was in profile now, this glowing Quintaglio.

It had no arms.

It was God.

But then the periphery of the light shifted, shimmered, and whatever form she'd thought she'd seen there was gone, lost in the glorious whiteness.

She wanted to approach closer, to be with the light, but new images were crowding her mind, a cascade of images, images blowing in the wind.

Her first pilgrimage voyage. The Face of God at the zenith, a magnificent banded crescent . . .

Getting her hunter's tattoo, holding her jaw firmly shut, determined not to yelp as the metal lance repeatedly pierced the skin on the side of her head . . .

She and her creche-mate, Daldar, running through the forest together . . .

A culling—surely not her own! One she must have seen at some other point. A group of eight hatchlings half-running, half-stumbling across the birthing sands, while a giant male Quintaglio—a bloodpriest—gave chase, his purple robes billowing about him. One after another, hatchlings were caught in his gaping maw and then slid down his distended throat . . .

A happier sight: her first meeting with gruff old Var-Keenir, when the master mariner had sought her out to acquire one of her far-seers. She'd beamed with pride at that, and all of Pack Gelbo had treated her with new respect . . .

The sight of Kevpel through the big far-seer she'd set up at the summit of the dormant Osbkay volcano. Kevpel's glorious rings, its retinue of moons, its beautiful banded cloud tops . . .

That first glorious time she'd beat her teaching master at a game of *lastoontal* . . .

Being there, aboard the *Dasheter,* to see her first clutch of eggs hatch, the eight babies using their little birthing horns to break through their shells, then tumbling out onto the wooden deck of the ship . . .

Soaring through the air during that incredible first flight aboard the *Tak-Saleed* . . .

And that time, long ago, with Afsan. Dear, wonderful Afsan. He'd seemed so awkward and gawky—just a skinny adolescent, really—when he'd shown up at her workplace in the old temple of Hoog. But what a mind he had! And what wonderful and startling truths they'd found by pooling their observations. And that night, when she suddenly found herself receptive, suddenly found herself with him inside her. That wonderful night—

Mokleb had co-opted Pettit, Afsan's apprentice, to do some research for her. Pettit knew what time Afsan's usual appointment with Mokleb was, and so she waited for Mokleb along the path that led to Rockscape. The young apprentice stood in plain sight, in the middle of the path, so that Mokleb would be sure to see her well in advance. After ritual greetings were exchanged, Pettit spoke: "I have that information you requested."

"Ah, good," said Mokleb. "Tell me."

"Empress Sar-Sardon arrived in Pack Carno on the nineteenth day of Dargo in kiloday 7096."

Mokleb's inner eyelids fluttered. "The nineteenth? Are you certain?"

"Oh, yes," said Pettit. "There's a commemorative stone in Carno's territory. There's a fine etching of it in the archives here; the date was easy to read."

"There's no chance that the Empress's arrival was delayed, so that the date was wrong?"

"None. They tell me the date was carved in the presence of the Empress, and that the Empress then added her own cartouche, chiseled with the aid of a stencil. I checked with Porgon, who's in charge of palace protocol. Of course, it was his master's master who handled such things back then, but he said that's the way it's always done: the date not carved until the Empress was actually there."

"And how long did Empress Sardon stay with Pack Carno?"

"Less than a day. Indeed, I spoke to one oldster who used to be with Carno but now lives here who remembers Sardon's visit well. She said the Empress was there for only the better part of an afternoon."

"Incredible," said Mokleb, shaking her head. "Did you also check the creche records, as I asked?"

"Yes. The originals are still with Carno, but copies are kept here in the Capital. I found the duplicate record of Afsan's hatching. The date is exactly as Afsan had said."

Mokleb stood their, shaking her head. "And the sequence of hatchings?" she said.

"Six clutches were laid that season in Carno; Afsan's was the second last to hatch."

"You're sure?"

"That's what the documents say. Allow me to approach closer; I've copied out the birth records for you."

"Hahat dan."

Pettit moved close, handed over a limp piece of writing leather, then backed off.

Mokleb was silent for a long time, staring at the sheet. After a while, Pettit said, "Um, will that be all?"

"Hmm? My apologies. Yes. Yes, it will. Thank you very much."

Pettit bowed. "I hope the information is of some use."

"Oh, yes," said Mokleb. "Yes, indeed."

Suddenly, Novato was awake.

Breathing.

Alive.

She opened her eyes.

The strip of black along the edge of the door was gone. The outer door of the double-doored room had closed; either she had pulled the handle or perhaps it had slid shut of its own volition.

She was floating again.

And there was air all around her.

Air and, drifting about, rounded globs of blood.

Novato ached all over, especially her eyes, which felt as if they'd been under great strain.

She touched her left earhole. It was caked with dried blood. Her right earhole was the same. She brought her palms together in a loud clap. She could still hear, thank God.

God.

She'd been dying. *Dying.* And she'd come back.

It had been so peaceful, so inviting.

And all those memories, those wonderful memories. Every moment of her life.

But it wasn't her time. Not yet. There was still work to be done.

She had to go back. Kicking gently off the outer door, she propelled herself back into the corridor. Further kicks pushed her through the cubic room with the wall of nine windows and out into the staging area. She found her lifeboat, got in, and touched the panel that made the door disappear. The lifeboat began its long trek down to the ground. Although her entire body ached, Novato floated serenely in midair, absolutely at peace with herself.

Chapter 24

Afsan spent most of his days now in consultation with Dybo and members of the imperial staff, preparing for the arrival of the Others. They had developed a plan for defending Capital Harbor, and the engineers and chemists were now hard at work devising the equipment needed. Still, Mokleb had impressed upon Afsan that the talking cure could not be interrupted, so every second day, for one daytenth, Afsan left the palace office building and came out to Rockscape.

"Remember one of our early sessions in which you discussed your childhood with Pack Carno?" asked Mokleb.

"No," said Afsan. Then, "Wait—yes. Yes, I remember that. Goodness, that was ages ago."

"Very early in the therapy, yes. Remember you said you had wished there had been other people like you, others who would have accepted you."

"I suppose I said that."

"You did. I keep verbatim notes." A rustling of paper. "Afsan: 'It didn't seem fair, that's all. It seemed that somewhere there should have been people more like me, people who shared my interests, people to whom my mathematical skill was nothing special.'

"Mokleb: 'But there was no one like that in Carno.'

"Afsan: 'No. Except perhaps . . . '

"Mokleb: 'Yes?'

"Afsan: 'Nothing.'

"Mokleb: 'You must share your thoughts.'

"Afsan: 'It's gone now. I've forgotten what I was going to say.' "

Afsan shifted uncomfortably on his rock. "Yes, I recall that exchange."

"Well, I know whom you were thinking of, Afsan. I know precisely whom you were thinking of."

"Oh?"

"In a much later session, you mentioned the visit of Empress Sar-Sardon to your home Pack of Carno."

"That's right. I didn't know it was Sardon at the time—guess I was too young to understand such things—but later I learned that it had been her. But, Mokleb, I can assure you that Sardon wasn't whom I was thinking of."

"No, of course not. Now, this is crucial: are you sure it was Sardon?"

"Yes."

"Absolutely sure? There's no chance that you witnessed the visit of some other dignitary? The provincial governor, perhaps? Or a lesser palace official?"

"No, I'm sure it was Sardon. I remember the blood-red sash; only members of The Family wear those. Why do you ask?"

"Do you know what kiloday that was?"

"I haven't a clue."

"It was 7196."

"Really? Then I would have been—"

"Less than a kiloday old. Much less, in fact, for, according to palace records, Empress Sardon visited Carno on a tour through Arj'toolar in the sixth tenth of that kiloday."

"Fascinating."

"Do you remember anything of your life *before* that?"

"It's hard to tell. I've got lots of memories, but as to which came first, I can't say."

"Do you remember the creche?"

"Of course."

"Do you remember clutches of eggs in the creche?"

"You mean while I was still living in the egg chamber? Goodness, that was a *long* time ago. Other clutches of eggs? No. No, I can't say that I—wait a beat. Wait a beat. Yes, I—now that you mention it, I *do* remember one other clutch. Eight eggs, laid in a circle."

Mokleb shook her head. "That's incredible."

"Oh?"

"You were part of the second-last clutch to hatch during that hatching season, were you aware of that?"

"No."

"Well, it's true. The bloodpriests keep meticulous records, copies of which eventually end up in the census bureau here in Capital City. There *was* one other clutch that hatched after yours."

"Indeed?"

"Yes. And it hatched *eight* days after your own clutch did."

"Eight days? But that would mean . . ."

"That would mean you have a memory from when you were just eight days old—maybe earlier, even."

"Is that normal?"

"Who can say? No one has really studied early memories before."

"Eight days, you say. It seems incredible, but I'm sure I remember those eggs. Not well, you understand—the memory is dim. But I'm sure of it nonetheless."

"Do you remember anything before that?"

"Like what?" Afsan clicked his teeth. "Like breaking out of my eggshell?"

"Yes. Do you remember that?"

"Oh, be serious, Mokleb."

"I am. Do you remember that?"

"I—no. I don't think so. I mean, I've seen eggs hatch before. In the very creche I was born in, for that matter, when I paid a return visit to Carno kilodays ago. So, yes, I have mental pictures of eggs cracking open in that creche, of little birthing horns piercing shells. But of my *own* hatching? No, no memories that I'm aware of."

"And what about the culling?"

"The culling by the bloodpriest?" Afsan shuddered. "No. No, I do not remember that."

"Are you sure?"

"That's something I wouldn't be likely to forget." Afsan seemed shaken. "I saw a culling once, you know. During that same trip back to Carno. I came through the wrong door into the creche. Most horrifying thing I've ever seen. Babies running across the sands, and a bloodpriest, his purple robe swirling around him, chasing them down, swallowing them whole, his gullet distending as each one slid into his stomach." Afsan shook his head.

"Did you say purple robe?"

"Yes—that's the color bloodpriests wear, at least in Arj'toolar, and I'd assume elsewhere, too."

"A purple robe . . . swirling around him."

"Yes, you know: swirling, flapping up."

"*Flapping.* Like wings of cloth?"

"I suppose."

"*Like a purple wingfinger?*"

Afsan pushed off his rock and got to his feet. "Good God."

"You saw a bloodpriest once as an adult. And we've already established that you have a memory that's at most from your eighth day of life. The culling of your own clutch of eggs would have taken place on your second, third, or, depending on the availability of the bloodpriest and on whether the alignment of the moons was appropriate for the sacrament, your fourth day of life. Are you sure you don't remember it?"

"I tell you I do not."

"Forgive me, good Afsan, but I suggest that you *do* remember it."

Afsan spread his arms. "You can see my muzzle, Mokleb. I'm sure it's as green as yours."

She held up her hands. "I meant no insult. I don't mean you can consciously remember it, but that subconsciously, perhaps, you do recall it."

Afsan sounded exasperated. "Surely a memory that can't be recalled consciously is no memory at all."

"I'd have agreed with you before I began my studies, Afsan. But events from our past *do* affect our present actions, even if we can't voluntarily summon up the memories."

"That makes no sense," said Afsan.

"Ah, but it does. It does indeed. Have you ever wondered why Quintaglios fight territorial battles to the death, when animals do not? Animals are content to engage in a bluffing display, or to quickly determine who is the strongest without drawing blood. Although we call ourselves civilized and refer to the animals as wild, it's we who don't stop when instinct tells us we should. Instead, we fight with jaws and claws until one of us—even if it is a friend or creche-mate—is dead. Why is that? Why do we do that?"

"I admit that question has puzzled me."

"And me as well—until now. Afsan, we're *traumatized.*"

"Traumatized? The kind of injury that leaves one in shock?"

"Forgive me; I'm using the word in a slightly different way. I'm not referring to physical injury, but rather to emotional injury. Something that causes lasting damage to the mind."

"Traumatized, you say? By what?"

Mokleb's tail swished. "By the culling of the bloodpriests! Each of us was once part of a . . . a family, of eight siblings. Each of us had brothers and sisters. We hatched together, we spent a day or two or three becoming used to each other, impressing each other, *bonding* with each other. And then what happens? An adult—a male, the first we've ever seen—swoops in and chases us, and seven of the eight die, gulped down by the bloodpriest. We *see* it happen, see our brothers and sisters devoured. You said that, even as an adult, watching a culling was the most horrifying thing you'd ever seen. Imagine the impact, then, of that sight on a child! And imagine, too, the guilt that goes with the eventual realization that you lived only because you outran your seven siblings, that the price of your life was that they died horribly."

"But I don't recall my culling!"

"Not consciously, to be sure. But it's there, Afsan, deep in your mind, beneath the surface, shaping your perceptions, your mental processes. You said, in that early therapy session, that there had been no one in Carno who shared your interests, no one to whom your mathematical skill might have been nothing special. No one . . . no one *except,* you said, and then you trailed off. No one except your dead brothers and sisters, Afsan! They would have been more like you than different; you learned that by seeing your own children. And you remember your brothers. You remember your sisters. *All seven of them.*"

"That's impossible . . ."

"They are there, in every one of your fears and bad dreams. You said my interpretation of your fear of Saleed was nonsense. You were afraid that he would dispatch you—the very word you used—just as he had dispatched his six other previous apprentices, to make room for the eighth and final apprentice you were sure must come. You said that couldn't possibly be related to the culling of a bloodpriest, who likewise judges youngsters, dispatching seven and only keeping the eighth. It couldn't be related to that, you said, because you hadn't learned about the culling until after you'd left Saleed. But you already knew about the culling. You'd seen it with your own eyes! You'd seen your seven brothers and sisters die, and it's the memory of the seven of them that haunts your dreams. Fourteen arms clawing at your own—the arms of seven siblings who died so you could live. The voices calling out 'I,' 'you,' 'we'—seven long-forgotten siblings, a part of you, yet separate, seven voices that no matter how hard you try, you can no longer hear. The birthing sands, soaked with blood—the blood of your dead brethren. And swooping over it all, the purple wingfinger, representing the ravenous bloodpriest!"

Afsan staggered back on his tail, his breathing ragged. "Maybe. Maybe."

"It's true, Afsan. Face it! What's the one purely joyous thing in your life, the one thing that gives you no trepidation, no fear?"

"I don't—"

"Your relationship with Novato, isn't that right? The only thing that calms you, relaxes you. You told me yourself that you used to fall into peaceful sleep by imagining her face. Of course you chose that image! She's the one thing in all your life that is untouched by the culling of the bloodpriests. Indeed, she represents for you the very opposite, for the egglings she and you jointly created were *exempted* from the culling. But everything else—from your old fear of being replaced as Saleed's apprentice to your guilt over the reinstatement of the bloodpriests—is related to that long-buried memory of seeing your seven brothers and sisters devoured so that you could live."

"I told you, I don't feel guilt over the reinstatement of the bloodpriests."

"Don't you? Do you remember when your bad dreams began?"

"You've asked me that before, and I've told you."

"Yes. Two kilodays before we began our therapy. During the time when the bloodpriests were in disrepute. During the time of the mass *dagamant*. During the time when Dybo was being challenged by his brother."

"Yes."

"And what was your role in all that?"

"I don't see what you're getting at . . ."

"Yes, you do. *You* came up with the solution to the challenge against Dybo. And what was that solution?"

"That he and his siblings . . . oh, my God—that he and his siblings undergo a culling, that they be chased around a stadium by a giant blackdeath, just as the hatchlings in a normal clutch are chased and devoured by a bloodpriest."

"And what was the result?"

"Six of Dybo's siblings were devoured."

"Devoured because of *your* suggestion."

"No . . . no, it was just . . ." Afsan was shaking, his whole body convulsing. "No, it was the only way. Don't you see? The only way—"

"*You* engineered a culling. *You,* in essence, became a blood-priest. You, whose low mind *remembered* the culling your own clutch had gone through, who later had stumbled onto another culling in progress, children swallowed whole in front of your eyes, you *became* a bloodpriest . . ."

"No . . ."

"And six died, on top of the seven siblings of yours who had already died so you could live."

"There was no other answer . . ."

"Exactly! You lamented that yourself when we discussed your *dagamant* aboard the *Dasheter.* Living our lives should not require killing others of our own kind. 'By the very Egg of God,' you said, 'it shouldn't!' "

"That's right! It shouldn't."

"But it *does*! Starting right in the creche: those of us who are alive today live because seven of our siblings died. And to solve the challenge to Dybo, you yourself, who hated the necessity of death so that others could live, you *became* a bloodpriest."

"No. We used a blackdeath . . ."

"A blackdeath is a dumb brute. *You* engineered the replay of the culling. *You* were responsible. *You* were the bloodpriest."

"No."

"And now you must face that truth. Do you see it, Afsan? *Do you see it?*"

"I can't see *anything,* Mokleb."

"Because your mind *refuses* to see. Even with working eyes, your mind refuses to look upon what you have done, what you have become."

Afsan's voice was growing shrill. "I don't believe you."

"Think! Most people are traumatized once by a bloodpriest, when their own clutch is culled. You've been traumatized *three* times: first at your own culling, then when you stumbled into Carno's creche as an adult, and finally again when you engineered the battle with the blackdeath—when you became that which you feared most. When you became a bloodpriest!"

"Shut up!" screamed Afsan.

"You became a bloodpriest, Afsan. In your own mind, that's what you are."

"Back off!" shouted Afsan, his claws coming out into the light. "Give me room!"

"A bloodpriest!"

"You're invading my territory!"

"That's the real trauma, Afsan—that's what's preventing you from seeing! The *shame* of what you became. In your own eyes you'd become evil, and now those eyes refuse to see."

Afsan was bobbing from the waist. "Back off! Back off now!"

"You refuse to see!"

"Back off before I *kill* you."

"The trauma!" shouted Mokleb.

"No!"

"Face the trauma!"

"I'll kill you!" Afsan's voice had changed to a low, guttural tone, an animal's tone. "I'll kill you!" he shouted again. And then, low, slurred, a voice from deep within his chest: *"I'll swallow you whole!"*

He bobbed up and down in full *dagamant,* enraged, wild, a killing machine.

Mokleb turned from Afsan, hiding her eyes so that she would not be drawn into the madness. She ran as fast as she could from Rockscape. Behind her, Afsan continued to bob up and down, up and down, unable to sight anything to kill.

Chapter 25

Garios had been counting the days until Novato would return. He did not know what to expect. He'd watched, amazed, as the long waves of the landquake had worked their way up the tower. Had Novato survived that? Even if she had, had some other tragedy befallen her in the twenty days she'd been gone? If nothing else, would having been cooped up in such a small space for that long have driven her mad?

Garios had brought to the base of the tower everything Novato might possibly need: water in case her supply had been exhausted; freshly killed meat in case she was hungry; leather blankets in case she was cold; wooden splints in case she had broken a limb. He'd also tethered a runningbeast outside the entrance so that he could make his escape if Novato had been driven to *dagamant* by her own pheromones and the tight confines of the lifeboat.

There was no way to know how long Novato had spent outside the lifeboat at the top, so Garios couldn't be sure when she'd return. The only warning of her impending arrival would be actually sighting the lifeboat coming down. Garios sat on the beach, looking up, and waited.

Garios saw many wingfingers, as well as pale spots behind the clouds that must have been moons, but, as the old saying went, a watched carcass never finishes draining. The sun was setting when at last he saw the lifeboat emerge from the bottom of the cloud layer. Garios was surprised to find his claws sneaking out; he was more apprehensive about Novato's return than he'd thought.

He hurried down the long blue corridor and arrived at the end of its 140-pace length just in time to see the lifeboat complete its journey, a faint whistle accompanying its reduction in velocity. It came to rest at the bottom of the shaft.

Nothing happened for an interminable time. Garios watched his own worried face being reflected back from the curving metal of the lifeboat. And then, at last, the hull appeared to liquefy and when it regained a solid appearance, a large doorway had appeared in its side.

Novato staggered out, apparently having some difficulty walking. She leaned back on her tail after each step. Almost from head to toe, her skin was the purple-blue of bruises, as if somehow her entire surface area had been subjected to an assault.

"My God!" declared Garios. "What happened to you?"

Novato's expression was totally serene. "Something wonderful," she said.

"I'll summon a healer. We'll get you fixed up."

"I'm fine," said Novato. "Really, I am." She beamed at Garios. "It's so good to see you again, my friend."

"You're sure you are all right?"

"I'm better than I've ever been before, Garios. How is everyone down here?"

"Most of us are fine," said Garios, "but there is some bad news, I'm afraid. It happened while you were away, during the landquake."

"I know," said Novato, an absolutely calm, peaceful look on her face. "Karshirl is dead, isn't she?"

An even-day passed, and then it was odd-day again. As the time for their appointment approached, Mokleb walked the path to Rockscape with trepidation. Had she gone too far in her last session with Afsan? She was normally not so brutal with her patients, but, by the Eggs of Creation, she'd had to make Afsan see her point.

It was a lackluster day. The gibbous Big One made a dull smudge behind a stack of clouds on the eastern horizon. The sun was a point drilling through other clouds as it slid down the western sky. Wingfingers of every color—every color except purple, that is—flitted across the gray firmament.

The path to Rockscape took a sharp bend to avoid a thick copse of trees just before it rounded out onto the field of carefully arrayed boulders. Mokleb was too far from Capital City to hear the drums from the Hall of Worship, but was sure that she was on time. She rounded the grouping of trees, and Rockscape was visible before her.

It was deserted.

Afsan wasn't there.

Mokleb felt her heart sink.

She *had* been too hard on him. He'd curtailed their sessions. The penalty of wasting part of a volume of Saleed's treatise was hardly enough in the face of what she'd made him go through last time.

She was about to leave when a thought struck her. She'd sat on a couple of the Rockscape boulders over the course of her long association with Afsan, but had never actually touched the one called Afsan's rock. She made her way across the field, through the ancient geometric patterns, and came to the large, proud boulder. Mokleb reached out with her left hand and lightly patted the stone. It was worthy of Afsan: strong, hard, weather-beaten, but, despite all it had been through, placidly surviving.

Surviving.

She wondered if she'd ever see Afsan again, if he'd ever forgive her for their last session. She had no desire to be near anyone else today. She began to amble on in the same direction, heading through Rockscape toward the lands beyond.

"Wait!"

Mokleb turned. Emerging from the mouth of the path, beside the dense copse of trees, was Pal-Cadool. "Wait!" he shouted again, and ran toward her, his long legs covering the distance quickly. Mokleb stood dumbfounded as Cadool came within eight paces of her. "Don't go," said Cadool. "Afsan is coming."

She looked back toward the mouth of the path. Soon Afsan did indeed appear. He held his walking stick in his left hand, and his right was on Gork's harness. Mokleb hurried over to Afsan as fast as she could with her bad knee, Cadool loping alongside. Once the distance between them had closed as much as it reasonably could, Mokleb blurted out, "I thought you weren't coming."

Afsan's face was a portrait in joy. "I'm sorry, Mokleb," he said. And then, with a deep bow, *"I overslept."*

Chapter 26

Mokleb and Afsan headed back to their usual rocks. Afsan was eager to understand all the implications of what Mokleb had revealed in their last session.

"If your low mind remembers your culling by the bloodpriests," said Mokleb, "then the same is probably true for all Quintaglios. I suspect our suppressed memories of the culling manifest themselves most in the territorial challenge. When we end up in a fight with another, we *don't* behave sensibly or logically or instinctively. Instead, our minds, our traumatized minds, cause us to fight uncontrollably until we or our opponent is dead."

"You sound like Emperor Dybo. He thinks that trait in us will allow us to defeat the Others."

Mokleb nodded. "He's probably right."

"But it sounds like you're saying we're insane."

"That's a strong word. I might say 'irrational' instead. But yes, as a race, we're deranged."

"But by definition the majority is always sane. Insanity or irrationality is an aberration from the norm."

"That's a semantic game, Afsan, and a dangerous one to play. There was a time when many of our ancestors practiced cannibalism. Today, we find that concept abhorrent. There *is* a higher arbiter of conduct than simple mob majority."

"Perhaps," said Afsan. "But what does the culling of the bloodpriest have to do with the territorial frenzy of *dagamant*? It sounds as though you're trying to link the two."

"I am indeed. It's the traumatizing effect of the culling that causes us to have such a wild reaction to territorial invasions. Think about it! The very first time we see someone invade our territory—that someone being the bloodpriest—it results in death and destruction and unspeakable horror right in front of our eyes! No wonder our reaction to future invasions is so strong—far stronger than any animal instinct would require."

Afsan's tail shifted as he considered this. "It's a neat theory, Mokleb, I'll give you that. But you know what you suggest is only a pre-fact, only a proposition. You can't test it."

"Ah, good Afsan, that's where you are wrong. *It already has been tested.*"

"What do you mean?"

"Consider your son Toroca."

"Yes?"

"We've discussed him before. He has no sense of territoriality."

"He doesn't like people talking about that."

"Well, doubtless it causes him some embarrassment. But it's true, isn't it? He feels no need to issue a challenge when another encroaches on his physical space."

"That is correct."

"And when he sees the Others, he, alone amongst those who have encountered them, has no adverse reaction. What was it his missive said? 'Mere sight of them triggers *dagamant* in all of us except me.'"

"Yes."

"Well, don't you see? Don't you see why that is? What's different about Toroca?"

"He's—ah! No, Mokleb, it can't be that simple . . ."

"But it is! I'm sure of it. What's different about Toroca is that he did *not* undergo the culling of the bloodpriest. None of the offspring of yourself and Wab-Novato did."

"But not all of them are without territoriality," said Afsan.

"No, that's true, although as near as I've been able to determine, none of them has ever been involved in a territorial challenge."

"It pains me to bring up this subject, Mokleb, but what about my son Drawtood . . ."

"Ah, yes. The murderer." Mokleb raised a hand. "Forgive me, I shouldn't have said that. But, yes, Drawtood poses a problem. He killed two of your other children."

Afsan's voice was small. "Yes."

"But consider, good Afsan, exactly how he committed the, ah, the crimes."

"He approached his siblings," said Afsan, "presumably with stealth, and slit their throats with a jagged mirror."

"You've said that before, yes. Let's consider that. He was able to come very, very close to his siblings apparently without triggering their territorial reflexes."

"He snuck up on them," said Afsan.

"Perhaps. Or perhaps their own senses of territoriality were so subdued as to allow him to approach them openly."

Afsan said nothing for a long time, then, slowly, the word hissing out like escaping breath: "Perhaps."

"And do you remember, Afsan, the mass *dagamant* that ensued while the bloodpriests were temporarily in disrepute?"

"How could anyone forget that?" Afsan said, his voice heavy.

"Indeed. But who quelled the madness? Who rode into town atop a shovelmouth, leading a stampede of prey beasts so that the violence could be turned away from killing Quintaglios and onto hunting food?"

"Pal-Cadool."

"Cadool, yes. A trained animal handler, and, if you'll forgive me for saying so, one who has subsumed his personal sense of territoriality into defending *your* territory. His actions were dictated by the fact that he perceived you to be in danger. But who else aided in the quelling of the rage? Who else rode atop a shovelmouth, this time from the imperial stockyards?"

Afsan's head snapped up, his muzzle swinging toward Mokleb. "Why—Emperor Dybo."

"Dybo! Indeed. And what do Dybo and your son Toroca have in common?"

"I don't see . . ."

"Think about it! What caused the bloodpriests to be banished from the Packs?"

"The revelation that there had been malfeasance involving the imperial creche," said Afsan. "All eight imperial egglings had been allowed to live."

"Precisely! All eight egglings got to live. Just like Toroca, Dybo never faced the culling of the bloodpriest, never suffered the trauma of seeing his infant brothers and sisters swallowed whole."

"Perhaps," said Afsan. "Perhaps." And then: "But I've seen Dybo on the verge of *dagamant*. Aboard the *Dasheter,* during our pilgrimage voyage, when he was attacked by Gampar."

"But you told me it was you, not Dybo, who killed that sailor. Nothing you said indicated that Dybo would have, of his own volition, fought Gampar to the death. I believe he would not have, except if necessary in rational self-defense. But on his own, when it mattered most, during the mass *dagamant* of kiloday 7128, Dybo did *not* succumb to the madness. He was able to function rationally because he had never been traumatized by witnessing the bloodpriest's culling."

Afsan looked thoughtful. "Incredible," he said at last. "So what you're saying is—"

"What I'm saying is that no future generation must go through the trauma of the culling of the bloodpriests. You said it yourself, Afsan. Parenting is the key: the relationship between ourselves and our children. We must find another way to control our population. Never again must children have their minds shocked that way. We *can* change this, this *madness* within ourselves. It's not instinct that we have to overcome—not at all! Rather, it's *abuse* of our children that we must put an end to."

The *Dasheter* was finally close enough to Land that Keenir felt he could risk pulling away from the Other ships, confident that they'd follow the same course the rest of the way in. He unfurled the *Dasheter*'s two remaining sails, and his ship leapt ahead of the armada, letting the Quintaglios arrive back at Land five days before the Others would get there.

As soon as the *Dasheter* had docked, Toroca and Keenir hurried to an audience with Emperor Dybo.

Garios had immediately told Novato of Dybo's summons for her to return to Capital City. Garios, of course, wasn't about to let Novato go back alone to where Afsan was, so they boarded a fast ship and headed out together. But once back in the Capital, Novato had left Garios and gone to see Afsan anyway. When Garios next saw her, she was walking with the blind sage, who was accompanied by his large lizard.

"Hello, Garios," said Novato as they drew nearer. "May we enter your territory?"

Garios looked up, his long muzzle swinging from Novato to Afsan, then back again. *"Hahat dan."*

"It's a pleasure to be with you again, Garios," said Afsan.

"Afsan," said Garios, somewhat curtly. Then, perhaps regretting his tone, he added, "I cast a shadow in your presence."

"And I in yours," said Afsan.

There was a protracted silence.

"I've made my choice," said Novato.

Garios's voice betrayed his hope. "Yes?"

Novato's tone was soft. "I'm sorry, Garios, but it has to be Afsan again."

Garios's tail swished. "I see."

"I know you were hoping otherwise," said Novato. "Please understand, I never wanted to hurt you."

"No," said Garios. "No, of course not."

Afsan's toeclaws were churning the soil. "However," he said, "it would be a loss to our species to not have more offspring from one so gifted as you."

"That's kind of you to say," said Garios, his tone neutral.

"Will you walk with us?" said Afsan. "There's someone I'd like to meet. Someone I've, ah, grown quite close to myself."

"Who is it?"

"Her name is Mokleb," said Afsan. "Nav-Mokleb."

"Oh?" A pause. "May I be so bold to ask how old she is?"

Afsan shrugged. "I really don't know. I've never seen her."

"Oh. I thought perhaps you were getting at . . . Never mind."

"But I think you will find her quite, ah, open to new acquaintances," said Afsan. "I've had a certain amount of trouble resisting her myself. Come along, Garios. She really is a fascinating person."

Despite territoriality, Quintaglios in Capital City favored apartment blocks over individual dwellings because they withstood landquakes better and were easier to repair. Novato had been pleased to find her own apartment just as she'd left it when she'd departed the Capital for the Fra'toolar dig; of course, she'd taken all the usual precautions, such as moving breakables off shelves and placing them on the floor before departing on her long trip.

But all those objects had now been put back up on the shelves, leaving a wide open expanse of floor—an expanse of floor that was just right for what was about to come. She and Afsan lay together on it. The windows were closed, letting Novato's pheromones build up in the room. They lay there, five paces between them, talking about things that were important to them, about experiences they'd shared together, joys they'd known, and some sorrows, too, talking softly, warmly, intimately, as Novato's pheromones wafted over them.

They talked for daytenths on end, teeth clicking freely at fondly remembered times they'd spent together. Finally, intoxicated by the pheromones, his dewlap puffing, Afsan pushed off the floor and, despite his blindness, moved unerringly toward Novato. He placed his hand on her shoulder, touching her, feeling the warmth of her skin. His claws remained sheathed; so did hers. He stroked her shoulder lightly, back and forth, feeling the appealing roughness of her hide. Novato moaned softly.

And, at last, more than twenty kilodays after the first time, Afsan moved even closer to her still. The two of them savored every moment.

The next morning, Afsan and Novato woke slowly, their tails overlapping, the euphoria of the night before still upon them. Afsan was expected back at what was now called the war room in the palace office building; final tests of his designs were to be conducted today. He could not touch Novato again, but there was a warmth in her voice that thrilled every part of him. He bade her good day, and called for Gork to lead him on his way. But as they were walking along, Afsan heard the sound of feet approaching. "Who's there?" he called out.

"Hello, Afsan. I've been looking all over for you."

"Toroca!" Afsan's voice was warm as he reigned Gork in. "*Hahat dan,* boy, *hahat dan.* It's good to hear your voice again."

"And yours, Afsan." Toroca, taking advantage of Afsan's blindness, allowed himself the luxury of approaching within four paces of the older Quintaglio. Gork padded over to Toroca, tasting the air with a forked tongue.

"This is a time for reunions," said Afsan. "Novato is back, too."

"I haven't seen her yet," said Toroca, "but I'm looking forward to it."

"I take it the *Dasheter* is safely docked, then?" Afsan said, leaning back on his tail.

"Yes, late last evening. I've spent most of the night briefing Dybo."

"And did Dybo tell you what we've got planned?"

"Planned—no, I did all the talking. We tried to summon you to join us, but you weren't at either Rockscape or your apartment."

Afsan looked away. "This message you sent by wingfinger— what news about that?"

Toroca looked his father up and down. It was so very good to see him again. "The *Dasheter* had no trouble outrunning the Other ships, but they are indeed in hot pursuit. They will be here in four or five days, Keenir estimates."

"We will be ready for them," said Afsan, his voice uncharacteristically hard.

Toroca's tail moved nervously. "That's what I came to speak to you about."

Afsan waited.

"This whole thing, Afsan: it's our fault. We were the aggressors."

"So your missive indicated." Afsan scrunched his muzzle. "But there's nothing to be done about that now."

"I can't agree with that," said Toroca. "I feel an obligation to try to prevent the coming battle."

Afsan tilted his head. "Is that possible?"

"I can interact with the Others, Afsan. My—my lack of territoriality, I guess . . . it lets me be with them. But so far, I'm the only one they've had direct contact with."

"If I understand this correctly, you're the only one they *could* have contact with."

"I don't think that's completely true, Afsan. It's not pheromones that trigger the violent response; when Keenir and I first encountered an Other, she was downwind of us. No, it's a reaction to the *appearance* of the Others. The appearance doesn't affect me, because of the way I am. And, good Afsan, you are blind: it could not affect you."

Afsan was quiet for a time, digesting this. At last he spoke. "Come over here, so you are downwind of me." Toroca obeyed. "There are not many people I can say such things to, but come closer. Come stand right by me."

Toroca moved nearer. "Yes?"

Afsan turned his muzzle to face his son, then lifted his eyelids.

"My . . . God," said Toroca. "Are they—are they glass?"

Afsan clicked his teeth lightly at the unexpected suggestion. "No. No, they're real."

"But eyes don't regenerate, and . . . and, anyway, it's been ages since you were blinded."

"I had an accident while you were away. I was kicked in the head by a hornface. There was substantial tissue damage. Healer Dar-Mondark thinks that may have something to do with it."

Toroca nodded. "Miraculous. I'm sorry; forgive me, Afsan. I should be jubilant for you. It's just that I was sure that if you could talk to the Others, you could help me prevent a slaughter. With the world coming to an end, there are more important matters than fighting. But now that you can see again . . ."

Afsan's voice was soft. "I cannot see, Toroca."

"But your eyes . . ."

"Do not work."

"That's . . . that's . . ."

"The phrase 'that's a kick in the head' comes to mind," said Afsan gently. "Unfortunately, the particular kick I got seemed to do only half a job."

"I assume there's something wrong with the way they regenerated, no?" Toroca stared intently into Afsan's dark orbs, as if trying to see their inner workings. "It has been such a long time, after all."

"No. As far as Dar-Mondark can tell, they regenerated perfectly. The problem, he suspects, is in my mind."

"Is there nothing that can be done?"

"I am, ah, undergoing therapy. There's a chance my sight will return."

"How long has this therapy been going on?"

"Forever, it seems."

"What are the chances of the therapy being successful in the next five days?"

"We've had, ah, a major breakthrough. But I still cannot see."

"Then perhaps you will risk coming with me to try to meet with the Others."

"What could I do?"

"Your whole life has been devoted to championing reason over emotion. It is irrational for us to be at war. There is an old proverb: only a fool fights in a building that's on fire. By working with the Others, we can perhaps save both our peoples. I have some vague ideas about how some of their technology could be adapted to spaceflight. But by wasting time on a conflict with them, none of us may get off this world. If they see that more Quintaglios than just myself want peace, perhaps we can convince them to turn back."

"And you think these . . . these Others will be receptive to an envoy of peace?"

"I don't know for sure. There is one Other who would be— Jawn is his name—but I'm not even sure if he's on board one of the boats coming this way. I thought I caught a glimpse of him once through your far-seer, but I can't be sure."

"And what will happen to us if the Others are not receptive?"

Toroca's voice did not waver. "They may kill us."

"You have never had much stomach for killing, my son," said Afsan. "I, on the other hand, have been revered as a great hunter."

"Of animals, Afsan. The Others are not animals."

"I suppose not."

"I can't believe you don't share my view that peace is the way. Dolgar said it: 'The intelligent person must abhor violence.' If there's any chance for peace, I must pursue it."

Afsan was quiet for a time. "What do you propose?"

Toroca's tail swished. "That we take a small boat out to meet the Others. If my friend Jawn is among them, he will come to talk with us. I know it."

"The chances of success are slim," said Afsan.

"I know that, too. But I must pursue the possibility."

"Nav-Mokleb, the savant helping me with my therapy, believes that anyone who did not undergo the culling of the bloodpriests might be able to interact with Others without falling into *dagamant*. That would mean your siblings, as well as the Emperor, and his sister Spenress, could have contact with them, too."

"What?" said Toroca. Then: "Hmm, an interesting suggestion. But we can't risk testing it aboard a boat. I'm positive you will be immune because you are blind. And besides, none of those people you mentioned could convince the Others of the danger facing the world. You've convinced the Quintaglio population of this; surely you can convince them, too."

"All right," said Afsan slowly. "All right. I will go with you."

Toroca had an urge to surge forward and touch Afsan. "Thank you," he said. "Thank you, Father."

Chapter 27

After his meeting with Toroca, Afsan went to find Pal-Cadool, who, much to Afsan's surprise, was just returning from his own meeting with Emperor Dybo. Afsan asked Cadool to take him to the Hall of Worship.

"You? To the Hall of Worship?" Cadool was incredulous.

"Yes," said Afsan. "I, ah, have need of a priest."

It was quite a distance to the Holy Quarter, and Afsan, as always, walked slowly, feeling his way with his stick. At last they entered the small antechamber of the temple, Gork waiting outside.

Det-Bogkash, the old Master of the Faith, had been fired by Dy-Dybo in 7128: as part of restoring order after the scandal involving the bloodpriests, Dybo had dismissed all senior clergy serving in the capital. Standing in the antechamber, Afsan called out the name of Bogkash's successor. "Edklark! Det-Edklark!"

A heavy, jovial priest, clad in plain white robes, came through a small doorway to greet them. "Do my eyes deceive me," said Edklark, "or has a miracle occurred right here in my Hall? Has Afsan come to church?"

Afsan ignored that. "Twenty kilodays ago," he said, "when I was held prisoner in the palace basement, I was visited by Det-Yenalb, who was Master of the Faith back then."

Edklark still seemed bemused. "Yes?"

"He strongly implied something that shocked me, something I'd never suspected."

"And what was that?" said Edklark.

"Yenalb implied that some priests, including himself, could lie in the light of day—that their muzzles did not flush blue with the liar's tint."

Edklark looked startled. "Yenalb said that?"

"Not in so many words, but, yes, he did imply it. I still remember exactly what he said: 'Not every person can be a priest. It takes a special disposition, special talents, special ways.' "

"And did you believe him?" said Edklark.

"At the time, my immediate reaction was that he was trying to frighten me, but now I must know the truth about this. Tell me, Edklark, can you lie openly?"

"Why, no, Afsan. Of course not."

"Cadool?"

"His muzzle remains green," said Cadool.

"Unfortunately, that proves nothing, since if you were capable of lying, you could be lying now."

Edklark clicked his teeth in what seemed to Afsan to be forced laughter. "Well, then you'll have to take my word for it."

"That is the one thing I cannot do," said Afsan. "Tell me a lie."

"Oh, be serious, Afsan. I—"

"Tell me a lie."

"Afsan, I cannot lie inside the Hall of Worship. That would be sacrilege."

"Then step outside."

"It would be sacrilege there, too, I'm afraid. Once ordained, a priest promises never to speak anything but God's own truth, even in the depths of night."

Afsan pushed his claws out of their sheaths and held his hand in plain sight. *"Tell me a lie, you worthless plant, or I will rip your throat out."*

Cadool's jaw dropped. "Afsan . . ."

"Shut up, Cadool. Priest, I will hear you lie. Don't provoke me further; three of us here in this confined space is enough to drive anyone to *dagamant*."

"Afsan," said Edklark, "I cannot lie . . ."

Afsan tipped forward from the waist and bobbed his torso, slowly, deliberately. It was clearly a mockery of the instinctual movements, but it was also well known that such play-acting often erupted into the real thing without warning.

"*Lie*, priest. The very future of our people is at stake."

"You have no authority to give me orders," said Edklark.

"I have all the authority I need," said Afsan, stepping closer to the priest. "You will do as I say."

The part of Edklark's tail visible beyond the hem of his robe was swishing in naked fear. "I have every wish to cooperate," he said.

"Then lie, animal dropping! Tell me—tell me that you are the Emperor."

"His Luminance Dy-Dybo is Emperor," said Edklark. "It is my honor to serve—"

Afsan stepped forward again, encroaching further on the priest's territory. "Claim," he said, "to be the Emperor yourself." Afsan left his mouth open after speaking the words, showing serrated teeth.

"Afsan, I . . ."

"Claim it! Claim it *right now* or die!"

"I—" Edklark's voice was attenuated by fear. "I am the Emperor," he said tremulously.

"Say it forcefully. Assert it loudly."

Edklark swallowed. "I, Det-Edklark, am the Emperor."

"Again! With full titles!"

"I, Det-Edklark, am the Emperor of all the Fifty Packs and the eight provinces of Land."

Afsan swung around. "Cadool?"

Cadool's voice was full of wonder. "I've never seen anything like it," he said.

"What happened?" demanded Afsan. "Exactly what happened?"

"Nothing," said Cadool. "His muzzle didn't show even a hint of blush. It's as green as yours or mine."

Afsan slapped his tail hard against the marble floor, releasing pent-up energy through the blow, the sound of the impact reverberating throughout the antechamber. "Excellent! Edklark, come with us. There's a job only you can do!"

Later that day, Toroca caught sight of Cadool in the Plaza of Belkom, Cadool's long legs carrying him quickly over the paving stones. "Ho, Cadool!"

Cadool turned. "Toroca!" He gave a little bow. "*Hahat dan.* It is good to see you again."

Toroca closed some of the distance between them, but left a large—for him—territorial buffer. "And you. Good Cadool, ah, it is said that there is nothing you will not do for Afsan."

"It is my honor to be his assistant."

"And you know that I am his son."

"One of his sons, yes."

"I, ah, I know I have no right to ask this, but I wonder if any of your sense of duty to Afsan carries over to me?"

"What do you mean?"

"I mean, you are a good and loyal friend to my father, and I would like to think that perhaps I, too, can count on you."

"I don't understand."

"Well, I mean, Afsan and I are related. Since you help Afsan, I thought perhaps you might also be willing to help me."

Cadool's tone was pleasant, but confused. "I don't see what being related to Afsan has to do with anything."

"I don't really know myself," confessed Toroca. "But I need to ask a big favor of someone, and, well, I thought perhaps, because of your relationship with my father, that maybe . . ."

Cadool held up a hand. "Toroca, if I were to do a favor for you it would be because of who you are, on your own terms. Why would you want it to be anything but thus?"

Toroca nodded. "You're right, of course. Forgive me." A pause. "Afsan has told you what we are doing, I presume."

"Yes," said Cadool. "I'm not enthusiastic about the idea—despite the efforts of that Mokleb person, Afsan is still blind. What you have proposed is very risky."

"That it is. But peace must be given a chance."

Cadool grunted noncommittally. "In any event," he said, "what favor would you ask of me?"

"I have in my custody a child," said Toroca. "I need someone to look after him while I am gone."

"Surely room can be found for him in the creche?" said Cadool.

"No, this child is, ah, not Quintaglio. He is an Other."

"An Other! Toroca, we are at war with the Others."

"The child is innocent. He was hatched aboard the *Dasheter,* just as I myself was. I need someone to care for him while I am gone."

"Surely you are not asking me to regurgitate meat," said Cadool.

"No. He's big enough to swallow hunks whole now, although perhaps you could cut small pieces for him."

"Wait a beat—if he is an Other, won't the sight of him drive me to *dagamant*?"

"I honestly don't know if children have the same effect, but, yes, you'll have to take precautions. See him only in the dark, perhaps."

"But Emperor Dybo has given me my own assignment to take care of. I'm going to have to leave the Capital, too, in a couple of days."

"I should be on my way back by then. Taksan—that's the child's name—Taksan doesn't require constant supervision, of course. He's already used to being left alone. If you could simply check on him a couple of times before you go. He's in my apartment."

"Well, if that is all, I suppose I can manage it."

"Ah, no, that isn't quite all there is to it. Good Cadool, I find myself facing a problem no other Quintaglio has ever faced. I am responsible for another's life. I am concerned about what will happen to Taksan if I don't return from this peace mission. Cadool, I ask you to look after Taksan if I don't come back."

"That is a lot to ask."

"I know it. But you were the only Quintaglio I could think of to approach. You look after my father; I thought perhaps you'd understand . . ."

"I freely confess that I *don't* understand," said Cadool. "I will do this: I will make sure this, this Taksan, is fed and kept safe until I leave the Capital. Beyond that, I make no promises."

Toroca nodded slowly. It was all he could expect. "Thank you, Cadool."

Toroca and Afsan left Capital City early the next morning aboard a small sailboat, the *Stardeter*. The ship was only seven paces long, barely big enough to accommodate two people. Toroca was amidships, controlling the rigging for the two sails. Afsan sat in the stern, holding the tiller steady, and occasionally moving it in response to instructions from Toroca. They had to tack into the wind, and, despite the huge amounts of time he'd spent aboard the *Dasheter*, Toroca was by no means an expert sailor. Still, the boat handled well, and soon the cliffs along Land's shore were receding over the horizon.

They sailed for a full day and a night before Toroca caught sight of the first mast poking over the eastern horizon. It was difficult to make out the approaching ships against the rising sun, but Toroca had soon counted fourteen vessels spread out along the horizon, and he had every reason to think there were many more still behind them.

Would Jawn be aboard the lead ship, or another one? Was he even here at all? Jawn was the only one who spoke even some of the Quintaglio language; surely they would have brought him along.

Before departing Land, Toroca had painted Jawn's name across the *Stardeter*'s main sail; it was one of the very few words he knew how to make, having seen it over and over again on Jawn's name-tag necklace. If the Others had far-seers, surely they'd be able to see the word "Jawn" and understand that a meeting was being requested with him. That is, if they'd even noticed the tiny sailboat yet.

As their little craft moved closer to the armada, Toroca used his own far-seer to examine the big ships. Small colored flags were running up a guy from each ship's bow to its foremast. Toroca at first thought that these identified individual vessels, but he soon counted three that were displaying the same sequence of flags. At one point, Toroca saw the old flags brought down and new ones hoisted. Apparently this was a signaling method used to communicate between the ships.

Wingfingers occasionally swooped down from the sky to look at the *Stardeter*. Many others were flitting above the Other ships, perhaps feeding on garbage thrown overboard.

And then, at last, one of the big ships changed course slightly, heading directly for the *Stardeter*. Toroca was deliberately not wearing his sash; instead he had on the same swimmer's belt he'd worn that day he'd first arrived in the Other city. He suspected all Quintaglios looked alike to the Others, just as all of them looked pretty much the same to him, and he wanted to do everything possible to aid identification.

The big ship was approaching quickly. Toroca described its alien shape for Afsan, who seemed amazed by the differences from standard Quintaglio design. Toroca could see several Others on its deck. They were all standing in the shade of an overhanging tarpaulin; Toroca guessed they weren't used to equatorial sun. Even in the far-seer, the faces were indistinct, but—

There.

Waving at him.

Jawn.

Toroca tied off the sail cord and, holding the mast for support with one hand, waved wildly in reply with the other. As the ships came closer together, Toroca could tell that not everyone on deck was pleased to see him. Two individuals were pointing metal tubes at him, and a large black cylinder, one of the much bigger weapons that had earlier taken shots at the *Dasheter,* had been swiveled in a wooden mount to face the *Stardeter*. Still, Jawn's face was one of open delight at seeing his old friend. Two Others were putting a rope ladder over the ship's side; weights on its ends kept it taut as it descended toward the waves.

"They're letting down a ladder," Toroca said to Afsan. "You'll have to go up first; I'll need to stay behind to tie off our boat."

Afsan nodded. Toroca shouted up at Jawn in the Other language, while pointing at Afsan: "No eyes! No eyes!"

Jawn looked perplexed for a moment, then seemed to get Toroca's meaning. Shouting back at his own shipmates in the Other language, he said, "The big one is *lees-tash*"—presumably the word for "blind."

One of the Other sailors shouted out, "Then what is he doing here?" but Jawn ignored that and motioned for Toroca and Afsan to come aboard. Toroca helped Afsan get hold of the rope ladder. "It's about thirty rungs to the top," he said. "Remember, they can touch you without difficulty; let them help you get up on deck."

Afsan grunted and began to climb. He had trouble with the first couple of rungs, but soon got the hang of it, and before long was up on the Other ship. Toroca tied his little sailing boat to the rope ladder in hopes that it wouldn't bash against the big boat too much; the Other vessel could doubtless take the impacts, but the *Stardeter* had a fragile hull. He then made his own way up the ladder, banging his knuckles as it swung back against the ship when a big wave came by. Finally, he was on the deck, too. Toroca bowed deeply in Quintaglio greeting, then spoke the standard salutation used by the Others: "It is my good fortune to see you." One of the Others made a derisive sound, but Toroca thought he was more likely mocking his halting command of their language than the actual sentiment.

Jawn repeated the greeting, then asked in his own language, "Who is this?"

"My . . . father," said Toroca. "Afsan."

Jawn bowed at Afsan, and, in heavily accented Quintaglio, said, "I cast a shadow in your presence."

Afsan tilted his muzzle toward Jawn, impressed.

"Enough of this," said the same one who had snorted earlier, speaking the Other tongue. "Ask him why they attacked us, Jawn."

Toroca faced the fellow directly, and spoke in the same language. "That is what I have come to . . . to . . ."

"Gan-noth," said Jawn. Explain.

"That is what I have come to explain," said Toroca. "My people want no fight. We not good feel about what happened."

The belligerent fellow let loose a vocal barrage containing many words that Toroca didn't know, but he realized part of it was a body count of how many had been killed by the Quintaglios aboard the *Dasheter*.

"We are sorry for that," said Toroca. "It is moving by the hand of God," he said, an Other idiom meaning, we couldn't help ourselves. "Your appearance causes a . . . a violent reaction within most of us."

"Appearance," said Jawn. "Then your father . . . he can be here because he is *lees-tash,* yes?"

"Yes."

Jawn faced Afsan, and spoke in halting Quintaglio. "Toroca says he does not want to fight. Do you?"

"No," said Afsan. And then repeating himself in the Other style of amplification, which Toroca had taught him during the voyage out: "No, no."

"How," said the belligerent one, who Toroca had come to suspect must be the captain, "is not fighting possible between our peoples?"

"We can have no direct contact," said Toroca. "But my people are good at interacting *without* contact. We could trade, exchange documents, learn more about each other—"

"Enough!" The captain spit a string of words at Jawn so rapidly that Toroca could only pick out a few terms. Jawn looked upset.

"What did he say?" asked Toroca.

"He said you are—not the absence of good, but the opposite of it. You live out of the sight of God. We cannot trust you, he says."

"Ah, but you *can* trust us, Jawn. You saw it yourself back in your city. I cannot lie without my muzzle turning blue; none of my people can. You know that."

"Joth-shal," said the captain.

"What?"

"A trick," said Jawn. "He thinks you've tricked us into thinking that about yourselves."

"Do you think it is a trick?" said Toroca.

Jawn looked thoughtful, then said slowly, "Among those who died trying to visit your ship was my sister."

"We told you to stay away."

"Yes, you did. You—"

"How?" snapped the captain, his face suddenly suspicious. "How—" and then a string of words Toroca couldn't follow.

Jawn looked at Toroca. "My friend asks a good question," he said. "How did you know what effect our appearance would have on you? How did you know enough to warn us not to visit your ship?"

Toroca's heart sank. Not knowing what to do, he turned to Afsan and quickly filled him in. Afsan shrugged.

"Because," said Toroca slowly, "that day I arrived in your city was not the first time Quintaglios had seen your peoples. We had landed on another one of your islands a few days before—"

The captain spoke again and Toroca recognized the name of one of the islands.

"Oh, God," said Jawn. "You killed two people there, didn't you? There was a massive search; one body was found, and another was never recovered."

"Now the test!" said the captain. "If you killed them, you must die for it. Prove you cannot lie, *thash-rath*. Tell us you killed them."

Toroca briefly explained to Afsan what was going on.

"Not a great experiment," observed Afsan. "You die either way."

"I did not kill them," said Toroca in the Other language, "but, yes, ones of my kind did. We feel not good about it." Toroca held up a hand, and was relieved to see his claws were still sheathed. "If you believe that we did kill them, you must also believe we are sorry. Sorry, sorry."

"If you knew the effect of our appearance, then why did you come back to our islands?" said Jawn. "Why did you risk killing more of us?"

"That is why Afsan is here," Toroca said. "He is one of our greatest thinkers, and is influential with our Emperor. He has something to"—he tried to recall the word he'd just learned—"explain to you about what will come for our world. Let him show you; I will translate what he says."

The captain's tail swished. "You are dangerous. Your kind must be eliminated if my kind is to be safe." He moved in closer. He was no bigger than Toroca; the young geologist could surely take him in single combat. But other sailors had weapon tubes trained on him. "We attack you tomorrow, *thash-rath*. Tell me where your weakest point is."

Toroca crossed his arms over his chest. "I do not wish for this conflict to go on," he said, "but I will not . . ." His noble speech faltered as he realized he didn't know the Other word for *betray*. "I will not *not* help my people."

The captain held out his right hand, motioning to one of the armed sailors to give him his tube. "Tell me, or I'll shoot you," he said.

"No!" said Jawn. "Do not!"

"I would rather die than not *not* help my people," said Toroca.

The captain grunted, a sound of grudging respect. "Finally a quality to admire in your kind," he said. "No matter. Tell me where your people's weakest point is, or I shall kill the large one." He swung the mouth of his tube toward Afsan.

"No!" said Toroca, first in Quintaglio, then in the Other tongue. "He is blind."

"So you say," said the captain. "He is also much bigger than any of us, and that makes him dangerous. Now, tell me, where exactly should we attack? Where are you least fortified?"

"I cannot reveal that," said Toroca.

The captain did something to the tube. It made a loud click.

"Tell me, or I will *kas-tak*." A word that presumably referred to operating the weapon.

"Do not," said Jawn again. "They came here in peace."

"There will be peace," said the captain. "When they are all dead, and the *jar-dik* to our people is over, there will be peace." He looked at Toroca again, his yellow eyes thin slits against his yellow face. "Tell me!"

Toroca closed his eyes. "The docks." The Quintaglio word exploded from him.

The captain looked at Jawn, who provided the equivalent Other term.

"The docks," Toroca said again. "The harbor."

"Where?" snapped the captain. "Exactly where?"

"Dead ahead, at the easternmost tip of our land," said Toroca. "You cannot miss it. Our Capital City is built on cliffs overlooking those docks. They are unfortified and unguarded."

"Thank you," said the captain. "Thank you very much." And then he casually aimed the mouth of his tube at Afsan and moved his fingers. A flash of light leapt from the barrel's mouth and wingfingers who were roosting on the ship's rigging took to flight. Afsan fell backward against the raised wall around the edge of the ship, and collapsed to the wooden deck.

"You said you wouldn't shoot him!" shouted Toroca in Quintaglio.

The Other captain must have been anticipating the question, because he answered it even though he couldn't possibly have understood the words. "You may not be able to lie," he said simply, "but I can."

Chapter 28

Toroca ran over to the fallen Afsan. A neat round hole, with blackened edges, was visible on his upper-left chest. Blood was seeping from the wound. Toroca lifted Afsan's sash from over his shoulders, wadded it up, and pressed it against his chest, trying to stanch the flow. Afsan groaned.

"Why?" Toroca said, but he realized that wasn't the question he really wanted to ask. He fixed his gaze on the captain and spoke the eighth Other interrogative word: *"Glees?"* How righteous is this?

Jawn, too, was looking at the captain in naked disgust. He turned to Toroca. "How is he?"

"Bad," said Toroca, his Other vocabulary lessons failing him. "Bad."

Afsan tried to lift his head. There was some blood in his mouth; the metal pellet had probably torn into his lung or windpipe. "I . . ." His voice was raw, pained. "I do not wish to die here."

"Nobody's going to die," said Toroca, glad for once that his father was blind and could not see his muzzle. He turned to Jawn. "I am not a healer," he said. "I have to get him back to my people."

"No," said the captain. He gestured at some of his sailors. "Take them below."

Jawn protested in language Toroca couldn't follow, but soon weapon tubes were being waved at them. Toroca put an arm around his father and helped support his massive weight as they were taken down a ramp into the ship's interior. Large skylights were inlaid into the ceiling; there were no signs of interior lamps.

Afsan was groaning slightly with each step. While helping him walk, Toroca could no longer hold the leather sash against his father's wound, but Afsan himself was doing it now. They soon found themselves at the doorway to a little room. Even aboard ship the Others favored any floor plan that wasn't square; the room was five-sided. A circular skylight admitted late-afternoon sun.

There were coarse sacks stacked in three of the five corners. Toroca helped Afsan lie on his side, leaning against one of the sacks. The door was closed, and Toroca heard the sound of metal hitting metal. He tried to open the door but found he couldn't shift it.

"Locked," said Afsan faintly.

"What does that mean?" said Toroca.

"Secured . . . so it can't be opened."

"Oh." Toroca came back to where Afsan was lying. "How are you?"

"Cold," he said. "Cold. And thirsty."

"The *hak-al* is still inside you?"

"*Hak-al?*" said Afsan.

"It's an Other word. A piece of metal, fired from a weapon."

"Oh." Afsan groaned. "I think I prefer a society that doesn't often use locks, and has no word for such weapons." He winced as his fingers probed his wound. "It's stopped bleeding." He shuddered. "How long . . . how long until they attack Land?"

"They're only a day's sail away now," said Toroca. "But they're not used to real darkness; I suspect they'll attack early in the morning of the day after tomorrow."

Afsan grunted, but whether in pain or acknowledgment, Toroca couldn't say. Soon, he slipped into unconsciousness. Toroca leaned back against the opposite wall and watched Afsan's shallow breathing.

Much later—Toroca had lost all track of time—he heard footfalls in the corridor outside, and the sound of metal against metal again. It was now quite dark; only pale moonlight filtered in through the skylight. Cautiously, Toroca got up and walked across the room. He tried the door again. It swung open. He peered out into the corridor. No sign of anyone.

Jawn, he thought. Jawn understood not wanting to die away from home. Toroca hurried over and touched Afsan's shoulder. No response. He shook it lightly. Again nothing. He placed a hand on his father's chest. It was still warm, still moving up and down with respiration. Toroca let out a sigh of relief, and gently shook Afsan once more. If Afsan had been well, he never would have woken him thus; he could have regained consciousness startled, jaws snapping. Soon, though, Afsan did slowly lift his muzzle.

"The door," whispered Toroca. "It's open. Come on, let's go."

"A trap?" said Afsan weakly.

Toroca shook his head. "A friend, I think." He reached a hand out and grasped Afsan's arm, helping him up. "Hurry."

Toroca looked out the corridor again, then, cupping Afsan's elbow, led him up on deck. The nighttime breeze was cool. Clouds covered about half the sky. The sound of water slapping the ship's hull and of the sails rippling in the breeze masked their footfalls.

Toroca jogged ahead to look over the edge of the ship. The rope ladder was still there leading down to the *Stardeter*. He looked back at Afsan, who was walking slowly, a hand clasped over his wound. Toroca hurried back to him, once more cupping his elbow, and led him to the ladder.

"I'll go down first; you'll need help getting aboard. Give me about twenty-five beats, then follow me down."

Afsan grunted in pain. Toroca slipped over the side of the ship and started the descent. The rope ladder was wet, having been in the spray kicked up by the ship's movement for many daytenths now. Finally, Toroca made it into the boat. The *Stardeter* had taken on a small amount of water, either from spray or rain. Toroca almost slipped as he stepped off the ladder. He looked up. Afsan was coming over the side of the ship now. The ladder seemed to sag under his weight, and at one point, Afsan missed a rung and almost fell the remaining distance to the ship, but he managed to steady himself and make it down the rest of the way. Toroca could barely discern Afsan's face in the darkness, but his expression was one of agony, as if with each movement of his arms or legs, spikes were being driven into his body.

At last the older Quintaglio was aboard. Toroca unfurled the tiny ship's sails. Afsan collapsed against the *Stardeter*'s stern, holding the tiller with one hand and his chest with the other. The ship slipped away into the night.

Doubtless at least one of the ships in the armada would have a lookout on duty, but hopefully that person would be scanning the horizon, not the waters close by. "I can't take you directly back to Land," said Toroca. "For one thing, we can't outrun their ships, and for another, they'll be watching the waters ahead carefully. Will you be all right if I sail south for a bit first, and then takes us in near Fastok?"

Afsan grunted. His voice was faint. "I'll be fine." In the dim light, though, there was no way to tell if he was speaking the truth.

The next morning, Afsan and Toroca were still out on the water. The night's rest seemed to have done Afsan some good. Toroca had briefly gone swimming to catch some fish, and although Afsan had trouble swallowing—further evidence that the metal pellet had clipped his windpipe—he seemed to regain some strength after the meal.

"I feel like one whose shell had been too thick," said Toroca. "I was so sure we could convince them. Now they know our weakest point. I've doomed our people."

Afsan's voice was raw and faint. "You knew the docks were undefended because you'd heard that at that briefing just before we left."

"Yes. If only we'd missed that briefing." He raised a hand. "I know, I know: you were right in insisting we attend."

"Indeed," said Afsan. "Didn't you find the choice of who was giving the briefing unusual?"

Toroca, paying out rope to change the angle of the mainsail, nodded. "At first, yes. But then I figured Dybo was no strategist. I assume this other fellow had a flair for that sort of thing."

"Actually, Dybo's contributions were invaluable. But do you know who that other fellow was?"

"I recognized him, of course: Det-Edklark. We'd had our share of run-ins over my theory of evolution."

"He's the Master of the Faith."

"Yes."

"A priest."

"Yes."

"He can lie in the light of day."

"What?"

"I said, he can lie in the light of day."

"I heard you. That's not possible."

"It is for him. It is for some priests."

"Then why have him give the briefing? I mean—oh! Afsan, no."

"What he told you about the docks being our most vulnerable spot was a lie. We are in fact waiting in ambush for the Others there."

"My God. It will be—"

"A slaughter, I suspect."

"But how did you know the Others would force information from me?"

"I didn't know it for sure." Afsan shifted slightly, a grimace crossing his face as he did so. "You said you trusted this Jawn completely. But I'd been in a similar situation once before myself." He paused, catching his breath. "I had trusted my friend Dybo. That had cost me my eyes. Dybo was pushed aside by Yenalb, the High Priest at that time." Another grimace as the boat was rocked by a large wave. "I was concerned that your associate, Jawn, would be only one voice."

"A slaughter, you say?"

"Unquestionably."

Toroca looked sad. "I didn't want this to happen."

"Nor did I, which is why I went with you on your mission of peace." He paused while pain worked its way across his face. "But as I once admonished Dybo, a leader rarely has any choice in what he or she does."

"But how did you know I'd talk, even if the Others tried to coerce me? You didn't recant, despite Yenalb's threats."

"No, but back then no one I cared about was being directly threatened. Your kindness was your weakness."

"You're wrong, Father," said Toroca, his voice firm. "It is my greatest strength."

Afsan shrugged. "Regardless, if this works, at least Mokleb will be happy."

"I don't understand," said Toroca.

Afsan's muzzle scrunched as he fought again against raging pain. "She thinks I'm The One, and as Lubal said, 'The One will defeat demons of the land *and of the water*.'"

Chapter 29

The first wave of Other ships was sailing in toward the harbor of Capital City. Emperor Dybo had already ordered all Quintaglio vessels removed from there. Even if the Others hadn't fallen for Afsan's trick, the target would be too tempting; the docks provided easy access to the city itself via ramps carved into the rocks.

Standing on the top of the cliffs just north of the docks, Dybo used a far-seer to watch the approaching vessels. He was amazed at how their decks swarmed with the yellow beings. They were approaching at a good speed, the steady breeze toward Land driving the strange triangular sails of their ships.

Closer. Closer still. At last, Dybo raised his left hand, just like a hunt leader about to give a command. As he did so, the three metal bracelets he wore that indicated his rank slid down toward his elbow. And then, at last, he brought the hand down in a chopping motion, signaling the attack.

The *Lub-Kaden,* one of the small fleet of gliders built based on Novato's plans, swooped over the edge of the cliff, sailing high above the ships below. The glider resembled a wooden-frame replica of a giant wingfinger, with a wide triangular canopy and a small hollow undercarriage containing a Quintaglio lying on her belly. The pilot could steer the ship by moving her tail; a harness connected it to the glider's pointed prow which could move left or right on hinges.

The pilot did much better today than Novato had done a few

kilodays ago when she had become the first Quintaglio to take to the air; this female had no trouble staying on her planned course, and she could keep airborne for an extended period, taking advantage of the upcurrent as the wind blowing against the cliffs was deflected toward the sky.

Dybo could see the tiny yellow beings on the deck pointing upward. He hoped it was in astonishment; flight was so new to the Quintaglios, he was betting that the Others hadn't yet discovered it. Indeed, Novato hadn't been able to work it out until she had actual bird specimens to work from, and they could only be found in the blue ark, something the Others had no access to.

Dybo could see some Others trying to maneuver the heavy weapon tubes on their decks, hoping to aim at the airship swooping above. But these tubes weren't designed to point that far overhead; their rear ends butted into the deck before they could swing that high.

Some Others were firing their handheld sticks up at the flyer, too, but so far, no shot had connected.

The *Lub-Kaden* was circling now over the lead ship. Dybo watched as the first bomb dropped from its central chassis: a heavily weighted ceramic container, divided internally into two parts by a wall, each section containing a different chemical. When the container hit the deck of the ship—which it did *now*— the ceramic shattered and the chemicals mixed, bursting into flame.

Dybo watched as a ring of fire widened on the sailing ship's foredeck and soon began climbing the mast. Fire touched the triangular lead sail, and the whole thing went up in flames. Several Others dived into the water, but their big weapon tubes and supply of other devices on this ship would soon be lost.

The *Lub-Kaden* was now over a second ship. It dropped another ceramic canister, but this one missed, plunging beneath the waves. The pilot circled around again and dropped her third bomb. This one actually hit the top of the mast, and fire spread down the triangular sail in a widening path toward the deck.

Dybo made a chopping motion with his arm again and a second glider soared off the cliff. This one, the *Irb-Falpom,* sailed straight and true farther out from the docks, toward some of the ships in the rear. In a beautifully executed arc, the glider dropped bombs in rapid succession onto the three farthest ships. They started to burn slowly but persistently, and soon yellow beings were trying to get away in lifeboats or by swimming.

From a nearby ship, one of the Others had scrambled up to the lookout's perch atop the mast and was carefully aiming his weapon tube. He squeezed off three shots. One missed completely. The second tore an insignificant hole in the leather covering of the *Irb-Falpom*'s wings. But the third hit one of the ceramic bombs directly. A chain of liquid fire dribbled downward from the craft toward the waves, but enough had splashed up as the canister blew open to set the whole glider ablaze. Burning brightly, like an apparition from one of the sacred scrolls, the glider pilot bravely took aim on an Other ship and let her flaming vessel plow into its decks, the fragile glider breaking apart like kindling wood as it skidded along, finally smashing into the base of the foremast. Within moments, the Other ship was engulfed in flame.

A huge explosion split the air. Dybo brought his hands to his earholes. Below, a giant ball of fire was expanding upward, and thick smoke was everywhere. One of the ships must have been carrying a supply of blackpowder, and the fire had set it off all at once.

Three Other ships had turned now and were heading out of the harbor, desperately trying to get away.

Dybo launched a third glider, the *Sor-Denkal,* but it failed to catch the wind properly, and, spinning wildly, it spiraled down toward the waves. As it hit the surf, one of the Others' big weapons blew it and its pilot apart, sending a huge spray of water onto the Quintaglio docks.

With another chop of his arm, a fourth glider, the *Jal-Tetex,* took to the air, swooping out to drop a series of bombs.

Meanwhile, the *Lub-Kaden* had bombed four more ships; the water was now thick with flaming timbers and yellow backs swimming for shore. The glider swooped up once more, catching the air current perfectly, and swung around to drop the last of its bombs in a neat series—*plink! plink! plink!*—onto three more boats. The pilot then swung her glider back in a giant arc that swept her over the cliff tops, buzzing Rockscape before coming in for a smooth landing on an open field.

Besides the three ships that seemed to be making good their escape, there were only two Other vessels left below. Dybo had just one glider left: the *Tak-Saleed,* Novato's original flyer, salvaged from the waves and rebuilt after its first flight. It was smaller and less sturdy than the others, and Dybo had hoped he wouldn't have to use it, but there was no choice. His arm came down in a chopping motion again, and the *Tak-Saleed* soared over the cliff's edge. The glider shuddered visibly as it rose higher and higher, and Dybo thought briefly that it was going to fall apart. The pilot seemed to be having some trouble with the harness that controlled the prow—it had been seizing up in tests, but Dybo had been assured that the problem had been corrected. The prow oscillated left and right, causing the ship to waver in its flight. Soon, though, the pilot had the craft under control and she swooped out over the waves, overshooting the armada, then executing a turn and sweeping back in.

In the meantime, one of the remaining sailing ships had been taken care of. Another ship, engulfed in flame and completely abandoned, had careened into it, the second ship having been unable to get out of its way in time. Not only had the impact ripped open both ships' hulls, but both were now burning brightly.

The *Tak-Saleed* was completing its final run, but its pilot had been too intent on the spectacle below. Dybo shouted, "Look out!" but there was no way for anyone to hear him over the wind. He watched in horror as the rickety *Saleed* collided in midair with the *Jal-Tetex*. For a brief moment he thought they were going to just lightly touch, but no, the *Saleed* crumpled, its wings folding up into a corrugated mess, the wooden slats of its undercarriage snapping like twigs. For its part, the *Tetex*'s left wing snapped off and began spiraling in toward the waves while the rest of the ship was pushed sideways through the air for several beats by the force of the impact with the *Saleed*. The *Saleed* had been carrying four bombs. Two dropped free of the ship, their amphora shape providing little air resistance as they fell. They hit the waves and simply kept on going down. Moments later, the two aircraft crashed into the water as well. Dybo dipped his head in silent prayer. Surely the two pilots were dead.

But no—a green form was slicing through the waves. One of them still lived; it looked like Quetik, the pilot of the *Saleed*. Her airship had impacted not far from the one intact Other ship, but Quetik wasn't swimming toward it. Nearby was another ship whose decks showed sporadic fires but whose sails had not yet burst into flame; Quetik's tail whipped through the water, propelling her toward that vessel.

Three Others on the intact ship tried to fire at her; the big cylinders couldn't be aimed that fast, so they were using handheld tubes. Through the far-seer, Dybo saw Quetik gulp air, then dive beneath the waves. When he next caught sight of her, she was climbing up a rope ladder dangling over the side of the burning boat, a ladder its crew of Others had used to escape into the water. Moments later, she was on the deck.

Quetik used her jaws to chomp through a rope tying off a boom. The sail swung around, and the ship swung, too. She then found the massive tiller and threw her shoulder and back against it, pushing, pushing, steering the ship. The neighboring Other vessel, the only one in the harbor still intact, was desperately trying to turn as well, but its options were limited; the harbor was full of ships aflame. The fire on the deck of Quetik's ship was spreading, and—there!—it leapt onto the sails. But the ship was moving under inertia and a good wind now, and Dybo watched as the inevitable collision played itself out, the burning ship ramming into the one remaining target vessel. Flame spread to the intact Other ship, and Dybo saw Quetik slump to the deck of the one she was on, perhaps overcome by fumes.

And then the air was ripped apart by another deafening blast. This last ship, too, had had holds full of blackpowder. The explosion tossed wooden boards and bodies high into the air. Quetik had completed her objective at the cost of her life.

The sun had set by now, but the harbor blazed more brightly than at high noon as the thirty hulks below continued to burn wildly. Ships had drifted into the wooden docks by now, and the docks, too, were aflame. The three Other ships that had fled earlier were sitting on the horizon; they'd have to be dealt with separately.

Surviving Others were straggling onto the rocky shore far below, but with no weapons they presented little threat to the twenty-five Quintaglios who had been waiting on the beach for them to arrive. Dybo left them to their business.

Chapter 30

Pal-Cadool and several butchers were riding atop their running-beasts. That they were skilled in handling animals was clear: the runningbeasts were terrified of being crushed under the giant feet of the thunderbeasts, and yet they moved with precision, responding to the gentle tugs on their harnesses, the subtle prod-dings with heel spurs into their bellies, and their riders' shouted instructions—shouted, because they had to be audible over the deafening footfalls of all those thunderbeasts.

The thunderbeasts hadn't liked being driven at first, and Cadool's team had lost several excellent members: slaps from massive tails had literally flattened them against the rocks, or sent them flying through the air, every bone in their bodies shattered even before they hit the ground. But eventually even animals as stupid as these realized that the riders had been driving them toward lush forests, filled with *hamadaja* trees, their favorite fodder. And now they accepted herding with reasonable passivity. Why, Cadool had lost only one handler so far today . . .

But, unlike the last several days, today the thunderbeasts were not being driven toward fresh trees. Cadool's team was now riding in rough circles around the five giant animals whose heads were held dizzyingly high overhead, and whose tails were lifted so high off the ground that rider and runningbeast had no trouble galloping beneath the endless tubes of muscle and bone and flesh.

The thunderbeasts had an advantage that Cadool had forgotten in planning the drive. Although from the ground the next valley was invisible, from the vantage points of the thunderbeasts, whose eyes were held twenty times higher up than were Quintaglio orbs, they could plainly see over the low hills, and could see, and perhaps even smell, the vast tracts of succulent vegetation. Everything would be lost if they went that way.

Cadool was screaming at the lead thunderbeast, trying to get it to turn and go the other way. Two more riders were shouting out as well. Faster and faster they ran around the group of five beasts, hoping to draw their dull attention away from the nearby forest.

"Come on!" shouted Cadool. "This way! This way!"

At last the lead thunderbeast—the bull male of this herd— tipped its long neck down, the great expanse of it slicing through the air with an audible *whoosh,* and its head, about the size of Cadool's torso, loomed in at ground level, coming up behind Cadool's runner, and letting out a yell of its own. The sound reverberated as air was pumped through the tunnel of its throat. Its breath stunk of plants. But by the time it had come down to ground level, it had likely forgotten what it had been look- ing at a moment before. Cadool continued to ride in a circle, and the neck, an impossibly huge snake, sliced through the air to follow. The peg-like teeth could do little harm to anything except foliage, but Cadool's mount plainly did not like having the thunderbeast's head floating behind it. It bucked. Cadool moved his hands across the back of the runner's skull, calming it. At last, the thunderbeast's neck was pointing in the direction Cadool wanted the animal to go. He stopped circling and, with a cry of *"Latark,"* headed out through the gully between two steeper hills. The bull male began to lumber on, and the others— three females and a juvenile male—fell in behind, although one of the females kept looking plaintively back at the vast tracts of uneaten treetops behind them.

The giants' footfalls echoed off the hillsides, but in the distance Cadool could already hear another kind of thunder. Big weapons being fired. Cadool picked up the pace; no matter how fast he made the runningbeast go, the thunderbeasts had no trouble keep- ing up, for their legs were four times as long as Cadool was tall.

The gully was narrowing, and it was clear the thunderbeasts didn't like that; these animals hated going where they'd have trouble turning around, and although their necks could be held straight up, to rotate comfortably they'd need an opening at least eighty paces wide. The gully had already narrowed to only half that width.

As long as the bull male didn't panic, everything would be fine. If he did, if he decided to back up, the resulting cascade of huge bodies would doubtless crush Cadool's team.

Soon, Cadool could hear the slapping waves and the occasional report of weapons being operated. *Closer now, closer. Around this bend. Come on, beasts! Don't fail me now . . .*

And then, at last, an open expanse of beach, rich with black volcanic sands. And beyond, out in the waters, the three Other ships that had escaped the bombing, and farther from shore, two wide, flat Quintaglio barges.

Cadool rode off to the left, getting out of the thunderbeasts' way. The Others, no doubt, had clicked their teeth together—or whatever it was that they did to laugh—when they'd seen what the Quintaglios were going to answer their three remaining ships with. Barges! Simple barges!

Cadool, now, was clicking his teeth . . .

Barges overflowing with freshly cut *hamadaja* leaves, with ripe yellow *henkar* melons, with fronds from succulent *pistaral* plants . . .

With every kind of thunderbeast fodder.

Two giant barges full of it, floating now, just beyond the three Other ships, the barge crews now diving overboard, swimming out of the way . . .

The bull male, hungry after the long march, caught sight of the barges and—Cadool clicked his teeth harder when he saw this—stuck a long, dry tongue out of its flat mouth and licked its face in anticipation—

And then it charged, huge waves of water being sent up as it plowed into the surf, barreling out toward the barges . . .

More waves as the largest female crashed into the water as well . . .

And then the juvenile . . .

And then the other two females . . .

Great walls of water splashing everywhere, Cadool now thoroughly soaked on the beach . . .

Huge waves being kicked up, the water now touching the bottom of the bull male's belly . . .

The three Other ships rocking back and forth wildly in the turbulence . . .

Two of them directly in the path of the large male, pounding his way along, his tail slapping the water, huge gouts shooting up behind it . . .

The females fanning out behind him, trying to avoid being splashed in his wake . . .

A wall of flesh now, five giants pounding through the water . . . Ships rocking wildly . . .

Water up to the middle of the bull's belly now, the juvenile swimming freely, its head and neck sticking up above the waves . . .

And then, the first of the Other ships capsizing as it was hit by the giant waves kicked up by the charging thunderbeasts . . .

A big weapon on the deck of the second Other ship swinging around and firing at the bull male, the ship rocking back and forth so badly that the metal ball went almost straight up, then came plummeting down just slightly to starboard of the vessel, the splash of its impact nothing compared to the roiling waves already buffeting the ship, but still enough to momentarily get the bull's attention, its long neck swinging around to look at the ship and then, almost nonchalantly, tapping the ship—just tapping it—with its long tail, the vessel breaking open as though it had been made of paper . . .

And then the bull was upon the first barge, swinging his neck down to virtually suck the fronds and leaves and melons into his elongated gullet . . .

And moments later, two females arriving at the same barge, moving to the far side to get better access, their long bodies rotating through water that came up to their shoulders, their tails stretching out endlessly behind them. The third battleship was desperately trying to get away, moving as fast as the wind would propel it but not fast enough to avoid being slapped by one of the tails, the ship actually lifting clear of the waves, its keel briefly visible, and then smashing back down into the surf, and cracking in two like a dropped egg.

The juvenile and the third female made their way to the second barge, while Others tried to swim for shore, a shore now lined along its entire length with Quintaglio hunters, each one ten paces from the next, torsos tipped forward in fighting posture, just waiting for the enemy survivors to try to come onto dry land . . .

For the rest of the afternoon, the thunderbeasts feasted on choice greens and frolicked in the crashing surf, oblivious to the carnage on the beach.

Chapter 31

Afsan was finally taken back to the imperial surgery, where Dar-Mondark tended to his wounds. There was no doubt that Afsan had internal injuries; in addition to his collapsed lung and spitting up blood, he had now passed bloody stool. The healer cleaned the wounds but didn't risk digging after the metal pellet lodged in Afsan's chest. Afsan slept for a time, and when he awoke, Nav-Mokleb was waiting to see him.

"How are you?" Mokleb asked.

Afsan, lying on his belly on a raised table, groaned. "Not well," he said. "I don't think the talking cure will help me get over this."

Mokleb's tail swished. "I've brought you a present," she said.

"Oh?"

"The volumes of Saleed's *Treatise on the Planets*. I'm returning them."

"You earned those, Mokleb."

"Aye, I did. But they mean much to you. And besides—"

"Besides, I might wish to bequeath the complete set to someone."

Mokleb's tail swished again. She changed the subject. "I've been thinking more about what we were discussing, and about why we react to the Others the way we do. I've developed an idea." She leaned back on her tail. "By having the bloodpriests, generation after generation, select for strength and speed, we've bred ourselves into a race with, well, an exaggerated sense of masculinity."

"Masculinity?" said Afsan.

"That's a word we rarely use, of course," said Mokleb. "The sexes are equal. Oh, females grow at a slightly slower rate than males do, but since Quintaglios grow throughout their lifetimes, that makes little difference. Jobs requiring strength and physical prowess can as easily be done by males as females. But in the animal world, we do often see differences between males and females. Take shovelmouths, for instance: the male is always much larger than the female, and has a much more ornate head crest. Or thunderbeasts: a bull male will control a harem of several smaller females. Or hornfaces: the length of the horns and the height of the neck shield are much greater in males. And in almost every kind of wingfinger, it's the male who stakes out a territory, defending it against all other males, but allowing females to come and go as they please. But we Quintaglios are different. We've unwittingly bred for a tendency toward strength and aggression, and a by-product of that has been to minimize the differences between the two genders."

"But surely having equality of the sexes is laudable?"

"Oh, indeed," said Mokleb. "No question of it. After all, according to legend, females were formed from the fingers of one of God's severed hands, and males from the fingers of the other. No reason one should be better than the other. But here's the rub: *equality* doesn't necessarily mean being the same. It's possible to be different but equal. Yes, the male may be more ornate or more powerful in many cases, but the female controls mating, choosing the male, and also, of course, it is the female who brings new life into the world. Which is better? No one can say. Equal, but different."

"All right," said Afsan.

"But we've made ourselves, essentially, an all-the-same race, in attitudes and attributes. There's little difference between a male and a female. And the traits we've accentuated through the culling are, in many ways, the worst and most antisocial traits of the male. And we've distilled those traits in *both* genders."

"I've never thought about it that way."

"And now, consider this: the Others are, well, less overtly *masculine* than we are. They're physically smaller, they have less prominent jaws, and smaller teeth. They're drably colored compared to us and they have only a weak sense of territoriality."

"So you're saying they're more like females?"

"Ah, but if they *were* like *our* females, perhaps we'd have no problem facing them. But they aren't; they don't have the exaggerated masculinity of our females. And there's something deep, something dark, within our spirits that can't stand the sight of what we perceive as *lesser* males. We've exaggerated our own masculinity to the point where we've become a threat to anyone that doesn't meet the same standards of robustness or aggression. I've seen plenty of Other corpses now. *All* the Others appear to be males; even female Others have folds of skin about the throat reminiscent of a dewlap sack."

"Then there's nothing inherently evil about the Others," said Afsan.

"Nothing at all. The evil is within us. In fact, I'll suggest that we know that on an instinctive level; that Toroca knew to hide his difference from his fellow Quintaglios because he knew how we might react to one we perceived as not as *male* as we expect."

"We destroyed every one of the Other ships," Afsan said. "I doubt they'll dare send more. So what do we do? You tell me we are bred to hate the Others because we see them as lesser versions of ourselves, or—I don't know—perhaps as something we fear becoming. But if we can't help how we feel, what do we do? You know the old saying, you can't change Quintaglio nature."

"Ah, good Afsan, but we must. We're going to need to do that if we're to go to the stars."

The ruling room was empty except for Dybo, lying on the throne slab, and Toroca. "I take it you've finally got an answer for me?" said the Emperor.

"Yes," said Toroca.

"Well?"

"As you recall, the problem you set for me was to find a way to choose which eggling should survive. Almost every clutch consists of eight eggs; most females produce two or three such clutches in a lifetime. Obviously, to maintain a stable population, only one eggling may be allowed to live from each clutch."

"Yes, yes," said Dybo. "But which one?"

"I've given this matter much thought, Emperor. I want you to know that."

"I expected no less, Toroca. Now, what is your answer?"

"My answer, Your Luminance, is this: it doesn't matter which eggling we choose."

"What?"

"It makes no difference. Or, perhaps said better: to refrain from artificially imposing selection criteria makes for *more* difference. More variety."

"I don't understand," said the Emperor.

"It's simple, really. You know my theory of evolution?"

"Yes, of course. That's why you were chosen to come up with a way to select which eggling should live. Survival of the fittest!"

Toroca scratched the underside of his neck. "A regrettable phrase, that . . . Our bloodpriests have been selecting for physical robustness for countless generations. And what has that selection process made us? Territorial beings, savage beings."

"Then we should select based on intelligence," said Dybo.

"Forgive me, Emperor, but that, too, is wrong. Consider Afsan, for instance. A finer mind we've never known, but you yourself have teased him for his scrawniness. In a rock slide, he might die, whereas a bigger but dumber fellow might well be able to dig himself out. The point is, Emperor, there is no hard-and-fast criterion for fitness. As the environment changes, so, too, does the list of requirements for survival. And we're about to change our environment more than ever before, for we are soon to leave this world and seek another. It would be folly to breed for any one particular characteristic, since we don't know what sort of demands the new environment will put on us. No, good Dybo, what we need is variety, and the best way to ensure that is by selecting which egglings get to live *at random*." He turned his muzzle so that there could be no doubt that his black eyes were falling on Dybo. "Some will be strong, some brainy, some perhaps neither of those things but nonetheless possessing qualities we might someday need."

Dybo nodded. "At random," he said. "It's not the sort of answer I expected, Toroca."

"I know, sir. But it *is* the right one."

"Every eggling would have a one-in-eight chance."

"Yes, Your Luminance. But more than that, there should be no culling of hatchlings. I've spoken at length now to Nav-Mokleb— I had no idea of the incredible damage we've done to ourselves through that ancient rite. No, instead we must simply select one egg—one egg, not one eggling—from every clutch, and let only that one egg hatch." He paused. "I only hope that in the generations left before our world dies we can regain some of the other qualities we'll need."

• • •

The pain in his chest made it difficult for Afsan to sleep. He'd nod off for a time, only to wake again, the discomfort too much for him. The third or fourth time that happened, he let out a frustrated growl and slapped his palm against the lab table. With his other hand he scratched his chest, trying to relieve the itching caused by his scabbed-over wound.

He lay there and opened his eyes. He'd been doing that more and more lately; since his eyeballs had grown back, there was no pain associated with having the lids open.

Across the room, he saw a faint light.

He saw—

Across the room!

A faint—

No, a trick of his tired mind. He scrunched his inner and outer lids closed, rubbed them with the backs of his hands, and then opened them again.

No mistake! A light . . . a faint rectangle against the darkness.

A window. An open window, its shade left undrawn.

Afsan pushed himself off his table and let himself down to the floor. Pain sliced through his side but he ignored it. He hobbled over to the window and gripped its ledge with both hands.

It was the middle of the night—and, better still, it was odd-night, the night most Quintaglios slept, the night Afsan always preferred because the outdoor lamps were doused, letting the heavens blaze forth in all their glory, the phosphorescent band of the great sky river arching overhead. Four moons were visible, but they were all thin crescents, doing little to banish the stars.

The night sky, cloudless, pitch black, resplendent, glorious. Just as he'd remembered it. All the nights he'd spent staring up at the sky came back to him: childhood nights, full of wonder and awe. Adolescent nights, full of longing and yearning. Nights as an apprentice, full of study and slowly gleaned understanding.

His tail was fairly vibrating with joy. The pain, unbearable earlier, was now all but forgotten, pushed from his high mind by the magnificent sight. Old friends were beckoning. Why, there was the constellation of the Hunter, which had been called the Prophet in his youth. And, there, arching up from the horizon, Lubal's hornface Matark. Straddling the ecliptic, the Skull of Katoon.

Afsan thought about shouting out, about waking the others, about declaring to one and all that he could see—he could see!—he could see!

But, no, this was a moment to be savored by himself. The stars tonight were for him and him alone. He leaned back on his tail and drank in more of the spectacle.

It came to him, after some time of enjoying the sight: the reason his low mind had finally relented, had finally given up the fight, had finally allowed him to see. It, too, now knew what Afsan had come to understand on the conscious level.

His time was almost up.

Still, he reveled in the sight, the glorious sight. He watched silently as a meteor made a tiny streak across the firmament.

Chapter 32

They crowded together in the room, their love for Afsan enough to keep the territorial instinct at bay for a short time. Novato was there, the mother to his children, the person with whom he had discovered the truth about the universe. Emperor Dybo was there, too, Afsan's longtime friend. Huge, vastly old Captain Keenir, who had first introduced Afsan to the far-seer, was also there. And others, as well . . .

Afsan had eventually gone back to sleep, and when he awoke, it was morning, the brightness, the glorious brightness, stinging his eyes. He called for Dar-Mondark, who immediately summoned Afsan's friends.

Although he could now see, Afsan's condition was worsening. He'd vomited blood this morning, and the pain in his chest was spreading. He lay flat on his belly, his breath coming out in long ragged hisses. "Dybo?" he said.

The Emperor nodded. "It's me, Afsan."

"It is good to see you."

Dybo clicked his teeth. "It is good to be seen."

Afsan turned his head slightly. "And Novato—I'd know that face anywhere."

"Hello, Afsan."

"You look—" He paused, as if wondering whether to give voice to his thought. "You look *wonderful*. Beautiful."

Novato dipped her head. "Thank you."

"And Captain Var-Keenir." Afsan rallied a little strength. "Ah, the times we had aboard the *Dasheter*!"

"Greetings, eggling," said Keenir, his gravelly voice cracking slightly.

Afsan clicked his teeth. "Don't you think I'm a bit old to still be called that?"

"Never," said Keenir, a twinkle in his eye.

"And this long-shanked fellow," said Afsan, "is doubtless my good and loyal friend. Cadool, the kilodays have been kind to you."

Cadool bowed deeply.

Afsan was quiet for a moment, but then his tail began to twitch as if he were very, very sad.

"What's wrong?" said Novato.

Afsan shook his head. "I—I don't know who the rest of these people are. I should know, but I don't."

One male stepped slightly closer, and then, ignoring the sharp intakes of breath around him, reached out and briefly clasped Afsan's shoulder. "I'm Toroca."

Afsan's voice was breaking. "My son."

"Yes, Father."

"What a fine, handsome Quintaglio you are."

"Thank you."

"I want you to know how very, very proud I am of you."

"I know it, Father. I have always known it."

Afsan turned to the next one, a female who, incredibly, had a horn growing out of her muzzle. "And you are?" he said.

"You mean you can't tell?"

"Well, I can now: I recognize your voice, Babnol."

"Toroca had never mentioned my, ah, horn?"

Afsan shook his head, and saw that Babnol was pleased.

Afsan's tail was shaking again, beating back and forth with the strength of his emotions. "It is good of you all to come," he said. "I know I don't have much time left, but of all the sights I could have seen once more, none means more to me than seeing the faces of my friends . . . and my family."

There was no point in even trying a comforting lie; Afsan could see the color of their muzzles now. "I'll miss you, Afsan," said Dybo. "I'll miss you terribly. You'll not be forgotten. There will be statues of you in every province."

"To be remembered by my friends is enough," said Afsan, and they saw from his muzzle that the sentiment was sincere.

"You will be remembered by all Quintaglios," said Novato.

"You saved us. You saved us all. We're making enormous strides, Afsan. We have our own flying machines and the tower into space, and we're studying the projectile weapons salvaged from the Other ships. We will get off this world before it disintegrates. I promise you that."

Afsan was quiet for a moment. "I have a small request," he said, his voice ragged. "Dybo, this would mean more to me than any statue. I know it will be generations hence before our ships leave this world, but when they go to their new home have them take something of me with them. Let something that I have touched be taken to the soil of our new world."

"Your far-seer," said Toroca at once. "You gave me your far-seer kilodays ago. What could be more appropriate than that?"

Afsan clicked his teeth. "Thank you, son."

"I'll make it happen, Afsan," said Dybo. "Your far-seer will travel to our new home."

Afsan nodded but then his body racked. "I don't think I have much time left," he said. "I care about you all deeply, but you can't all stay here until the end. It's too crowded, too dangerous. Go. Go, knowing you are in my thoughts."

"I want to stay with you," said Novato.

Afsan's voice was faint. "I'd like that. The rest of you, Dybo, Keenir, Toroca, Babnol—I'll miss you. Goodbye, my friends."

"Afsan—" said Dybo, his own voice breaking. "Afsan, I—I must know, before you . . . before you . . ."

Afsan nodded once. His voice was soft. "I forgive you, my friend. I forgive you for everything."

Dybo bowed deeply. "Thank you."

"Now," said Afsan, "please, all of you—God be with you."

"God be with you," said the Emperor. Keenir and Babnol repeated the phrase. The three of them left, along with Toroca.

"Afsan," said Novato, moving closer than territoriality would normally allow, "don't be afraid."

"I'm not afraid," he said, his voice wan. "Not exactly. I don't wish to die, but I'm not afraid."

"I have seen it, Afsan," she said, her voice full of wonder. "The other side. What lies beyond. I have seen it."

Afsan tried to lift his head, but couldn't manage it. "What?"

"At the top of the space tower, I accidentally opened a door that led right out into space. The air rushed out, and I thought I was going to die. In a way, I *did* die. I felt myself leaving my body, and traveling down a long tunnel toward a magnificent light." She spread her arms. "Heaven . . . heaven is peaceful, Afsan. A place without pain, without concerns."

"You saw this when the air ran out?"

"Yes."

"Novato, good Novato . . ." His voice was gentle. "When a person is drowning or otherwise starved for air, the mind often plays tricks."

"This was not a trick, Afsan. This was real."

"I find that difficult to believe," he said.

She nodded, not offended. "I knew you would. But you of all people should know that the simple idea is often not correct. There is a heaven, Afsan, and it is more wonderful than our sacred scrolls ever said."

Afsan's tone was neutral. "Perhaps," he said. "Perhaps."

Novato was serene. "And there's more, Afsan: on the other side, I saw people that I'd known before. Lub-Kaden from my old Pack, our daughter Haldan, others. Do you know what that means, Afsan? Someday, we'll be together again. And you know what the sacred scrolls say about heaven: in the afterlife, there is no territoriality. That's why we must hunt in packs, to prepare ourselves for the ongoing camaraderie of the next existence. We'll be together again, Afsan, you and I. And it will be different. Different and better. We'll be able to walk side by side. We'll be able to touch one another at any time." Her face was calm, beautiful. "It will be wonderful."

"I hope you're right," said Afsan. "My dear, beautiful Novato, I hope you are right." But then his body convulsed. "I—I think it's time," he said at last.

Novato reached out to him, placing a hand on his arm. "I *am* right, Afsan. You'll see."

And then once again for Sal-Afsan, savior of the Quintaglios, everything went dark.

Two kilodays later

The large stone-walled enclosure had once been used to house a blackdeath but it had been extensively modified for its new purpose. A second stone wall had been built around the first. The door in the outer wall faced east; the one in the inner wall faced south. There was no way anyone could accidentally wander inside.

It was late afternoon. Toroca came here every day at this time, going past the warning signs painted on the walls, entering through the eastern door, walking along between the two walls until he reached the entrance onto the field from the south.

The field was two hundred paces in diameter. Most of it was covered by grass, kept short by Pasdo and Kendly, two old shovelmouths who lived inside here. They were tame beasts, as gentle as could be, and the children were crazy about them.

Toroca stood at the entrance, looking in. There were children everywhere in the playground. Nearby, four of them were playing a game with a ball, kicking it back and forth. Farther along, he saw five youngsters intently building structures in a pit of black sand. Over there, two females were chasing each other. The one in pursuit finally closed the gap, and, with an outstretched hand, *touched* the other girl on her back, then turned around and began running away. The one who'd been touched now took up the pursuit, her turn to try to catch the other one.

Toroca watched in amazement. Such a simple game, he thought, such an *obvious* game. And yet, no one of his generation had ever played it. But here he'd seen it spontaneously invented time and again.

He caught sight of a movement out of the corner of his eye— something sailing through the air. A ball. One youngster had thrown it and another had caught it. The one who'd caught it was now running with it. Two others gave hot pursuit, leaping onto his back and propelling him to the ground. Jaws swung open, but only so teeth could clack together, and one of the boys reached out a hand to help the felled player back to his feet.

Toroca beamed. In the center of the field, he saw his sister, Nov-Dynax, formerly a healer, formerly of Chu'toolar, who now worked here in this, the new creche. Toroca bowed toward her and she waved back. And there, off in the distance, carrying two youngsters, one on each shoulder, was Spenress, sister of Emperor Dy-Dybo.

Toroca was sorry that only adults such as these—adults who, like these children, had been spared seeing the culling of the bloodpriests—could come in here. The sight of such intimate contact between individuals (even if they were juveniles) could drive most Quintaglios to *dagamant*. And, of course, there was always the question of—

"Father!"

Toroca turned. The little yellow boy was running toward him, stubby tail flying out behind. "Father!" he called again. Toroca bent his knees and held out his arms. The child ran to him, and Toroca scooped him up.

"How's my boy?" Toroca said, holding him close, feeling his warmth.

Taksan looked at him with golden eyes. "Fine, Father," he said.

"And can you say that in the Other language?"

Taksan nodded. "*De-kat, rak-sa.* But, Father, I still don't understand why I have to learn to talk in two different ways. I mean, there's nobody except you who can understand me."

Toroca set the boy down and crouched beside him. "Someday, you will go somewhere where people speak like that." He patted the child on the shoulder. "Now, run along and play some more."

Taksan gave him a quick hug and went off to join his friends. Toroca watched him go, beaming with pride. Someday Taksan and some of this new generation of Quintaglios would go to see the Others again. He wanted Taksan to be able to say hello to them in their own language. But, more than that, he wanted him to be able to tell the Others just how very, very sorry the Quintaglios were.

Epilogue

The rest of the starships had left at various times over the last few kilodays. But this last ship hung in orbit above the innermost moon of the fifth planet. Liss extended her forefinger claw and used it to move a selector control. The viewscreen snapped to an image of that moon, waxing gibbous. A vast ocean covered almost everything except the frozen polar caps and the single continent with its archipelago of volcanic islands trailing off to the west, and another, smaller, archipelago in the nearside hemisphere. Many chains of volcanoes had popped up recently along fracture lines in the sub-sea crust. They looked like sutures on the skull of some strange round-headed beast.

Twisting white clouds moved in neat east-west bands as the moon spun rapidly on its axis. Intertwined with these were trails of black volcanic smoke, the dying gasps of this world.

Behind the moon was the massive planet they still called *Galatjaroob,* the Face of God. It, too, spun rapidly, causing its methane and ammonia clouds—gold and orange, brown and yellow—to play out into latitudinal bands. An awesome sight, thought Liss. She could understand how her ancestors, five hundred kilodays ago, had fallen into hypnotic stupor when they first saw it.

Liss would be sorry to leave the Face behind, to never bask in the sight of it again. Soon, very soon, this ship, too, would head off into interstellar space. But it was their job to wait, to actually watch the breakup of the Quintaglio moon.

An alarm sounded. The sensors left on various parts of Land

were beaming up signals, warning that the final breakup had begun. At that moment, the door to the instrumentation room opened and in floated Geman. He touched Liss on the shoulder. "The computer can look after the cameras," he said. "Come on up and watch it with the rest of us."

Liss checked the controls one last time, then pushed herself off the wall and followed Geman out into the corridor. They soon came to the observation deck. Thousands of green bodies, and hundreds of yellow ones, floated together beneath the vast bubble of the observation dome. Around its edges, ten giant viewscreens showed close-ups from the ship's external cameras, from free-flying probes, and from cameras left on the surface. Between two of the viewscreens was a glass case, holding the far-seer that had once belonged to Sal-Afsan.

Liss looked at the screens. The volcanoes in the southern part of the great ocean flared first, each in turn, like a chain of lights coming on one by one.

On one of the viewscreens, vast walls of water—waves the height of mountains—crashed against the rocky terrain, smashing the ancient ruins of the old Capital City, then flooding over the damage, sinking it all beneath the waves.

Soon, other volcanic chains, some with cones still submerged beneath the vast worldwide ocean, lit up. The moon Liss had been born on, always somewhat oblate because of its rapid spin, now took on the appearance of a cracked egg, the fissures aglow in red.

Another viewscreen was showing the coastline of Fra'toolar and the blue pyramid that anchored the space elevator. The ground was shaking, and the elevator shaft, an impossibly long blue finger reaching up toward the L3 point, was shifting back and forth. Although from the ground the vibration at first seemed minimal, another viewscreen showed the top of the shaft swinging in a vast arc.

The land was buckling and soon the stone ground beneath the pyramid started to crack. The blue material was virtually indestructible, but slowly the tower's base began to separate from the rock strata. It didn't topple, though. Rather, it gently rose up into the sky. The tower had begun to rotate around its midpoint, some 6,600 kilopaces above the surface of the dying moon. Although soon there would be nothing at all left of Quintaglio civilization, the blue tower, a calling card from those strange five-eyed beings who had transplanted life to this and other worlds millions of kilodays ago, would apparently survive the breakup of this moon.

When Liss's world at last fell apart, it did so with each component trailing glowing red streams of magma, like fiery entrails. The globe split into three large chunks and two smaller ones. Each began to move at a slightly different speed. The same differential tidal forces that had torn the world asunder now caused each piece to find its natural orbital velocity based on distance from the Face of God.

It wasn't long before the two largest hunks touched together again, silently shattering into hundreds of smaller pieces, the water that had covered them both scattering everywhere, freezing into droplets in space like a trillion new stars, twinkling as they tumbled in the blue-white light of the distant sun.

In successive orbits, the large chunks, tugged this way and that by gravitational interactions with each other and with the remaining thirteen moons, brushed and bounced together, grinding into smaller and smaller fragments. Already the pieces of debris were spreading into a thin band covering a few percent of the circumference of their orbits around the Face of God.

As the process continued, the shattered remnants of the home world would grind into hundreds of thousands of chunks, ranging from flying boulders to gravel-sized pieces, slowly distributing themselves into a vast, flat ring around the orange-and-yellow-banded planet.

The ship's central computer was an artificial intelligence whose mind simulated that of the greatest Quintaglio thinker of all time. Its neural nets had been configured and reconfigured until they had been trained to give the same responses to the question that the original had, three hundred and thirty kilodays ago, when his words had been recorded by Mokleb, the founder of modern psychological research, who had probed his every thought, every emotion.

The observation deck was crowded, but Liss was close to one of the pairs of glossy black hemispheres that were the computer's stereoscopic cameras. "Afsan," she said, "how long until the rubble actually forms a continuous ring around the Face of God?"

The computer's voice was deep and smooth, reassuring with its quiet confidence and the hints of serenity and wisdom that legend said were the hallmarks of the original Afsan. "I'm afraid we won't be able to stay for it," said the voice. "It'll take at least a hundred kilodays." And then a little sound effect issued from the speaker, a clicking like teeth gently touching together. "But when it's done, it will be a glorious sight—a beautiful reminder that, once upon a time, our home world did indeed exist."

The ship tarried a few days more, taking measurements. Then, at last, with everyone strapped onto his or her cushioned dayslab, the engines were brought on-line. Liss felt something she hadn't felt for a long time—the first faint sensation of her own weight— as the ship gently nudged out of orbit.

They had tried establishing colonies in this solar system, tried living under pressure domes on the third moon of Kevpel and on the rocky surface of Gefpel, tried living in orbital habitats. But none of those was a proper existence; they wouldn't do forever.

And so now they were leaving, all of them, green and yellow, Quintaglios and what had once been called Others, looking for a suitable home, a world on which they could run and play and hunt in the open air.

It would be a long voyage, and Liss would be dead well before it was over. But someday the children of the children of the eggs she now carried within her would arrive at their new home.

Their new home.

And their old home.

The monitoring room at the top of the space elevator had shown them pictures of the thirty-one worlds that the ark-makers had seeded, as well as pictures of the original home world, the crucible on which life had originally arisen. An antenna running along the tower's 13,000-kilopace height had picked up images continually broadcast by self-repairing probes left on those worlds by the ark-makers millennia ago.

Most of the Quintaglio generation ships had gone to new worlds discovered by orbital far-seers; a few had been dispatched to some of the worlds that had life already seeded on them; but this one ship, the last, had a very special mission.

It was going home.

Liss wondered whether the strange tailless bipeds, those long-lost cousins of the Quintaglios, would be glad to see them when they arrived back at their original world.

Time would tell.

The full-acceleration alarm sounded.

And the starship *Dasheter* surged ahead.

Appendix:
A Quintaglio Concordance

Dates given use the old pre-Larskian calendar, and are in kilodays after the hatching of the Eggs of Creation as told in the first sacred scroll.

Individuals are alphabetized under their common names (without praenomen syllables); full names, when known, are given in parentheses.

After each reference, the book in which the item was first presented is indicated: [1] for *Far-Seer*, [2] for *Fossil Hunter*, [3] for *Foreigner*.

adabaja: type of tree; since it is easy to waterproof, its wood is used in sailing ships and exterior scaffolding. [1]

Adkab: (7093–   ) a male Quintaglio, the fifth of seven apprentices to Tak-Saleed. [1]

Afdool: a Quintaglio name meaning "meaty legbone." [1]

Afsan (Sal-Afsan): (7096–   ) a male Quintaglio, the seventh and final apprentice to Tak-Saleed; he became known as "The One." He was hatched in Pack Carno, Arj'toolar province, the son of Pahs-Drawo. The name Afsan means "meaty thighbone." Blinded by Det-Yenalb in 7110, he later became an advisor to Emperor Dy-Dybo. [1]

Afsanian revolution: the intellectual, political, and religious upheaval following the discovery by Sal-Afsan in 7110 that the Face of God is a planet. [1]

Afsan's rock: a particular granite boulder (technical designation: Sun/Swift-Runner/4) at Rockscape favored by Sal-Afsan. [2]

Anakod: a male Quintaglio psychologist; once a promising student of Nav-Mokleb, now a professional rival. [3]

anchor: armless wingfinger-derived reptile indigenous to the south pole. [2]

Apripel: the eighth and outermost planet of the Quintaglio sun, a small, rocky world whose presence was first suggested to the Quintaglios by a system map seen in the observing room atop the Jijaki space elevator. [3]

Arbiter of the Sequence: the individual responsible for overseeing "the Sequence"—the official ordering of all information. Var-Osfik held this post during Sal-Afsan's time in Capital City. [2]

Arj'toolar: a province in northwest Land, home of Sal-Afsan, known for orange-and-blue-striped shovelmouths and the contemplatives of its holy land. Provincial color: white. [1]

ark-makers: Quintaglio term for the Jijaki. [3]

arks: hydrogen ramjet starships used by the Jijaki to transport plants and animals from Earth to the thirty-one destination worlds; the final ark, the *Ditikali-ot,* crashed into the Quintaglio moon. [2]

armorback: ankylosaur; herbivorous armored dinosaur. [1]

artifact, alien: a Jijaki handheld computer found by Kee-Toroca at the Bookmark layer in 7126. [2]

aug-ta-rot: Quintaglio term for "demon," literally meaning one who can tell lies in the light of day. This term was applied to the followers of the original five hunters who refused to accept Larsk's view of the world; the borders of the Tapestries of the Prophet show *aug-ta-rot* beings. [1]

Avenue of Traders: one of Capital City's widest thoroughfares. [2]

Baban (Ho-Baban): a Lubalite songwriter, best known for "The Ballad of the Ten," which tells the story of Lubal's original Pack. [1]

Babnol (Wab-Babnol): (7110–   ) a female Quintaglio from Pack Vando in Arj'toolar province who joined the Geological Survey of Land in 7126. She retained her birthing horn into adulthood. [2]

banded swift: a species of wingfinger with white fur and pale orange stripes. [3]

Bay of Three Forests: a small bay in Jam'toolar at the westernmost tip of Land; the *Dasheter* landed here after its first circumnavigation of the world. [1]

beat (or heartbeat): the shortest standard unit of time, equal to about 0.42 Earth seconds; this unit was eventually standardized by the Arbiter of the Sequence at 1/100,000 of a Quintaglio day. [1]

Belbar: one of the five original hunters, symbolized by the color blue. [1]

Belbar, Cape of: a storm-ravaged cape in Edz'toolar whose tip is the southernmost point in mainland Land. [1]

Belbar, Song of: a song about one of the original five hunters; one of its verses says, "If beasts confront you, slay them. If the elements conspire against you, overcome. And if God should call you to heaven before you return, then heaven will be the richer for it, and those you leave behind will honor you and mourn your passing." [3]

Belkom, Plaza of: a public square in Capital City. [2]

Big One, The: second of the Face of God's fourteen moons, orange in color. [1]

Biltog (Mar-Biltog): the *Dasheter*'s longest serving mate; a short-tempered male frequently stationed in the lookout bucket, given to telling endless stories about the old days. [1]

birds: extinct flying creatures, known only from fossils and specimens found aboard the crashed Jijaki ark. [2]

birthing horn: located on the upper surface of the muzzle, this fluted cone is the only one of the facial horns normally associated with tyrannosaurs that Quintaglios still develop. A birthing horn is usually lost about thirty days after hatching. [1]

blackdeath: tyrannosaur; the largest carnivorous dinosaur. [2]

blackpowder: explosive, used for clearing rocks. [2]

Bleen (Det-Bleen): the *Dasheter*'s bombastic male priest. [1]

bloodpriest: *halpataars,* a special priest, always male, who devours seven out of every eight hatchlings in each clutch; sometimes referred to as "a disciple of Mekt," the first bloodpriest. [1]

Bogkash (Det-Bogkash): male who succeeded Det-Yenalb as Master of the Faith; fired by Dy-Dybo in 7128. [2]

Boodskar: a volcanic island, westernmost member of the archipelago to the west of Land. [1]

Bookmark layer: in a coastal cliff face on the eastern shore of southern Fra'toolar province, nine-tenths of the way up to the top of the cliff, this chalk seam marks the oldest fossils ever found, and was taken by some to indicate the point of divine creation. [2]

Book of Rites: a standard Lubalite religious text, banned by Larsk. [1]

Brampto: a Pack in Arj'toolar; Bor-Vanbelk, inventor of the small-seer, comes from there. [3]

Bripel: the sixth planet of the Quintaglio sun; a ringed gas giant with sixteen moons. [1]

Cadool (Pal-Cadool): A lanky, illiterate male butcher at the imperial palace who becomes Sal-Afsan's personal assistant. A Lubalite. Cadool means "hunter of runningbeasts," but Wab-Novato calls him "Cadly," meaning "long of leg." [1]

Cafeed: apprentice bloodpriest under Mek-Lastoon in Pack Tablo in Edz'toolar. [2]

calthat'ch: Quintaglio word for "fraud." [1]

Capital City: the city built on the site of Larsk's landfall after returning from discovering the Face of God. The largest and most populous city in all of Land. [1]

Capital province: the easternmost province in Land. Population: 7,000. Provincial color: red. The Emperor is *ex officio* governor of this province. [1]

Carno: Sal-Afsan's home Pack, in Arj'toolar province; Carno roams along the northern shore of the Kreeb River. At the time Afsan left, its governor was Len-Haktood. [1]

Carpel: the innermost planet of the Quintaglio sun, a small and rocky world with no moons. [1]

Cartark (Bon-Cartark): a member of Pack Tablo in Edz'toolar. [2]

cartouche: personal identifying mark; an oval shape containing symbols or glyphs. [1]

ca-tart: Quintaglio word for "toys." [1]

Catekt (Tol-Catekt): a past leader of the imperial hunt. [1]

census bureau: official repository of records, located in Capital City. [3]

centiday: a unit of time equal to one one-hundredth of a Quintaglio day; about seven minutes. [2]

centipace: a unit of linear measure equal to one one-hundredth of a pace; about one centimeter. [2]

central square: a large open area in Capital City where Larsk had made many speeches. Afsan was blinded there, and the battle between the Lubalites and the palace loyal took place there in 7110. The arches of Dasan and the First Emperor were located there, as was Pador's famous marble statute of Larsk, but all were destroyed in the great landquake of 7110.

Ch'mar volcanoes: a range of active volcanoes to the west of Capital City. [1]

Chu'toolar: a large province in north-central Land, known for its glassworks and resort beaches. Provincial color: light green. [1]

coiled mollusk: ammonoid; a chambered, shelled cephalopod. [1]

Colboom: (7112–   ) a male member of Capital Pack, creche-mate of Bos-Karshirl. [3]

creche: communal nursery. [1]

creche, imperial: the nursery for members of The Family. Egg-shells of past Emperors are on display there. [1]

creche master/mother: terms used for Quintaglios who work in the communal nurseries. [1]

creche-mates: individual surviving members of each clutch of eggs laid in the same hatching period. Quintaglios are closer to their creche-mates than to anyone else, hence the saying "creche-mates are as one." [1]

Crucible: the planet Sol III (Earth), the only known world in the universe on which life arose naturally. [2]

culling: the sacrament performed by bloodpriests, swallowing seven of every eight hatchlings. [1]

Dabo (Gar-Dabo): an ancient female maritime explorer. [1]

dagamant: territorial bloodlust. [1]

Dagtool: apprentice to imperial bloodpriest Mek-Maliden. [2]

Daldar: a creche-mate of Wab-Novato. [3]

Dancer: one of the Face of God's fourteen moons. [2]

Dancing the Night Away: an astronomy book about the moons by Tak-Saleed. [1]

Dandor: a creche-mate of Sal-Afsan. [3]

Dargo: one of the five original male mates; the first healer. The sixth tenth of the kiloday is named after him. [2]

Dasan: an ancient land surveyor, famed for her ability to resolve territorial disputes without bloodshed; author of the *Hahat Golarda*. There was an arch in her honor in the central square of Capital City. [1]

Dasheter: large sailing ship captained by Var-Keenir, co-opted to the Geological Survey of Land. [1]

dat-kar-mas: a ceremonial dagger made from obsidian, normally used for cutting hide from an anointed kill to make copies of the sacred scrolls; one was used by Det-Yenalb to blind Sal-Afsan. [1]

Davpel: the third planet of the Quintaglio sun, a small and rocky world with two moons. [1]

day: the time it takes for the Quintaglio world to complete one orbit around the Face of God; eleven hours and forty-three minutes of Earth time. Days are subdivided into ten parts, called "daytenths," the first of which begins at dawn. [1]

dayslab: a hard platform of wood or stone mounted at an angle on a heavy pedestal, it supports the torso and legs while the user lies on his or her chest. [1]

Dedprod: (7098–7128) the female apprentice governor from Kev'toolar. [2]

dekaday: ten Quintaglio days, or about five Earth days. [1]

delbarn: a philosophic discipline related to the organization of knowledge; one of Nov-Dynax's professions. [2]

Delplas (Bar-Delplas): (7096–   ) a female member of the Geological Survey of Land; she wears a distinctive blue and orange sash. [2]

Derrilo, Pack: one of three Packs in Fra'toolar that periodically occupy stone buildings near the edge of the cliff exposing the Bookmark layer. [2]

Detoon: "Detoon the Righteous," the first priest, one of the five original mates, mated to Mekt. [1]

dewlap: Quintaglio secondary sexual characteristic. Males have a sack of skin on the front of the throat which inflates and shows red during sexual arousal; both sexes of Others have dewlaps. [1]

dispatch: euphemism used for the culling of the bloodpriests. [1]

Ditikali-ot: the final Jijaki ark, which crashed into Land. [2]

diver: ubiquitous indigenous fauna of the south pole, a swimming, fish-eating reptile based on the wingfinger body plan; dissecting one gives Kee-Toroca his first clue about evolution. [2]

Doblan (Pos-Doblan): a female Quintaglio, the keeper of the maritime rookery north of Capital City, where homing wingfingers are raised. [3]

Dolgar: ancient philosopher, the founder of psychology. Among his observations was that "the intelligent person must abhor violence." [1]

Donat (Pal-Donat): Pack Carno's bloodpriest. [1]

Doognar: a spring-fed lake in Arj'toolar province. [1]

Dordool (Tar-Dordool): leader of Pack Carno. [1]

downrock: sedimentary rock. [2]

Drawo (Pahs-Drawo): (–7110) Sal-Afsan's father, a Lubalite gored to death by Det-Yenalb's hornface. [1]

Drawtood: (7110–7128) a male Quintaglio, one of Sal-Afsan's children, a dockworker in Capital City. He committed suicide. [1]

Dybo (Dy-Dybo): (7098–   ) as Dybo, crown prince under Empress Len-Lends; after her death, Emperor Dy-Dybo. Hatched in Capital City. The son of the daughter of the daughter of the son of the daughter of the son of Larsk, the prophet. [1]

Dynax (Nov-Dynax): (7110–   ) a female Quintaglio healer, one of Sal-Afsan's children. She lived for a time in Chu'toolar. [1]

Edklark (Det-Edklark): A male Quintaglio priest, appointed Master of the Faith in 7128, succeeding Det-Bogkash.

Edz'toolar: the most isolated province, with a rocky, storm-swept coastline. Located in south-central Land. Provincial color: brown. Governed by Len-Ganloor until 7126; governed by Dy-Rodlox from 7126 to 7128. [1]

Egg of God: an egg from which God herself supposedly came; never referenced by the sacred scrolls, but proposed by Spooltar in his famous discourse on theology. [3]

Eggs of Creation: according to the first sacred scroll, the eight eggs laid by God from which all things in the universe, except the Quintaglios themselves, came. [2]

Empress/Emperor: the head of Quintaglio state, always a direct descendant of the Prophet Larsk. Referred to as "Your Luminance." [1]

Emteem: (7098–7128) male apprentice governor from Jam'toolar. [2]

even-day: an even-numbered day within a kiloday. [1]

even-night: the night of an even-numbered day; sometimes called "liar's night," since most Quintaglios are awake then but it's too dark to see their muzzles. [1]

exodus project: the effort, led by Wab-Novato, to get the Quintaglio people off their doomed world. Symbolized by a sash consisting of a lower green strip and an upper black one. [2]

Face of God: *Galat-jaroob,* the fifth planet of the Quintaglio sun, a gas giant world with fourteen moons, the innermost of which is the Quintaglio world. Diameter: 60,000 kilopaces (similar to Saturn's). Mass: 236 times that of the Quintaglio world (intermediate between Jupiter and Saturn). [1]

Falpom (Irb-Falpom): (7060–7126) the palace land surveyor who had an office near Tak-Saleed's. She was Kee-Toroca's teaching master and, from 7111 until her death, first leader of the Geological Survey of Land. [1]

Family, The: The Royal Family, the direct descendants of the Prophet Larsk. [1]

fangjaw: a type of carnosaur that evolved after the transplantation from the Crucible, a quadruped with two giant teeth growing up from the lower jaw. [1]

far-seer: telescope, invented by Wab-Novato of Pack Gelbo in 7105. [1]

Fastok: a port south of Capital City. [3]

Fetarb: a butcher at the imperial palace. [2]

Fifty Packs: "The Fifty Packs" is a general expression, referring to all the Quintaglio people. Each of the original five hunters had a Pack of ten members, and each of those ten members founded a Pack, for a total of fifty. However, many subgroups were subsequently formed, and there are now far more than Fifty Packs. [1]

first ancestor: an oblique reference to Lubal, thought to be first-formed of the original five hunters. [1]

First Edict of Lubal: "A Quintaglio kills with tooth and claw; only such killing makes us strong and pure." [3]

first Emperor: term sometimes used for Larsk; the Arch of the First Emperor stands in the central square of Capital City. [1]

fish-lizard: ichthyosaur. [1]

Forgool (Dak-Forgool): (7095–7126) eminent geologist from Pack Vando, expert in erosion, assigned to the Geological Survey, but died of fever before taking his post; Wab-Babnol joined the Survey in his place. [2]

Foss: assistant to imperial hunt leader Lub-Galpook. [2]

Fra'toolar: a province in southwest Land where the alien ark was unearthed. Provincial color: dark blue. [1]

gabo: a type of nut, with three seeds within. [1]

gadkortakdt: the point in a game of *lastoontal* in which neither player can force a win. [1]

Galadoreter: ill-fated sailing ship; blown out to sea by a storm, unable to land for dekadays. With no way to release the territorial instinct, the crew fought until everyone aboard was dead. The ship blew back to shore near the mining town of Parnood. [1]

galamaja: a type of tree with pale wood. [1]

Galat-jaroob: Quintaglio term meaning "the Face of God." [3]

Galpook (Lub-Galpook): (7110–   ) a female Quintaglio, one of Sal-Afsan's children. Succeeds Jal-Tetex as imperial hunt leader. [1]

Gampar (Nor-Gampar): (7090–7110) a male mate aboard the *Dasheter* who went into *dagamant* and was killed by Sal-Afsan. [1]

Ganloor (Len-Ganloor): (7079–7126) female governor of Edz'toolar, sister of Len-Lends, killed in a hunting accident. She was succeeded by Dy-Rodlox. [2]

gaolok: sap used to waterproof ship hulls. [1]

Garios (Den-Garios): a member of the exodus project staff who mated with Wab-Novato in 7112, producing a daughter, Bos-Karshirl. [3]

Garsub (Jal-Garsub): the middle-aged female hunt leader of Pack Tablo in Edz'toolar. [2]

Gatabor: a hunter who belongs to Pack Derrilo in Fra'toolar. [2]

Gathgol (Var-Gathgol): Capital City's undertaker, a male who assists Sal-Afsan in investigating the murder of Afsan's daughter, Haldan. [2]

Gefpel: the seventh planet of the Quintaglio sun, small and rocky. [1]

Gelbo: Wab-Novato's home Pack, in western Jam'toolar. [1]

Geological Survey of Land: project to provide a complete inventory of natural resources that might be of use to the exodus. Proposed by Wab-Novato, authorized in 7111 by Dy-Dybo, and directed first by Irb-Falpom and later by Kee-Toroca. [2]

Gerthalk: "Gerthalk the Miracle Worker," an ancient healer. [1]

glowgrub: beetle larva capable of bioluminescence. [1]

glyph: Quintaglio written character; "stone-glyphs" are an ancient writing form. When a word is to be emphasized, its constituent glyphs are written facing to the left rather than the right. [1]

God: the deity of the Quintaglio people, personified as a giant armless female Quintaglio. [1]

Godglow: light visible on the horizon before one actually sights the Face of God. [1]

God's eyes: shadows cast on the Face of God's cloud tops by its coterie of moons. [1]

Gork: Sal-Afsan's large pet monitor lizard. [2]

government, Quintaglio: the Emperor or Empress is the head of state and governor of Capital province; each of the seven other provinces has its own governor. The principal branches of Quintaglio government are the church, civil works, the exodus, interprovincial trade, the judiciary, portents and omens, and tithing. [1]

Gray Orb: one of the Face of God's fourteen moons. [2]

Greeblo: (7057–   ) an elderly female member of the Geological Survey of Land. [2]

groundfruit: the succulent fruit of a low-growing plant. [1]

Guardian: one of the Face of God's fourteen moons. [2]

guards, imperial: security officers charged with protecting members of The Family. [1]

***guvdok* stone:** torus-shaped stone carved with one's professional credentials and award citations. [1]

Hadzig (Irb-Hadzig): a member of the *Dasheter* crew, swallowed by Kal-ta-goot. [1]

***hahat dan*:** standard abbreviation of the Quintaglio phrase *"hahator pas da dan,"* meaning "permission to enter my territory is granted." [1]

***Hahat Golarda*:** an ancient scroll written by Dasan that apportioned provincial territories. [3]

Haktood (Len-Haktood): (7080–   ) the governor of Arj'toolar at the time Sal-Afsan left there. [1]

halbataja: a tree whose leaves are used for medicinal purposes. [1]

Haldan: (7110–7126) a female Quintaglio, one of Sal-Afsan's children. She was a naturalist who studied animal populations. Murdered. [1]

Hall of Stone Eggs: a corridor in the old palace in Capital City lined with cut geodes. [1]

Hall of Worship: a Quintaglio church. Major services are held every fifth even-day. On odd-days, daytenths are marked by the appropriate number of drumrolls; on even-days, by the appropriate number of bells. [1]

halpataars: Quintaglio term meaning "bloodpriest." [1]

Halporn: a port city in Fra'toolar province near the Jam'toolar border. [1]

haltardark: a liquid used to clean lenses; deadly poison (symbolized by a drop shape with the outline of an animal lying on its side); Drawtood commits suicide by drinking this. [2]

Haltang: a male, third of seven apprentices to Tak-Saleed. [1]

hamadaja: a type of tree, its leaves are the favorite fodder of thunderbeasts. [1]

hamrak: a philosophic discipline concerned with morals and ethics; one of Nov-Dynax's professions. [2]

Hapurd (Bal-Hapurd): an old member of the palace staff. [1]

Harnal (Pas-Harnal): a metallurgist who lives in Capital City. [2]

Helbark: (7110–7110) a male Quintaglio, one of Sal-Afsan's children; he died of fever shortly after hatching. [1]

henkar: a plant producing yellow melons that thunderbeasts like to eat. [3]

Hoad-Malat: a past imperial hunt leader. [1]

Honlab (Len-Honlab): the stubborn governor of Chu'toolar. [3]

Hoog: one of the original five hunters, patron of butchers. Associated with the color yellow. [1]

Hoont'mar mountain chain: a chain of mountains on the border between Chu'toolar and Mar'toolar. [3]

Horbo, Pack: one of three Packs in Fra'toolar that periodically occupy stone buildings near the edge of the cliff exposing the Bookmark layer. [2]

hornface: ceratopsian dinosaur; herbivorous. Often domesticated and used in caravans. "Triple hornface" refers to the genus *Triceratops*. [1]

hornface, bossnosed: pachyrhinosaur ceratopsian dinosaur; herbivorous. [1]

Howlee, Tower of: a mythical tower to the stars, twenty-five kilopaces tall, with a base fifty paces wide, told of in the fiftieth sacred scroll. [3]

Hunter: a constellation named in honor of Lubal; during the Larskian era, it was known as the Prophet in honor of Larsk. [1]

Hunter's Shrine: a structure made of the bones of previous hunt leaders built atop a giant rock pile near Capital City. According to legend, each of the original five hunters had brought one stone to this pile for every successful kill throughout their lives. [1]

hunting spirit: a Lubalite term for "soul." [1]

hunt leader: leader of a Pack's hunting parties; almost always a female who is in perpetual heat. [1]

imperial jack: a breed of wingfinger, flocks of which fly in a distinctive three-pronged formation. [3]

Inlee (Vek-Inlee): an ancient female maritime explorer. She was the first to sight the north polar cap, but mistook it for the icy shore of the River. [1]

Irb-Falpom: one of the five Quintaglio gliders used in the battle against the Others. [3]

Jal-Tetex: one of the five Quintaglio gliders used in the battle against the Others. [3]

Jam'toolar: a province in northwest Land. Provincial color: gold. [1]

Jawn: an Other who teaches Kee-Toroca their language. [3]

jerboksaja: a type of tree with branches that trail into the wind. [1]

Jidha: (7112–   ) a member of Capital Pack, creche-mate of Bos-Karshirl. [3]

Jijak: (plural, Jijaki) extinct beings evolved from transplanted *Opabinia,* with six legs, five phosphorescent eyes each on a short stalk, plus a long flexible trunk ending in a pair of cup-shaped manipulators. The first intelligent form to emerge in this universe, used by The Watcher to transplant life from the Crucible. [2]

Jodor (Fas-Jodor): (7079–   ) the hunt leader of Pack Derrilo. [2]

Jostark: one of the five original male mates; the first crafter, mated to Katoon. [2]

Jostark's Day: a holiday, celebrated with a parade, in honor of craftspeople. [2]

Jostor: a famous musician who was a creche-mate of Sal-Afsan. [3]

Julor (Cat-Julor): a creche mother from Pack Carno who knew Sal-Afsan. [1]

kadapaja: a type of tree; its wood is used in fires because of its even flames and slow consumption. [1]

Kaden (Lub-Kaden): female, a hunt leader from Pack Gelbo. She was deceased by 7131. [1]

kalahatch: a traditional call to the hunt. [2]

Kal-ta-goot: a giant plesiosaur (aquatic reptile) that twice did battle with the *Dasheter*. The first time, in 7109, it chomped off Captain Var-Keenir's tail; the second time, in 7110, it was slain by Sal-Afsan. [1]

Karshirl (Bos-Karshirl): (7112–7131) a female structural engineer from Capital City, assigned to the exodus project; daughter of Wab-Novato and Den-Garios, she was killed in a landquake. [3]

katadu bench: bench on either side of the throne slab, used by imperial advisors. [1]

Katood (Dath-Katood): an old male mate aboard the *Dasheter*. [1]

Katoon: one of the original five hunters. Associated with the color green. [1]

Katoon, Skull of: a constellation. [1]

Keebark: a creche-mate of Sal-Afsan. [3]

Keenir (Var-Keenir): (7047–   ) captain of the *Dasheter* and influential Lubalite, he was a creche-mate of Tak-Saleed. [1]

keetaja: a type of tree with golden wood. [1]

Keladax: ancient male philosopher, known for the dictum "Nothing is anything unless it is something." Also coined the saying "Time crawls for a child, walks for an adolescent, and runs for an adult," and wrote a famous polemic on battles in which he observed that the most important thing you can have on your side is being right in the eyes of God. [1]

Kelboon (Af-Kelboon): (7110–   ) a male Quintaglio mathematician, one of Sal-Afsan's children. [1]

kev: an old Quintaglio word for "bright." [3]

Kevo: one of the original Fifty Packs. [3]

Kevpel: the fourth planet of the Quintaglio sun, a ringed gas giant. [1]

Kev'toolar: a province in southeast Land. Provincial color: light blue. [1]

kiit: Jijaki term for the super-strong blue building material developed for their interstellar ramjets. [2]

Kijititatak Gikta: a Jijaki children's television program, featuring an animated character named Tilk. [2]

kiloday: one thousand Quintaglio days (about one and a third Earth years). [1]

kilopace: one thousand paces (about one kilometer). [1]

Klimsan: "Klimsan the Scaly" (Sar-Klimsan), a previous imperial hunt leader; also "the smooth-skinned Klimsan," another previous imperial hunt leader. [1]

Kreeb River: a meandering river that forms part of the border between Arj'toolar and Fra'toolar; Pack Carno roams along its north shore. [1]

Kroy: (7098–7128) female apprentice governor from Arj'toolar. [2]

kurpa **leather:** fine leather taken from wingfinger bodies. [1]

lancer: a wingfinger-derived reptile indigenous to the south pole with elongated fourth fingers that it uses for spearing fish. [2]

Land: name given to the single continent of the Quintaglio home world, roughly oval in shape, measuring some 3,000 kilopaces from the harbor of Capital City to the western-most tip of mainland Fra'toolar and 1,200 kilopaces from its northern edge to the Cape of Belbar in the south. [1]

landquake: earthquake. [1]

Landquake, Great: the larger of two landquakes to rock Capital City in kiloday 7110. [1]

language, Other: in the language of the Others, successive degrees are shown by repetition. The introduction of the syllable *"na"* into the middle of a word signifies negation. Among the words Kee-Toroca learns are *de-kat* (fine), *eb* (plus), *ga-san* (sailing ship), *gan-noth* (explain), *glees* (interrogative for "how righteous is this?"), *hak-al* (bullet), *hoos-ta* (good), *hoos-na-ta* (bad), *jar-dik* (threat), *joth-shal* (trick), *kas-tak* (discharge a weapon), *lees-tash* (blind), *lesh* (face), *rak-sa* (father), *sas* (your), *sek-tab* (correct), *sek-na-tab* (incorrect), *sil-don-kes-la* (rowboat), *tar* (is), *thash-rath* (an epithet), and the numbers *bal* (one), *lod* (two), *ker* (three), and *farg-sol* (twelve). [3]

language, Quintaglio: related nouns usually end in the same suffix, for example: *-aja* (most types of wood), *-'mar* (mountain chain), *-o* (Pack), *-pel* (planet), *-staynt* (type of building), *-ter* (proper name for a sailing ship), *-tok* (small town), *-'toolar* (province). [1]

Laree (Dee-Laree): the officer in charge of palace accounts under Dy-Dybo. [3]

Larsk: A sailor who came to be known as The Prophet. In kiloday 6959, he was the first Quintaglio to sight the Face of God. He returned to Land at what later became Capital City and established a religion and a dynasty based on worship of the Face. [1]

Lastoon (Mek-Lastoon): (–7126) the bloodpriest of Pack Tablo in Edz'toolar. [2]

lastoontal: a strategic board game. [1]

latark: Quintaglio term equivalent to "giddyup." [1]

Lee (Len-Lee): the governor of Kev'toolar. [3]

Lends (Len-Lends): (7079–7110) Empress, the mother of Dy-Dybo; she was killed when a roof collapsed on her in the small landquake of 7110. [1]

liar's night: even-night. [2]

liar's tint: a reference to the color blue. [1]

lifeboat: name given to the cabs traveling up and down the Jijaki tower. [3]

limpid floater: jellyfish. [3]

Lirpan (Nom-Lirpan): a senior palace advisor in Dy-Dybo's administration, in charge of provincial relations. [2]

Lizhok: a female, second of seven apprentices to Tak-Saleed. [3]

Loodo: a Pack in southern Mar'toolar; Nav-Mokleb hatched there. [3]

Lubal: largest of the original five hunters. Associated with the color red. She was gored by a hornface. As she lay dying, she prophesied the coming of The One. [1]

Lubal, Temple of: an ancient temple in Capital province, located on the west side of the Ch'mar volcanoes; known for the Spires of the Original Five. It was mostly buried by lava in the eruptions of 7110. [1]

Lubalite: an adherent of the Hunter's religion, a worshiper of the original five hunters following the precepts outlined in the Edicts of Lubal. [1]

Lub-Kaden: one of five Quintaglio gliders used in the battle against the Others. [3]

madaja: a type of sacred tree, the wood of which is used for the floors of Halls of Worship. [1]

Madool (Cat-Madool): a member of Pack Tablo in Edz'toolar. [2]

***makaloob* root:** holding one of these roots in the mouth can quell nausea. [1]

Maliden (Mek-Maliden): (7047–7128) a male Quintaglio who served as imperial bloodpriest until his death. [2]

maritime rookery: a breeding facility for homing wingfingers situated north of Capital City and run by Pos-Doblan. [3]

Matark: Lubal's hornface riding mount; also a constellation depicting same. [3]

Mar'toolar: an almost completely landlocked province in central Land, known for its great plains. The only place on Land where agriculture is practiced extensively. Provincial color: pink. [1]

Master of the Faith: the High Priest and spiritual advisor to the Emperor or Empress; presides over Capital City's Hall of Worship. During Afsan's lifetime, the Masters of the Faith were Det-Yenalb (up to 7110), Det-Bogkash (from 7110 to 7128), and Det-Edklark (beginning in 7128). [1]

Mekt: one of the original five hunters; she was the first bloodpriest until she repudiated the job as inappropriate for a layer of eggs. Associated with the color purple. [1]

Mekt, Cape of: in southern Fra'toolar, near the site of the space ark. [2]

Mokleb (Nav-Mokleb): developer of "the talking cure"; a female psychologist from Pack Loodo in Mar'toolar who treats Sal-Afsan. [3]

Mondark (Dar-Mondark): the palace healer. He treated Sal-Afsan in 7109 after Afsan had felled a great thunderbeast and again in 7130 when Afsan's head was kicked by a hornface. [1]

moons: the Face of God has fourteen natural satellites orbiting around it, including the Quintaglio world (the innermost moon), Big One (second closest to the Face), Sprinter, Swift Runner, Dancer, Gray Orb, the Guardian, and Slow-poke (the outermost moon). [1]

Morb: (–7131) the chief of security for the Others. [3]

Nasfedeter: the sailing ship that in 7110 transported Dy-Dybo from Jam'toolar to Capital City to take the throne. [1]

Nesster: (7098–7128) male, the apprentice governor of Mar'toolar. [2]

newsrider: a Quintaglio who travels from Pack to Pack on a runningbeast, bringing news. [1]

nictitating membrane: the semi-transparent inner Quintaglio eyelid. [1]

Noltark (Pal-Noltark): a male painter whose book *The Wing-fingers of Land* supposedly contains a painting of every species of wingfinger. [3]

Novato (Wab-Novato): (7094–   ) a female Quintaglio from Pack Gelbo who invented the far-seer in 7105 and became leader of the exodus project in 7110. [1]

Nunard rift: part of the subduction zone between the two tectonic plates that form the continent of Land; an old royal marble quarry, known for pristine white stone, was located near it, but was closed after a series of landquakes. [1]

odd-day: an odd-numbered day within a kiloday. [1]

odd-night: the night of an odd-numbered day; most Quintaglios sleep on odd-nights. [1]

One, The: prophesied by Lubal, a male Quintaglio who would be the greatest hunter of all time. The name "The One" is sometimes applied to Sal-Afsan. [1]

Orange Wingfinger: an inn near Capital City's docks, favored by discerning mariners. [1]

original five hunters: Lubal, Mekt, Katoon, Hoog, and Belbar; according to the first sacred scroll, these five females were created from the fingers of the severed left hand of God. [1]

original five mates: Varkev, the first explorer; Dargo, the original healer; Takood, the first scholar; Jostark, the craftsperson before all others; and Detoon the Righteous, the first priest. According to the first sacred scroll, these five males were created from the fingers of the severed right hand of God. [2]

Oro (Pod-Oro): (7067–7128) male; aide to Governor Dy-Rodlox of Edz'toolar, killed by Sal-Afsan in the mass *dagamant* of 7128. [2]

Osbkay volcano: a volcano near Pack Gelbo. [1]

Osfik (Var-Osfik): a female Quintaglio holding the post of Arbiter of the Sequence. [2]

Others: a species of carnosaur closely related to Quintaglios but smaller in stature and with yellow skin and eyes, living on an archipelago north of the equator on the nearside hemisphere of the Quintaglio moon. [3]

Otok: a port town in Fra'toolar. [2]

pace: standard Quintaglio unit of linear measure, used for both length and height. Approximately equal to one meter. [1]

Pack: the principal Quintaglio social group. Also **pack**, a hunting party. [1]

Pador: the sculptor who made the statue of Larsk in the central square of Capital City. [1]

Pakta tannery: a large facility for tanning hides located near Yabool's home in Capital City. [2]

Paldook: a mate aboard the *Dasheter*. [1]

Palsab (Gerth-Palsab): a pious, illiterate female citizen of Capital City who engages Sal-Afsan in an argument about his worldview. [1]

Parnood: a coastal mining town; the ill-fated sailing ship *Galadoreter* was blown back to shore near it. [1]

Passalat sandstones: the finest grained sandstones in all of Land, known for their magnificent fossils (including bird fossils). [2]

Patpel: the second planet of the Quintaglio sun, small and rocky. [1]

Paturn: a young male Quintaglio nurse working at the imperial surgery. [1]

Pettit: Sal-Afsan's female apprentice. [3]

pheromones: airborne chemicals secreted by Quintaglios that elicit behavioral responses in other members of that race. [1]

pilgrimage: ritual retracing of Larsk's ocean voyage of kiloday 6959 in which he first sighted the Face of God. A Quintaglio must be at least ten kilodays old to take the pilgrimage; a pilgrimage ship holds station beneath the Face for ten even-days and ten odd-days, during which thirty-seven penances are performed and the nine sacred scrolls devoted to Larsk's journey are studied. [1]

Pilgrimage Guild: founded by Larsk, an organization certifying sailors to perform pilgrimages; all mariners of note belong to it. [1]

Pironto (Dem-Pironto): a deceased imperial hunt leader, gored by a triple hornface; succeeded by Jal-Tetex. [1]

pistaral: a type of plant thunderbeasts like to eat. [3]

planets: the planets of the Quintaglio sun, in order out from it, are Carpel, Patpel, Davpel (all rocky worlds), Kevpel (a ringed gas giant), the Face of God (a gas giant), Bripel (another ringed gas giant), and the rocky worlds of Gefpel and Apripel. [1]

Polemic on Battles: a famous writing by Keladax; it says that the most important thing you can have on your side is being right in the eyes of God. [3]

Porgon: individual in charge of palace protocol. [3]

Pradak (Gan-Pradak): the chief palace engineer. [2]

praenomen syllable: a component of an adult Quintaglio's name; a prefix chosen by the bearer upon completing the rites of passage. It is usually the first syllable of the name of the individual's patron or of an admired historical figure. Examples include *Det-*, a common praenomen for priests, derived from Detoon the Righteous, and *Mek-*, frequently chosen by bloodpriests, in honor of Mekt. Sal-Afsan's praenomen is in honor of Tak-Saleed, his teaching master; Saleed's commemorates Takood, the first scholar; Var-Keenir's is in honor of Varkev, the first explorer; and Kee-Toroca's is in honor of Keenir himself. Provincial governors always take a praenomen in honor of the current Emperor or Empress (as in Len-Haktood and Dy-Rodlox), whereas the head of state always takes a praenomen in honor of himself or herself (as in Len-Lends and Dy-Dybo). [1]

Prath: funereal site a half-day's march southwest of Capital City; a basalt field where bodies are laid out for predators to claim. [2]

prayer neckband: a leather band worn during prayer by those who haven't yet received the two tattoos marking completion of the rites of passage. [1]

Prophet: name given to Larsk; also, for a time, the constellation of the Hunter was renamed this in honor of him. [1]

provinces: the provinces of Land, as apportioned by the *Hahat Golarda,* are Jam'toolar, Fra'toolar, Arj'toolar, Chu'toolar, Mar'toolar, Edz'toolar, Kev'toolar, and Capital. [1]

Punood: a hunter who was killed by a slap from a thunderbeast's tail during Sal-Afsan's first hunt. [1]

Quebelmo, Pack: one of three Packs in Fra'toolar that periodically occupy stone buildings near the edge of the cliff exposing the Bookmark layer. [2]

Quelban (Len-Quelban): (7080–   ) the governor of Fra'toolar. [1]

Quetik: (–7131) the female pilot of the rebuilt glider *Tak-Saleed*. [3]

Quintaglios: an intelligent species of tyrannosaur, derived from the Earth genus *Nanotyrannus*; the name means "The People of Land." [1]

Quintaglio world: the twenty-seventh world seeded by The Watcher. A tectonically active globe mostly covered a single ocean, it has one large continent and by two polar ice caps. Originally the third of fourteen moons of the Face of God, chaotic orbital dynamics made it the innermost moon. Mass: approximately the same as Earth's. Diameter: 12,000 kilopaces. By the time of the Afsanian revolution, its center orbits at a mean distance of 162,600 kilopaces from the center of the Face of God (2.71 times the Face's radius). [1]

raladaja: a type of tree. [1]

raloodoo: a delicacy from Chu'toolar province, consisting of shovelmouth eyes dipped in the rich, sugary sap of a *raladaja* tree. [1]

Reegree (Ter-Reegree): Dy-Dybo's father (deceased). [1]

Reestee (Gar-Reestee): a male charioteer in Capital City whose hornface accidentally kicks Sal-Afsan in the head. [3]

Regbo (Dar-Regbo): a Lubalite hunter who participates in the battle with the palace loyal in 7110. [1]

Retlas: (7112–   ) a female member of Capital Pack, crechemate of Bos-Karshirl. [3]

Rewdan and the Vine: a children's story from Mar'toolar. Rewdan planted some magic seeds and from them a vine grew up into the sky. Rewdan climbed the vine and was attacked by a giant blackdeath living at the top, but he managed to escape with a wingfinger that laid eggs of gold. [3]

Rikgot: a female, fourth of seven apprentices to Tak-Saleed. [3]

River: ancient name for the vast, world-spanning ocean covering almost all of the Quintaglio world. [1]

robe: clothing worn by priests and, on ceremonial occasions, by the Emperor. Until the Afsanian revolution, normal priests wore banded ones imitative of the Face of God's clouds; junior priests wore red and black ones; bloodpriests wore purple ones. After the revolution, all priests wear simple white robes, except for bloodpriests, who continue to wear purple. [1]

Rockscape: just north of Capital City, ninety-four granite boulders arranged in geometric shapes; the oldest known evidence of a Quintaglio settlement. [2]

Rodlox (Dy-Rodlox): (7098–7128) male governor from Edz'toolar who challenged Dy-Dybo for the Emperorship. [2]

royal marble quarry: near the Nunard rift, famed for its pristine white stones; closed after a series of landquakes. [1]

runningbeast: stocky ornithomimid dinosaur with a round body, stiff tail, legs built for great strides, long neck, tiny head, and giant eyes. Several species exist; the fastest can run at speeds up to sixty-five kilopaces per daytenth, and can carry a single Quintaglio rider. [1]

sacred scroll, 1st: written two thousand kilodays ago, it tells of the origin of the world. [2]

sacred scroll, 4th: tells of Mekt killing an armorback. [3]

sacred scroll, 11th: talks about working together to rebuild, and says that God sends landquakes not out of spite or anger, but to give Quintaglios a reason to hold their instincts at bay and cooperate. [1]

sacred scroll, 17th: discusses Mekt's repudiation of being a bloodpriest and the establishment of the all-male bloodpriest order. [3].

sacred scroll, 18th: forbids discussion of dispatched hatchlings and declares that "children are the children of the Pack." [2]

sacred scroll, 23rd: also called the Scroll of the Hunt, it defines the hunt as the ritual through which emotions of hate and violence are purged; the endeavor through which Quintaglios gain self-sufficiency; the activity that brings them together in camaraderie and cooperation. It implies that in heaven Quintaglios will no longer feel territoriality. This scroll also forbids the killing of animals that will not be eaten, as well as the use of weapons in hunting, saying, "That which is at hand is there by the grace of God; use it if need be, but take not a weapon with you on the hunt, for that is the coward's way." [1]

sacred scroll, 50th: tells the story of the Tower of Howlee. [3]

sacred scroll, 111th: declares "for there is grace in all Quintaglios, but none more so than the skilled hunter." [1]

Sacred Scroll of the Hunt: another name for the twenty-third sacred scroll. [1]

Sacred Scrolls of Jostark: a series of scrolls setting out the religious rituals devoted to various crafts. [3]

Sacred Scrolls of the Prophet: the final nine sacred scrolls, describing the life of Larsk. [1]

salabaja: a type of tree. [2]

Saleed (Tak-Saleed): (7047–7110) male court astrologer under Emperor Len-Lends; Sal-Afsan's teaching master; a creche-mate of Var-Keenir. Author of *Dancing the Night Away* and the eighteen volumes of the *Treatise on the Planets*. [1]

Sardon (Sar-Sardon): Quintaglio Empress prior to Len-Lends; Dy-Dybo's grandmother. She visited Pack Carno briefly on 7096/6/19. [1]

sash: the only clothing normally worn by a Quintaglio, often adorned by insignia indicating one's profession. Blood-red sashes are reserved for members of The Family; gray for master mariners; the combination of orange and blue for imperial staff; and green and black for members of the exodus project. Prior to the Afsanian revolution, senior priests, when not wearing robes, wore sashes with swirling, colorful patterns imitative of the cloud banks on the Face of God. [1]

scooter: a wingfinger-derived reptile indigenous to the south pole that shoots across the ice on its belly, kicking its powerful hind feet for propulsion. [2]

Seenuk (Mar-Seenuk): one of the hunters comprising Belbar's original Pack of ten; founded the Pack that Carno is descended from. [1]

semi-ten: a Quintaglio term for "five." [1]

Sequence: the order of knowledge; since the Quintaglios don't have an alphabet, they have no concept of alphabetical order; all knowledge instead is organized into this linear progression. The Arbiter of the Sequence is responsible for determining the order. [1]

Serkob (Rej-Serkob): from Pack Carno, an individual Sal-Afsan thought might have been his father. [1]

Shanpin foothills: an inhospitable land of scorched ground and basalt. [2]

shawl: a wingfinger-derived reptile indigenous to the south pole; tall and thin, shawls wrap themselves in their thick rubbery wings to keep warm. [2]

ship's call: a distinctive pattern of drumbeats and bells used to identify a ship; when a ship is at rest at sea, the part of its call normally done by drumbeats is done with bells, and vice versa. [1]

Shoveler's Inlet: a passage leading inland on the border between Fra'toolar and Mar'toolar, at the north end of the Bay of Vatastor. [3]

shovelmouth: duckbilled dinosaur (hadrosaur), herbivorous and docile. Despite having stringy meat, they are a staple of the Quintaglio diet. [1]

sinner's doorway: portal in a Hall of Worship, outlined by a black basalt arch, set perpendicular to the channel of holy water. Through here, penitents enter and perform the sinner's march. [1]

sinner's march: ritual walk through holy water in a Hall of Worship. [1]

skimmer: a wingfinger-derived gliding reptile indigenous to the south pole. [2]

Skull of Katoon: a constellation on the ecliptic. [1]

Slowpoke: the outermost of the Face of God's fourteen moons. [1]

small-seer: microscope, invented by Bor-Vanbelk of Pack Brampto in Arj'toolar. [3]

Sor-Denkal: one of the five Quintaglio gliders used in the battle against the Others. [3]

south pole: southern ice pack; Kee-Toroca led an expedition there in 7127. [2]

Spalton (Gan-Spalton): (7197–   ) a male member of the Geological Survey of Land, known for his sly sense of humor. [2]

Spenress: (7098–   ) female apprentice governor from Chu'toolar, and, later, a worker in the new creche in Capital City. [2]

spikefrill: styracosaur ceratopsian; an herbivorous dinosaur. [1]

Spires of the Original Five: at the Temple of Lubal west of Capital City, five giant stone columns representing the upward-stretched fingers of the hand of God from which the original five hunters were formed. [2]

Spooltar: ancient female religious philosopher who said, "A true belief is stronger than the mightiest hunter, for nothing can bring it down." She proposed the existence of an Egg of God. [1]

Sprinter: one of the Face of God's fourteen moons. [1]

Stardeter: a small sailboat used by Sal-Afsan and Kee-Toroca on their peace mission to the Others. [3]

Stark (Kad-Stark): a deceased imperial hunt leader. [1]

starweed: common plant with orange flowers. [3]

stilt: giant reptile indigenous to the south pole, derived from wingfinger stock. [2]

Sun/Swift-Runner/4: technical designation for Sal-Afsan's rock at Rockscape. [2]

superposition: theory developed by Irb-Falpom stating that the lower rocks in a sedimentary sequence are the older ones. [2]

Swift Runner: one of the Face of God's fourteen moons. [1]

Tablo, Pack: a Pack on the outskirts of Edz'toolar. [2]

Tagleeb (Gat-Tagleeb): fantasist; a contemporary of Sal-Afsan. [1]

Takood: one of the five original male mates; the first scholar. [2]

Tak-Saleed: the first Quintaglio glider, originally dubbed "Novato's folly." First flown in 7128; rebuilt and used again in the battle against the Others in 7131. [2]

Taksan: (7131–   ) a male Other child, adopted by Kee-Toroca. [3]

talking cure: a psychological therapy technique resembling psychoanalysis developed by Nav-Mokleb. [3]

Tapestries of the Prophet: famous paintings on leather by Hel-Vleetnav that depict Larsk's voyage; they are kept behind sheets of thin glass in the basement of the palace office building in Capital City. [1]

Tardlo (Bog-Tardlo): a mate aboard the *Dasheter*. [1]

Tasnik: a female, first of seven apprentices to Tak-Saleed. [3]

tattoo of the hunt: a purple-black tattoo located above the left earhole, received upon successful completion of one's first hunt. [1]

tattoo of the pilgrimage: a tattoo received upon completion of one's first pilgrimage. [1]

Teevio (Pog-Teevio): Sal-Afsan's predecessor as Tak-Saleed's apprentice. From Chu'toolar, he lasted only thirty days before he was sent back home. [1]

telaja: a type of tree with red wood. [1]

Tendron (Hoo-Tendron): a merchant in Pack Vando, dealing in gemstones and fossils; Wab-Babnol's teaching master. [2]

Terdog (Tep-Terdog): an old member of Pack Carno, no relation to Sal-Afsan. [1]

terrorclaw: a *Deinonychus*-like carnivorous dinosaur that hunts in packs. [1]

Tetex (Jal-Tetex): imperial hunt leader at the time Sal-Afsan took his first hunt; a Lubalite. She eventually died during a hunt and was succeeded by Lub-Galpook. [1]

thunderbeast: sauropod; giant herbivorous dinosaur. Their oil is often burned in lamps. [1]

Tilk: an animated character on the Jijaki children's television program *Kijititatak Gikta*. [2]

Tipna (Tol-Tipna): a deceased imperial hunt leader. [1]

Toroca (Kee-Toroca): (7110—) a male Quintaglio, one of Sal-Afsan's children. Toroca became leader of the Geological Survey of Land at the age of sixteen kilodays. He lacks the instinct for territoriality. In kiloday 7128, he was named putative head of the bloodpriests, following the death of Mek-Maliden. [1]

Toron (Val-Toron): a hunter from Pack Gelbo who loaned Dy-Dybo her mount. [1]

Tower: space elevator extending from equatorial Fra'toolar to the L3 point, 13,000 kilopaces above the Quintaglio moon, built in 7130 by Jijaki nanotechnology. [3]

Tralen: a member of the Geological Survey of Land who wears a blue sash. [2]

traveler's crystal: a six-sided deep red crystal that serves as a good-luck charm for travelers. [1]

Treatise on the Planets: a scholarly work in eighteen volumes (three per planet); the most famous work by Tak-Saleed. [1]

twist-saw: a saw used for amputations. [1]

uprock: igneous rock. [2]

Vanbelk (Bor-Vanbelk): inventor of the small-seer. [3]

Vando, Pack: a Pack in Arj'toolar, home of Wab-Babnol. [2]

Varkev: one of the five original male mates; the first explorer. [2]

Vatastor, Bay of: the large bay between the capes of Mekt and Belbar; the cliffs exposing the Bookmark layer are on its western shore. [2]

Vleetnav (Hel-Vleetnav): ancient artist who painted the Tapestries of the Prophet. [1]

vocational exams: administered at the age of ten or eleven; used to determine the profession one will be assigned. [1]

Voyage of Larsk, The: a ballad telling of Larsk's discovery of the Face of God. [1]

Watcher, The: a god-like entity whose consciousness has survived from the previous cycle of creation; responsible for seeding lifeforms from Earth around the galaxy. [2]

water serpent: plesiosaur. [1]

waterweed: seaweed. [2]

Wendest: (7098–7128) the female apprentice governor from Fra'toolar. [2]

wingfinger: pterosaur; flying carnivorous reptile. [1]

Wingfingers of Land, The: a book of paintings by Pal-Noltark. [3]

Withool: a junior palace page. [2]

writing leather: although the Quintaglios have paper, it is rare; thin sheets of leather are more commonly used for writing. [1]

Yabool: (7110–7126) a male Quintaglio, one of Sal-Afsan's children; a mathematician and naturalist. Murdered. [1]

year: the time it takes for the Face of God to complete one orbit around its sun; between 18,310 and 18,335 Quintaglio days. A Quintaglio female becomes sexually receptive at the end of each year of life. [2]

Yenalb (Det-Yenalb): (7067–7110) Master of the Faith; he blinded Sal-Afsan using a *dat-kar-mas*. He was killed during the skirmish between the palace loyal and the Lubalites. [1]

Zamar (Det-Zamar): one of Pack Carno's senior priests. [1]

About the Author

Robert J. Sawyer is the author of three previous science fiction novels, a dozen SF short stories, and over 200 nonfiction pieces. Orson Scott Card called Rob's first book, *Golden Fleece*, the best SF novel of 1990; it also won Canada's Aurora Award for best English-language SF novel of 1990/91.

Rob is also the author of *Far-Seer* and *Fossil Hunter* (the first two books in the Quintaglio trilogy) and *End of an Era* (an unrelated and quite different novel about dinosaurs to be published in November 1994 by Ace). *Far-Seer* won the 1992 HOMer Award for best SF novel of the year, voted on by the 18,000 members worldwide of the Science Fiction and Fantasy Forum on the CompuServe Information Service.

Rob's short SF has appeared in *Amazing Stories, The Village Voice, Leisure Ways, Dinosaur Fantastic* (edited by Mike Resnick), and *100 Great Fantasy Short Short Stories* (co-edited by Isaac Asimov). Rob also writes and narrates documentaries on SF topics for CBC Radio's *Ideas* series, is *The Canadian Encyclopedia*'s authority on science fiction, and is Canadian Regional Director of the Science-fiction and Fantasy Writers of America. He lives in Thornhill, Ontario (just north of Toronto), with his wife, Carolyn Clink.

"Redwall is both a credible and
ingratiating place, one to which readers
will doubtless cheerfully return."
—New York Times Book Review

BRIAN JACQUES

SALAMANDASTRON
———————— A Novel of Redwall ————————

"The Assassin waved his claws in the air. In a trice
the rocks were bristling with armed vermin behind him.
They flooded onto the sands of the shore and stood like
a pestilence of evil weeds sprung there by magic: line
upon line of ferrets, stoats, weasels, rats and foxes.
Banners of blood red and standards decorated their
skins, hanks of beast hair and skulls swayed in the light
breeze.
    The battle for Salamandastron was under way...."
—excerpted from Salamandastron

__ 0-441-00031-2/$4.99